No Going Back

A novel by Jonathan Langford

ZARAHEMLA BOOKS
Provo, Utah

ISBN 978-0-9787971-9-5

Cover design by Jason Robinson

Published by
Zarahemla Books
869 East 2680 North
Provo, UT 84604
info@zarahemlabooks.com
ZarahemlaBooks.com

Author's Note

The city of Arcadia Heights, Oregon, is my own invention, as are all the characters in this story. None of them are directly based on real people.

No one but myself is responsible for any of the views or events portrayed in this book. In particular, although I have strived to accurately represent the views of the various organizations depicted in this book, I do not speak for The Church of Jesus Christ of Latter-day Saints; Boy Scouts of America; Parents, Families & Friends of Lesbians & Gays (PFLAG); the state of Oregon; or anyone else.

A final note: The issue of same-sex attraction is a difficult and complex one, particularly for those (such as believing Mormons) who don't find that living a gay lifestyle is an acceptable choice for them. In this book, I haven't tried to depict any (mythical) "typical" experience for such individuals. Instead, I've attempted to reflect some of the complexity of that situation as it might play out for a particular set of characters in a specific set of circumstances. If, in the end, readers come to like and feel for those characters — mostly well meaning, as I see them, even when they don't agree with each other (or with me, always) as to how to express those good intentions — I'll be content.

Chapter One

Paul had no intention of telling Chad that he was gay. Not anytime soon. Not ever, if he could get away with it. Eight years as Chad's best friend told him Chad's reaction wouldn't be good. So why did he keep thinking about doing something he already knew was really, really stupid?

Paul glanced over at the fifteen-year-old sitting next to him. Pretty average looking. A bit shorter than Paul, even though he was several months older. Heavier, but only because Paul was so skinny. Dark-brown hair cut as long as his mom would let him, which wasn't very long. Uncombed as usual. Zit on his forehead, and another one coming up on his chin.

Face more familiar to Paul than his own. After all, he didn't really spend that much time each day looking in a mirror. Thirty seconds, maybe, to get his hair combed. More like fifteen. Not long at all.

Chad, concentrating on his video game, was oblivious to Paul's attention. *No surprises there.*

Paul thought back on their friendship. He'd been in third grade when he and his mom moved to Arcadia Heights, just a couple of months after she and his dad had separated in 1996. He hadn't liked this place. Western Oregon wasn't like Arizona, where they'd lived ever since he could remember. He hadn't *wanted* to like it.

And then that guy from their new church who kept coming over turned out to be the father of one of the biggest jerks in Paul's class at school. The first time Chad's dad brought him over for home teaching because his regular companion couldn't make it, the two boys wound up in a fistfight. Paul's mother and Chad's dad were both appalled. Chad seemed surprised that the geeky little kid had actually hit back. But Paul was pretty fed up with the world right about then, and he wasn't in a mood to take anything from anyone. When Chad threw the first punch, Paul was more than ready to respond.

A week later, they were best friends.

Paul had absolutely no romantic feelings about Chad. None. It would be like . . . having a crush on his mom. The very thought made his stomach crawl.

But Chad was important to him. More important, maybe, than if Paul had been attracted to him that way. Being Chad's friend was part of how Paul defined who he was, even if Chad didn't know *all* of who he was.

One time back when Paul was thirteen, he dropped a rock on their glass-topped coffee table. He knew what would happen before he did it, but somehow he couldn't stop himself. It was like he'd been hypnotized by the thought of the breaking glass. When his mom asked why he'd done it, all he could say was "I don't know."

I've gotta be crazy for even thinking about telling Chad that I'm gay. But no matter how much he kept telling himself that, he knew that sometime soon he'd open his mouth and it would just come popping out, whether it was a good idea or not. Sometime *very* soon, he guessed from the way his stomach couldn't stop clenching.

I wonder if today's the day I lose my best friend.

"Prepare to die."

"Not a chance, doofus. Once I let go with this . . ." Chad fired. It missed. He bit back a swear word.

"Stupid!" Paul jeered, imitating the worms' high, thin voices. *It's kind of creepy just how well he does that,* Chad thought.

It was after school, May 2003. Chad and Paul were at Paul's house, playing *Worms Armageddon* on his game system.

"This game really sucks," Chad said a couple of minutes later, as Paul wiped out the last of his forces.

"You're just saying that 'cause you lost."

"We've been playing this stupid game since we were in sixth grade."

"True classics never get old."

"So, you wanna break out *Twisted Metal*?"

"I said *true* classics."

"*Twisted Metal*'s a classic!"

"Classic waste of time," Paul said. As they talked, both boys were flipping through Paul's collection of games.

"Hey, it's all about smashing things. What could be better than that?"

"Sometimes I worry about you."

Chad thought for a second. "Okay, then. How about *Gran Turismo 3?*"

"Fine."

Paul dug it out while Chad vented. "So fifth period — you know, Mrs. Zeller's class. I'm minding my own business when that ass — I mean, when that jerk Brett Davis trips me on my way to my seat. So I kick him, and then he calls me a fag. I would have punched him, except I saw Mrs. Zeller looking at me and I was pretty sure I'd get a detention. So instead I just said he was the faggot, not me, except real quiet so Zeller couldn't hear. You should have seen the look on his face. It was sweet."

Paul rolled his eyes. "He called you a name, so you called him a name back. Real mature."

"Hey, I thought you'd be happy I didn't get a detention for once."

"Whatever. Pick your car."

"Viper. Totally." Chad paused, then noticed Paul's choice. "Wait a minute. A Zonda? You're picking a Zonda?"

"Some of us don't like to pick the same car every time we play."

"But a Zonda? I swear, Paul, you're an alien."

"Hey, it has a cool name."

"Hopeless."

They started the race. "So why'd you call Brett a faggot?" Paul's voice sounded strange.

"He called me one first."

"So you don't think he really is gay."

Chad snorted. "You gotta be kidding. Davis may be a jerk, but he isn't a fag."

"How do you know? You flash him in the locker room or something, see if he got excited?"

"Geez, Paul! It's just obvious, okay? I mean, we've known the guy since sixth grade. Don't you think we'd know by now if he was queer?"

"How do you think you'd know?" Paul persisted. "If Brett was a fag?"

Chad was starting to get annoyed. "Geez! I dunno! I mean, he doesn't act all faggy or anything. He plays soccer. He's a normal guy, you know? Not like Seth."

Seth Porter had gotten teased a lot in middle school for being a wimp and for liking drama and art instead of sports. Chad and Paul were both there one day in seventh grade when Seth actually started crying at lunchtime because everyone kept giving him a hard time. Chad remembered that Paul got really mad when Chad laughed about it.

"You know, Seth's dating Esther Watkins," Paul said. "So maybe your gay-o-meter is as lousy as the way you drive your Viper." He sounded ticked off.

For the next couple of minutes, they played in silence. Finally Chad asked, "So why're you all spazzing about who's gay and who's not? I mean, why do you care?"

There was a pause. Then Paul's voice quietly said, "I'm gay."

Startled, Chad looked over at Paul. He was staring straight ahead at the TV screen, fingers working busily at the controller. The tight set of his mouth was the only thing that suggested he'd just said anything out of the ordinary.

"What the fuh—"

Before Chad could even finish the word, Paul's fist shot out. Pain exploded in Chad's shoulder.

"Why the hell did you do that?"

"You know why." Paul still wasn't looking at him.

Chad's brain was still trying to catch up with what Paul had said. "You just told me you're a fag. My best friend is a *fag!*" Chad didn't realize how loud he'd gotten until he heard himself shouting the last word.

Paul was staring at him. "Look. Let's just pretend I didn't say anything. I mean—"

"Shut up, you faggot!" Chad roared. He knew his reaction was out of control, but he couldn't seem to do anything about it.

Paul's face tightened with anger. He threw down his controller. "All right. You can leave, asshole." He stood up, grabbed Chad's backpack, and threw it at him. Hard.

Chad sat there for several seconds, struggling to control his temper. He didn't want to make things worse by punching his best friend, even if Paul was a fag. The whole time, Paul was glaring at him. Finally, Chad got up and left.

• • •

Yeah. That went okay. Not.

Paul wiped his mouth. He'd just finished throwing up his lunch, plus the Doritos and root beer he and Chad had been snacking on after school. It got really old sometimes, having a stomach that decided to barf each time he got nervous.

Back when Paul first realized he was having feelings about boys that he was supposed to have about girls, his reaction had been sheer, petrifying terror—followed quickly by denial. He was a Mormon kid. He wasn't supposed to be that way. He was supposed to get married—to a woman. That was God's plan. It had been months before he'd been able to think about it for more than thirty seconds at a time without wanting to throw up. Like now.

A small, optimistic corner of Paul's brain reminded him that Chad always blew up like that when he got hit with something he wasn't expecting. Maybe things would be better once Chad cooled down.

Yeah. But he's never found out that his best friend's a fag before, either.

Paul stood and walked back to his bedroom, being careful not to close any doors in case he had to make another fast bathroom run.

Walking home from Paul's house, Chad was still angry. Mostly, though, he felt confused.

Gay. He knew what the word meant. Thanks to his eighth-grade health unit—and the stuff he'd heard from other kids—he knew what gay guys did for sex, though he thought it was pretty gross. He'd seen gay couples when he went into downtown Portland to buy something. He really didn't want to think about Paul doing any of that stuff, walking around holding hands with another guy, making out—

And Mormon. How did that happen? Paul followed the rules. Better than Chad did, most of the time. Not like Tim Geary, who went to church just because his folks made him but who Chad was pretty sure smoked pot with his friends on the swim team. Paul was a teacher in the Aaronic Priesthood, just like Chad. He'd been ordained by Chad's dad a little over a year ago right after he turned fourteen, a couple of months before the end of eighth grade.

Chad had been jealous, actually. That had been a few months after Chad's dad was made bishop. Chad had been mad about that. After his dad's call, it seemed like Chad kept getting into trouble because he couldn't follow all the rules that the church and his parents and the school and everybody expected him to follow. Watching Paul sitting there in his suit, with his dad's hands on his head, he'd thought how much easier it all was for Paul. He didn't have a dad for a bishop. He didn't have a bratty little sister who loved to get him in trouble and a little brother who pestered him all the time. His mom didn't have rules about things like not having a TV or computer in his bedroom.

It was just easier somehow for Paul to follow the rules, or that's the way it seemed to Chad. Paul didn't have a temper that got him into trouble with pretty much everyone. Adults *liked* Paul. It wasn't like that for Chad. Whenever he tried to tell his side of the story to his parents or teachers, it seemed like they just wound up getting mad. "I don't get why you don't keep your mouth shut and think a minute before saying stupid stuff," Paul had said to him one time, shaking his head.

Thinking back to what had happened later on the day Paul was ordained a teacher, Chad had to agree. That afternoon after church, he'd let go with one of his new cuss words in front of his mom, just to see how she'd react. She'd gone ballistic and sent him to his room, and then she sent his dad to talk to him when he got home.

That conversation hadn't gone the way he'd expected. His dad grounded him for a week, but then he spent more than an hour listening to Chad and asking him how things were going. It was the most time they'd spent talking, just the two of them without any interruptions, since his dad had become bishop.

At one point in the conversation, his dad had asked why he didn't spend as much time with Paul anymore. Chad muttered something about being interested in different things now and how he'd started spending more time with guys who weren't such science-fiction freaks. Even as he said it, though, he felt guilty. He knew that wasn't the reason they'd stopped hanging around so much. Mostly, Chad had realized later, it was just because he wanted to be around kids who weren't Mormons and didn't know how he was supposed to act, so he could pretend he wasn't Mormon for a while. It was a pretty lousy reason for ditching someone he'd been friends with since third grade. He didn't even like spending time with those other guys that much anyway.

He'd apologized to Paul a few days later. That was when they'd made a bargain about Paul slugging him whenever he cussed. He'd gone around with a sore arm for at least a month after that. He hadn't realized how much he'd started using that kind of language until he tried to stop.

During that same conversation, Chad had admitted feeling like following the rules was so much easier for Paul and how he was a lot better of a Mormon than Chad was. Paul had laughed in a kind of strange way Chad hadn't known how to interpret. Then he said Chad didn't have any idea what he was talking about. Chad guessed he knew what Paul meant now.

Which didn't help him any in figuring out what to do.

Paul's a fag. My best friend's a faggot.

So what you gonna do about it?

Chad didn't know.

"You're late!" Chad's mom's words greeted him as he entered the house, kicking off his shoes just inside the entryway.

"What the—" He swallowed and bit back the words.

"It's a quarter after five. You know you're supposed to be here at five on school nights."

Chad looked over at the clock. Sure enough, it was 5:15. He still sometimes forgot that his mom had reset it ten minutes fast "to make sure we get ready for things on time" after that one Sunday a couple of months ago when they hadn't gotten to church until the sacrament hymn was playing. It was embarrassing, she said, for the bishop's family to arrive late to meetings. When Chad complained that it messed up his schedule, she suggested that he reset his own watch to match the living-room clock. He didn't say anything about it after that. Instead, he just tried to remember that their house now ran on Mortensen Family Time, which was just a little different from everywhere else in the known universe.

"Go get started on your homework. I'd like it if you were done by 6:30. That's when we're having dinner tonight."

"I thought I was supposed to mow the lawn today."

"It's drizzling. Tomorrow, maybe. Or Saturday."

"But Dad—"

"I'll tell him I talked to you. Okay?" She smiled at him.

He smiled back a little cautiously, wondering if he ought to be nervous. *Parents smile like that when they want you to do something.* As soon as she turned away, he ran upstairs toward the relative safety of his bedroom.

• • •

Homework went slow. Chad had a paragraph to write for English and a set of problems for algebra, together with a chapter to read for social studies. He did his best to concentrate, but his thoughts kept drifting.

Paul. Gay. The more time he had for it to sink in, the more confused he got. It was just . . . something he couldn't really believe. Paul didn't act like a fag. How could he be a fag?

By dinnertime, Chad still had half a chapter to finish reading. Thankfully, his mom was too busy telling his dad, who'd just gotten home from a two-day trip, about all the chores that needed doing to ask Chad about the state of his homework.

"What are we having for dinner?" his dad asked, ruffling nine-year-old Emily's hair as he passed her on the way to the table. "I'm sure it's great, just like usual." Chad's dad was a sales manager for a company that manufactured computer components. He'd heard his dad say that each time you talked to someone, you should include a compliment. Unfortunately, that meant his dad's compliments didn't always mean much.

"Pork chops," his mother responded. Chad was pleased. He liked pork chops. "And green beans, applesauce, and potatoes and gravy."

His dad shook his head. "Why people think applesauce goes with pork is beyond me."

"You don't have to have any." She was grinning.

"I'll just save it for dessert." His dad grinned back, in kind of a . . . Were Chad's mom and dad flirting with each other? Chad closed his eyes.

"Can we eat already?" he muttered.

"Yeah!" shouted seven-year-old Jeffrey, already bouncing up and down in his chair even though he'd been sitting for only about thirty seconds.

"Someone needs to feed that kid some Ritalin," grumbled Chad.

"Let's have dinner," his dad interrupted. "Is it all right if I say the prayer?"

Why does he always ask that? wondered Chad. *It's not like we're gonna say he can't.*

His mom nodded, and they all bowed their heads.

"Dear Heavenly Father. We thank thee for the many blessings you've given us this day . . ."

Chad tuned out what his dad was saying, noticing only when

he slipped from the *thees* and *thous* to *you* and *your*. His dad hadn't become Mormon until he was seventeen, and the church he'd attended before then didn't use *thees* and *thous* when they were praying. His dad had even found an old article from the *Ensign* about the language of prayer and turned it into flash cards to practice with, but he still couldn't get it right.

"Amen."

"Amen," answered Chad automatically, together with Emily and—after a warning look from his mom—Jeffrey.

"I'm sorry it's been such a stressful time at work," his mom commented as they started eating. For a minute, Chad felt guilty. Had his dad said something about work during the prayer? Then he shook it off.

"I almost got in trouble today, except it wasn't really my fault— it was Eric's fault," announced Emily. Eric was a boy who sat near her in class and always seemed to be causing trouble for Emily and her friends. If they were older, Chad would have suspected that maybe Eric had a crush on some of the girls. Thank goodness they were only in third grade.

A couple of minutes later, Emily was still talking.

"—and then Rita went and got the teacher, but the teacher hadn't seen Eric do it, so she said we had to go and sit at another table, but that was okay because I didn't want to sit next to Eric anyway—"

Jeffrey had pretty much finished his pork chop and was now busy building a fort out of his mashed potatoes and gravy, supported on two sides by the bone from the pork chop, with green beans stuck around the top like a picket fence. "Eat it, don't play with it," Chad hissed, then glared when his brother grinned mischievously back.

From the other end of the table, Chad's mom gave him a look that he knew meant it was his job to keep his little brother under control. He clenched his fists. *Why is it always me that gets stuck with the brat?* Looking at his mom, though, he knew that if he objected, he'd be in trouble. Turning to Jeffrey, he said, "You wanna play on my GameCube after dinner?"

"Yeah!"

"Then eat your food."

"Aww." But Jeffrey stopped playing and started eating, though he still had to be talked into each bite. Thankfully, after six bites Chad's mom nodded permission for Jeffrey to leave, and he was off like a shot.

"He's a menace," Chad said the minute Jeffrey was out of sight.

It had taken all his self-control not to yell at the kid when he took almost five minutes on the last two bites.

"You were worse," his mom responded. Privately, Chad doubted this, but he didn't argue the point.

"We appreciate your patience, son," his dad added. Behind his back, Emily stuck out her tongue at Chad.

"Richard, I was wondering if you could help Emily with her math this evening. The teacher sent a note home saying she needs more work on carrying in subtraction."

"I need to go up to the church for a while this evening."

Chad's mom lost her smile. "That's the third time this week."

"I'll be back in about an hour."

"Well." She paused. "If you have to go up to the church, then I suppose you'd better take off, so you can get back more quickly." She swept out of the room and into the kitchen.

"I guess I'd best get going," Chad's dad replied in a gruff tone. It was another minute before he stood up and headed off.

Chad wound up playing *Super Smash Brothers Melee* with Jeffrey for about a half-hour in the downstairs TV room, until it was Jeffrey's story time. Then Chad went upstairs to finish up the rest of his homework. Emily, he guessed, was off playing in her room. He put on his headphones and started on his homework.

He'd just gotten done and was putting his books away in his backpack when the door to his room opened and his dad's head poked in. Chad glanced over at the clock. It was a little after nine.

"How you doing? Finished with homework?"

"Yeah." He scowled. "You said you'd knock before you come in my room."

"I did," his dad said calmly, sitting on Chad's bed. "You didn't hear." He poked a thumb at Chad's CD player. "What are you listening to?"

"Some stuff Tony at school copied for me."

His dad raised his eyebrows. "Isn't that illegal?"

Chad felt a sudden, sharp spike of anger. With difficulty, he controlled it. "It was a present," he said. "Some songs he thought I'd like."

"But copied. Not bought."

Chad clenched his fists and swallowed. "Look, it's just one CD."

"It's not the size, it's the principle of the thing. You're just as much a thief if you steal only one CD as if you steal a million dollars."

"So you're saying I'm a thief."

"That's not what I'm saying." Chad could tell that his dad was starting to get ticked off. "But you *are* the one who's listening to it. And even if everyone is doing it, you need to set a better example."

"I'm sick and tired of being an example! Just because you're the bishop—"

"Chad!" His dad took a deep breath, then continued. "You're a priesthood holder, and it's your responsibility to act like one." He paused. "Clearly this isn't a good time to have this conversation. We'll talk about it later, after you've had a chance to think it over."

The two of them stared at each other. After a few seconds, Chad felt his pulse start to calm down. Then to his own surprise, Chad heard himself ask, "What makes people fags?"

His dad looked surprised. "Where did that come from?"

Chad shook his head. His dad gave him a serious look. "Is there something you need to talk to me about as the bishop?"

"No!" The very idea horrified him. "Never mind. Just—forget about it, okay?"

His dad just kept looking at him. After a minute, Chad reluctantly continued. "Just, some guys at school, you know? Nobody I know really well. Everyone says they're fags."

"I'd rather you didn't use that word."

"Fag?"

"Yes."

"It's what all the guys at school call them."

"I'm sure. Regardless, that's not a word I think you should use." He paused. "You sure you don't have anything to tell me?"

Chad's temper flared again. "I'm not a fag, so you can just stop it with the accusations!" he snarled.

"Whoa!" His dad stared at him. "I wasn't accusing you of anything. You need to get a better handle on that temper of yours."

There was an awkward silence before his dad continued. "Anyway, getting back to the question you were asking. I don't know why some people turn out gay." He looked at Chad again. "You really want to hear what I think about this?"

Chad nodded.

"A lot of gays say they're born that way. I don't know. I can't believe God would create someone gay. But then, I can't believe that God would create someone handicapped or psychopathic, either."

He shook his head. "I'm not even sure it's something I think can be labeled all that easily. I think it's not really uncommon for boys to sometimes have crushes on other boys when they're young. Sometimes it may not even have anything to do with sex. Just a kind of hero worship."

Chad snorted, thinking about the way Colin Creevey followed Harry around all the time in the Harry Potter books. *Hero worship. That sounds about right.*

His dad continued. "Maybe it's partly genetics. Maybe it's how someone is raised. Back when I was younger, they used to say that growing up without a strong father could make people homosexual. I don't think they're saying that anymore." He paused. "I think the church has materials for helping people who struggle with homosexuality. I haven't really had to look at them yet. I suppose I should."

Yeah, well, you might need them sooner than you think, Chad thought.

"Even if homosexuality isn't something people choose, I do know that homosexuality isn't a lifestyle that can bring happiness to people. Not real, eternal happiness. That's what the gospel teaches. From the church's perspective, the really important thing is how you choose to live. Satan tries to tell us that just because we feel something, we have to act on it. The gospel is all about self-control — doing things in God's own time and in the way God wants us to do them. Even if people have those kinds of feelings, they don't have to act on them."

Chad recognized a favorite theme of his dad's. He was really big on self-control, especially since he'd been made a bishop.

"Anyway, that's what I think about it. Sorry if that doesn't answer your question."

Chad shrugged.

"So, about that music CD."

Chad tensed up again. He'd almost forgotten about that.

"I'll make you a deal, okay? Pick one of the songs you especially like, and I'll see if we can get you a legal copy. Just don't tell Emily about it, or she'll want another Britney Spears CD."

Chad swallowed and nodded. He supposed it was better than nothing.

"I'm glad you're doing the right thing."

Not like you gave me any choice, Chad thought. *Why does doing the right thing always have to suck?*

"Take care, tiger." Chad's dad smiled and gave him a quick hug—which Chad did his best not to return—and then left.

Down in the family room, the smile melted off Richard's face as he settled onto the couch and closed his eyes.

I remember back when Chad was this easy kid to listen to and understand. Now he's like a stone. An angry, sullen stone. Half the time we talk, it seems like it turns into another argument. And then he comes out with this gay question—

Richard wasn't a fool. His time as bishop had taught him a lot about young men and what they would and wouldn't talk about to someone they saw as an adult authority. He thought about his son, with his shuttered face and eyes, and knew he'd reached the age where he'd hang onto his privacy with every bit of determination a sullen teenager could muster.

Someday maybe he'd find out what had been behind Chad's question tonight. He just hoped it wouldn't be one of those conversations parents have nightmares about. "Dad, I'm gay." "Dad, I got a girl pregnant." "Dad, I blew up the school." He shook his head. There were just too many horrible options to choose from, teenagers being as young and stupid as they were. He'd been that stupid himself.

At least his son had good friends.

Back at the beginning of third grade, Chad had been running wild, without any friends Richard and Sandy could feel good about. Getting a head start on teenage anger and sullenness, and at only nine, too. Then he started spending time with Paul, and their cheerful, sometimes wacky, headstrong, active, but mostly well-meaning son had been back.

Chad was a happier person when Paul was around, more the kind of person Richard hoped he might grow up to be once the teenage morass was past. Richard hadn't realized how much of a difference it made until that time about a year ago when Chad had been hanging out with those stoners-in-training. Thank God that stage was over and Chad was spending more time again with Paul and his other church friends. Their family's life had truly changed for the better when Paul and his mother moved to Arcadia Heights.

Chapter Two

Paul was more tired than usual the next morning when he woke to the sound of his mom's voice.

"Paul! You have ten minutes before Sister Tanner gets here."

He looked at his clock. It was 6:00. Oh, dang. He was supposed to be up twenty minutes ago to get ready for seminary. He threw on his clothes, grabbed his backpack, and was down the stairs within two minutes, taking three stairs with each step.

"You're going to kill yourself one of these days," his mom observed. She sounded remarkably calm at the thought.

Paul was stuffing toast into his mouth and didn't answer. Five minutes later he was out the door, climbing into Sister Tanner's van.

Unfortunately, the ten-minute drive to the church gave him plenty of time to worry about what had happened the day before.

Paul was glad Chad wasn't there yet when he got to their seminary classroom. He sat in his usual place, wondering if Chad would choose to sit somewhere else today. He was surprised but pleased when Chad slid into the seat next to him a minute later, just before class was supposed to start.

Paul couldn't stop himself from smiling. Chad glared back, then turned toward the front of the class.

Paul winced. It was going to be a long day.

When Chad got to seminary that morning, he sat down next to Paul without even thinking about it. Noticing the huge smile on Paul's face, he scowled. *This doesn't mean I'm okay with you being a fag.* Paul evidently got the message, judging by how quickly his smile vanished.

Serves him right, Chad thought. Then he felt guilty.

Tony Westergren, the seminary class president, stood at the front of the room. "All right. The opening song today . . ."

The rest of seminary was awkward. Every few minutes, Paul would glance sideways at Chad, then quickly look away again. By the third time, it was getting old.

"What's with you?" Chad hissed. Then he whispered, "Did you get an extra scoop of Purina weirdo-chow in your bowl this morning?"

Paul's eyes got bigger. "Sorry!" He looked away again.

Chad looked away as well, growling to himself. *Not only is Paul a fag, he's spazzing as well.*

"And then Wash said, 'I was gonna watch. It was very exciting.' And—"

It was lunch. Paul was retelling one of his favorite scenes from the *Firefly* series to several of their friends, using rapid, half-finished sentences. Chad was sitting several seats down from him at the lunch table, watching and listening.

Mysteriously, the collection of girls at their lunch table didn't seem to mind Paul's manic enthusiasm. In fact, they seemed to like it, although hearing Paul giggling like that just made Chad want to slug him. Somehow, though, Paul was able to get away with acting like a goofball. Chad knew that if he was the one acting that way, several of the girls would be quick to tell him just how immature he was being. It really wasn't fair.

Just one more thing to be irritated with him about.

Suddenly Chad's frustration got the best of him. "I've got some stuff to do before next period. Paul, I'll see you after school." Chad stared at him. "We'll walk home."

Paul gulped. Chad knew he'd heard the unspoken *or else.*

As he walked away, he heard Paul's voice resuming his plot summary. "And it turned out they were hauling *cows*—"

They met in front of the school after last period, where they stood around talking with friends until the first set of buses pulled out. Then they set out for Paul's house.

Paul gave Chad a quick, frightened look, then turned away. They started walking.

All during the school day, Chad had kept thinking about Paul and the whole gay thing. He wished he could just ignore it. But he knew that wasn't an option. If he did, Paul would just keep freaking out, waiting for Chad to say something.

And Chad really did want to keep Paul as a friend. He just didn't see how he could handle the gay thing. What if Paul had a crush on *him*? But whenever he thought about not being Paul's friend anymore, Chad got a kind of sick feeling inside. Ditching Paul was something Chad would really regret.

Chad waited until they were a block away from school before he started talking. "So. I'm guessing what you said yesterday wasn't just a trick to make me lose at *Gran Turismo 3*."

There was a pause. "No."

"So. You're really gay."

Paul glanced around quickly. "Don't say it!" he hissed.

"No one else is here."

"Still."

They walked in silence for another couple of minutes. Finally Chad spoke. "You've been freaking out all day, dude. Acting all hyper-boy."

"Hyper-boy?"

"Lunchtime, you were like a six-year-old on a sugar high."

Paul laughed a bit, but there wasn't much humor in it. "I dunno. It's just . . . I guess I've just been worrying about it, you know? Telling you and everything."

"Well, duh."

They both fell silent again. Chad thought again about how much he didn't want to have this conversation. *Yesterday was bad enough. Now I'm trying to get him to talk about it some more? I must be nuts.*

As soon as they got to Paul's house, they went straight to his room and dropped their backpacks on the floor. Paul flopped onto the bed while Chad took the chair in front of the computer.

Chad spoke first. "So. Uh, gay. So that means you, uh, have the hots for guys?"

"Duh."

"Okay." Chad took a deep breath. "So, how long have you been gay?" Seeing the look of withering contempt on Paul's face, he quickly corrected what he'd just said. "I mean, when did you find out you're gay?"

"Remember health class, fall of eighth grade?"

"It was only a year and a half ago."

"Right," Paul answered. "You remember that unit on, uh, gays and lesbians and stuff?"

"And transvestites."

"Yeah."

Chad remembered. His parents had argued about it for several days before they decided to sign the permission form.

Paul was still talking. "You know that bit about 'Are You Gay?' they did? You know, when they said you couldn't tell just by looking at some kind of checklist, and then they gave us a checklist anyway?"

"Yeah." They'd joked about it at the time.

"Yeah. So I, uh, looked at it. You know, the things about, like, what you think about."

"You mean, when you jack off?"

"Yeah." Paul's face was bright red now, and he wasn't looking at Chad at all. "So I thought about it. And, uh . . ." His voice trailed off.

Chad swallowed. "You sure? I mean, you aren't, you know, girly or anything like that. And, uh, they said that even straight kids sometimes—"

Paul rolled his eyes. "I'm not *girly* 'cause I'm not a *girl*. Got it?"

"But—"

"Chad. Think about Alisha Thompson standing in front of you without any clothes on," Paul said.

Chad felt himself blushing. Alisha was a sophomore who lived a couple of doors down from him. She was really hot. He adjusted his pants. Sometimes it wasn't good having a best friend who knew so much about you.

"See, thinking about Alisha Thompson naked makes me kind of embarrassed, but it doesn't make me start to drool and want to make babies with her. Actually I think it's kinda gross, to tell the truth."

Chad hesitated. He really didn't want to know, but— "You've never—I mean, you, uh, have crushes on guys, right?"

"Well, yeah." Paul's face started to turn red.

"You don't, uh . . ." His voice trailed off.

"Dude. You trying to ask if I have a crush on you?"

"I guess."

"Not really."

"What does that mean?" Almost without realizing it, Chad sat back in his chair, pulling farther away from where Paul was sitting.

"It means I know you're not gay, and you're my best friend, and I don't think about you that way." Paul rolled his eyes again. "Your pimply body is safe from my carnal lust."

"Hey! You get as many zits as I do."

"Keep telling yourself that."

There was an awkward pause.

"So," Chad continued at last. "You're gay. But you're Mormon. How is that gonna work?"

"What do you mean?"

"Dude! Last time I looked, the church doesn't really approve of being gay."

"Well, duh."

"So how are you gonna handle being gay and Mormon both?"

"I dunno! Look! I—" Paul ran his hand through his hair. "Maybe I can just, you know, not ever act gay."

"You mean, not ever have sex with anyone?"

"Yeah."

"Huh." Chad was doubtful. He didn't think he'd be able to go without sex his whole life. Sometimes he wondered if he was going to make it through high school. Not that any girls had expressed an interest, but still—

"Or maybe things'll change later on."

"You mean, like you not being gay anymore?"

"Yeah."

"You really think that'll happen?"

"I gotta hope." Paul's voice got softer. "Look, it's not like—I mean, I still believe in the church, you know? I want to get married, have kids."

"Pretty hard to manage that if you're gay."

"Well, yeah. That's kind of the problem."

They were both silent for a couple of minutes. Finally Paul continued. "See . . . basically what I figure is, there's something wrong with me. Something wrong with the part of me that wants to get together with guys, instead of girls. That's not something I can change, but maybe it'll change someday, if I try to do my best and follow the church's rules."

"So what you're saying is that guys turn you on, but you wanna stay in the church, but you can't have guys if you wanna stay in the church."

"Basically."

"Sucks to be you."

"Not really. About the sucking part, I mean. Not unless I want a one-way ticket to the bishop's office."

Chad was shocked for a moment. Then he snickered. Paul joined in.

"So I guess that's your official first gay joke." Paul hit him in the arm.

"So, does anyone else know you're gay?"

Paul shook his head. "Who else would I tell?"

Chad thought about that. Paul's mom and dad had gotten divorced back when Paul was about eight, before his mom moved from Arizona to Oregon and started coming back to church. Chad's dad had been their first home teacher. He'd baptized Paul, who was eight and a half at the time.

Paul didn't talk about his dad very much, though he traveled out to visit him a couple of times a year in Minnesota, together with his dad's second wife and their two young kids. Chad was pretty sure Paul wouldn't want to talk to his dad about this. As for talking to his mom . . . Chad knew that he himself would rather stab himself in the eyes with a hot poker, or even carve them out with a blunt spoon, instead of talking to his mom about anything related to sex. He figured Paul felt the same way.

There was another pause. Then Paul cautiously asked, "So, are we cool?"

"This is still freaking me out."

"Yeah, well, imagine what it feels like for me."

"I don't wanna imagine anything about it at all."

Paul threw a pillow at him. Chad grabbed it and tossed it back. "Jerk." They were both grinning, though.

Chad spoke again. "You know, I really don't get that you're gay."

"What do you mean?"

"Like, you're not femmy at all. I mean, yeah, you read all that science-fiction stuff, but mostly you seem pretty much like everybody else."

"Ordinary Paul, that's me."

"Yeah. I mean, you went out for soccer last fall, even though you suck at it." Chad smirked.

"Yeah, well, I didn't see you scoring a ton of goals either."

"Point." Chad hesitated. "I talked to my dad last night. Asked him about gays."

"You—"

"I didn't say anything about you. I just said there were a couple of guys at school who were gay."

"What did he say?"

"No real surprises. Said we don't know why some guys turn out to be gay. Said the church doesn't approve. Said that if I was gay, he hoped I wouldn't fall for you, because you're so butt-ugly." Chad was snickering by then.

"You know, it's a good thing you laugh at your own jokes, 'cause no one else would."

"You're just jealous of my astounding wit and studly body."

"Your ugly body, you mean."

"Anyway, he didn't seem too freaked out by it."

"That's good."

The conversation stalled again.

"I'd better get home now," Chad finally said, looking at his watch. His dad's work schedule had him traveling a lot during the week, so they had family home evening lessons on Sunday instead of Monday and "family fun night" on Friday, except when there was something going on for school or church. Sometimes Paul and his mom were invited over for that, but not this week.

"Right. See you, man."

"Okay."

Chad gathered up his stuff and left.

After Chad left, Paul lay back on his bed, closed his eyes, and took a deep, shuddering breath.

It was way better than yesterday. No question about that. Chad still seemed a little freaked out by it, but overall it had turned out about as well as Paul could have hoped.

Being gay really sucked, but things could be a lot worse.

Thinking it over after he left, Chad thought Paul seemed a lot more relaxed by the end of the conversation. *I guess something worked.*

Chad wanted to be a good friend—he really did—but trying to be cool about Paul being gay was seriously one of the hardest things he'd ever done.

Thank goodness that's over. Maybe if I'm lucky, we won't ever have to talk about it again, and I can just pretend nothing's really changed.

• • •

Choosing a new music CD turned out to be a bigger deal than Chad had expected.

For one thing, Chad didn't even know who'd sung half the songs on Tony's CD, or even what the song titles were. He solved that by taking the CD to school and having Tony listen and write down the titles and band names. That took most of one lunch period. But Tony didn't know what albums they'd come from—he'd downloaded them himself or gotten them from other people. Chad realized, a little uncomfortably, that this supported his dad's point about the record companies not making any profits if everyone just copied the songs without paying for them.

Several of the songs were obvious choices to drop. Chad hated rap, so that eliminated a couple right there. He also couldn't stand the whiny sound of the singer on "Addicted."

And "Sk8er Boi" was right out just on principle. He couldn't stand the title, he couldn't stand the story, and most of all he couldn't stand Avril Lavigne the Hyperactive Emo Tomboy. The fact that Paul liked her stuff was just another sign that his best friend's musical taste had been surgically removed at birth.

And then there were the songs he knew would get him in trouble if his parents ever really listened to them. "Your Body Is a Wonderland"—yeah, right, that would go over *really* well. He liked "Minority" by Green Day, but if his mom or dad happened to come in the room when they were saying "F— 'em all," it wouldn't be a happy scene.

Then he realized he'd have to look at the lyrics for all the other songs on each album as well, in order to make sure they wouldn't flunk the parent test. At that point he almost gave up.

But that evening, Chad's dad happened to ask if he'd picked out his new CD yet. He said he was still narrowing down the possibilities. His dad commented that it couldn't be too difficult, since all the stuff he liked sounded pretty much the same anyway. Chad was pretty sure he meant it as a joke, but it still ticked him off. After that he was determined to go ahead with it, no matter how much time and energy it took.

At the ward father-and-son campout the next weekend, he asked some of the boys what kind of music they liked that didn't bother their parents too much. Unfortunately, most of their answers were bands he hated, had never heard of, or had already decided his parents wouldn't approve.

"Your folks let you listen to Nelly?"

The other boy—Jason Devlich, a thirteen-year-old—shrugged. "They don't pay much attention to my music," he said. "I don't think they really care, as long as they don't have to hear it."

Chad shook his head. Neither of his parents were like that at all.

"Hey, don't mention it to your dad, okay? I mean, I know he's the bishop, and—"

"Don't worry about it."

Why did people insist on seeing him as an extension of his dad, now that his dad was the bishop? It made him mad that Jason thought he had to say anything about it. That was one nice thing about Paul. He'd known Chad and his dad long enough that it didn't change things when his dad was made bishop.

Chad finally decided maybe Creed would work. He really liked the guitar work on "One Last Breath." He decided that after he got home, he'd go online and see if he could check out the lyrics for the other tracks on *Weathered*. Hopefully, he'd have a final decision by Monday.

He and Paul talked about it that night in the tent they were sharing. Chad's dad was in another tent with Jeffrey. For a moment while they were setting up the tent, Chad had wondered if Paul would try anything weird, but he quickly forced the thought away.

"That whole music thing's a real bummer," Paul commented as they were climbing into their sleeping bags.

"Yeah. At first I thought it was kind of cool that I'd be getting a new CD, but I'm starting to think it's more hassle than it's worth. I mean, it's just one CD, right?"

"You know your dad would be laughing his head off if he knew how much time you're putting into this."

"He'd say it was good for me. But yeah, he'd be laughing while he said it."

Paul lowered his voice. "So I've been wondering. How did your dad get this campground on Memorial Day weekend? I mean, like, first they were saying the father-son campout would have to be canceled, and then your dad said it was taken care of. Nobody could figure it out."

Chad hesitated. "He paid the campground owner. Out of his own pocket, I mean. He told me not to tell anyone, though, so don't say anything about it, okay?"

"You dad does that sort of thing a lot, doesn't he?"

Chad grimaced. "Not so much anymore. He and Mom have argued about it. I don't know if she knows about it this time."

"Ouch." Paul paused. "They still arguing a lot?"

"Not as much as a few months ago."

"That's good, right?"

"Dunno. My mom's still upset about a lot of stuff, I think, but they don't talk about it. Sometimes things are okay, sometimes not. My dad just pretends everything's normal. Some ways, I think it's worse than when they were arguing." He sighed. "I wish they'd never made him a bishop."

"He's a good bishop," Paul said quietly.

"Yeah. But I'd rather have my dad back."

In the other tent, Richard lay listening beside the sleeping body of his younger son, Jeffrey. Sound carried better than the boys realized. He'd been amused to hear about how hard it was for his son to figure out a new CD to buy, though he hadn't been able to figure out just what was causing him so much trouble. It was good to know Chad wasn't just trying to put things off in hopes that Richard would forget about the illegal CD.

Then the boys had started talking about other things. Richard had been dismayed to realize just how much Chad—not the most sensitive or perceptive person when it came to noticing things about other people—had picked up on the tension between him and Sandy. It was a good thing Chad had Paul to talk to. Richard remembered how much it had helped when he was able to talk to his best friend when his parents had gotten a divorce, back when he was thirteen.

Not that he and Sandy were anywhere near getting a divorce. This was just the normal kind of tension couples had to work through, especially when both of them were under stress. He knew that his being bishop hadn't helped, though he'd had no idea Chad resented it. The boy had never said anything to him.

Still, it was a warning sign. Things had to start going better on the home front. He had to readjust his priorities—while not neglecting his duties as a bishop as well. And his work. And he had to somehow stay sane through it all. Richard sighed.

"And we're *outta* here!" yelled Rich Grober, punching the air with his fist.

It was June twelfth. About half a dozen of them were walking down the sidewalk, heading toward their houses. Since the last day of school was only a half-day, they still had all afternoon free.

"Who's coming to the sleepover tomorrow?" one of the boys asked. The group of them had been doing end-of-school sleepovers ever since sixth grade.

"I can't make it," said Tony. A couple of others said they couldn't either.

"Why'd we have to wait until tomorrow anyway?" Mike asked.

" 'Cause my dad said he didn't want us keeping him up late when he has to get up early the next day," Tyler replied.

"Whatever. So anyone wanna hit that new gaming place on Columbia Boulevard?"

"Can't," replied Chad with regret. "I've gotta watch my little brother and sister."

"I'll go," Paul said.

Chad was surprised. He'd been counting on Paul coming over to keep the afternoon from being completely boring.

The other guys seemed a little surprised as well. Mike said to Paul, "Thought you'd be attached at the hip to Mortensen here, like usual."

"We spend time with other people," Chad replied irritably.

"You maybe. Paul, not so much," Mike said.

Paul shrugged. "Sometimes I do stuff on my own, sometimes I don't. Anyway, I'm looking forward to playing some games."

Chad stood there watching as the others went off. Then he turned and walked home.

"It wasn't that big a deal. I just wanted to play games with the other guys for once. I heard about that place, but I've never been there before."

Chad scowled. Paul had shown up at his house about 5:30. It had been a rotten afternoon, with Emily and Jeffrey both whining and arguing about every little thing and not letting Chad sulk in peace about being on his own the first afternoon of summer vacation. Finally his mom had come home and he'd gone into the backyard to cool down. That's where he was when Paul found him.

"We do stuff with them all the time," Chad said. Even while he was saying it, though, Chad realized it wasn't really true. This past year, he hadn't spent very much time with his non-Mormon friends from middle school.

"*You* do stuff with them all the time. Me, not so much. Like Mike said."

"I don't really hang out with them that much anymore."

"Yeah, well, I pretty much never hang out with them at all if you're not there. So when do I get a chance to see them?"

Chad scowled but didn't say anything.

"You know my mom likes me to be home when she's there," Paul said. "And she doesn't like me to go places she doesn't know about when she's not home."

"You can come over here."

"And I do come over here. All the time. It would be nice, though, if I could go other places, too."

"You did today."

"Yeah, well."

"Didn't she say you had to go straight home today?"

"She thinks I was over here."

Chad glared at him. "You jerk. You used me as a cover with your mom, then you ditched me to play video games with the guys."

"It's not like you haven't used me as a cover before."

"Yeah, and you liked it so much when I did it to you." Back in eighth grade, Chad had told his folks he was spending time with Paul when actually he was with Steve Sessions and his friends. Paul hadn't known about it until Chad's mom called one day and told Paul that Chad was late. Paul had covered for him but refused to talk to him for a week afterward.

Paul was breathing deeply. "I'm sorry, okay! It just—I just really wanted to get away from everything for a while, you know? Just have fun, and not think about being gay, and . . ."

One look at Paul's face and Chad realized Paul had said more than he meant to say. "What? Being around me reminds me you you're gay?"

"Well, yeah." Paul wasn't looking at him.

"Why?"

Paul shrugged. " 'Cause you're the only other person who knows."

"Not my fault. Telling me you're gay was your own stupid idea."

"It's just—the way you look at me sometimes. I can tell you're thinking about it."

"Well, forgive me for remembering this freakin' huge bomb my best friend dropped on me."

They glared at each other for a minute before Paul looked away. "Anyway, I'm sorry," he repeated.

"Yeah, well, like you said, it's not like I don't act like a butthead, too, sometimes." Chad paused. "So how was the game place?"

"It was fun." Paul shrugged.

"Fun? Dude, fun is what you say when the second-grade teacher brings modeling clay and you get to play in the mud all afternoon. What was it like, really?"

"Dunno. I guess the best word to describe it was . . . fun." Paul snickered at him.

"Jerk." They both started laughing.

Paul came over a little after noon the next day. Then at about 3:00 they took off to Tyler's house for the sleepover.

"Welcome to the nut house," Tyler said as he opened the door. Then he laughed. He always said that. Chad had no idea why.

"Who else is here?"

"Rich. Mike's on his way."

"Anyone else coming?"

"No."

"So how'd you do on that last math test?" Paul asked Tyler.

"Okay, I guess. Good enough to get a B."

As they were talking, Tyler led them downstairs to the large area that included his bedroom and a separate TV room. That was one reason why they always had the sleepovers here.

"Did you hear what happened in fifth-period P.E. with McCloskey last Friday?"

"What?"

"This girl wound up ripping her shirt. Showed her boobs. Well, her bra anyway."

"Bet you liked that."

"I didn't get to see it."

"What did McCloskey do?"

"Told her to go change."

"Bet he was drooling over it."

"He's a pervert."

"You're a pervert."

"I'm fifteen."

"That's what I said."

"Right. So what was all that crap about what happened second lunch?"

"Some effin' idiot pulled the fire alarm."

"Well, yeah, I heard that part—"

The first couple of hours went like that, with the guys all playing video games while snacking on chips and soda pop and trading stories about stupid things that had happened the last few weeks of school. It was nice.

They also talked about summer plans. Paul would be spending the first few weeks as a counselor-in-training at Beaver Lodge Scout Camp. All the other guys thought he was nuts to want to spend time with a lot of twelve-year-olds. Later, he and Chad would both be going on the weeklong high adventure at Diamond Rock, where Paul hoped to finish off his last requirements for advancing to Life Scout. A couple of the other guys had part-time jobs or travel plans.

For the traditional movie with pizza, Tyler had picked *Goldmember*, the Austin Powers movie. Chad hadn't seen that one before. It was really funny, though Chad thought the dancing and singing got kind of old. During the part when Dr. Evil was talking about Preparation H, Paul snorted soda pop through his nose. Then later on, everybody snickered when the guy that Foxxy Cleopatra was using as a cover kissed Austin Powers. Chad glanced briefly at Paul but couldn't tell if his reaction to seeing one guy kiss another guy was different from everyone else's.

The final credits rolled up through the part with the outtakes. Then Tyler turned it off.

"Shit, that was lame," Chad commented.

"Well, no duh. That was kind of the point," Tyler responded. At the same time, Chad felt the inevitable punch from Paul on his arm.

The other guys noticed. "Hey! Is it Ficklin's job now to make sure the other Mormon boys don't use potty language?"

"Knock it off, Walters," Chad said.

"I heard your dad got made the bishop or something. I thought he was a salesman with Dynamo."

"Still is."

"So he's, like, part time or something?"

"Hell, no," interrupted one of the others. "Don't you know anything? Mormons don't pay their preachers."

"That's pretty dumb. Why do all that extra work if you aren't gonna be paid for it?"

Chad knew what Mike thought about churches, but he couldn't help but get a little ticked off. He didn't say anything, though.

Unfortunately, Paul did. "Chad's dad is a good guy," he insisted.

"Yeah, sure. Whatever. Just as long as he doesn't preach his religion at me."

Paul shut up then.

"What's with Ficklin?" asked Tyler a bit later, as Paul was off using the bathroom.

"Yeah. He's always been a dweeb, but now it's like he's all on your case and everything. Why do you hang around with him, anyway?"

Chad shrugged. "He's a friend," he said at last. Thankfully, they dropped the topic.

Next morning the guys slept in, then played video games and ate cold cereal. About noon, things broke up and Chad and Paul walked over to Paul's place.

After almost a day of pretty much nonstop talking—except when they'd been watching the movie or actually sleeping—Chad was pretty much talked out. So he hardly noticed how quiet the first part of the walk was. Then, out of the blue, Paul said, "I'm not gonna be your mouth monitor anymore."

"Huh?"

"Bargain's over. No more punches in the arm. You wanna stop swearing, find some other way."

"Okay." Chad was surprised, but he figured it was a good idea if it would avoid scenes like the guys hassling him the night before. Still, the way Paul said it, it was clear he was ticked off about something else as well.

A minute later, Chad found out what it was. "Why didn't you stick up for your dad?"

"What do you mean?"

"When Mike was going on about your dad being bishop and how dumb it was."

"He wasn't talking about my dad. He was just, you know, kind of making a general comment."

"They're lowlifes. Tyler and the rest."

Chad wondered where all this was coming from. "A couple days ago you went to the game place with them. Why trash them now?"

Paul shrugged. "It's nothing." He looked uncomfortable. "Just—the whole thing kind of made me realize that, you know, they don't really look at things the same way we do."

Chad wondered what had happened Thursday afternoon that made Paul and the other guys go off on each other. *I'll probably never know.*

Chapter Three

THE NEXT MONDAY, PAUL TOOK OFF for his three-week training at Beaver Lodge Scout Camp.

The time passed slowly. Chad spent some of it hanging out with Tyler and the others. After what happened during the sleepover, though—with them trashing Paul and everything—he didn't feel quite as comfortable with them as he had before. So he did a few things with them but also spent quite a bit of time with his family. Jeffrey in particular got a lot of time with his big brother. The kid always liked that, and it made their mom happy, which was an extra bonus.

For the Fourth of July, Chad went to the three-ward potluck and sat around eating fried chicken and watermelon and platefuls of desserts until he was stuffed, washing it all down with soda pop. It was at the pavilion in Somerset Park, as usual. After a while, most of the boys took off to play dodge Frisbee, but Chad didn't want to move away from the dessert tables yet. Instead, he let himself be talked into playing a game of bocce ball. No one was very good at the game, but Chad's team beat the team his dad was on.

Chad decided to sit out the next game while he let the last three brownies he'd eaten settle in his stomach. After a couple of minutes, his dad plopped down beside him.

"Paul gets back soon, right?"

Chad hadn't seen his dad much since school got out. He'd been working long hours training a new batch of salesmen.

"Tomorrow. Why?"

"Tell me, President Mortensen. You turn sixteen in August. Who should we call to be the next teachers quorum president?"

Chad shrugged. He'd been surprised when he was called as

quorum president back in March, though probably he shouldn't have been. Most of the other guys were hopeless or were still only fourteen, like Paul had been.

"I'd like your recommendation."

"Paul, of course."

His dad looked at him. Chad wondered if his dad was going to ask if he'd said that just because Paul was his friend. Really, though, Paul was the only choice that made any sense. Except for the gay part, which his dad didn't know about.

Don't think about that, he told himself.

His dad nodded. "Thanks," he said, then stood and walked off.

The next day was a Saturday. Paul arrived home that afternoon, and he and his mom came over for a barbecue at Chad's house that evening, although Chad's dad had to duck out partway through. Then Paul went home for what Chad assumed was going to be a marathon reading session with *Harry Potter and the Order of the Phoenix,* which had come out while Paul was at camp.

They spent a lot of the next few days playing video games and watching videos and biking around town. Sometimes Paul would come over and help Chad with babysitting his little brother and sister. Paul had lots of stories to tell about Beaver Lodge, like the time when one of the younger scouts got stuck in the latrine or when an idiot put a soda pop can—which they weren't supposed to have anyway—into the fire so that it exploded and sprayed hot Dr. Pepper over everyone. It almost made Chad wish he'd gone—until he remembered that he would've had to spend the time with twelve-year-olds and thirteen-year-olds. *Not to mention next year, when Paul gets to be a real counselor for the whole summer. I'd go nuts.*

That Wednesday night at Young Men was mostly spent preparing for the upcoming summer camps. Most of it was for the younger scouts, who would be going to Beaver Lodge in a couple of weeks, followed by the Diamond Rock trip for the older scouts the week after that. Chad and Paul spent most of the time sitting in the back, talking and cracking jokes.

Partway through the evening, Chad's dad poked his head through the door and waved Paul over. After a minute, Paul was back.

"What was that all about?"

"Your dad wanted me to make an appointment with Brother

Esplund to see him on Sunday," Paul grumbled. "Talks with the bishop aren't ever good news."

Chad couldn't help but smirk.

Paul stared at him. "Okay, out with it."

"Well, you know, I'm the teachers quorum president. And I'm turning sixteen in about a month . . ."

Paul closed his eyes. "Oh, no."

"Oh, yeah."

He opened his eyes again. "You know, I like your dad. But I really don't wanna have a conversation with him right now."

"My dad as in my dad, or my dad as in the bishop?"

"Either one."

"Are you gonna talk to him about . . . ?"

"Dunno. I don't really want to. But, well, I suppose it has to happen sometime." He swallowed nervously.

Next Sunday after church, Chad saw Paul waiting in front of his dad's office. He waved and gave him a thumbs-up. Paul waved back, his face almost as pale as his Sunday shirt. He looked really, really nervous. *Good luck,* Chad thought.

Later that afternoon, Chad was up in his room listening to his new Creed CD when he heard a knock on the door.

It was his dad. He didn't look mad, but he had a serious look on his face. Chad turned off the music.

"I guess now I know where all those questions about gay people were coming from," his dad said. Chad didn't say anything.

"Paul said you're the only one he's told about being attracted to guys. It sounds like you've been a good friend. I'm proud of you." He paused. "I could tell that was important to him. He's a really good kid. I'm glad he has a friend like you. And I'm glad you have a friend like him."

His dad stopped. Chad tried not to feel guilty when he remembered how badly he'd reacted when he first found out Paul was gay.

After a minute, his dad continued. "This thing Paul's going through is really tough. He's going to be making a lot of choices over the next few years that will make a difference for—well, forever. I'll help him as much as I can as his bishop. But I think how you act as his friend may make a bigger difference than anything I can do."

Chad wondered with a sinking feeling if his dad was somehow expecting him to help Paul get over being gay. Talking to Paul, he didn't think that was even possible, and he wouldn't have the slightest idea how to try.

Apparently some of what he was thinking showed on his face. "Just be his friend," his dad said. Then he patted Chad on the shoulder, gave a small smile, and left.

"So I guess you told my dad," Chad said to Paul the next day.

Chad had done several chores that morning, including reading two stories to Jeffrey and helping with his train set while his mom went to the hairdresser's, then mowing the lawn and fixing lunch. As soon as that was done, he'd biked over to Paul's place, stopping just long enough on his way out the door to get his mom's okay. She'd laughed and waved him off, telling him to make sure he was back by dinner. She also said he could invite Paul and his mom over if they didn't have other plans.

"You were right," Paul said, looking away. "Your dad wants me to be the next teachers quorum president, just like you said. And, well, yeah. I mean—"

"You figured you had to tell him before you said yes."

"Yeah."

"What did you say?"

"I told him I was gay. He got a really weird look on his face and asked if I've ever done anything, you know, gay with someone else. And then—" Paul chewed on his thumb. "It looked like he was thinking. Then he said he figured that as long as I was doing what I should, it didn't make much difference what I was *tempted* to do. Then he said I could still be a good teachers quorum president if I follow the same standards everyone else is supposed to follow. We talked awhile. He said he didn't know why some people turn out gay, but I shouldn't be too quick to decide I'm really gay. Except he called it same-sex attracted, which apparently is what some people in the church call it. Whatever."

"He didn't have a problem with you being gay?"

Paul stared at him. "Of course he had a problem with me being gay. 'Cause it's, you know, against church standards. Remember that part? Like where two guys can't get married, and sex outside of marriage is wrong? Duh. I didn't think you needed a rehash of the whole 'Let's look it up in *For the Strength of Youth*' bit. You know, just to make sure I knew, absolutely one hundred percent, that having sex with guys is not allowed."

"He did that?"

"Of course."

Chad could believe it. Each time his dad talked to the youth, he'd start by quoting from the church's pamphlet for teenagers and their parents. He did the same thing in one-on-one interviews, too. He always said the best way to start was by making sure everyone understood what the rules were.

"He also said I should tell my mom about it."

Chad winced.

Paul continued. "There's this part in *For the Strength of Youth* where it talks about telling your parents and your bishop. So I told him I'd talk to her sometime. He said it was up to me, but I should let her know. Like I'm really looking forward to *that*."

"Sucks to be you."

"So you've said before." Paul shook his head. "No way am I telling my dad, though."

"No duh."

Paul was nervous about something. And Barbara knew it had to do with her.

It—whatever it was—had started last Sunday after Paul's interview with the bishop. Barbara had been pleased when Bishop Mortensen told her he wanted to extend a calling to Paul to serve as the teachers quorum president. She didn't imagine there would be any problem with Paul accepting.

But then the short fifteen-minute interview the bishop said they'd be having had stretched to twenty-five minutes, and then thirty-five minutes, before Paul came out the door. He was smiling, though, as he shook the bishop's hand.

"So. New teachers quorum president?" she'd asked, on the way home.

"Yeah." He was looking out the window.

"You were in there an awful long time," she ventured.

"Yeah. We were talking about some stuff."

She waited, but Paul didn't say anything more. Instead, he just kept looking out the window. *I guess whatever it was, I won't be finding out any more about it,* she thought. *Teenagers. Always a mystery. Boys especially.*

Paul had remained unusually quiet in the days since then. Several times, she'd seen him giving her a strange look that she had no idea how to interpret.

Dinner tonight was quiet, too. Usually, eating together was a chance to catch up on things: schedules, funny stories from her work, how Paul had kept busy that day. Talking to each other, sharing things, kept them functioning as a family, not just two people living in the same space. Tonight, though, the conversation kept falling flat.

Just as they were finishing up, Paul said, "Mom, I need to talk to you."

I guess this is it. Barbara's stomach tightened. "Should we go into the living room?"

He nodded.

Barbara pulled out a couple of multilayer Jell-O-type desserts from the refrigerator. They stacked their dirty dishes in the sink, then moved into the other room.

Barbara pulled her legs underneath herself on the couch as she opened her dessert, ignoring thoughts about what she'd say to her physical therapy patients if they sat like that. It was comfortable. From the way Paul was acting, she got the feeling she might need that comfort.

Paul sat on the edge of his chair. He'd pulled in one of the kitchen chairs, she saw, rather than sit in one of the big overstuffed chairs that were already in the living room. He put his dessert on the floor without opening it.

And then she waited, while Paul looked down at his lap. Looked up. Looked down again. Shifted in his seat, and shifted again.

"Paul?"

"Sorry. It's . . . kind of hard to talk about."

With an effort, Barbara stopped herself from saying anything. Finally, a minute or two later, he looked up and started talking.

"There's no really easy way to say it." He paused and licked his lips. "I . . . don't like girls, Mom."

She waited a minute to see if Paul was done. Then, carefully keeping her voice calm and even, she asked, "Are you trying to tell me you're gay?"

"Yeah. That's what I'm saying."

Barbara nodded slowly. Inside, she felt her mind go into a deep freeze. *I have to be a mom right now. I can fall apart later.*

Meanwhile, her voice kept talking, asking questions to buy time while she figured out what to do next. "That's what took so long, when you talked with the bishop on Sunday?"

"Yeah."

"What did he say?"

Paul shrugged, but the rest of his body screamed just how tense he was. "He said it was a temptation just like any other temptation. He said as long as I follow church standards, I can still be a worthy member of the church."

"That sounds sensible." She paused. At times like this, she wished she'd grown up in an active LDS family. Maybe there would have been a talk or lesson somewhere along the line that would have given her a clearer idea how to handle this.

Well, first things first, she thought. *Triage.* "Paul?"

"Yeah?"

"This isn't what I expected our conversation to be about. Actually, I don't know what I expected," she admitted. "But you need to know this. You're still my son. I still love you. Whatever happens in your life, I'm on your side. Okay? This doesn't make me love you any less or think less of you."

"Thanks." He drew a deep breath. "I—hoped you'd say that. It's good to hear it, though."

"Come here and give your old mom a hug."

As she felt his arms wrap around her, Barbara reflected that from a mother's perspective, nothing could be too wrong with the world if your teenage son was still willing to hug you. She wasn't surprised, though, when Paul pulled away half a minute later.

Okay. Time to gather some information.

"Who else knows about this? Bishop Mortensen, of course. Anyone else?"

"Chad. He's the first one I told."

The two boys were awfully close. "Is Chad gay, too?"

Paul burst out in a nervous laugh. "No way! He's, uh, like, totally straight."

"But you're still friends?"

"Yeah. He freaked out about it at first, but he's okay with it now. He still thinks it's pretty weird."

"What's so weird about it? After all, I liked boys when I was your age."

Paul stared at her. "Bad joke, Mom."

"There were lots of boys in my class that I thought were cute."

"I really don't want to hear this."

"There was this one boy with really pretty green eyes and long eyelashes who I had a crush on my sophomore year—"

"Aagh!" Paul ran out of the room and slammed his bedroom door behind him, while Barbara broke up laughing. *Mom one, kid zero.*

A minute later he peeked out of his bedroom door. "Is it safe to come out now?"

"I promise. The bad, evil teenage-mom stories have all gone away."

"Good." They looked at each other. There was a reluctant grin on Paul's face. Barbara felt some of the tension start to drain away.

"So what does it mean to you, when you say you're gay?"

Paul blushed. "Part of it's like you said. Thinking guys are cute, and all that."

"You don't think girls are cute?"

"Not that way."

"Not romantically."

"Yeah." Paul's face was bright red. "I don't, you know, get crushes on girls."

"But you do get crushes on boys."

"Oh, yeah."

"Who?"

"Mom! Just—some of the guys at school, okay? That's all you need to know."

"You want to surprise your mom when you bring home your first boyfriend?" Barbara was proud of herself for keeping her voice light.

"That's not gonna happen, Mom."

"You don't want to have a boyfriend?"

"Not if I want to stay in the church."

That sounds pretty definite. Barbara thought carefully about how to phrase her next question. "So what *do* you want out of life, now that you've figured out you're attracted to boys?"

He looked unhappy. "I don't—I mean, it's not like being gay changes who I am, you know? There's part of me that really wants to go to BYU, I guess, and go on a mission and get married and have kids. Being gay hasn't changed any of that. It's just—" He gestured helplessly.

"You don't know if you can really have all that?"

"Yeah." He paused. "And, well, there are other things I want, too. Even if I know I'm not supposed to."

"Like having a boyfriend?"

"Yeah."

Barbara hesitated. "You know, I'm under the impression that a lot of what boys think about at your age has to do with sex, not relationships. Usually, it's teenage girls who want the romance."

"I guess." Paul's reply sounded reluctant, but at least he was responding.

"So when you say you're attracted to males, is this all about sexual attraction? Or is there more to it than that?"

"How should I know? I'm a guy!" Paul grimaced and ran a hand through his hair. "Both, I guess. I mean, yeah, a lot of it's about who I think is hot. But it's about being together with someone, too." He paused. "A few months ago there was this stake fireside where they brought in a couple who just got married, like, a year or two ago while they were both students at BYU. I remember the woman saying that being married to the right person was like filling a part of yourself that you didn't even know was empty. And then she talked about being alone, and how that's part of what being a teenager is all about. She said being lonely can be a good thing if it makes you think about the person you want to be and the choices you have to make in order to be that person. And then she said a lot of the mistakes teenagers make are because they aren't patient enough to wait for good relationships. Instead, they just settle for something that will fill that empty spot."

"Sounds like a smart lady."

"Yeah. See, though, the thing is . . . I'm not planning to get married anytime soon. But when I'm lonely and wish there was someone I could be with to make the loneliness go away, it's guys that I think about."

Both of them were quiet for a minute after that. Finally Barbara continued, "So what's it like, when you think a boy is cute or sexy or whatever?"

"Mom! You don't really want to know *that*!"

"Why not?"

Paul buried his face in his hands and mumbled something.

"What did you say?"

Paul looked up. His face was red. "It's like — sometimes I'll see a guy smiling, you know? And it'll be like, *wow*. Or sometimes I'll see someone who's really good looking, and it's like someone's traced around him with a marker so he just stands out from everything around him."

"It can be like that," Barbara found herself agreeing.

Paul winced and looked away. "One time—there was this kid in eighth grade who was really shy, and his friend embarrassed him at the lunch table. And he blushed, but he was kind of laughing at the same time, you know? And so I cracked a couple jokes just to try and cheer him up. And then he smiled at me, and I got this feeling in the pit of my stomach that was like—I don't know, eating a big double-fudge sundae or something."

Boys and their stomachs, Barbara thought. *I shouldn't be surprised that even romantic feelings get translated into thoughts about food.*

"So next thing I know, it was the end of lunch and Chad was really mad at me 'cause I never showed up to do stuff with him. It was like I didn't even want to do anything else as long as I could stay there and goof around with this other kid."

"Sounds like a crush."

"Yeah." He blushed.

"Hmm." A sudden memory struck her. "Was that Tony, by any chance?"

Paul looked at her warily. "Yes."

"He *was* a cute one. Freckles, too, if I recall. I can't fault your taste in boys." She grinned at him.

Paul's look turned to a glare. "You're going to hell for torturing your child," he said. "And I will look down on you and *laugh.* And God won't even blame me."

"No doubt." Barbara snickered at him. Paul grinned back at her.

Barbara took a deep breath. "I'm sure I'll have more questions later on, but for right now, I think we've talked about this long enough. Want a bowl of ice cream? That Jell-O thing really wasn't much of a dessert."

"It really wasn't," he agreed.

"How would you know? You didn't even eat yours." She pointed down to where it was still sitting unopened on the floor next to Paul's chair.

"Oops."

An hour later, Barbara collapsed inside her bedroom.

It had been a good evening, she thought. Especially when she considered what it might have been like.

They'd laughed. They'd talked. When she'd asked later how

long he'd known he was gay, Paul, blushing, admitted that he'd noticed some boys were cute back in seventh grade. He hadn't realized what it meant, though, until eighth-grade health class.

She couldn't really imagine what it must have been like for him, figuring out something like that about himself. Wishing it wasn't true. Praying for it not to be true. Having it finally sink in that it *was* true. Small wonder he'd waited a year and a half before telling anyone.

Part of her desperately wanted to talk to someone else about it. Her sister, maybe. She missed spending time with Sheanne ever since she'd moved back to Southern California a couple years ago. It would be a comfort to talk to her about all this. But she couldn't do that to Paul, talking about this to someone else — especially another family member — without his permission.

Maybe she should have stayed together with Frank. Having a dad in the home might have helped. As soon as she thought it, though, her mind rebelled. *That's not the way being gay works, Barbara. You know that.*

Besides, she couldn't really imagine that Frank would have been any help at all with this situation. Paul had told her that he didn't plan to tell his father about it. She thought that was a very good idea. Who knew how he'd react?

Absent father and controlling mother. That's what they used to say caused homosexuality. She didn't know if they were still saying that. Some people said it was genetic, but she didn't know anyone in her family or Frank's who was gay. It made her nervous, wondering if there was some way she'd contributed to making him gay. She didn't think so, but she'd probably never know.

He's still my son. That, she was sure of. She'd come out of the evening with a clear sense that he was still the same boy she'd spent the last fifteen years growing to love and enjoy. When it came right down to it, that was all she really needed to know.

And now that she wasn't focused on trying to be the mother Paul needed her to be, she could let her own emotions out. Finally.

She shuddered. Not entirely to her surprise, she felt tears gathering.

Paul would have a hard life. A lot of the things he said he wanted — mission, family, activity in the church — would be possible only if he could ignore some of his own deepest instincts.

She tried to put herself in his shoes, imagining what it would be like if God required her to have a relationship with another woman.

The thought horrified her. She doubted it would even be possible for her to do.

And then she was crying in earnest, crying over the little boy she'd raised and her hopes and dreams about the life he'd lead, all of which seemed so much less likely now. She could mourn now, alone in her bedroom without Paul there to see and misunderstand.

"So she was okay with it?" Chad asked.

"Yeah." Paul glanced over, and Chad saw a sly look on his friend's face. "Maybe even a little relieved, you know? I mean, it's not like she has to worry about me coming home and telling her I got a girl pregnant. Not like you in a couple of years." Paul snickered.

"Ha, ha, you're so very funny. Just don't say anything like that around my parents, or they'll kill me. And then who'll beat you at *Bust-a-Move*?"

"You wish." Actually the two of them were pretty closely matched, with Paul usually doing just a bit better.

They started another game.

"It's really weird, you know?" Paul said, keeping up a steady stream of fire on his side of the screen.

"What is?"

"Now you know, and your dad knows, and my mom knows. It's like I was hiding before, but now I'm out in the open. It's kind of freaky."

"Yeah. I can kind of see that." *Actually, I'm amazed you're not throwing up in the toilet over it,* Chad thought. He didn't say it, though, in case the words set Paul off.

Just then, Paul got off a lucky shot that dropped a bunch of bubbles, sending them over to Chad's side faster than Chad could drop them. He grumbled a little at his loss. To Chad's surprise, though, instead of starting another round right away, Paul paused the game, though he still wasn't looking directly at Chad.

"Sometimes, you know, I just want to go back to pretending it's not really real. I can't, though. It's different now, because I know that other people know I'm gay. No going back."

Paul stopped talking. Chad wondered if he was going to start the game again. He didn't, though. Instead, he stared off into space, as if he was still thinking about the last thing he'd said. Finally, just as Chad was about to ask if he wanted to go do something else, Paul shook himself, looked down at the controller, and pressed the start button.

Neither of them brought up the gay thing again for the rest of that summer.

High adventure with the scouts. Swimming, hiking, camping. Merit badges and campfire conversations. Funny stories about near-encounters with bears, or animals some of the scouts thought were bears. Then back home again. Chad's release, and Paul getting set apart as the new teachers quorum president. More summer activities. Dusty afternoons spent getting all scratched up chopping down massive blackberry thickets for Chad's Eagle project. Two and a half weeks in Minnetonka for Paul with his dad and second family, then back to Arcadia Heights. Late-summer bicycling and swimming. Late-night video-game marathons. Chad's birthday around the middle of August, together with getting his driver's license and being ordained a priest. Chad's Eagle board of review, followed by his court of honor. Preparations for the new school year.

And then summer was over and it was back to the regular routine, classes and homework and after-school activities, and a chance to see what had changed and what hadn't changed and what would keep on changing as they moved forward into the future.

Chapter Four

"You totally should come to GSA. It's all about tolerance, which is a good thing. And the people are neat, and no one will think you're gay just because you come to the meetings, especially if you come with me."

Paul looked around the lunch table. Most of the other guys were carefully looking away. A few were snickering surreptitiously at him for being caught by Sarah Donnelly in a crusading mood.

It was three weeks into Paul's sophomore year. This year, Paul and Chad's schedules had given them different lunches, though Paul found he didn't mind as much as he'd expected.

Paul had decided not to go out for soccer this year. Since Chad was still on the team, that meant the two of them weren't seeing much of each other right now. Paul had expected to feel bored, but instead it was turning into a nice opportunity to get to know other people. It was about time Paul picked up some new friends, anyway.

First day of the school year, he'd picked a lunch table with several people he recognized from last year and pretty much got along with. It had turned out to be a good choice. A lot of them were semi-geeks, like Paul, and they were mostly tolerant of people's personality quirks. Like Eric Swanson's fanaticism over *Final Fantasy Tactics* and the way Joel Reynolds would make the same stupid jokes about cafeteria food each day.

That tolerance had its good and bad sides, Paul thought, looking now at Sarah. On the one hand, if they'd been at a table full of jocks—like the one where Tyler and several other of Chad's idiot friends were sitting, across the commons—Sarah might have approached him anyway, but she probably would have been driven off by the dyke and faggot comments before he had to answer her. On the other hand, if he did find himself dragged off to the Gay-Straight Alliance, he didn't think the other guys at this table would tease him about it. Much.

"I'm waiting," Sarah said. Her eyes narrowed. "Are you homophobic?"

Paul choked on a bite of food. *That is so much* NOT *what my problem is with going to GSA,* he thought.

Back when he'd first come out to Chad, he'd just been relieved that it hadn't ended in disaster. The same thing had been true after he told his mom and the bishop. Since then, though, he'd started to wish there was someone else he could talk to about what it felt like to be gay.

Not his mom or the bishop. And Chad really didn't want to hear anything about what it was like to look at a cute guy or anything like that. Things with Chad had been okay over the summer, but Paul knew it was better not to push it.

Part of him really wanted to try out GSA, if he could do it without everybody knowing he was gay. And now Sarah had given him the perfect excuse.

"There you are." It was Sarah. "I thought for a bit that you weren't going to come."

"My last class is across the school from here. Other side of the gym."

"It's a good thing you showed up when you did. Another minute and I'd have left without you and then broke your arm the next time I saw you."

They started walking, with Sarah leading the way because Paul didn't know where the club met.

"Can't we just say no to all the violence?" he asked. "I mean, you know, violence in the cause of tolerance. It really doesn't look good."

"Just for that—" She punched him on the arm.

"Oh! I'm wounded!" In fact, the punch had landed with more force than he expected, though it was still nothing compared to what he and Chad did to each other, even when they were just kidding.

"Why did I bring you, anyway?"

"Because the other guys dodge faster, because you need a punching bag, because I'm a sucker for girls who beat me up."

"Har, har. Laugh it up, fuzz ball." She stopped. "Here we are."

They had reached two classrooms in the art wing with a divider pulled open between them, combining them into one big room. About twenty people were already there, more than half of them girls, standing and talking in groups. Up toward the front of the room, a woman who looked like she was in her forties was sitting and slowly leafing through papers in a manila folder.

"That's Ms. Allington, the advisor."

"Art teacher?"

"Counselor. She's new this year."

Paul was surprised. He'd never heard of a counselor being a club advisor.

"Last year's advisor was an art teacher, but she took a job in another district. Ms. Allington was already helping with tolerance issues for gay students, so she volunteered to be the new advisor."

"You were in GSA last year, too?"

"Yeah." Sarah continued more quietly, "My big brother's gay, so it's kind of important to me. He's a sophomore now at U. of O. studying journalism." She shook her head. "Let's get you introduced to some people."

"Sarah—"

But it was too late.

Over the next five minutes, Paul was introduced to about half of the other kids, almost none of whom he had the slightest chance of remembering.

He had to give credit to Sarah for truth-telling in her introductions. Mostly she introduced him as "Paul, this guy who sits at my lunch table who I dragged out to this meeting." The introductions he received in turn were equally short and blunt. "Tom, who's here to pick up girls. Kathryn, who makes friends with everyone who comes through the door. Ellen, who's friendly and nice and has a brown belt in something or other and is just possibly the most intimidating person I've ever met."

"More intimidating than you?" Paul asked.

"Shut up, you, or I'll punch you again. Fred, who's here because Elaine dragged him out and he's too scared of her to stop coming. Steve, our resident lech."

"Thanks for bringing such a cute guy," Steve said.

Embarrassed, Paul looked away.

Sarah rolled her eyes. "Ignore him. We all do. And Trevor, our resident goofball."

"Hi."

"Hi back," Trevor responded. "Hey, aren't you in my Spanish class?"

"Mr. Dickey? Third period?"

"Yeah."

"How do you stay awake long enough to see who's in the class?"

"Simple," Trevor said. "I look at everyone else instead of listening to Dickless."

Right about then, a girl who was apparently the club president stood at the front of the room and started talking. Even then, a lot of the conversations didn't stop, and Paul was able to make out only a few words. Finally, a boy he hadn't met yet stood up and yelled, "Shut up, people!"

In the sudden near-quiet, it was easy to hear the girl say, "Thank you, Jared."

"Any time."

"Welcome to the Arcadia Heights Gay-Straight Alliance. I see a few people here we haven't had out before — you're especially welcome. And now for the first thing we have to talk about today . . ."

"So how did you like it?"

Paul shrugged. "It was okay."

"You didn't seem too uncomfortable."

I guess that's true, Paul thought. Throughout the meeting, he'd felt like an outsider, but it hadn't really been uncomfortable. Mostly, he'd just sat back and watched — kind of like an anthropologist observing the habits of some new tribe. *The GSA tribe.* He grinned.

Sarah noticed the grin. "So you'll be back, then?" she persisted.

"Maybe." His grin got wider.

"Paul . . ."

"All right, all right, already! I give in. It was fine. It was great. I'll probably even go back sometime, maybe. If only to avoid getting punched again."

"Better believe it."

The whole thing had been quite a bit different from what Paul expected. In the back of his mind, he'd thought it would mostly be about being gay, and maybe talking with other gay kids about what it was like to be gay. Instead, most of the meeting had been about activities the club was helping organize for the school's AIDS

Education Week starting December first, which—Paul had found out—was World AIDS Day.

Somehow, Paul had wound up on the committee to do posters about AIDS statistics and safe behavior. He supposed that was fine, so long as no one outside the club ever found out he'd worked on them.

During the meeting, Paul had been startled to notice at least two pairs of girls holding hands, though he did his best not to stare. He hadn't seen any guys who were obviously in couples, but some of the comments he heard were pretty gay. That included some from Trevor, who'd cracked a couple of really funny jokes about being caught looking at guys—and about which guys he wouldn't be caught dead looking at. Paul had actually laughed out loud at one of them.

Some of the boys were a bit . . . effeminate. Most of them seemed pretty normal, though. To Paul's surprise, the normal-seeming ones included Trevor and several others who had been making gay comments. Paul wouldn't have ever been able to tell they were gay except for what they were saying.

He'd been really surprised to find out that Jared—the guy who yelled at everyone to shut up and who wound up sitting next to Paul for a lot of the meeting—was gay. Partway through the meeting, while the groups were supposedly working but most people were talking instead, a girl had come over and asked Jared how things were going with his folks.

"Pretty much the same as always," he said.

"That's too bad." She'd patted his arm sympathetically, then wandered off.

Jared caught Paul looking at him. "I came out to my folks last year. They said they were okay with it, but things haven't really been the same since."

"Sorry."

"Wasn't your fault."

Paul rolled his eyes. "You know what I mean, doofus."

Jared snickered. "Do you know how long it's been since someone called me a doofus? I swear, if it didn't sound like your voice had changed, I'd think you were twelve."

"I *have* gone through puberty, thank you very much."

"Or so you claim. I'm Jared Esters. I'm a junior."

"Paul Ficklin. Sophomore."

"Good to meet you. This your first time here?"

"Yeah. My friend Sarah dragged me out."

They spent the next five minutes talking about movies from the summer. Both of them had seen *The Hulk*, though Paul liked it better than Jared had. When Jared found out that Paul hadn't seen *Matrix Reloaded*, he went on about how great it was. Paul didn't tell him that he'd wanted to see it but hadn't because it was rated R, though he loved the first Matrix movie when he saw the edited version on cable.

Just then, the leader of the group had called for everyone's attention. As Paul turned to look at the latest idea for a poster, he noticed Jared grinning at him. He grinned back. It wasn't like a crush or anything — but Jared seemed like someone who might turn into a friend.

After Jared Esters got home that afternoon, he had a hard time concentrating on his homework. Instead, he kept thinking about Paul, the new kid who'd shown up at GSA.

Jared had started attending GSA pretty early in his freshman year. Back in eighth grade, he'd figured out that he was attracted to boys. He hadn't come out then, though. Going through the door to the GSA his freshman year was the first time he'd acknowledged to anyone else that he was gay — except for a couple of pen pals he'd picked up at a gay-teen website who knew him only by his e-mail nickname. Even at the GSA, it had been a couple of months before he actually told people he was gay. Still, just going through the door had felt like coming out to him.

His real coming out to his own family hadn't happened until he was a sophomore. With the support and encouragement of friends he'd met at GSA, he'd told his parents that he was gay. His dad had just grunted. His mom hadn't had any obvious problem with it. When his older brother found out, he'd given Jared a disgusted look but hadn't said much about it aside from a few comments about pansies. Afterward, though, there somehow didn't seem to be as much conversation in his house anymore. It was as if a kind of space had opened up between him and the rest of his family.

Or maybe things were just different because Jared was growing up and had become more vocal about making decisions for himself. He wasn't ready to leave home yet, but part of him was already looking forward to when he would finally be on his own.

Jared had a fairly wide circle of friends. Only some of them knew he was gay, though he wasn't paranoid about trying to hide it. He just didn't like to talk about it with anyone who didn't have a reason to know.

He didn't get into the political side of being gay that much, the way a lot of the other GSA kids did. Jared went to the meetings, but he didn't have much in common with most of the members. He was gay, and they were gay — or rather, some of them were gay and the rest were gay-friendly. That was it.

When it came right down to it, whether you liked boys or girls or both didn't really say very much about what you did in your spare time or the kind of music you liked or what type of jokes you laughed at. Mostly, he just felt like if he could be there for someone else who was gay, it was something he ought to do. Especially after the help the GSA had given him the year before when he came out to his folks and before that in helping him feel comfortable being gay.

Like he could do for Paul, maybe. Paul kind of reminded Jared of himself last year or the year before. He'd said that his friend had dragged him out, but he hadn't spent much time with her after that. Instead, he'd spent the time watching and looking around, as if he was evaluating what he was seeing. As if he was trying to figure out whether he'd fit in.

And he seemed pretty cool. He liked science-fiction movies and video games, but he wasn't too much of a freak about it. He seemed to have a pretty good sense of humor. And he was cute, too. Jared hoped he'd have a chance to get to know him better, even if he didn't turn out to be gay.

GSA met every other week, officially. Unofficially, there was apparently a get-together pretty much every week in the same place. On the weeks when there wasn't an official meeting it was mostly a social gathering, with some informal planning on the side.

The next week, Paul didn't go to the informal meeting. Afterward, Sarah asked him why he hadn't shown up. "Several people asked about you. Trevor and Jared both did."

"Sure they did."

"Really. I think Jared thinks you're cute." Sarah was definitely laughing at him.

"That's supposed to make me want to come out? To the meeting, I mean?"

She snickered at his unintentional joke. "Girls think it's a compliment when a boy thinks they're cute, even if it's not someone they want to go out with. I don't see why guys can't treat it the same way."

"Believe me, Sarah, it's not the same."

"What, you'd feel better if I told you Jane Weston thought you were cute, too? Should I set you up with her?"

"No! I can handle my dating and social life on my own, thank you."

She laughed again, then asked, "What's that ring you're wearing?"

It was Paul's CTR ring. Several people in his seminary class had started wearing them this year. "It's, um—it's something for a group I belong to."

"What kind of group?"

"A church group," he said reluctantly. Back when he'd decided to wear the ring, he'd thought it would provide a cool and easy way to explain about being Mormon. He hadn't imagined it turning out like this, with the first person who asked about it being the girl who'd dragged him out to GSA.

"Oh," Sarah said. To his relief, she didn't ask him any more questions. "Anyway, you *will* be there next week, right?"

"Yeah."

"Good. Jared said you helped keep them organized."

"I didn't do that much. Just wrote down some of the different ideas people had for the posters."

"Believe me, that's a lot better than they would have done without you there. I've seen that group try to get stuff done before. Penny's good at bossing people around, but not so good at organizing things. Usually it winds up with two or three people over on the side doing stuff, while everyone else talks the whole time."

"We talked a lot, too," Paul pointed out.

"Yeah, but that was after you'd made your list, read it, and then asked for people to do up some samples."

Paul blushed. For a few minutes the week before, it had felt like he was trying to run a patrol meeting in scouts. Once he realized what he was doing, he'd stopped and hoped no one noticed. Apparently some people had.

"You know, we really should put you in charge of the poster group. That's not really Penny's thing. They just needed someone to keep that group on track, and she got stuck with it."

"No! I'm not even a member of GSA."

"Actually, you are. You show up at a meeting, you're a member. There's no official signup sheet or membership list or anything."

"Great. But no on the poster thing."

"We'll see."

At the next meeting, Paul did manage to avoid being put in charge of the poster group, though it was a close thing. He finally agreed to be the group's record keeper. He had the uncomfortable feeling that whether he had the position or not, he'd probably end up in charge anyway, practically speaking.

About the first twenty minutes were taken up with announcements and general discussion. Apparently, one of the club leaders had a list of gay-related events in the Portland area. A few of them sounded interesting, like the guest lecture about the Holocaust at the Arcadia Heights Public Library. Paul hadn't even known the Nazis targeted gay people as well as Jews. They spent a while talking about organizing rides to some of the events.

Then the meeting broke up into groups. They spent most of the rest of the time figuring out different things they wanted to put on the posters and trying out designs that would get the message across without being too busy with information.

Going home that afternoon, Paul realized he was in a really good mood. He'd felt a lot more comfortable jumping in this time. Not so much like he was visiting, but more like he was a member of the group. He'd laughed more openly at Trevor's comments and the jokes told by some of the other club members, without worrying so much about whether someone might think he was gay. *No one here would care*, he realized. *They'd be fine with it either way*. It was a liberating thought.

Paul was feeling so good about GSA that he decided it would be a good time to let his mom know. So that evening at dinner, he introduced the topic.

"Mom."

"Yes?"

"I've, uh, started going to the school GSA club. A friend from my lunch table dragged me out for a meeting a couple of weeks ago, and I went again today. I'm helping with some posters they're making."

"Sounds great! What's the GSA, anyway?"

"It's the Gay-Straight Alliance at the high school. You know, for kids who are gay, as well as straight. They're really big into tolerance for people."

As Paul was speaking, his mom got a worried expression on her face, just the way he'd known she would.

"It's okay, Mom. Nobody there knows I'm gay. There are lots of straight kids. Sarah, the girl who dragged me there—I'm pretty sure she's straight herself. She thinks I'm straight. And they do really great stuff. Like, these posters I'm helping with, they're all for AIDS Education Week, to help the kids be more aware about AIDS and safe behavior."

Paul took a deep breath. "Besides, sometimes I'd like to talk about the way I feel with other people who feel the same way. It's not like I'm planning to get all active in gay liberation, or whatever."

"I guess I can see that," his mother responded. "Just make sure you don't get involved in something that will push you away from being the kind of person you want to be, okay?"

"I'll be careful, Mom."

The next week, Paul went to the unofficial meeting.

The first thing he noticed was that there were only about half as many kids as at the normal meetings, fewer than twenty total. They were in the same room as usual but hadn't bothered to open the divider.

Ms. Allington was sitting in an overstuffed chair on one side of the room, reading a book. Paul guessed that she had to be there to supervise because they were meeting in a regular classroom, but it didn't look like she was paying much attention.

"Hey, Paul! Good to see you!" It was Trevor, sitting on one of the desks and wearing . . . was that a cloak?

"Hey."

"Sarah isn't here yet."

"I thought I'd surprise her."

"So, she isn't your girlfriend or anything, is she?"

"Do I act like her boyfriend?"

"You let her punch you."

"So do you."

"That's because she's scary."

"Who's scary?" put in Jared, wandering over from another conversation.

"Sarah," they both said.

"I heard that!" It was Sarah, who'd just entered the room. "Hey, Paul. Good to see you."

"So Trevor already said."

"And what's so great about Trevor?"

"He doesn't punch me."

"So Paul, what's that ring?" Jared asked.

"It's, um, my CTR ring. Choose the right." He'd thought about taking it off after Sarah's question the other week but decided that might lead to more questions, both from Sarah and from the kids in his seminary class. Now he was wishing he had.

"It's something from his church," put in Sarah.

"What church do you belong to?" asked Trevor.

No way to avoid it. "I'm Mormon."

There was a pause. "Aren't they, like, anti-gay?" asked Jared finally.

"Not really. Just, well . . . it's kind of complicated. Let's skip it for now, okay?"

"All right." Jared looked like he wanted to say something but was choosing not to.

The conversation turned to movies again. Jared told them about *Kill Bill*, which he'd seen over the weekend and which sounded really strange to Paul. After Jared's third description of yet another violent scene, Sarah wandered off, saying she lacked the Y chromosome to think dismembered body parts were all that interesting.

After about ten minutes, Jared said, "Hey! You know what? We could all go see it tonight, if you want."

"I can't," said Trevor. "Too much homework."

"I better not go either," said Paul. "I can't stay out late on school nights. Maybe some other time."

"Tough."

The rest of the meeting continued in pretty much the same mode. Trevor wandered off after a while, but Jared and Paul kept talking about movies. When Paul discovered Jared hadn't seen *Firefly* when it was broadcast last year, he spent about twenty minutes talking about the series. Eventually Jared agreed that he'd have to see it sometime—partly, Paul guessed, just to shut him up. To his surprise, Paul found himself inviting Jared over to his house to watch it on video. After a minute, Jared agreed. Not too long after that, things broke up and everyone took off for home.

• • •

"So this is where you live."

"Yeah. It's the one on the right." Paul gestured toward the yellow duplex.

It was Thursday, a couple of days after the GSA social meeting. Much to Paul's surprise, he'd gotten a call from Jared on his cell phone the night before, asking when would be a good time for him to come over and see "that freaky science-fiction show you were all excited about." Since Jared had a car and a license, he'd volunteered to drive them both to Paul's house after school.

They clambered up the steps to the front door, then into the living room. "Have a seat," Paul said, gesturing as he continued into the kitchen. "What can I get you? Root beer? Orange juice? Milk? Sprite?"

"Do you have any Coke?"

"No." Paul could feel himself blushing. *No way am I gonna explain that Mormons aren't supposed to drink stuff with caffeine. Especially since half the Mormon kids I know do it anyway.* For some reason, he really wanted to make a good impression on Jared.

"Orange juice, then."

"Great."

Paul brought out two orange juices, a package of cookies, and some chips and salsa. He set them on the coffee table, then went over to where the *Firefly* videotapes were stashed.

"So, just you and your mom?"

"Yeah. Mom and Dad divorced about seven years ago."

"So what do you do for fun?"

"You mean, aside from attending our illustrious high school?" Jared grinned at the sarcasm. "Regular stuff," Paul continued. "I was in soccer last year, but I decided not to go out this year. I'm in scouts, working on my Eagle. Not too much else. Read a lot, play video games, that kind of thing."

"Any other clubs? Besides GSA?"

"Nah."

"You said something about belonging to a church?"

"Yeah. That's where I do scouts." Thinking about trying to explain the church and its position on gays made Paul nervous, so he turned the question back to Jared. "What about you? What do you do for fun?"

"Let's see. I like dirt biking."

"Is that with motorcycles?"

"I wish. Mountain bikes. You know, those bicycles with the fat tires. There's some places you can ride around not too far outside of town. Or sometimes I get together with friends and we drive a few miles farther out and then ride around."

"Sounds cool."

"You ever been?"

"No."

"I'm thinking of going this Saturday. Weather's supposed to be good. Might be the last chance to get out before everything turns all wet and muddy. Wanna come?"

"Sure!"

While they were talking, both of them ate plenty of chips, salsa, and cookies.

Paul gestured toward the TV. "So, ready for your first episode of *Firefly*?"

They spent the next hour watching "The Train Job." Joss Whedon's story and the actors' performances worked their usual magic, and Paul was pulled into the story again even though he guessed he'd seen it nearly ten times already.

At the same time, Paul was also watching how Jared reacted. To his relief, several of the funniest bits got chuckles out of Jared, which meant he was getting into the story at least a little.

"So what did you think?" Paul asked as the credits were running.

"It was pretty good."

Paul winced at the lukewarm praise. "Sorry. Sometimes I forget not everybody likes science fiction as much as I do."

"No, really. I can see why you like it, though it's not completely my thing. It was almost like a Western sci-fi story."

I guess he won't be coming over to see the other episodes, Paul thought. Still, it didn't look like Jared was in any hurry to leave right away.

"So. You a pretty good student?" Jared asked.

"I get mostly B's." *And A's,* Paul thought but didn't say. "You?"

"Yeah, pretty much. A few A's and C's." Jared paused. "What are your favorite classes?"

"Science and math. I like English pretty much too, except when we have to read stupid stuff like *Of Mice and Men*."

"I don't remember that one."

"It's this story about two guys, one of them's like mentally retarded, and he kills this girl without meaning to, and his friend has to kill him."

"What a downer."

"Yeah. It's like, the teachers go on all the time about teen suicide and depression and all that stuff, and then they make us read junk like that. It's like they *want* to get us all depressed."

Jared snorted. "Now there's a science-fiction plot for you. High school teachers are secretly trying to get teenagers to off themselves, because really they hate us all."

"It explains so much! I think we're onto something."

"You're on something, all right." They both snickered. "So who do you have for English this year?"

"Ms. Steinbraun."

"I had Erwin my sophomore year. She's really insane."

"In a good way or a bad way?"

"Good way. Mostly." Jared seemed to hesitate. "Back before I came out to my folks last year, I wrote an essay for her class talking about *Romeo and Juliet* and how their families were all mad about them getting married, and how much worse it might have been if they were both guys named Romeo and Julius. She said it was an interesting idea but didn't really fill the assignment. I got a B-minus."

"Wow! I couldn't ever write an essay like that." As soon as he spoke, Paul wondered if he'd made it sound like he was gay as well. *Oh, well,* he thought. *It's not like I was planning to keep it a secret.* He still didn't feel ready to just say it, though.

"Actually it was kind of a relief, being able to write about being gay."

"So, who all are you out to?"

"Everyone, pretty much. Most of my friends at school. Mom, Dad. My older brother." He shrugged. "I think my grandparents and most of my cousins know, too."

"You didn't tell them?"

"I don't see them that much. Cousins I saw last summer called me a faggot, though, so someone must have told them."

"That sucks."

"Totally. Still, it's better now that I can talk about it with people who understand, even if some people are jerks about it. It's really important to have someone you can talk to about how you're feeling." Jared stared at Paul as he spoke the last few words.

By then it was almost 5:00. They talked a few more minutes about the *Firefly* episode, then Jared said he had to be getting home. On his way out the door, he said, "We'll have to get together again sometime soon."

A smile lingered on Paul's face for at least fifteen minutes after Jared left.

Chapter Five

It was several weeks into the new school year before it occurred to Chad just how little time he was spending with Paul these days.

At first he thought it was just because of soccer season. He missed having Paul there but really couldn't blame him for quitting, especially since Paul didn't like the game that much. *I wonder if being gay makes him less competitive about stuff like that?* Then he thought about how Paul was when they were playing video games and immediately discarded any idea of calling him uncompetitive.

He still saw Paul each morning for seminary and each Wednesday for scouts. A couple of times Paul and his mom came over to their house for dinner, and they'd played video games and talked afterward. Mostly, though, Chad was just too busy, between soccer and homework.

One Saturday, Paul asked if they could get together after Chad got back from soccer—maybe go over to the mall, then hang out and play video games—but it just hadn't worked out. It was Chad's family's turn to clean the church that day, and then there were errands Chad had to run for his mom, including dropping off Emily at a friend's house. By the time he was done, it was dinnertime, and Paul said he had other stuff to do that evening. It was all a big change from the summer, when he and Paul had hung out pretty much all the time when they were both in town.

Chad was shocked to realize he didn't know what Paul was keeping busy with these days. Books and video games, he guessed. And Paul had said something about taking driver's ed after school. Still, it seemed strange not to know what his best friend was up to. *I can't wait for soccer season to be over.*

• • •

Richard approved of sports. They helped build team spirit and a strong work ethic. They provided a focus for boys' energy and competitiveness, giving them a chance to learn how to express their aggressiveness in socially acceptable ways. But he was starting to count the weeks until soccer season was over.

Part of it was simply that Chad was so busy. Between practice, games, and homework, it seemed the only time they saw Chad outside his room was when he was on his way to or from something. When he was home, he seemed to spend a lot of time studying. Either classes were harder this year or Chad was taking his homework more seriously.

Another big part of it, though, was that Paul Ficklin wasn't around as much. Chad had explained that Paul wasn't playing soccer this year and so it was harder for them to get together. It made a bigger difference than Richard had expected.

The two were still friends, but it seemed to Richard that without Paul around so much, Chad was acting a little differently. He was more stressed and impatient. He laughed less often, and when he did laugh it sounded more—well, sarcastic, really. Not as much like he was enjoying himself. Less open.

Overhearing Chad around the other members of the soccer team, it struck Richard just how similar they all sounded: the boasting, jeering putdowns and carefully casual tone, as if nothing they were saying was really that important. *Adolescent posturing,* Richard realized. *Protective coloration.* It wasn't new. What was different was that he and Sandy—and the two younger children—weren't seeing the other, more pleasant side of their son that much anymore.

Chad doesn't really let himself relax when Paul isn't around.

It wasn't a terribly welcome insight. Richard wanted to believe that Chad could be himself around his family. Still, he knew better than to be surprised by it. Parents were adults—representatives of the world teenagers were trying to launch themselves into. Some wariness and caution was inevitable.

Back when he was seventeen, Richard had overheard a conversation between his best friend and his friend's mother. His friend had said she felt like a small boat pushing off against a big ship. "It's not like I want to argue all the time. It's just that I have to put some distance between us, you know? Sometimes I have to shove pretty hard just to get out of your wake." She'd been an English major in college, he remembered—no surprise, considering how good she was at coming up with metaphors. He'd been impressed with her ability to explain what she was feeling without making her mother feel defensive about it. He hadn't done nearly so well at talking to his own parents.

Not that the thought was very comforting when you were the one on the parenting end.

Richard had been surprised, after finding out earlier that summer that Paul was same-sex attracted, that it didn't seem to make much difference in Chad's friendship with him. Just like previous summers, the two had spent large blocks of time doing things together. Richard hadn't seen any signs that either of them was bothered by Paul's situation. *I would have gone ballistic if one of my friends told me he was gay. I guess things really are different from the way they used to be when I was a teenager,* he decided.

And now here he was, looking forward to soccer season being over so Chad and Paul could spend more time with each other again. And Richard was counting on Paul — Chad's gay best friend — to be a good influence on him. *Go figure.*

Richard was sure the whole thing would have been a lot harder to accept if he hadn't known Paul so well already. As it was, it didn't seem completely real to him. Knowing Paul made it harder for him to feel alarmed or concerned about the boy and his influence on Chad.

Barbara sat on one of the workbenches in her exercise area. *I'm glad that's over,* she thought. She liked her job, but sometimes dealing with the patients could be frustrating.

Mr. Rawlins, for example. He knew he needed physical therapy and exercise if he wanted to regain his full back function. She'd told him often enough. Losing about a hundred pounds wouldn't hurt either.

But would he do his exercises between visits? No. Instead, all he did was come in and complain when his therapy hurt and then complain some more because he wasn't getting better as fast as he wanted. *Idiot.*

She glanced at her watch. Twenty-five minutes until her next appointment. Plenty of time to take a walk around the clinic, then pull the paperwork and get things ready for her next patient.

Barbara's route outside took her past the clinic's mental and emotional health section. Usually her eyes were fixed on the outer door, which she could just see beyond the bend in the hallway. This time, though, she happened to glance at the pamphlets and brochures that lined the wall on the other side of the receptionist's desk. One title in particular caught her eye: *Supporting Your Gay Teen.* With a quick glance to make sure no one was looking, she grabbed a copy and stuffed it into her purse. She'd read it later.

Her chance came the next evening, while Paul was off home teaching. Reading about depression and suicide rates, the risk of AIDS, and other challenges facing gay teens, Barbara realized that in some ways the reality of having a gay son still hadn't sunk in. *Possible factor in as many as thirty percent of teen suicides . . . I wonder where they got those statistics?*

She spent the next several minutes mentally cataloguing Paul's behavior over the last several months. Was he acting more depressed? She didn't think so. If anything, he seemed more relaxed around her since he'd talked about his feelings for other boys.

Not that it necessarily meant anything. Barbara remembered all too well from her own experience just how good teenagers could be at lying with their faces when they wanted to hide that something was wrong. There was no way of knowing for sure.

Barbara flipped over the brochure. On the back was stamped an announcement for a local support group for parents, family, and friends of gays and lesbians. *I guess if they have a club at school for supporting gay kids, it makes sense that they'd have organizations for family members as well.*

A lot of the problems and issues the brochure mentioned didn't seem particularly relevant to Paul's situation, since he wasn't planning to date or be sexually active. On the other hand, it certainly wouldn't do any harm for her to learn more.

Her thoughts were interrupted by Paul's arrival. "Hey, Mom!" he said, leaning over to give her a quick hug.

"How was it?"

"Pretty good. Sister Calhoun had us put up a bookshelf for her. She spent most of the time talking about her sick cat."

"Oh, my. I hope you were polite."

"Mom! I'm always polite."

"Hmm."

"So Mom, I was wondering . . . Tomorrow's supposed to be good weather. Do you think I could go out dirt biking with some friends?"

"Who? Chad?"

"Nah. He's still in the middle of soccer. Just some guys I met at school."

"Dirt biking?"

"With bicycles. You know, mountain bikes. They said I could borrow one."

"Hmm. Are you sure this is safe?" He rolled his eyes at her. "I'll take that as 'No, this isn't really safe, but I'm a stupid teenager and want to do it anyway.' "

"Mom. Going on a campout with the scouts isn't really safe."

"I suppose every teenage boy has some allotted ratio of stupidity he has to get through, one way or another."

"Come on, Mom. It'll be fun!"

She sighed. "Fine. Go ahead. Just make sure you take your cell phone and don't do anything illegal, and get all your homework done before you go. Oh, and make sure you change into clean underwear tomorrow morning, so the EMTs will know you came from a good home when they pry you out of the wreckage."

"Great!"

Barbara shook her head as Paul kissed her on the cheek and then went bounding off to his room. *Boys,* she thought.

Paul spent Saturday morning getting caught up on chores and homework, then made lunch for himself while he checked for updates at several of his favorite websites. He was laughing at a new Strongbad e-mail at homestarrunner.com when the doorbell rang.

"You ready to go?" Jared asked.

"Yeah."

"Your mom here?"

"Nah. She teaches this aerobics class on Saturday." Paul sometimes called it her ladies' gossip group. She'd grouch back at him about disrespectful children.

"You okay if that shirt and pants get ripped up?"

"Yeah. They're old." As they spoke, Paul and Jared were making their way to Jared's car. Jared started the car, then pulled out of the driveway.

"So where are we going?"

"East side of town. There's this huge housing development out past Franklin Boulevard. Big piles where they've bulldozed stuff. Lots of space to make our own paths. Big hills." Jared grinned. "No one minds if a bunch of kids ride around in the dirt."

They met Jared's friends at his house. Paul didn't know any of them. He wound up borrowing Jared's mountain bike while Jared took his dad's, which was larger. "I need to get a bigger bike for myself sometime," Jared commented. He also used his dad's helmet while passing his own to Paul.

It took a while for Paul to get used to the heavier bike with its thicker tires. He had to pump harder than he was used to. Still, he got a real rush out of riding up and around on top of the huge mounds of dirt, then plunging down the slopes. It was even kind of fun when he wiped out, which he did a fair number of times.

"So, you like dirt biking?" Jared asked several hours later, as he was driving back to Paul's house.

"It was great!"

"Wanna go again sometime?"

"Sure! Next Saturday?"

Jared laughed. "We were lucky this week. There were a couple days of good weather in a row. Next week everything will be turned to mud, I'm pretty sure. I've done that a couple of times, but it's a lot harder to control the bike. Not something for a newbie."

When Paul got home, his mom met him at the door. "I take it from all the scrapes and bruises and dirt, not to mention the state of your clothes, that you enjoyed yourself?"

"Yeah! It was a lot of fun."

She sighed. "If you were a little younger, I'd have you strip down right here so you don't drag dirt across the carpet. The next thing on your schedule is an appointment with a great many gallons of hot water. Leave your clothes, and I do mean *all* your clothes, on the floor outside the bathroom."

"Sure thing."

The shower felt good. Paul washed his hair three times just to make sure he'd gotten all the dirt out. Afterward, he changed into the clean clothes his mom had set out, combed his hair, and then went downstairs.

"What are we having for dinner?"

"Fried chicken."

"Yum."

"Let me look at you." She tilted her head to one side, then another. "Well, now the dirt's all washed off, you don't look quite so much like when you and Chad got into fights back when you were nine. It's an improvement, I guess. But you'll never be able to wear that shirt again."

"It was too small for me anyway."

"You got it less than a year ago!"

"Like you always tell me, I'm growing." He grinned. "Gonna grow more, too, eating your yummy fried chicken."

"Flattery will get you everywhere."

Dinner was good, and the peach cobbler they had afterward was even better. As Paul was getting up to leave the table, his mother asked, "So, who was that boy who brought you back in his car?"

"Jared. Jared Esters."

"Where'd you meet him?"

No way out of saying it. "GSA club."

"So he's gay then?"

"Not everyone in GSA is gay." Even to himself, Paul's voice sounded defensive.

"But he is."

"Yeah."

"What about the other people you were biking with? Were they from GSA, too?"

"I haven't seen them there. They're just friends of Jared's."

"So he's a friend, then."

"Yeah."

"Not a boyfriend."

"I told you before, I'm not looking for a boyfriend."

"Does he know you're gay?"

"I haven't told him." Paul paused. "What's with the whole cross-examination bit, anyway?" Even to himself, his voice sounded a little defensive.

"Sorry. It's just—this is the first time you've shown up with anyone who wasn't already a friend with Chad or someone you knew from church. I was curious."

"Yeah, well, it feels like you're giving me the third degree just for having some new friends."

"I'm sorry. And you need to stop being so sensitive." As she got up from the table, Paul winced at the look of irritation on her face. "By the way, you have dishes tonight," she added as she left the room.

"What happened to you?" asked Chad, as soon as Paul saw him the next day.

It was about five minutes before church was supposed to start. As teachers quorum president, Paul always tried to get there a couple of minutes early, just in case the teachers assigned to prepare the sacrament forgot, were late, or didn't bring bread.

That morning when Paul woke up, his face looked worse than it had the night before, all covered with scrapes and bruises. *Oh, well,* he thought. *Nothing to do about it.* He was just glad he didn't have to shave yet, since one of the scrapes went right across his chin.

"I ran into someone's face," he said to Chad. "You should see the other guy, though."

"That's a load of bull. I'm the only one you ever fight with."

"Well, yeah. I guess I should say, you should see the other pile of dirt, then."

"Huh?"

"Pile of dirt. Dirt biking. As in, what I was doing yesterday."

"Really?"

"Yeah.

"Who with?"

"Some guys I met at school. No one you know, I don't think."

Chad looked surprised and seemed to hesitate before replying. *I do have other friends, you know,* Paul thought a little irritably. "Cool," Chad finally said, then went up to sit behind the sacrament table. Apparently he was blessing this week.

As usual, there weren't enough deacons, so Paul wound up helping pass the sacrament. He got several strange looks from people when they noticed his face, but no one said anything until after the meeting, when he was on his way to his Sunday school class.

"Hey, Ficklin! Who cleaned your clock?" It was Scott Bradshaw, a senior at the high school and one of the more obnoxious teenagers in the ward. Fortunately, Paul didn't have much to do with him, now that the other boy had stopped showing up at scout activities.

"I was dirt biking."

"What, a pansy like you?"

"Knock it off, Bradshaw!"

A female voice chimed in. "You know what, Scott? He's right. Knock it off."

It was Janice Taylor. She and Scott had hated each other ever since he'd tried to blame her little brother for letting the air out of the scoutmaster's tires. After it came out that Scott was lying, she'd hauled him back behind the church and punched his lights out. She'd been twelve. He was thirteen.

Paul and Janice went down the hall one direction. Scott, fortunately, took off the other way.

"Bet he's ditching Sunday school."

"Probably." Then another thought occurred to Paul. "You know,

Scott talks an awful lot about other people being pansies. I wonder why?"

"Omigosh! You're exactly right!" Janice exclaimed, her face lit with an unholy glee. "It explains so much!" She opened her mouth. "Hey—"

"Shhh! Geez, you can't just belt it out like that."

"Why not?"

"It's embarrassing."

"He deserves it. Guy's an ass."

Paul's eyebrows shot up. It wasn't any news that Janice felt that way, but hearing her actually say it was a surprise. At least, hearing her say it at church.

"Oh, come on. You gotta agree," she continued.

"Yeah. I guess. Though I don't suppose he really *is* gay."

"Of course not! What would be the point of yanking his chain if it was true?"

"Whatever." He eyed her warily.

"Look. I have a friend at school who's gay." She looked at him curiously. "Actually, one of my friends told me she saw you at a GSA meeting. What's that all about?"

Paul could feel his heart rate speeding up. He really, really didn't want his involvement in GSA getting out at church. "Nothing much, really," he heard himself saying. "A girl at my lunch table dragged me along to a meeting."

"Sarah Donnelly, right?" Janice snickered. "Pushy, isn't she?"

"Yeah." He grinned. "She's okay, though."

"Do I detect a crush?"

"No, not really."

They made their way into the classroom, where Paul sat down beside Chad, with Janice on his other side. Usually Janice and Chad were in the class above his, but today their teacher wasn't there, so the two classes had been combined. Brother Campbell called on someone for an opening prayer and started the lesson.

Paul felt sorry for Brother Campbell. He always tried to get them involved in a discussion, but this week's lesson—about the book of Hebrews in the New Testament—didn't give him much to work with. The bits and pieces they read sounded like the author of Hebrews was making some kind of complicated legal argument.

Finally, during the last ten minutes, Brother Campbell closed the lesson manual and talked directly to the class.

"Part of what makes it so hard for us to understand the book of

Hebrews is that it keeps talking about things related to the Jews and their history. Why do you think that's the case?"

No one said anything. "Think about the title of the book," he urged. He flipped back a couple of pages. " 'The epistle of Paul the Apostle to the Hebrews.' An epistle's a kind of letter. What does the title tell us about who this letter was written to?"

Finally Janice spoke up. "The Jews?"

"That's right. This is a letter that Paul the Apostle wrote to the Jews who had converted to Christianity. So he's talking about their traditions, and he's explaining to them how Christ doesn't replace all the things they knew before, but instead fulfills them. He's trying to convince them that being good Christians is the best way to be good Jews."

Brother Campbell paused, then continued. "The Jews had been the chosen people of God. They had the gospel, at least as much as it was known at that time. Yet many of them found it hard to accept Christ. Why was that? Elaine?"

"Maybe it was hard for them to accept that there was something they didn't already know?"

"I think that was probably part of it. Chad?"

"Maybe Jesus wasn't what they expected."

"That was certainly part of it. The Jews were expecting someone who would deliver them from political oppression. The kingdom of heaven Jesus spoke about wasn't like that, and so they found it hard to accept him.

"Now, let's switch forward and apply this to Joseph Smith's time. The Bible was on the earth, but the true church of Christ wasn't here. Why did people have such a hard time accepting Joseph Smith's message?"

"Satan deceived them."

"Right. Paul?"

"They thought they had all the truth already."

"Exactly. And so, like the Jews in Jesus's time, they weren't open to receiving new knowledge about God, especially when it went against what they thought they already knew.

"Now, switching back to the book of Hebrews. This was written to people who were already members of the church. They'd accepted the gospel of Christ. And yet they kept holding onto their ideas from back when they were only Jews."

Brother Campbell folded his arms and looked around the room. "Comparing that to today, we live in a culture that has figured out a lot of things about the universe through science and study. We're not expected to reject all the good things that come from being part of that culture. At the same time, we've been given spiritual knowledge the rest of the world doesn't have. Sometimes what we know about spiritual truth gives us a perspective the rest of the world doesn't have, on things like drugs and morality and honesty and chastity.

"That's something we need to remember when we go out into the world—when we're talking to our friends, at work and school, and so on. No matter how much good information the world has about a lot of things, we need to reject the world's ideas when they contradict revealed truth. Like the Jews who converted to Christianity, we need to be careful about holding onto ideas that come to us from the culture around us, instead of relying on the light and knowledge we have through the restored gospel."

Brother Campbell continued for another minute or so before calling on someone for the closing prayer and then dismissing the class. During that time, though, Paul mostly wasn't paying attention. Instead, he kept thinking about Brother Campbell's comments about not accepting the world's ideas when they contradicted the gospel. He was still thinking about it as he walked down the hall after class.

Paul liked going to the GSA. He liked the people—well, a lot of them anyway. Like pretty much any group, GSA included its fair share of idiots and people Paul didn't particularly want to be around. Mostly, though, the people Paul didn't like were easy enough to ignore. Easier than in scouts, in fact.

And Paul had something in common with them, or a lot of them, at least—being gay. He liked being around other people who shared that part of himself, even if they didn't *know* he was that way.

At the same time, it was pretty obvious that a lot of things the church taught wouldn't be very popular at GSA. Obviously, what the church said about homosexuality was one of those things. But also stuff like the church's teachings about marriage and eternal families. A lot of the time at GSA, Paul felt like his Mormonism was an invisible bubble surrounding him, separating him a little bit from the other kids—even if no one but him knew it was there.

"So, President Ficklin. How are things going?"

Paul looked up. "Good, Bishop."

"Glad to hear it." He gave Paul a firm handshake, then gestured into the room. Paul went in to priesthood opening exercises.

• • •

As Richard made his way in to start priesthood meeting, his eyes fell again on Paul, who was sitting at the front of the room together with the rest of the priesthood quorum presidents. *The file leaders,* he thought to himself. *I may have responsibility for the whole ward, but these are the ones who lead the boys and men.*

At least, that was the way it was supposed to work.

Just that morning in priesthood executive committee meeting, they'd been talking again about a number of families in the ward who weren't being home taught regularly. The elders quorum president had shrugged at him apologetically but didn't have any plans for how to improve.

It wasn't just a problem because of the families who weren't being seen. How would the boys learn to be good home teachers and priesthood holders if the men in the ward didn't show them how it was done?

Then there was the problem of trying to staff the Primary. Several callings hadn't been filled for a couple of months now. Some of the larger classes really needed to be split, according to the Primary president—especially those that included children with behavior problems. Unfortunately, the people the Primary president wanted to teach those classes already had callings in the Young Women and the Relief Society. Everyone, it seemed, was able to clearly see the challenges faced by their own organizations, but fewer members of the ward understood that all the other organizations faced similar challenges.

Richard sighed. The youth, and especially the young men, were supposed to be his particular responsibility as bishop, but sometimes it felt as if he was too busy taking care of the adults and running the ward organization to do the sorts of things he imagined that he should be doing with the youth.

Seeing Paul that morning, for example, Richard realized he hadn't gotten together again with him the way he'd intended after their conversation back during the summer. He'd wanted to talk to Paul some more about being same-sex attracted and what Paul thought it would mean for his future—college and mission and marriage and such—and whether Paul thought his feelings might ever change. Richard wanted to make sure Paul knew that even if they didn't change in this life, he could still be a worthy member of the church if he just refrained from acting on those feelings in any way.

That conversation hadn't happened. Instead, Richard had to make do with short exchanges like the one today, guessing how

Paul was doing by the firmness of his handshake and whether the boy was willing to look him in the eye.

It wasn't a lot. Still, based on those clues it seemed like Paul was doing well. Richard took what comfort he could from that thought.

"Today's lesson is on sexual purity."

Paul slumped in his chair. *Oh, great.* From the stony expressions and uncomfortable shifting around him, he could tell that none of the other members of the teachers quorum were any happier about it than he was.

"When Jesus was twelve years old, his parents took him to the temple in Jerusalem. After they left, he stayed behind, talking to the scholars in the temple. This was a sign that he wasn't a child anymore but was starting to become a young man."

Oh, no.

"About the time a young man turns twelve or thirteen, he starts to change. His body starts to mature."

Just kill me now.

"His voice starts to change. He starts to get stronger and taller. Other changes start to happen as well."

Duh. In case Brother Williams didn't notice, we're all at least fourteen. Why is he giving us this lesson that was clearly written for deacons?

Back when Paul was eleven, his mom had given him a pamphlet about growing up, titled something like *You and Your Changing Body.* At that point he already knew about the basic biology of sex, but there was a lot of stuff he hadn't known about puberty and all of that. It was also the first time he'd heard about masturbation, aside from snickering half-understood references from other boys. Later that year, he'd started to become intensely curious about his body and what was happening with it. The inevitable had happened. He'd been overwhelmed by the feelings and started repeating the experience frequently.

Then there'd been a lesson on chastity at church. Afterward, Paul had felt horribly guilty about his habit and had gone in to talk to his bishop about it. The bishop—not Chad's dad, but the one before him—had been very calm, not disgusted or shocked as Paul had expected. They'd talked about ways for Paul to control his thoughts and feelings, including singing hymns when he was feeling tempted. The bishop had given him a pamphlet by Boyd K. Packer titled *To Young Men Only,* and they'd gone over some of that together. The bishop had also said that the goal was for Paul to develop long-term self-control and that if Paul did slip up he should just do his best to pick himself up and keep trying to do the right thing.

Talking about how he was doing in that area was one of the embarrassing but unavoidable parts of the regular interviews that all the young men were supposed to have with the bishop. The fact that it was *boys* Paul thought about when it was happening just made it worse.

"Elder Boyd K. Packer said that our bodies have a power of creation—a light, so to speak, that has the power to kindle other lights. This gift is supposed to be used only within the sacred bonds of marriage. Dale, can you tell us why?"

The boys were sitting in a half-circle, with Dale seated almost directly opposite Paul. Out of the corner of his eye, Paul noticed Dale twitch when Brother Williams mentioned his name. He looked miserable. Quickly glancing around the room, Paul saw that Alan, a new member of their quorum who had moved in about a month before, had turned bright red. The other boys were doing their best to pretend they weren't there.

Paul sighed. It was gonna be a long lesson.

Chapter Six

"TRICK OR TREAT!"

"Oh, don't you look absolutely precious! A princess and a were-wolf. And two teenage boys—my goodness, how scary."

It was Friday night—Halloween. Chad's mom had decided it was his job this year to take Emily and Jeffrey out trick-or-treating while she stayed home and passed out candy.

Fortunately, he'd managed to talk Paul into coming with him. The plan was that Paul would stay over tonight and they'd spend Saturday playing video games and celebrating the end of soccer. At least, Chad would be celebrating. The last few weeks, he'd felt so busy he could hardly breathe, between soccer and homework.

Back in September, there'd been a visitor to their seminary class from the Church Educational System. He'd talked about requirements to get into Brigham Young University. Chad hadn't been happy when he realized just how far his own GPA was from the average for entering BYU freshmen. He'd pretty much have to make straight A's for the rest of high school if he wanted to get in. So he'd decided to try an experiment this year and see just how well he *could* do if he really put a lot of time and effort into it.

Over the past month he'd seen some improvement, but trying to concentrate on grades during soccer season had pretty much killed him. And no matter how hard he tried, it seemed like he couldn't get above a B-plus in some of his classes.

But tonight he was going to forget about all that and relax with Paul. At least, they'd be able to relax as soon as they got the two candy-holics back home and out of their hair. *Just to the end of the street,* Chad thought, looking at the size of Emily and Jeffrey's bags and noticing how dark and cold it was getting.

"So, how was soccer season?" Paul's voice was bright and cheerful.

Chad scowled at him. "It sucked. As I'm sure you know."

Paul laughed. "Really? And after we had such a good season last year!" A second later, he was dodging Chad's halfhearted punch. "Wuss."

"Right, Mr. Sarcasm. Just because you couldn't tough it out—"

"Hey, leave me out of it. I'm not the one who kept bragging how much better the team would do this year."

"Someday someone's gonna pound you for saying 'I told you so'—"

"I told you so, I told you so," Paul chanted in a singsong voice.

"—and it just might happen tonight, if you keep this up."

Paul stuck out his tongue at him. "Try it."

The words, *No thanks, I'm not into that,* ran through Chad's head. He shuddered. "You know, you're acting like a ten-year-old."

"Must be the company I'm keeping."

Just then, Jeffrey started whining about how cold it was getting and how he was tired of walking. They did another couple of houses, then headed home.

"You're doing *what*?" Chad demanded.

Paul did his best to keep his voice steady. "I'm going to GSA. You know, the Gay-Straight Alliance club."

It was later that evening. They'd ditched the kids at the kitchen table, where Sister Mortensen was presiding over the inspection and trading of candy. Then they'd grabbed a couple of sleeping bags and taken over the downstairs TV room, where they launched into a round of *Super Smash Brothers Melee*. They'd been playing for about a half-hour now.

"See, you were all busy with soccer season, and I was bored. And then Sarah—she's this girl at my lunch table—she dragged me off to a GSA meeting. So I went. And, well," he shrugged, "I decided I kinda like it. So I kept going."

"Geez, Paul. I thought you said you didn't want to let people know you're gay."

"Hey! There's lots of straight guys at GSA. So far as they know, I'm just another one."

"Yeah, and I bet a lot of the others are just like you. They're gay, but they don't want to admit it."

Paul considered. "Yeah, probably."

"So is there anyone at GSA who admits they're gay?"

"Sure." Paul hesitated, then decided to go ahead and say it. "Jared, the guy I went dirt biking with. Him and his friends. I met him at GSA. He's gay. I don't think his friends are, though."

There was a long silence. "Whatever," Chad said finally. "Don't tell me about it. I don't wanna know."

"Geez, Chad! He's just a friend."

"Who happens to be gay."

"Well, yeah. So am I."

"That's kind of my point." Chad seemed to hesitate. "Don't do anything stupid, okay?"

"What do you mean?"

"Never mind, just drop it."

"Okay, I will." Paul didn't bother to hide his irritation.

"You know, I think that's the first group thing you've done without me since that Little Gym class back in third grade."

"That was so lame," Paul remembered. He smirked at Chad. "You could always come with me to GSA, you know."

"Not a chance."

"Don't complain about me doing stuff without you, then."

"I'm not complaining, I'm just—"

"Yeah, you're complaining."

"It just seems weird."

"See, this is what we talked about back at the beginning of summer. You do stuff without me, like soccer this year. It's just different because this time, it's me doing stuff that you're not doing."

Chad looked like he was trying to find some way to disagree with that but couldn't. After a moment, Paul decided to let it drop. Instead, he asked, "So what's this I hear about you studying all the time?" Chad's dad had made a comment about it as they came in.

To Paul's surprise, Chad blushed. "I just want to get my grades up," he mumbled.

"Is this about what Brother Elliott said about getting into BYU?"

"Yeah." Chad wasn't looking at him.

"So why're you acting all embarrassed about it?"

"I don't want my mom and dad getting on my case."

"It's not like they'd get upset with you just 'cause you're taking schoolwork more seriously."

"What if it doesn't work out? I don't want them stressing me."

"How's it going so far?"

"Okay." Chad shrugged. "I'm still doing crappy on my English papers."

"You tried getting any help? Like taking them into the writing lab or talking with the teacher? Or even just getting a computer for your own room, so you don't keep getting distracted by Jeffrey's video games?"

"No."

"Idiot."

Chad looked hesitant. "You mind looking at the paper I'm working on for Monday?"

"You really must be desperate."

"Will you do it?"

"Of course, doofus."

"Great."

They returned to the game. About midnight, Chad's dad came downstairs and told them to get to sleep, since he was going to bed and it was high time they did as well.

And things were okay between them, as far as Paul could tell.

Spending time with Paul on Halloween had been weird.

Chad had wanted to have fun — just goof off and have a relaxing evening. And they'd done that, mostly. After going out with the little kids, they came back and ate most of the leftover candy and generally acted several years younger than they were. Paul on a sugar high was pretty much always a crackup. It'd been nice to hang out with him, like slipping on a comfortable pair of shoes.

Well, except for the gay thing.

It wasn't like Chad could forget about Paul being gay. No way. But spending less time with Paul the last couple of months, he'd been able to . . . push it out of his head, sort of. At the same time, he'd been spending a lot of time around the soccer guys. A lot of fag jokes got told in the locker room. So when Paul started talking about that GSA thing, it was kind of a shock.

Thinking about Paul, Chad felt almost like two different people. One was the guy who'd been Paul's best friend for seven years. The other was a guy who thought it was too weird being friendly with a fag. Chad hoped he could keep that second part hidden while Paul was around.

• • •

It was a couple of minutes past 6:30 when Barbara slipped into the community center.

The foyer was deserted, but someone had helpfully taped up a PFLAG MEETING sign with an arrow pointing to the left. She followed the hallway down to where it opened into a large, classroom-like space where about half a dozen people were milling around, pouring themselves coffee from a machine at the back of the room and sampling doughnuts from a nearby tray. Evidently the meeting hadn't started yet.

A blond-haired woman who looked about Barbara's age came over. "Hi. I'm Connie Hammer, president of the local chapter of Parents, Families, and Friends of Lesbians and Gays. I haven't seen you here before, so welcome to PFLAG." She grinned. "If you're looking for Weight Watchers, well, the doughnuts probably already told you you're in the wrong place."

"No, the doughnuts certainly didn't scare me off. I'm Barbara Ficklin, and you're right, this is my first—how did you say it? P-flag?—meeting, here or anywhere else."

"So what brings you here?"

"I, ah, recently discovered that a family members is gay. I saw a notice about your meetings and decided to find out more."

"That's great." The other woman's smile seemed sincere enough, but Barbara got the impression that whatever she said, the answer would still have been the same. "Let's get you a name tag here, with a red dot since it's your first time."

Barbara wrote her name, while Connie continued talking. "Usually we start with some kind of presentation. This week we have Dr. Forcade from Arcadia University. He's done research on media images of people with unconventional sexualities. Then there's the support group, if you want to stay for that. It's a general group for parents, friends, family members—whoever wants to participate. People can confidentially share issues they may be having, get suggestions, vent, that sort of thing."

"Yes. I think that might be interesting."

"Great!" She glanced up at the clock on the wall. A couple of other people had drifted in while they were talking. "I guess I'd better go and get things officially started. Talk to you later!"

Connie hurried up to the front of the room. "Welcome PFLAG members and visitors. Tonight, for our program, we have Dr. Evan Forcade . . ."

• • •

A little over two hours later, the meeting was over. Barbara shook hands, smiled politely at several people who encouraged her to come back, and left as quickly as she felt she could without being rude, citing her need to get back to her family. On the way home, she pulled over into a vacant parking lot and turned off the car.

The whole thing was a lot more . . . political . . . than she'd been expecting. Lots of talk about gay rights. The main speaker gave a presentation about movies and television programs and how gay people were depicted in them. A lot of what he said made Barbara uncomfortable, though it was interesting in a horrifying kind of way. It certainly didn't make her feel any happier about the thought that this was the kind of world, the kind of attitudes, that her son would have to deal with in his life.

Then the support group had started.

Barbara had imagined that a lot of it would be about the challenges of raising gay teens, helping them make good choices and learning how to understand what they were going through. And part of it had been like that. One person talked about how hard it was dealing with questions at family get-togethers about whether her daughter was dating yet, since she wasn't out. Another talked-ed about supporting a son through the hassles he was getting at school.

A lot of it, though, seemed to be talking about ways that homosexuality and lesbianism and things like that could be accepted better by society. No one seemed to have a problem with the idea that their children were that way — or if they did, they weren't saying anything about it.

Barbara did her best not to say anything about herself and Paul and their situation. When asked to introduce herself, she'd simply repeated what she told Connie Hammer: that she had a family member she'd recently discovered was gay. A couple of times when someone asked if she wanted to contribute anything, she just said that she was learning a lot by listening.

Which certainly was true. By the time she left, one of the things she'd learned was that there was a much bigger gap between the world's view of homosexuality — at least, the view of the people in that meeting — and the church's view than she had realized. The longer she listened, the more she felt there was an awful lot they were saying that she just couldn't agree with.

Partway through, she had what seemed like an epiphany. *These are good people. A lot of them are parents, just like me. All they want is for their children to be happy. But they're trying to get there by supporting them in things the church teaches will ultimately make them only miserable.* By the time the whole thing was over, Barbara was feeling worse about Paul being gay, not better.

Barbara shook her head. Figuring out all about homosexuality and whether things were really that different for people who weren't members of the church wasn't what she cared about. All she wanted was to know what was best for her own son. It didn't look like this group would be much help in doing that.

"So, just how do I get Chad's attention, anyway?"

It was Janice. She, Chad, and Paul—along with most of the other youth in the ward—were at a Saturday-night stake dance. Chad was shooting the breeze with some of the other priests over by the refreshments, while Paul was actually dancing. With Janice.

"I'm wounded," he said with a grin. "Dancing with me, and asking about my best friend?"

"He's sixteen—he can date. You can't," she replied calmly.

"Mercenary," he accused, still wearing his grin.

"Better believe it. I want someone I can con into taking me out to a movie every now and then. Get me out of the house."

The dance ended, and Paul started over to the refreshment table. Janice grabbed him and pulled him back onto the dance floor. "Hey! You never answered my question!"

The next song started, and they started dancing again. "What's in it for me?"

"Besides another dance with wonderful *moi*? I'd think you'd be happy to do a favor for your best friend."

Paul snorted. "Just how many boys do you know, anyway?"

"Obviously, at least one too many. And who were you calling a mercenary just a minute ago?"

"Everything that boys know about treachery and double-dealing is stuff we learned from girls." Janice was one of the few girls he felt comfortable saying something like that to.

"True enough."

"Seriously, though. You can hint all you want, but nothing's really likely to work on Chad unless you flat-out tell him, 'Hey look, if you want to invite me to a movie next Saturday, I wouldn't say no.' That would probably get the message across."

Janice shook her head. "Boys. The death of romance."

"Yeah, well, if you girls really want romance, it'd be a better idea to keep us males out of it entirely."

"Believe me, if we could, we would."

They danced the rest of the dance in silence. As it ended, Janice said, "I think I'll try the indirect approach a while longer. If all else fails, I'll do what you said."

"I'll look forward to seeing it." He snickered at her.

"Go away."

Paul went back to the refreshment table, where Chad was standing by himself at the moment.

"You danced two dances. With Janice Taylor."

"Well, yeah."

"Why would *you* want to dance with her?"

At first, Paul just thought Chad was talking about him being gay. "I like dancing," he replied evenly, a little ticked off that Chad would refer to it in a public place, even indirectly. Then his eyes widened in sudden realization. "You're jealous," he breathed. "You have a crush on—"

"Shut up," Chad hissed. "I do *not* have a crush on her." Then he whirled around and stalked off to another part of the cultural hall.

Chad avoided Paul for the rest of evening. Paul, for his part, couldn't stop grinning. *This is going to be so much fun.*

Barbara Ficklin enjoyed her calling as a Young Women personal progress counselor.

Part of it was the chance she had to work with the young women themselves. Back when she'd been younger, she'd looked forward to having a little girl of her own. That specific wish had faded over time, and despite her current worries about Paul, she couldn't be any happier with having him as her son. Working with the young women, though, meant she could temporarily enjoy other people's daughters without the problems that went along with being an actual parent. Certainly Barbara had given her mother enough gray hairs when she was a teenager.

Even better than that was the chance to work with the other Young Women leaders, Barbara thought as she looked around the room.

They'd finished the business part of the leadership meeting, talking about the individual girls and planning for next month. She'd made her report on how the young women were doing with their projects and how some of the Young Women activities could be tied to specific program requirements. After that, it had turned into a story-swapping session about the challenges of being a mother.

"I remember reading an interview with someone who'd been named Mother of the Year for her city," one sister said. "The interviewer asked the secret to her patience. She smiled and said, 'Each night after the children go to sleep, I kneel down beside my bed and say, Dear God, thank you for not letting me kill one of them today.' "

Most of them laughed, though Sister Jensen, sitting off to one side holding her six-month-old, looked vaguely horrified. On the other hand, Sister Ericson, who had three boys six and under, just looked tired.

"Please tell me it gets easier as they get older." Barbara thought she heard a hint of desperation in Sister Ericson's voice.

"I'd tell you that, but it would be a lie," said Sister Moseley. She was the oldest of them all, with five grown children.

"So what happened today?" someone asked Sister Jensen.

"The three-year-old and six-year-old decided to make brownies," Sister Jensen replied. "I was in the bedroom trying to put a screaming two-year-old down for a nap. You'd be amazed just how big a mess two kids can make in the kitchen in ten minutes."

"No, we wouldn't," several of them chorused simultaneously.

"Teenagers are worse in some ways," put in Sister Rathbone. "Last Saturday after the dance, my sixteen-year-old spent an hour and a half telling me, in great detail, about everything that happened at the dance, including who insulted whom, which of her friends danced with which cute boys, and how the boys she was interested in didn't pay any attention to her. It wouldn't have been so bad except that I was trying to get to sleep."

"I don't suppose I'll have to worry about any late-night confidences, since all of mine are boys."

"You'd be surprised," muttered Barbara. No one else seemed to notice, but Janet Moseley gave her a measuring look.

About then, Sister Jensen's baby started crying again. She shot everyone an apologetic look, grabbed her baby bag, and left the room.

"By the way, it sounds like yours is starting to attract girl attention," Sister Rathbone said to Barbara. "Denise said several of the girls were talking about how cute he is, though I gather she thinks he's a bit young for her. Has he mentioned anything about it?"

"No," Barbara said.

"He's, what, fifteen? I'm sure he's still pretty clueless about realizing when girls are interested in him."

"Probably," she responded, her throat tight. *I don't know. Would being gay make him more likely to notice things like that?* She shook her head, trying to clear away thoughts about her son's sexual orientation.

"Still, late night and dancing and dating and all, that's just normal wear and tear," put in Sister Phillips. "What with the way society's going these days, I worry about my kids coming home and telling me they're gay, or pregnant, or leaving the church—"

"Excuse me." Barbara stood and walked quickly down the hall.

Fortunately, there was no one in the women's restroom. She stood in front of the sink, closed her eyes, and let go the tight hold she'd been keeping on her emotions ever since Sister Phillips had said the word *gay*.

Several minutes later, she heard the restroom door opening. "What's wrong?" said Sister Moseley.

Hearing the sympathy in the older woman's voice, something inside Barbara cracked. She'd thought she was doing so well with it. And then going to that PFLAG meeting had gotten her all confused and worried about whether she was doing the right things. She had to have someone she could talk to about it, another woman.

"You don't know what it's like, having your son tell you he's gay," Barbara whispered.

Unexpectedly, Barbara felt the other woman's arms wrapping around her. Tears streamed down her cheeks more freely as she leaned into Sister Moseley's embrace. The other woman's hand moved in a slow circle on Barbara's back as she murmured, "There, there, it's okay, it's all right. You're gonna make it."

"You don't know what it's like," Barbara repeated a couple of minutes later, as she finally started to calm down.

"No, I don't." Something in Sister Moseley's tone made Barbara pull back and open her eyes. "But I do know what it's like to have my son-in-law, someone I'd come to love like my own son, call me in tears to say that he's gay and he and my daughter will be getting a divorce because he can't live a lie anymore." Barbara looked at her, eyes wide. She knew one of Sister Moseley's daughters had gotten a divorce but hadn't heard any details about it. "I still love the boy, and sometimes I want to tear him limb from limb for what he put my daughter and their kids through. And I wish to God he'd talked with someone about it back when he was a teenager, instead of just hiding it and hoping it would go away." She gave Barbara a fierce look. "Don't let Paul do that."

The door opened, and another sister came in. "Leadership meeting's over," Sister Moseley said in a more normal voice. "Let's go back and get our stuff." Barbara nodded and dried her cheeks before hurrying out.

Neither of them spared a thought for the door that was slightly ajar between the women's restroom and the mother's nursing room.

"I don't know how you can do it all, Sister Mortensen."

I don't, Sandy thought. *I just fake it.* "You get used to it," she said. "You're doing just fine."

Sandy and Sister Jensen had been out that morning, visiting one of the older sisters in the ward. Ever since being assigned as Sandy's visiting teaching companion, Ellen Jensen had latched onto Sandy as if she were some kind of wise and experienced older woman figure—which Sandy found hilarious, although it was true that being around the younger woman made Sandy all too aware of just how long it had been since she was twenty-three. *Thank goodness,* she thought. *Was I ever that sincere and innocent?*

Well, no. Probably not.

She did her best to be patient with the younger woman.

"The other day, I overheard someone talking . . ."

"Yes?" Clearly, there was something on her mind. Maybe if Sandy encouraged her, she'd get it out faster.

"I mean—I'd just find it so hard. I don't know if I could let my son spend so much time with someone who's gay."

Sandy's mind felt paralyzed. "What do you mean?" she heard herself say.

"Oh! I thought you—never mind. I guess I shouldn't have said anything."

"No, you probably shouldn't have. But now that you've started, you'd better finish." The words came out almost in a snarl. Sister Jensen looked shocked. *Get a good look, kid. This is what I'm like when I'm taken by surprise and don't have time to pretend that I'm nice.*

"It was—I was in the nursing room at church a couple nights ago, after the Young Women leadership meeting, when I heard Sister Ficklin and Sister Moseley talking. They were saying Sister Ficklin's son Paul was gay. I was sure you'd know about it, since Chad is such good friends with Paul."

My son's best friend is— Sandy forced herself to restrain her shock and growing anger so she could speak relatively calmly. "That's really not the kind of thing you should talk about with anyone, whether or not you think they might already know," she said, a hint of steel in her voice. "I'm sure you won't mention it to anyone else, will you?"

"No!" The younger woman's eyes were wide.

Sandy waited a minute, then spoke again. "Well! The morning really is getting along, and I need to get back home." She forced her voice to sound faintly regretful, instead of showing the impatience and frustration she was feeling. "Next Thursday?"

"That's good for me." Sister Jensen collected her six-month-old and his baby carrier from the backseat, giving Sandy a hesitant smile, then she walked up to her apartment door while Sandy watched, a carefully sculpted smile on her face. After the door closed, she let the smile fade.

I wonder if there are any Tylenol in my purse.

Chapter Seven

It was 5:30 when Richard pulled up the driveway. He'd made sure to get home on time today since he had an appointment at the church later.

Opening the door, Richard heard raised voices from the kitchen. It was his wife and older son. He sighed. Chad was often sullen with him in a low-key, typical teenage sort of way, but that was nothing compared to the arguments Chad and Sandy got into when both their tempers boiled over. There was something about Sandy's way of dealing with Chad that just seemed to rub him the wrong way these days — and vice versa.

It didn't help that the two were so very much alike when they got mad, in ways they would both hotly deny. Mentally, he prepared himself to act as a peacemaker.

Then Richard heard what Chad was saying. "It's not that big a deal, Mom! Being gay doesn't change who Paul is!"

Quickly he walked into the dining room, his eyes taking in Sandy's stance, her hands on her hips, and the way Chad's hands were clenched into fists at his side. *This isn't going to be good.*

Sandy looked Richard's way as he entered the room, her mouth set in tight, grim lines. "I just found out something we didn't know before about Paul Ficklin." She paused. "Did you know he's homosexual?"

The question was obviously meant to be rhetorical. Richard was trying to figure out just how to respond, when Chad broke in. "Yeah, sure, he's gay. Big deal."

"Yes, I think it is a big deal that the person my oldest son spends the most time with is a homosexual." Her eyes narrowed. "Obviously, that has to change."

"Mom! He's my best friend! I'm not gonna ditch him like that."

"You will if I tell you to!"

"Chad. Sandy. Nothing should be settled in anger or haste. Let's all sit down and—"

"I don't think there's anything to talk about."

"Neither do I." Chad's eyes were cold. "You don't have anything to say about who my friends are."

Richard took a deep breath. "Obviously, there's—"

"Now you listen to me, young man!"

"Just because you're acting like a bitch—"

There was a sharp *smack* as Sandy's hand struck Chad's cheek, followed a second later by a much louder *crack* as Richard's fist struck the top of the dining table. To his surprise, it split down the middle. The two pieces, unbalanced, crashed onto the floor, taking with them the placemats, flower arrangement, bowl of fruit, and pile of today's mail. *I guess it wasn't as sturdy as it looked,* Richard thought in a daze.

"Richard! That—the table—" Sandy started. From the look on her face, Richard wasn't sure she even knew what she was trying to say.

"I'm a lot less worried about the damned table breaking than about the way we're all acting!"

Off to the side, he saw Chad rubbing his hand over one cheek. The look on the boy's face was almost admiring as he gazed between Richard and the mess on the floor.

Just then, Emily appeared at the bottom of the stairs. "What made all that noise?" she asked. Then she saw the table. "Oh, my gosh!" She disappeared in the direction of the family room. They heard her yelling, "Jeffrey! You gotta come see this!"

"Stay out of this room until I say you can come back in!" Richard yelled after her.

The three of them looked at each other. Richard shook his head. "Chad, could you please pick things up? Especially the mail. Try to dry it off—it looks like the water got on it." As he was talking, Sandy walked toward the stove, her face blank.

"Why me?" Chad demanded.

"Just do it, okay? Your mother has to get dinner ready, and I have to see if I can find another table."

Heading out toward the garage, Richard winced as he heard Jeffrey yelling from the other room, "You mean *Dad* did that?"

• • •

Dinner that night was strained, to say the least. After all the time Sandy had put into redoing the kitchen the year before, Richard didn't dare go out and buy a new table on his own. He wound up cleaning off a work table that he'd made in wood shop his junior year in high school. Judging by the expression on her face, Sandy was unimpressed, though she went ahead and served dinner on it after covering it with a tablecloth.

After dinner, Sandy moved to clear off the plates while Chad headed up to his room. Richard had been hoping the three of them could get together and work things out, but one look at the grim expression on Sandy's face made him change his plans. Instead, he announced that he'd be heading off to the church for a while. Sandy's mouth tightened at his words, but she didn't say anything.

As it turned out, Richard's meeting with the Young Women president that night left him even more exhausted. It started with Sister Moseley's first words: "Bishop, the phone calls still haven't been made for the service project this Saturday. If people don't get called tomorrow night, no one will show up and it'll be a disaster."

What do you want me to do about it? Richard thought. *I'm not the Young Men president.* "I'll talk to Brother Sanders," he said, hoping his reluctance wasn't obvious to her.

"Good," she said firmly, and nodded at him before moving on to the next item on her list.

What is it about Young Men leaders that they always seem to irritate the Young Women leaders so much? he wondered. Certainly that had been true for him when he was Young Men president. *And why are the Young Women leaders always so surprised when Young Men leaders still act a lot like teenage boys?*

By the time Richard got home, both the younger children were in bed and Sandy was reading a novel in the living room.

She looked up as he came in. "I'm going out tomorrow to get a new table. Do you care what kind we get?" It was disconcerting to see her acting almost as if nothing was wrong. Only a slight tenseness in her voice signaled that she was still upset.

"Whatever looks good to you."

She continued reading. Richard wondered if he ought to say something else but eventually decided against it. Instead, he wandered back into the dining room and worked for a couple of hours on his presentation for a meeting the next day.

• • •

"So then Dad whacked the table and it broke, and the next day Mom went out and bought another table. And they haven't talked about it since, as far as I know."

Paul shook his head, still stunned by what Chad was telling him. "So what does it all mean?"

"I'm not gonna pay any attention to her saying I can't hang out with you, dude, if that's what you're asking about. It's probably better, though, if I come over here, instead of you coming over to my house. At least for a while." He paused. "I can't believe she wigged out like that."

It was Sunday afternoon. At seminary on Friday, Chad had muttered something about things being weird at his house right now, and it would probably be a good idea for Paul not to come over. Then at the service project yesterday—which Paul had forgotten about until the bishop's call on Friday night—Chad said he'd explain the whole thing Sunday after church. Paul hadn't expected anything like this, though.

"So how did your mom find out?"

"I dunno. I guess she heard from somebody who heard your mom talking to someone else. She didn't say who else knows."

"I'm screwed."

"Sounds like it."

Paul paused. It really wasn't Chad's fault, but Paul could feel himself getting mad about it anyway. Better change the subject. "So how's the whole studying-till-your-brain-falls-out project coming?"

"It sucks. I work on homework for an hour or two, then I get bored and my eyes start crossing and my brain turns to snot and drips out my nose."

"Wow. *That's* a vivid image."

Chad grimaced. "I work on homework a couple of hours, then I go nuts unless I do something else for a while. It's like my brain can process only so much schoolwork at once." He shook his head. "It was almost better during soccer season. Back then, I had only an hour or two a day that I *could* spend on homework, so I really concentrated on it. Now I have four or five hours, but I just run out of steam."

"So what are you going to do?"

Chad shrugged. "Dunno. What can I do? Keep trying, I guess. See what works."

"You want to get together and study sometime?"

"I doubt that would help me concentrate. Besides, it's not worth the hassle with my mom."

"I thought you said it didn't matter what she said."

"Dude, it's one thing not to stop seeing my best friend just because my mom's gone crazy and hit menopause, or whatever. It's something else to start spending a lot more time away from home, which you know she'd notice, and then have her all over my case about where I've been. It's just not worth it. Especially not for homework." He grinned. "Now, if you were a cute girl asking me to get together with you behind my mom's back . . ."

Paul picked up a pillow and threw it at him. Chad dodged, laughing.

"So if you don't want my help with studying, why don't we play some video games?"

Barbara knew Paul was upset with her as soon as he came down the stairs, a little while after Chad left to go home.

Her first glimpse of his face reminded her of Paul as a six-year-old, scowling like a thunderstorm because she hadn't fixed cookies when he wanted her to. She fought back her impulse to giggle.

"How did Chad's mom find out about me being gay?"

Uh, oh. She wasn't tempted at all to laugh now.

"I didn't know she had. Is that what Chad was telling you about?"

"Yes."

"I didn't talk to her."

"She told Chad she heard you talking to someone at church about it. In the girls' bathroom."

How could I have missed someone else being there when Sister Moseley and I were talking? Sandy Mortensen wasn't even at the church on Tuesday night! Obviously, though, someone *had* overheard them, or Paul wouldn't be talking to her right now.

"Did you?"

"What?"

"Talk about it. In the girls' bathroom at church."

"Yes." There was really nothing else she could say.

"Why?"

Barbara hesitated. "A couple weeks ago, I went to a PFLAG meeting. An organization for parents and families of lesbians and gays."

"You outed me to a whole stupid—"

"I did no such thing. I never told anyone my last name, and I never told anyone who you are or even that it was my son who was gay. I'd never seen any of them before, and I doubt I'll ever see them again." She paused. "So anyway, the whole thing got me thinking about what you'd been telling me before, about how hard it is to be Mormon and gay. And I realized how hard it was going to be for you."

"So you decided to make it a whole lot harder by blabbing about it to someone else?"

"I didn't—I wasn't thinking this was something that would make it harder for you. I just wanted to be able to talk to someone about it."

"Sure." His voice sounded infinitely bitter. "I'm the one who's gay, but you decide to talk to someone else about it, because it's all so hard for *you*. And now I'm the one who has to live with the consequences."

"What do you mean?"

"Just that Chad's mom decided he isn't allowed to spend time with a faggot anymore. She and Chad's dad got into an argument about it, with Chad stuck in the middle. And now I'm not allowed to go over there anymore."

Barbara was stunned. She'd never imagined Sandy Mortensen might react like that. "Oh, honey, I'm so terribly sorry. Do you suppose if I talked to her—"

"You've done enough talking to people already, I think." With that, Paul turned and left the room. A minute later, she heard his bedroom door slam.

"Where have you been?"

Chad looked up. He hadn't expected to be interrogated the minute he came in the door.

What the heck. "Paul's house."

Clearly, that wasn't the answer his mom wanted to hear. "All right. If you can't be bothered to follow the rules of the household, then I guess you can go without supper."

Chad was afraid that if he said anything, he'd start cussing or spout something that would get him into even more trouble. Instead, he went upstairs into his room, closed the door, and propped up the chair under the doorknob so no one could come in. Then he put on his headphones, turned his radio to the hardest rock station he could stand, and cranked up the volume.

"Where's Chad?"

"I sent him up to his room without supper."

I really don't need this after a day like today. Richard had been in interviews for several hours, including a particularly frustrating unscheduled one with a church brother whose family seemed constantly to be teetering on the edge of financial disaster but who couldn't be persuaded to stick with a budget. He kept saying "Yes, bishop, yes, bishop," but then a few more months would pass and he'd be back in Richard's office asking for help, and nothing would have changed.

"What happened?"

"He went over to the Ficklins'."

Richard sighed. Waiting for Sandy to calm down on her own hadn't worked. "Let's go up to our bedroom to talk about this."

"Fine."

Once the door was closed, he began. "Sandy, I don't see anything wrong with Chad spending time with Paul. They've been friends for seven years now, and as far as I can tell it's done them nothing but good."

"That's not the way I feel about it."

"Fine. What are your reasons?"

"Homosexuality is evil."

"I absolutely agree. It's a blight in the lives of good people. But let me point out a few things you seem to have missed. First, how did you find out about this?"

"Sister Jensen told me about it. She overheard Barbara and Janet Moseley talking about it at church."

"So first, any information you may have is completely second-hand."

"I haven't asked Barbara about it, if that's what you mean."

"So you have absolutely no idea what Barbara meant, or even what she actually said to Sister Moseley. You have no idea if Sister Jensen misunderstood something, or if this is something that's been blown completely out of proportion."

"Chad didn't deny it."

"You didn't listen to what Chad was saying. Don't you think if Chad already knew about this and wasn't worried about it, that's a pretty good sign it's not something we need to be worried about either?"

Sandy shook her head. "I really don't agree with that reasoning. For that matter, how do you know something hasn't . . . happened between Paul and Chad?"

"Because I've talked with them both about this. And I believe what they told me."

Sandy was silent for a long moment. Finally she asked, "How long have you known about this?"

"Since last summer."

"You've known for months. And you didn't think this was something I should know about?"

Richard struggled to contain his frustration. "Things that get told to me as bishop are supposed to stay in the bishop's office."

"So instead, I get to find out from one of the other sisters in the ward, who assumed that since Barbara's son and mine are such good friends, I *must* know about it already!"

He took a deep breath. "I'm sorry you had to find out about it that way." His temper flared. "In fact, based on how you're reacting, I wish you hadn't found out about it at all."

The way Sandy's mouth tightened, Richard could tell she wasn't pleased with the comment. "I had a right to know about it."

"No, you didn't."

"Anyway, sooner or later I would have found out about it anyway. It's not like you can keep something like this secret forever."

He shook his head. "That's not so. So long as Paul stays actively committed to the gospel, there's no reason why you or anyone else should know what he might be struggling with. In fact, I would think that having something like this generally known would make it harder for Paul to deal with this challenge." *Better spell it out.* "I hope you wouldn't do anything to make things more difficult for him. That includes talking with other ward members about it."

"Chad knows."

"Chad is Paul's best friend." He hesitated, then continued. "In some ways I'm surprised that Chad and Paul haven't played around sexually together. That kind of thing is a lot more common among boys than I suspect you realize. Still, I'm very glad it didn't happen, mostly for Paul's sake."

Sandy's eyes widened in what looked like surprise. After a moment, she asked, "Why *Paul's* sake? Why not for Chad's sake?"

Richard thought a moment. "Chad, from everything I can tell, is thoroughly heterosexual. I doubt that any kind of experimentation would change that. Paul, on the other hand . . . I can't help but think that sort of thing would have a much bigger impact on someone who was already attracted to boys." He stared at Sandy. "Which is a lot more than I ever would have said if you hadn't already found out more than you should know. I'm telling you this partly so you'll understand why I think letting them spend time together doesn't do any harm and is in fact a good thing for both of them. They both get friends who will support them in living gospel standards. It's a win-win situation."

Richard waited a long minute while Sandy thought. He knew she wouldn't be entirely convinced by anything he said, but her expression made him believe she was finally starting to think past her first emotional reaction.

"I don't like it," she said at last. "I don't approve of Paul being over here. And I really don't approve of you keeping important things like this from me, things that affect our family." She glared at him briefly. "But as long as you and Chad agree to be responsible for Paul's behavior while he's here, I won't object."

I wonder what "be responsible for Paul's behavior" means? She's still not making a lot of sense. Still, on the whole Richard was pleased. The conversation had gone better than it might have. *Now all I have to do is go listen to my sixteen-year-old rant and rave about how unreasonable his mother is being.*

"I really don't see why it's that big a deal for you."

It was the following Wednesday, time for Sandy's semi-regular lunch with Ella, her best friend from high school. Sandy had just finished pouring out the story of what had happened the past week: finding out her son's best friend was gay and then Richard and Chad refusing to take it as seriously as she did.

"What do you mean?"

"The world's full of gay people, Sandy. *Portland* is full of gay people. Sometimes it seems like half the people I work with are gay. Remember Justin? The guy I brought to the New Year's party that one time?"

"Yeah."

"He's gay."

"But you brought him as your date!"

"No. He was just a convenient friend I thought would enjoy

the party and keep people from seeing me as unattached — which would have attracted the wrong kind of attention at *that* party."

"Well, I don't want that kind of influence on my son."

"Maybe he'll pass on some good clothing taste."

Sandy grimaced. "It hasn't happened yet, and they've been friends since third grade. Anyway, Paul's taste in clothes is almost as bad as Chad's."

"Damn. Why is it always the stereotypes you *wish* were true that wind up not being true?" Ella took a drink from her diet Pepsi. "So are you worried your son might be gay? Or that this friend will turn your son gay?"

"Neither, really. Even Richard agrees that Chad is thoroughly heterosexual."

Ella raised an eyebrow. "So Richard's the authority on this?"

"As Chad's father, I'd think he would know."

"You can't always tell about these things. You remember Toby from high school?"

"Yeah."

"He was convinced his oldest son was gay, though the boy never said anything about it. Until he showed up with a pregnant girlfriend."

"How old was he?"

"Fourteen. They were both high school freshmen."

Sandy shook her head. "Toby always was particularly clueless."

"Even so." Ella smirked at her. "If you don't think this boy is any danger to Chad, then why are you so upset about it?"

"It's disgusting!"

"That's just your own prejudice showing."

One of the things Sandy valued about her friendship with Ella was the way the other woman said things Sandy wouldn't take from anyone else. They'd talked about it once. "I don't have to tiptoe around your feelings because I don't depend on you for anything," Ella had stated. "You know I'm going to tell things the way I see them, whether you like it or not. So you can avoid stuff you know I'll disagree with, or learn to take it. Or walk." She'd grinned. "The fact that you keep me around tells me that deep down inside, you know you need someone who won't let you get away with spouting bull."

Sandy hated it, even though she knew it was true. *But not this time,* she thought. She ignored the part of herself that reminded her that she *always* thought *But not this time* whenever she got into an argument with Ella.

"It's something about our religion," Sandy responded. "We believe that marriage between men and women is God's pattern."

"So you think I'm going to hell just because I haven't found a man worth hitching up with?"

Sandy shook her head. "You know what I mean."

Ella looked at her skeptically. "Sandra, if this was about your religion, Richard would be more upset than you are. No, I think I got it right the first time. This is about your prejudice." She gave Sandy a speculative look. "Or maybe it's about something else entirely that has nothing to do with this poor kid. Tell me, what made you maddest? The fact that Paul is gay or the way you heard about it? And then finding out that Chad and Richard both knew about it before you did and didn't tell you?"

"You're evil," Sandy mumbled.

Ella laughed. "And so are you. The difference is that you try to keep people fooled about it." She paused. "Actually, I admire that about you. Being nice to people doesn't come naturally to you, any more than it does to me. But you try anyway. And you pull it off a lot of the time, except for times like this when something catches you by surprise. Maybe that's why you're married and I'm not."

"Or maybe you just haven't found anyone like Richard."

She wrinkled her nose. "Boring!"

"But hot!" They both laughed. "Boring but hot" had been Sandy's capsule verdict on Richard when they first met.

"So I have to tell you about the e-mail I got from Eloise the other day . . ."

Another week, another GSA meeting.

Another GSA social meeting, more specifically. Since it was the Tuesday before Thanksgiving, there were even fewer people than usual. "But we make up in quality what we lack in quantity," Trevor asserted.

While people were still showing up, a girl named Alicia asked, "So why is it that people say 'You're so gay' or 'That's so gay' when what they really mean is 'That's so lame'? Is that, like, homophobia?"

"Nah," someone else said. "They're just being dumb."

"I think when people say that, they're not really thinking about gay people at all," put in Trevor. "Just—I don't know, kind of a generic term."

"Derogatory language can be damaging, even when it's not intended to be," said Ms. Allington. They looked at her in surprise. Paul wished she wouldn't throw in her opinion when they were talking about things like this, and he guessed the others felt the same way.

"I think it's kind of like a sign of acceptance," Paul found himself saying. "Like, being gay is just a generic insult. Not something people have to be all offended about anymore." As he spoke the words, he wondered if they would make sense to anyone else. To his relief, he saw several people nodding.

The conversation turned to television shows. Someone brought up *Boy Meets Boy*, a reality program that had aired over the summer on cable. Apparently this gay guy—James—was supposed to choose someone from a group of other guys, and then they'd get some money and a vacation to New Zealand. What James didn't know was that some of the guys were straight. If he wound up choosing a straight guy, then James wouldn't get the money or the vacation. Instead, everything would go to the guy who fooled him.

Paul was glad he hadn't known about the show. It didn't sound very good, but he doubted he would have been able to stop himself from watching it.

"Why do we even watch shows like that?" one of the girls was asking. "Is it sadism, because we want to see the look on the poor guy's face if he loses?"

"Masochism," one of the boys mumbled. The others looked at him. "Masochism, not sadism. That's why we watch TV shows like that."

"It's not like they were even all that good looking," Sarah said.

"You watched it?"

"No, but I saw the ads."

"Ri-i-ight."

Paul broke in. "I could never do that. Date somebody on a TV show, I mean."

"I could!" put in Trevor.

"Somehow we believe you." Sarah again.

"So I guess it's a sign of equality that there's a gay dating reality program on TV. So we should be happy about it."

"Yeah, but who really wants that kind of equality?" put in someone else.

"Did you watch it?" Paul asked Jared.

"Yeah." He snickered. "It was fun seeing guys make idiots of themselves."

"Like you do all the time," someone else called out.

"Can't we talk about something else?" complained one of the girls.

"I read a story about a year ago," broke in Gwenyn from Paul's left.

"What was it about?" he asked. Gwenyn often seemed kind of spacey—not like she was on drugs, but more like she just thought in a way that was different from everyone else. Paul always found what she had to say interesting.

"It was a fantasy story about a society where everyone could read each other's minds. Not all the time, but when they gathered for ceremonial occasions. Everything they thought and felt toward each other was all exposed."

Trevor shuddered. "That would be awful."

"Children were mostly shielded from it until they hit puberty. Then they had a choice. Over the next several years, they would be forced to open up more and more by their connection to the village and the magic of the ceremonies. The ones who couldn't handle it would leave."

No one spoke for several seconds. "Everyone would have to leave," Sarah finally said in a quiet voice. "No one could live with that."

"What if you'd been raised that way?" Jared responded. "Raised to think it was normal? Maybe it would be possible then."

"I thought it might be rather nice," Gwenyn said. "Living in perfect honesty. No secrets. No misunderstanding."

"It'd be like standing naked in front of God," Paul blurted out.

Everyone stared at him. "That's a really . . . disturbing image," Trevor said finally.

"I can honestly say that's not a thought that would ever occur to me," Sarah put in.

Paul couldn't figure out where it had come from either. Something he'd read in a science fiction story, maybe.

"No, I think Paul's right," Gwenyn said. "It *would* be like being naked in front of God. Except instead of God, it's being naked in front of everyone around you." She paused. "Which is kind of how things are anyway, if you think about it. You know, like a metaphor. Maybe that's what the author was trying to get across."

"Is it just my imagination, or do we talk about some of the weirdest things in GSA?" demanded Sarah.

Chapter Eight

AIDS Education Week went pretty much the way they'd planned it. There were rallies at lunchtime and guest lectures in some of the classes and a petition to increase funding for AIDS prevention and research. There was a school-wide assembly, too, where they talked about safe sex and where to get testing and other resources if you needed them.

The posters Paul's group made had been copied and put up around the school. They'd made a brochure as well with important AIDS facts and a section titled "What You Can Do" with ways students could help with AIDS awareness. Paul wound up learning a lot that he didn't know before about AIDS. He didn't suppose it would ever be important for him personally, but he guessed it was good to be informed.

Over Thanksgiving, he'd told his mother about what the GSA would be doing for AIDS Education Week and showed her the posters and brochure his group had made. She complimented him on the work they'd done. "A lot of the stuff I see in health care isn't really written so ordinary people can understand it," she said. "You and your friends did a good job of explaining things."

She paused. "A few years ago, back when we were visiting your great-aunt in Utah, I remember going to the funeral of a boy in her ward who had AIDS. He was hemophiliac—you know, the disease where you bleed really easily. He got AIDS from a blood transfusion. Just a young kid. She told me they had a church meeting where the boy's mother and his nurse talked about his health conditions and how people could be safe when he had nosebleeds. This was back before people knew as much about AIDS." She shook her head. "It was sad. Still, I couldn't help but be impressed with just how well the ward rallied around the family. That was back when we'd just started coming back to church. I remember thinking it wasn't true what people sometimes say about religious people, how intolerant they are. Really religious people, the ones who take it seriously, reach out to other people and help them." She smiled. "I'm glad to see you doing the same thing."

"I didn't want to help at first."

"But you did."

"Yeah."

"I guess this means I've got you well trained."

"Yeah. It's your fault I can't say no to bossy girls." He snickered and dodged the playful swat she aimed at him.

The week ended with a rally down at the college on Saturday. Paul hadn't really wanted to go but felt like he ought to, since it was officially being cosponsored by the GSA and they'd made a big push for people to come.

He was relieved to discover that the only people he recognized at the rally were a few other GSA members — fewer than he'd expected. After listening to boring speeches about gay activism and changing the laws — given by college students who were taking themselves way too seriously — Paul decided to ditch it and head home.

"Going my direction?" It was Sarah.

"Hey! I didn't see you."

"I was standing over on the other side. So, taking off already?"

"Yeah."

"Not your sort of thing?"

"Not really. I'm not into politics."

"Politics are important."

"Yeah, well, it's just not my thing."

They reached the parking lot where Paul had left his bike. "See you on Tuesday?"

"Sure!"

Sarah was grinning at him as he rode off.

GSA the following Tuesday was even less organized than usual. Ms. Allington had some meetings and couldn't be there. After the big push the week before for AIDS Education Week, the original plan had been to just skip the social get-together. Several people had complained, though, and so Ms. Allington had arranged with one of the art teachers to supervise while she was gone.

Most of the club presidency wasn't there. The ones who were there didn't seem too anxious to be in charge or try to organize things. Then Nara, one of the senior girls, spoke up.

"There was this activity we did at church camp a few summers ago where everyone got to hug someone else, just standing and hugging for, like, two minutes," she started. "It got me thinking. You know how guys can't hug other guys in our culture without people calling them queer or something, unless it's that kind of pounding-each-other-on-the-back half-hug? It's not as bad for girls, but still most of the time you just don't get hugs from other people unless it's your mom or grandma."

True enough, Paul realized.

Nara continued, "I saw this program the other day where a psychologist was saying we're starved for nonsexual touch in our culture. After we stop being little kids we don't touch each other much outside of sex or fighting. And so I thought about this activity from church camp. And I thought maybe we could try it here."

"How would it work?" someone asked.

Nara shrugged. "Put everyone's name in a hat, then draw pairs? We could do it a couple times. Think of it as being kind of like, I don't know, a psychology experiment or something." Several of the girls were nodding. They all seemed to like the idea, judging by the expressions on their faces.

Paul eyed the other guys warily. None of them seemed terribly happy with Nara's plan. Several of the straight guys, in particular, looked like they wanted to object but didn't quite dare—especially the ones whose girlfriends liked the idea. Paul felt like smirking at them until he noticed Sarah staring at him. The look on her face promised retribution if he dared to say anything against it. Hastily, he shut his mouth. *I guess you don't have to have a girlfriend in order to be intimidated by a girl.*

After a minute it became clear that they *would* be doing the hugging thing, basically because none of the guys was willing to be the first to refuse. Paul felt like he'd just gained an uncomfortable insight into the way the world worked.

One of the guys finally spoke up. "I'll give it a try." Nara beamed at him.

"I'm always up for a snuggle," another guy leered. *Trying to put the best face on it,* Paul thought.

"You start groping, your nuts'll be in pain," growled a girl sitting next to him. Paul thought she was his girlfriend.

"No groping," ordered Nara. Sarah, who was sitting next to her, nodded.

"Okay, so are we gonna get this started?"

Only about fifteen people were there—not counting the art teacher, who was sitting at her desk and ignoring them while she did some grading. All of them decided to try it at least once.

The first time, Paul wound up paired with Sarah, who looked pleased. She put her arms around his chest and leaned her head against his shoulder. He wrapped his arms around hers and leaned his head forward so that his cheek was against her hair.

It was weird. Nice, but weird. Standing with his chest against Sarah's, Paul was intensely aware that she was a girl—something he usually didn't think about. He was also more than usually aware of the four inches' difference in their height as he felt her face against his upper chest. Lower down, he could feel his body halfway react simply to being so close to someone else—as if it wasn't entirely sure what it ought to be doing in this situation. Desperately, he hoped his condition wouldn't be evident to Sarah. After a minute, his nose started itching, but he thought it would be rude to pull his hand away to scratch it.

"Time."

Paul pulled his arms away. Sarah held on a moment longer, gave Paul a final squeeze, then pulled away as well. While the second drawing took place, Paul stretched his arms.

"Well, that was different," said one of the girls, who'd been hugging another girl.

"It was good," insisted Sarah.

"I guess we really are the school's official touchy-feely club," one of the group's openly gay boys joked. Paul laughed a bit nervously. So did several others.

"Okay, round two," Nara announced.

This time, Paul was paired with Jake, a quiet, nervous-looking freshman who'd shown up a couple of meetings after Paul's first time. Paul had heard Trevor speculating to one of his other friends— after Jake had left one week—that Jake was probably gay but in the closet. *Like me,* Paul thought at the time.

At first, it felt even more awkward and embarrassing than it had with Sarah. The other boy was almost radiating tension. Hugging him, Paul realized that Jake was very skinny and almost as tall as Paul. It felt like hugging a wooden statue, or at least the way Paul imagined that would feel.

And then things changed. As Jake slowly relaxed, Paul became aware that everywhere the two boys were touching, Paul's skin had become extra-sensitive, almost like there was some kind of electric current passing between them. *I didn't feel anything like that when I was hugging Sarah.*

It was really good. He imagined little factories in his skin cells manufacturing happy drugs, sending smiley faces up the nerves to his brain. He almost felt dizzy. About the same time, Paul realized that he could feel Jake shaking slightly. Clearly, the other boy was nervous.

Paul squeezed lightly and felt Jake's arms tighten in response. Slowly, the other boy lowered his forehead until it was resting against Paul's shoulder. Feeling Jake tremble against him, Paul experienced a sudden surge of—affection, or maybe protectiveness—toward him.

It wasn't until then that Paul noticed his own erection. It didn't seem to him that what he was feeling had very much to do with sex, though. Instead, it just seemed like a natural side effect of being close to someone. Another boy. He felt himself relaxing as well. He hadn't even realized he was tense.

"Time."

Jake didn't seem any more anxious to pull away than Paul was. When the two finally did separate, they just stood staring at each other for a few seconds. Then Jake shook himself and turned away.

"Third round?"

Paul shook his head, then sat in one of the chairs over by the side of the room. What he'd just experienced was too intense to jump right back in again. Jake, he noticed, was also sitting out this round, standing over at the back of the classroom and looking out the window.

Looking at the other boy, Paul felt a lingering sense of—not quite affection. Friendliness, maybe. It wasn't like he had a crush on Jake or felt particularly attracted to him. Still, while they'd been hugging, it had been really . . . intense. *It was like I was, I don't know, almost falling in love with him, just for that couple of minutes,* he thought. *Wow.*

Paul couldn't help but wonder how much more intense it would have been if, instead of just hugging, they'd been doing something more specifically sexual. Part of him felt a sort of—*yearning,* he guessed was the right word—to experience that kind of closeness again. Not necessarily with Jake, but with someone. *Some guy,* he corrected mentally. *I can see why they say it's so easy to get caught up in physical feelings when you're with someone you like.*

The third round ended while Paul was sitting and thinking. Afterward, they all sat around talking about it.

"It was really cool," said one of the girls. "I felt, like, really connected to the other person." Several people nodded.

"It was, like, a hose, connecting Rachel and me," one of the guys added, grinning. The girl he'd named hit him in the arm.

"I'll bet it was like a hose," smirked one of the other guys.

"Why is it that boys have to joke around whenever someone wants to talk seriously about feelings?" one of the girls asked.

"Why do girls feel like they have to talk about feelings all the time?" one of the boys responded.

The girls looked surprised. The boy continued. "I mean, sure, it's important to talk about that sort of thing sometimes. With girls, though, it's like you spend so much time talking about feelings that it gets in the way of just enjoying them."

Around the circle, a couple of the guys were nodding. "You don't want to mess things up by talking too much about them," one said.

"Okay, I can see that. But it's not like guys do a very good job of just enjoying feelings, either," argued one of the girls. "I mean, look at this hugging thing. A couple of you looked like you were being sent off to fight bears or something — even here at GSA, where something like that should be okay, especially doing it as a group thing. But once it happened, you liked it, didn't you?"

None of the guys responded. "We don't want to talk about it," one of them finally said, with a grin on his face. "It would spoil the experience." Several of the girls groaned and shook their heads.

"We're not gonna get anything else serious out of you, now that Aaron thought up that excuse, are we?"

The guys, grinning, shook their heads, including Paul.

"I thought it was interesting how just hugging someone made me feel closer to that person, even if it wasn't someone I knew very well, at least while the hug was going on," one of the girls said. "Being close physically just, I don't know, made us feel closer emotionally as well."

"It was relaxing. I could feel the stress from school just kind of dropping away. It was pretty nice." That was Sarah.

As the discussion continued, Paul mostly was quiet. He really didn't feel like talking about what he'd felt while he was hugging

Sarah and Jake. He noticed that Jake wasn't saying anything either, though he seemed interested in what everyone else was saying.

Finally, things broke up.

"Walk with me," Sarah demanded as the group streamed out of the building.

"Okay," Paul responded, surprised. Usually Sarah spent the time after GSA hanging around and talking. Of course, usually Paul spent the time after GSA talking to Jared or Trevor, neither of whom were there that day.

They walked in silence for several minutes. Paul obligingly followed Sarah around to Garfield Street, instead of taking his usual route down Maple. Finally, after they'd gotten about half a block from the school, Sarah spoke. "You're gay, aren't you?"

Paul's first instinct was to deny it. Instead, he swallowed and asked, "How did you guess?"

Sarah laughed, but it wasn't a happy laugh. "That hug," she said. "It didn't feel like someone who was interested in me as a girl."

"Hugging you was nice," he protested.

"Yeah. Right. Nice," she said, and shook her head. "And then watching you hug Jake, right after me. It was like . . . You two aren't going out, are you?"

Paul was shocked. "No." *What gave her that idea?*

" 'Cause it looked like you were just, kind of, lost in each other. The difference was pretty obvious, at least to me. I don't know if anyone else was paying attention."

Paul rubbed his face with one hand. "Look. It's, well, it's complicated. Anyway, I have no idea if Jake is even gay."

"I'm pretty sure he's gay, after the way he was hanging onto you."

"Really?"

"Yeah. I was watching pretty closely. It was kind of—disappointing, actually."

"Watching him?"

"Watching you."

"Oh."

"Yeah. Up till then, I just kind of hoped that you were just clueless."

"Clueless?"

"I've been trying to show you I was interested since, like, the second week of school."

"Oh." He paused. "Sorry."

"So I guess you weren't just being polite and pretending not to notice."

"No."

"There's my answer, then. Gay *and* clueless both."

"Ouch."

"Well, yeah. Imagine how I feel."

Paul looked at her. "I'm sorry. You're a nice person."

"Don't even. 'Nice' is the kiss of death. You might as well just call me a very special person and get it over with."

Paul snickered. "In our church, they call it 'having a sweet spirit.' "

"Omigosh. Don't you dare tell me I've got a sweet spirit."

Paul stopped, put on his most serious look, and gazed at Sarah, one hand over his heart. "I would never think of calling you a sweet spirit. Sweet spirits don't punch as hard as you do." He dodged as she swung her fist at him. "See what I mean?" They both laughed.

"So if you're so clueless, how do you ever plan to get a boyfriend?"

"Uhh . . ."

"What? You're gay — you want a boyfriend, don't you?"

"Not really, no."

"That's not what it looked like while you and Jake were squeezing the stuffing out of each other."

"Sorry. I can't help what it looked like. I really don't want a boyfriend, though."

"Why not?"

"I'm Mormon. Remember?"

"Yeah? So?"

"My church doesn't approve of homosexuality."

"Ouch." She paused. "So you're not out to your folks?"

"It's just my mom. Actually, though, I *am* out to her."

"So what's the big deal, then?" Before Paul could answer, she continued, "Does she know about you coming to GSA?"

"Yeah."

"She's not upset about it?"

"I don't think so."

"So what's the problem with being gay? I mean, she already knows, right? It doesn't sound like she has a problem with it."

"It's just — I don't want to go against what my church teaches."

"Why not?"

Paul looked at her. It didn't seem like she was trying to argue with him. Instead, it looked like she was just trying to understand what he was saying. He sighed. "Look. As a Mormon, there are some—well, expectations—promises I've made about how I'm supposed to act. Heck, I'm not supposed to date *anyone* until I'm sixteen, girls included. Doing stuff with guys—it's not—" He took a deep breath. "We don't believe that's what God wants people to do."

"Wow." Sarah shook her head. "That's so messed up."

So much for tolerance, he thought. "Thanks so much for your respectful attitude toward my religious beliefs," Paul snarled, then turned back toward the direction of his house.

"Wait!" Sarah grabbed his arm. "Sorry! I didn't mean to insult your religion, I just—"

"Just what?" he demanded.

"Just—I don't know, okay? I mean, it sounds like you're getting down on yourself just because people think it's wrong to be gay."

"See, that's the thing. I *do* think it's wrong to be gay."

"How can you say that, when you're gay yourself?"

Paul paused, trying to think how he could explain. "Look. When you were a little kid, did you ever want something from the store? Something you didn't have the money for?"

"Sure."

"Did wanting it make it okay to steal it?"

"Of course not. But it's not the same thing."

"Why not?"

"How does being gay take something away from someone else?"

Paul thought for a moment. It all seemed a lot harder to explain than when they talked about this stuff at church. "It takes something away from *me*," he finally answered.

"What's that?"

"The person I can be if I live the way I should."

Sarah stood a moment with a thoughtful look on her face, as if she was trying to understand what Paul had just said. Then she shook her head. "I really don't understand how anyone can choose to live that way."

"What way?"

"Denying who you are. Trying not to be gay when you *are* gay."

"Look, it's my choice what I decide to do about my gay feelings. Individual choice, right?"

"I guess. But it doesn't sound healthy to me."

Now it was Paul's turn to shake his head. "See, this is part of why I haven't told anyone at GSA that I'm gay. It's hard trying to explain to someone who doesn't share my beliefs."

"You haven't come out to anyone in GSA? Jared or Trevor?"

"No."

"So who all does know, then?"

"My mom. My best friend. My bishop—that's kind of like a minister in our church. You."

"So what do they think about you being gay?"

"That's . . . complicated."

"Okay. So let's start with this best friend of yours. How did he take it?"

"He freaked. But he got over it."

"Do I know him?"

"I doubt it. His name's Chad Mortensen."

"You're right. I don't know him."

"He plays soccer. Has second lunch." Paul thought a minute, then continued reluctantly. "He's Mormon, too. In fact, his dad's my bishop."

"That has to be hard." Her eyes narrowed. "Wait a minute. His dad knows you're gay, and he lets him hang out with you anyway?"

"Why wouldn't he?"

"It's just—wouldn't he think you'd, like, contaminate him or something?"

"What are you talking about? It's not like anything gay is gonna happen between me and Chad. He's so straight it's ridiculous."

"That's not what I meant. Didn't you say your church thinks you're evil, since you're homosexual?"

He stared at her. "No, I didn't say that." He shook his head. "Look, getting turned on by guys isn't something I choose. Since I didn't choose it, it's not a sin. The sin would be if I acted on it. It's kind of like—" Paul thought for a moment. "Remember how in health class they said some people have addictive personalities, so it's really easy for them to get addicted to drugs or gambling or whatever? It's not those people's fault. On the other hand, if they don't ever take drugs, it won't become a problem for them."

Sarah was shaking her head again. "Not a really positive way to think about something you've already admitted you don't have any control over."

"I didn't say that. Just because I don't get to choose who I'm attracted to, it doesn't mean I can't control what I do about it. Otherwise, straight guys would be ripping the clothes off every pretty girl they see."

Sarah snickered. "I'm sure there are a lot of guys in this high school who'd do that if they thought they could get away with it."

"See, there you go. You admit that civilization depends on people being able to control their impulses. Especially guys." He grinned at her.

"Well, yeah."

"The way I see it, marriage is this kind of bargain. Guys get sex, and women get help raising kids."

"That's awful."

"That's *practical*," Paul replied. "Sure, there's more to it than that, but at base that's what it is." He felt vaguely amused that what he was saying, which seemed pretty straightforward and obvious to him, was so appalling to her. *I guess girls really are more romantic about this sort of thing.* "Anyway, my point is that the only reason we're even *here* is because people do a lot of things that aren't what they want to do. Being gay's like that for me."

"Like what?"

"Something I want to do, but I have to control myself so I don't."

Sarah was silent for a couple of minutes. "I guess I get where you're coming from," she said finally. "It still doesn't sound like any way to be happy, though." She paused. "So why do you come to GSA anyway, if you think you're so much better than all the other gay kids there?"

"I don't think I'm better."

"But you do think being gay is wrong and everyone else should just pretend they aren't gay, the way you're trying to do."

"I guess." That wasn't exactly what Paul thought he was doing, but he figured it wasn't worth the argument to try and explain it to her more clearly. "At least, if they all believed the same way I do." He shrugged. "But as far as I know, I'm the only Mormon in the GSA."

"That's hardly a surprise, from everything you've said."

"As for why I come to GSA—" He shrugged again. "At first it was because I was curious, and because you dragged me out. I kept on coming because, well, you're my friends."

Paul's final comment put a smile on Sarah's face.

For the last couple of blocks to her house, they talked about less controversial things, like who was dating who in their lunch group and who wanted to be dating someone but was too chicken to do anything about it. When they got to Sarah's house, she gave him another hug before hurrying up the walkway.

Wow. I wasn't expecting to have a conversation like that today, Paul thought as he turned back toward his house. *But I guess it turned out all right in the end.*

Chapter Nine

Coming out at the next GSA meeting was something of an anticlimax.

It happened during the general socializing and B.S. session after the main part of the meeting was over. Since it was the last meeting before Christmas break, there wasn't much to discuss. So after about a half-hour or so of talk about GSA events they'd be planning for the spring, the meeting pretty much broke up into a lot of different conversations. No one seemed particularly anxious to leave and Ms. Allington wasn't shooing them out, so everybody just sat around and talked.

Paul was sitting in a group of six or seven people that also included Trevor and Jared. Trevor—wearing his cloak as usual—was telling them all about something that had happened the previous weekend in downtown Portland, when he'd apparently been mistaken for someone's long-lost friend by that person's mother. "She kept talking and saying how happy her son Nathan would be that she ran into me, and could I give her my telephone number and e-mail so they could get in touch with me."

"You didn't tell her she had the wrong person?"

"Why should I? It's not like she bothered to ask. After the first couple minutes, I was having way too much fun to stop her."

"Did she ever figure it out?"

"That's the best part. I went ahead and gave her my telephone number and my e-mail address, trevorspacealien@geonode.net. She never even noticed my name wasn't Allen, which was what she kept calling me."

"Did you get a call or e-mail from this Nathan guy?"

"I did. He called me the next day. The guy sounded miserable.

I guess he'd noticed my name wasn't Allen, but his mom kept insisting he give me a call. So he finally did. He was really embarrassed."

"And?"

"And what?"

"Oh, come on. After an introduction like that, you can't just let it drop without even meeting the guy."

Trevor laughed. "You got me. I'm trying to arrange to get together in Portland sometime this next weekend. Maybe go to a mall or something. Don't know if he'll go for it, though. He seems a little bit weirded out by it all."

"Can you blame him?"

"Yeah, Trev. Not everyone has your complete lack of social embarrassment."

Trevor laughed again.

"Hey, guys," Paul put in. He was surprised to hear himself speaking.

"Yeah?"

"I, uh, wanted to say something."

"What? You're another one of Trevor's long-lost friends?"

"Not exactly. I'm, uh, gay."

Trevor shook his head. "Dude, and I thought it was gonna be something interesting." He paused. "I think we kinda all assumed that was the case, seeing how comfortable you are with us and how you never said you *weren't* gay." He laughed, but there was little humor in it. "It's funny how, even though we're supposed to be all about tolerance and stuff here, all the straight guys find ways to make sure everybody knows they're straight."

"Now, Trevor. You know how important it is not to make assumptions about people, regardless of what they do or don't say." This was from Ms. Allington, who'd apparently wandered over without Paul realizing it. Trevor rolled his eyes, though Paul noticed that his face was turned away so Ms. Allington couldn't see.

She looked now at Paul. "That's a brave thing you've done, coming out. I hope GSA can be a positive and supportive place for you. Everything you say here is confidential, you know." Then she drifted away again.

They watched until she was out of earshot before resuming the conversation. "How many other people know?" asked another kid who'd been on the poster committee with Paul.

"My mom. A couple of my friends. Sarah."

"Is that why she dragged you out to GSA?"

"No. I didn't tell her till, uh, last week. After the GSA meeting."

"I heard about that day," Trevor said. "Hugs. Weird stuff."

"It wasn't too bad." Paul shrugged. "Anyway, after talking with her, I thought I might as well tell other people in GSA."

Trevor grinned at him. "So Sarah really wasn't your girl-friend."

"Not hardly."

"I bet she wasn't too happy to find out you're gay."

Paul could see Sarah scowling at him from across the room and wondered if she'd heard what they were saying. "Look, guys, let's change the subject, okay?"

"Fine. Anyway, welcome to the warm and confidential enfold-ing arms of GSA, as Ms. Allington never fails to remind us. You planning to come out to the whole school?"

"Not a chance."

"So, you really are gay," said Jared. "I was starting to wonder."

The meeting had finally broken up. Paul and Jared were on their way out to Jared's car. He'd offered to take Paul home after the meeting, since it was cold and starting to drizzle.

Paul shrugged. "If anyone would have guessed, I thought it would be you. It's not like I was trying really hard to hide it."

"Yeah, but you never said anything either."

They got into the car. "So, what does it mean to you?" Jared asked. "Being gay, I mean? Being out now, at GSA at least?"

"I don't think anybody's asked me that before. Well, except my mother, when I told her."

"How'd she take it?"

"She was great. Even started teasing me about cute boys. I had to tell her I didn't really plan on dating guys."

Jared was silent for a moment. "Why not?"

It was Paul's turn to be silent. "I've made a promise," he said at last. "A religious commitment. Gay sex is against the rules of my church. I'm trying to live by those rules."

"Really?"

"Yeah."

"Wow. That's intense."

"You're not gonna go on about how I'm all wacko for believing in a religion that tells me it's wrong to be gay?"

Jared gestured with one hand while holding onto the steering wheel with the other. "I figure that's your call. You're the one who has to live with it, either way."

"Which means you think I'm crazy, but you aren't gonna say anything to me about it."

"Well, yeah. Crazy people are dangerous." They both laughed.

"Seriously, I figure you're the one who has to live your life," Jared continued. "Whatever floats your boat. It's like . . . some gay guys are cross-dressers. You know, they like to dress up like girls. That just totally freaks me out. For me, being gay has *nothing* to do with wanting to be like a girl, in any way. That's just so different from what being gay is like for me, it's hard for me to even understand it. But, hell, it's their thing, so whatever. I figure it's the same way for you." He paused. "Did someone give you grief about it?"

"Sarah."

Jared laughed. "Yeah, I can see her doing that."

"She's so busy taking up the cause, she doesn't always hear what you're actually saying."

"She seems like a good friend, though."

"We got to know each other just this year. But yeah, if things were going bad or I was being hassled about being gay, I can't think of anybody who'd be better to have on my side than Sarah."

"So you're happy being a Mormon?"

Just then, they pulled up in front of Paul's house. Jared turned off the car, but neither of them got out.

"Yeah. Mostly." Paul's voice sounded louder with the motor turned off. He hesitated, then continued. "Sometimes it's really tough." The words echoed strangely in Paul's mind, as he realized this was the first time he'd mentioned this particular set of doubts to anyone. *Maybe it's because I don't know Jared that well, so it's easier to talk to him about it.*

"What do you mean?"

Paul was silent for a moment. "It's just—there're these expectations, you know? I mean—" He hesitated, not sure how to explain about marriage and mission and BYU and all that stuff. "I've really started to wonder if I can live up to all that."

"Especially with being gay?"

"Yeah."

"So I guess that kind of answers my question on how you feel about being gay."

"Huh?"

"It's a problem for you. From what you've said."

Paul hesitated. "Well, yeah," he finally said. "It sure makes things a lot more complicated." He thought about all the mess with Chad's mom and shuddered.

"Ain't that the truth." Jared paused. "So why do you go to GSA, if this is something you don't really want in your life?"

Paul hesitated again. He wanted to come up with a better answer than he'd given Sarah the week before. "The biggest thing—it's like, there's this part of me that nobody else understands. I mean, my mom's been great, and my bishop, and my best friend's been okay about it too, even though it freaks him out. But—a minute ago, you were talking about being gay not meaning you want to be like a girl. And that's completely the way I feel, too. But I don't think my best friend gets it. He says he does, but really I don't think it's true. He accepts me, but there's this big part of me that he doesn't understand. At GSA, though—I can laugh when someone tells a joke about big cute blond football players, without worrying too much that someone will think I'm weird for laughing at the *cute* part." Trevor, in fact, had told a joke like that at the meeting today. Everyone in their group had laughed, including Jared and Paul.

"Especially now that you've come out at GSA."

"Especially now, yeah."

"So GSA helps you feel comfortable with who you are."

"Yeah. The non-Mormon parts at least. It's a relief, getting to spend time around people where I'm not a weirdo, just because I'm attracted to guys." He paused. "But I'm still Mormon, too. I don't plan on changing that."

"Sounds tough. The balancing act, I mean."

Paul shrugged. "I think it's worth it."

"Just let me know if I can help at all. Talking, or whatever."

"I might take you up on that." Paul grabbed his backpack, then hesitated. "You know, some of this is stuff I haven't been able to talk about with anyone else. Thanks."

"Any time."

It was the last Friday before Christmas break. Ms. Allington had gotten permission for them to leave the AIDS posters up for all of December, if they made sure to take them down before the break. Paul had volunteered to take down the one in the hall where the sophomores had their lockers.

The weather didn't look too bad. Paul waited in the library until the buses left in the hopes that there wouldn't be anyone around to hassle him while he was collecting the poster. After that, he was planning to go over to Chad's house and hang out for a while. He'd told Chad he'd be a little late.

When Paul reached the poster, he saw three guys with their backs to him clustered in front of the bulletin board. To his surprise, one of them was Chad. He looked like he was prying something off the bulletin board while the other two stood there and watched him. Paul thought he recognized Randy as well, one of the guys from the soccer team. He didn't know the third guy.

"You know, you could just rip it off," the third guy was saying.

Chad's reply was hard to make out, but it included the word *staples*. Paul grinned to himself. Chad hated it when people left staples stuck into things. He'd spent fifteen minutes one time using a table knife to pry the staples out of the telephone pole near his house. Chad's mom hadn't been pleased when he bent the knife.

"So what's the big deal with taking down the soccer schedules *now*?" Randy was asking. "I mean, it's been two months since the season ended."

"Coach said do it, so we do it," the other boy said.

"I think they're replacing the bulletin boards or giving them a new covering or something," Chad put in. "Ouch! Staple got my thumb."

"What a pansy," Randy said.

"You're the pansy," Chad grunted, pulling the staple out of his thumb. Then he pointed at the GSA poster. "You want pansies, what about this pansy poster here? Should we take it down too?"

"Leave it up," ordered the third guy. "Otherwise we'll be here all day."

"*AIDS Hurts Everyone*," Randy was reading from the poster. "What a bunch of crap. If the damn faggots would just keep their dicks out of each other's butts, there wouldn't be any AIDS."

"Geez, you're ignorant," muttered the third guy.

"Just as long as they keep their dicks away from me," put in Chad.

Paul had heard enough. Disgusted, he turned to walk away.

Just then, Chad called out, "Got it."

The soccer schedule sailed through his hands and onto the floor. Turning to pick it up, he saw Paul. "Oh. Uh, hi, Paul."

Paul glared at him. "Hi yourself, jerk."

"Weren't you, uh, supposed to meet me at my house?"

"That *was* the plan, but I guess it's changed."

Chad got a kind of trapped look on his face. "I'm, uh, busy right now, but if you come over later—"

"Sorry. Looks like I'm pretty busy too this afternoon."

"Uh, well, I can come by your place later—"

"Don't bother."

"Hey, Mortensen," Randy called from halfway down the hall. "More boards. Remember? Get your ass over here."

"Crap! I—"

"Just save it." Paul pointed at the other two guys. "You got soccer schedules to take down, right?"

Chad stood there for a couple of seconds, looking undecided. Finally, he took off after the other guys.

Paul waited a minute to make sure they were gone. Then he took down the GSA poster, folded it carefully, put it in his backpack, and took off for home, riding his bicycle as fast as it could go. *What a bunch of jerks.*

About twenty minutes after Paul got home, Chad showed up.

"I said I didn't want to talk to you. Loser." They were standing just inside Paul's front door. He'd deliberately locked it after he got home, just in case Chad came over. Paul didn't want a shouting match on his porch, but he also didn't want Chad to just casually walk in the way he usually did.

"Look, Paul, it didn't mean anything—"

"Whatever. Here I've been telling all the guys at GSA about how *cool* you are, what a great *friend* you are, after you stopped freaking out about me being gay—"

"Hey! It's not like I *want* people talking about me at GSA—"

"—but then I find out what you're like when I'm not around. Talking about pansies and how we'd better keep our dicks away from you!" Paul realized he was shouting. He swallowed a couple of times instead of saying more.

"Look, you know that's just the way guys talk. They didn't mean anything by it. *I* didn't mean anything by it."

"Sure. Whatever you say. And Randy didn't mean anything when he was blaming gay people for AIDS."

"Randy's an idiot. You know that. Besides, you have to admit that poster was pretty lame."

"I helped *make* the poster. Jerk." As Paul was speaking, he reached out to shove Chad on the shoulder. And Chad . . . flinched. Like he didn't want Paul to touch him.

All of a sudden, a lot of small things started adding up in Paul's mind. Like the short glances Chad would shoot his way sometimes when Chad was around his soccer buddies. The way he sat a little farther away than he used to when they were playing video games. The way he tried to change the subject when Paul started talking about the GSA.

A deep feeling of betrayal filled Paul as he realized this wasn't just about the poster or Chad making insulting comments about gays. It was like stepping onto something he thought was a solid surface and then having it vanish underneath him.

"There's a word for people like you," Paul snarled. "The word's *homophobic*. You act all like you're okay with me being attracted to guys, but you're really not, are you?"

Chad looked away and shook his head. His face was dark red.

"Then why the *hell* did you pretend you were all right with it?"

"I figured you had enough to worry about without me spazzing out on you."

Paul stared at him a moment. "Get out. Just go. I don't wanna see you, I don't wanna talk to you. Not now, not tomorrow, not next week."

Chad shook his head. "I'm sorry I insulted your poster. And about the rest of it." Then he turned and walked away.

Paul slammed the door behind Chad and went up into his room. He spent the rest of the afternoon and evening doing his best to zone out by playing video games, but his timing and all his reflexes were lousy.

It was a week later. Paul was frustrated and upset. And, well, bored.

Christmas at Aunt Jean and Uncle George's had been okay. Paul always thought it was funny how Kyle, the youngest boy, would leap on top of him — from chairs, stairs, the arm of the couch — each time Paul got near. Hyper little rug rat. It was easy to imagine that Chad must have been like that back when he was a little kid.

Which brought his thoughts back to just how mad he was at his best friend.

Chad had tried to apologize to him at church last Sunday. Paul hadn't said anything, just stared at him.

Part of him said he was being unreasonable. It wasn't Chad's fault that he was freaked out by Paul being gay. He'd even tried to keep Paul from finding out. Which was well intended, in a stupid kind of way. Right now, though, Paul was just too upset to be around him.

I thought I had this really cool, tolerant friend. But I don't. He was just faking it.

Since church, they'd seen each other once, on Tuesday night when Paul and his mom had dropped off Christmas presents. The two exchanged cautious words, enough to keep anyone else from knowing they were fighting. Neither of them wanted to get the adults involved.

Unfortunately, that left Paul without anything to do or anyone to do it with, two days after Christmas.

On a sudden impulse, he pulled out Jared's number.

"Hi, Jared? Yeah, this is Paul. Nope, no disaster. Just regular Christmas stuff. Yeah, I got some cool stuff. Listen, you want to hang out today? Cool. Your house? Great." Paul took a look outside. "Weather doesn't look too bad right now. I'll bike over, okay?"

"So, how'd Christmas do you?"

"Pretty good," Paul answered. "Good stuff all around."

Only Jared was home, as it turned out. His parents were out visiting some relatives they saw only at this time of year. Jared had stayed home since, as he put it, he couldn't care less about the things they talked about and the relatives couldn't care less about him, so everyone was happier if he did his own thing while they were doing theirs. Paul could sympathize, kind of.

"Good stuff?" Jared asked. "Or good getting stuffed?"

"That too. We had this huge turkey . . . Oh, wait, you're still here, aren't you."

"Yuk, yuk. You're such a comedian. Except, actually, not."

As they were talking, Jared pulled out some soda pop, chips, crackers, and a leftover cheese ball. "Help yourself," he said. Paul opened up a Sprite, then tried the crackers and cheese.

" 'Sgood," he slurred, his mouth full. Jared laughed.

"So here it is, la casa de Jared. What brings you over this fine December day?"

"Well, my bicycle, to start with."

Jared raised an eyebrow. "Oh, please. Your sense of humor can't possibly be as desperate as that."

"I was sitting home bored," Paul confessed.

"So you came over here to see if I could entertain you?"

"Well, yeah."

"At least you're honest about it."

"So what were you doing before I came over?"

"Seeing if there's anything decent on the tube."

Paul rolled his eyes. "I could do that at home."

"Demanding, aren't you?"

"That's right. I'm the irritating little brother you're glad you never had, until now."

"Lucky me."

"Yes, you *are* lucky to be entertaining a superior being such as myself."

"Fine. I give up." They both laughed.

"So if TV isn't good enough for you, how do you want to waste time today?"

"Got any good movies?" Paul asked.

"Some action movies." A sly look. "Ones with hot guys."

"But is there decent character development?" As Jared stared at him, Paul giggled. "Okay, I don't care about character development either. Just so long as the guys are hot."

"And there's a lot of violence."

"Well, of course. That goes without saying."

They wound up watching *X-Men 2*, which had just come out on DVD. Aside from Logan, the cast of hot guys was somewhat lacking. Still, it was a lot of fun. Paul had seen the movie back in May when it was in the theaters, but it was great watching it again.

"So, enough hotties for you?" asked Jared. He'd gotten some more soda pop for both of them.

"Not really."

"Plenty of action, though."

"And character development." They both snickered.

"Not to mention that coming-out scene."

"Oh, yeah. Like, 'Have you ever tried not being a mutant?' That was classic."

"You know, the really disgusting thing is how the teenagers in these movies all have perfect hair and no zits." Paul paused. "Still, Logan was hot."

"Yeah, but we didn't see nearly enough of him. Not enough bare chest," Jared said with a grin.

Paul sighed in satisfaction. "You know, this is what I was talking about."

"Huh?"

"You asked one time what I get out of GSA. It's this kind of thing. Being able to sit around and talk about, you know, which guys I think are hot, just like it's normal. That kind of thing. I couldn't ever do that with Chad."

"Hmm?"

"My best friend." Paul frowned. "At least, I thought he was."

"Yeah?"

"Until last week."

With Jared's encouragement, Paul told the whole story. How he'd come out to Chad last spring. How Chad had freaked out at first, but then seemed to be okay with it. How they hadn't spent as much time doing stuff during soccer season but got together again afterward. The whole thing with Chad's mom. And then the scene with the poster, and Paul's argument with Chad, and figuring out that Chad wasn't really as okay with everything as he'd been pretending.

After Paul finished, Jared was quiet for a moment. Finally he asked, "Dude, don't you think maybe you're being a little harsh with Chad, here?"

"What do you mean?"

"So, yeah, it sucks that he's not really okay with you being gay. But at least he cared enough about staying your friend that he went ahead and pretended."

Paul didn't say anything. The same thing had occurred to him, but he was still too upset to just let it go.

Jared cleared his throat. "So, what kind of guys do you like?"

Paul welcomed the change of subject. "You know, I really haven't thought about it. I mean, I know who I think is cute, but I haven't thought about body types." He thought a minute. "Guys who are fit. Muscular."

"Bodybuilders?"

"Not so much. Just . . . fit. You know."

"Yeah." Jared snorted. "The kind of guys they put in underwear commercials."

Paul blushed. "Yeah."

"There's this poster in my room . . ."

"What?"

Jared was blushing now. "I, um, had a poster made from a Calvin Klein ad. Not indecent or anything. Just, um, hot."

"Oh, this I gotta see." Paul started laughing.

"Fine. Just . . . you turd," Jared griped. But he got up anyway

Paul followed Jared up to his room. The other boy opened the door with a flourish. "Here we are. My little fortress from the world."

"Nice." The room was larger than his, with what looked like a much bigger and more impressive music system, though Jared's computer was an older model than Paul's. The poster Jared had mentioned was very prominent—and, Paul had to admit, quite good.

"So, what do you think?"

"Nice."

"I've got a catalogue with a bunch more of those ads . . ." Jared was digging around in a stack of magazines. "Here."

Paul started thumbing through it, pausing every so often in appreciation. "You're right," he breathed. "Those guys are hot." He could tell from the tightness in his pants that his body agreed with him.

Finally Paul got to the end of the catalogue. He handed it back to Jared. "Wow. That was, um, really something. Especially that Mexican-looking dude."

"Yeah. He's hot."

"They all are." Paul adjusted his pants.

Jared looked at him kind of sideways. "You know, I can get some pictures online that are hotter than that." He paused. "You wanna see them?"

Paul knew he was crossing a line, but at the moment it didn't seem to matter that much. He knew most guys his age looked at porn sometimes, including some of the guys at church. In fact, he was pretty sure Chad had looked at porn once or twice. If he hadn't, it was only because there wasn't enough privacy in the family room where his parents kept the computer. "Sure," he said.

Chapter Ten

The stake New Year's Eve dance officially started at 8:00. Chad, though, had to be there at 7:30 because it was his dad's turn to chaperone. That meant he had a chance to get bored before most of the other kids even arrived.

Paul got there around 9:30. Chad had started to think his friend wouldn't show up. He waved at Paul, but after one glance Paul looked away. *I guess he's still mad at me.* Paul stayed away from him the rest of the night.

Shortly after Paul arrived, Chad found himself over by the refreshments talking with Janice Taylor.

"You don't particularly look like you're enjoying yourself," she started.

"I'm not," he responded, after swallowing a mouthful of punch. He made a face. It tasted like Sprite mixed with Hawaiian Punch and prune juice.

She rolled her eyes at him. "You know, when someone asks you a question like that, you need to learn to be more diplomatic. Especially when a girl is the one asking."

"Why?" He grinned. Over the past several months—ever since the dance where Paul had accused him of having a crush on Janice—he'd noticed her going out of her way to talk to him. At first he hadn't known what to say, but over time he'd gotten more comfortable. It helped that Janice had a really sarcastic sense of humor. Sometimes it was almost enough to make him temporarily forget he was talking to a pretty girl.

She shook her head. "I would have sworn that Paul was exaggerating, but . . . Chad Mortensen, if you want to invite me to a movie next Saturday, I wouldn't say no." She paused, as he stood there blinking. "Or even next Friday. Or tomorrow. I'm not particular."

Chad tried to say something. "Huh?"

"For a date. You know, those things we're allowed to do now that we're sixteen. I've heard that boys are supposed to like them, though judging from the way you're reacting I'm starting to doubt that."

"Um, yeah." With an effort, he focused on trying to respond sensibly to what she'd said. "Janice Taylor, would you like to go to a movie with me, this, um—" He thought quickly. Today was Wednesday, tomorrow he was watching the pests . . . "This Friday?"

"I'd be delighted to go with such a gentlemanly young man. What movie will we be seeing?"

How should I know? I didn't even know I was going on a date until about thirty seconds ago. "I, um, I'll check and see what's playing. And then I'll give you a call. Okay?"

"That sounds reasonable." She smirked at him. "See, I knew you could do it, if I could just coach you well enough."

"I'm not that bad!"

"Yeah, you are."

Chad remembered what Janice had said just before she started talking about going out to a movie. "So what does Paul have to do with this?"

Janice laughed. "A couple months ago, I asked him what I had to do to get you to notice me. He said I'd have to spell it out for you. I didn't really believe him, but it turned out he was right."

"I thought you were interested in him," Chad blurted out.

"Like there'd be any point in that."

Chad froze. "What do you mean?"

Janice, in turn, got a kind of panicked look on her face. "Uh, nothing."

"No, really, what do you mean?"

Janice's expression quickly went back to normal. "Nothing, really. He's just, you know, such a geek."

Looking around quickly, Chad saw a spot where no one would be close enough to hear what they were saying. "Let's go over there." She nodded.

As soon as they got there, he started again. "Look. Paul's my best friend. If there's something you think you know about him that—"

"I'm pretty sure Paul's gay."

"What?"

"I said, I'm pretty sure he's gay." She looked at Chad carefully, then shrugged. "It doesn't make any difference to me. When I found out he was going to GSA, it got me thinking. Then I mentioned the GSA to Paul. He tried to laugh it off, but he didn't exactly say he wasn't gay, either. So I put two and two together." She looked directly at Chad. "Then just a minute ago I opened my big mouth, without thinking that even if it was true, it might not be the type of thing a guy would tell his best friend. But from the way you reacted, it's clear that you *do* know something." She bit her lip. "Uh, I was right, wasn't I? You did know already?"

"What? Oh, sure. Yeah, I knew."

She shook her head. "Geez, Chad, you have a lot to learn. See, just then is when you could have told me I got it all wrong. Instead, you confirmed it. I mean, I wouldn't have believed you anyway if you denied it, but at least you could have tried."

"Didn't figure there was any point."

"Right." She eyed him. "So now you've agreed to go out on a date and we've established the whole I'm-not-freaked-because-your-best-friend's-gay thing, what do you say we get out there and dance?" Without waiting for a response, she started pulling him toward the center of the cultural hall.

"But—"

"See, the music's starting again. Let's have some fun!"

It had all happened so quickly.

Paul had been feeling mad at Chad and guilty about staying mad. He'd wanted something to distract him from how he was feeling. Jared had been a distraction. And then . . . and then . . .

Even after several days, Paul couldn't really believe what had happened. How easy it had been to wind up doing something that went so completely beyond anything he'd ever thought he'd do. Part of him kept insisting that it couldn't really have happened after all. Except that it had.

And what did you expect, when you agreed to look at porn with Jared? part of him asked. *Did you think it would stop at that?*

The answer, of course, was that he hadn't really thought about it at all. He'd been doing his best *not* to think about what was going on. That hadn't stopped it from happening, though.

The worst part was that even though he felt awful about it—

and awful about himself for doing something like that—there was still a part of him that kept thinking about how great it had felt while it was happening and that wanted to do it again. Which made him hate himself even more.

Barbara had noticed that Paul was acting odd this Christmas.

The day itself went as usual, with the two of them opening presents that morning in front of the tree in their living room. Then in the afternoon they went down to Corvallis to see George and Jean and their family—relatives on her father's side who they mostly saw at Christmas, though each year they talked about getting together more often. They'd moved to Oregon a couple of years after Barbara and Paul, but somehow they'd never become particularly close the way Barbara had hoped. Still, it was nice to see them every now and then.

Paul had talked and joked and played and been unusually patient with his younger cousins and polite to the adults. Barbara could tell that he was out of sorts, though. After they got home, he went up to his room earlier than usual.

Paul continued to be unusually quiet the next several days. Barbara didn't know exactly what was wrong, though based on the fact that Paul didn't seem to be spending any time with Chad, she guessed they'd had another argument. *Kids and their friendships. Painful, messy territory.*

Two Saturdays ago, when Barbara got back from shopping, Paul wasn't there. He didn't get back until almost dinnertime. When she asked where he'd gone, he gave the kind of vague nonanswer that was teen talk for "I don't really want to say." He looked unhappy.

Barbara didn't start worrying until the next day at church, when she noticed that Paul didn't take the sacrament. That had happened before, of course, several times since he'd reached thirteen or so. Thinking about the sorts of things that might make teenage boys feel they shouldn't partake of the sacrament, she'd thought then— and thought now—that it probably wasn't a good idea for her to ask any questions about it.

Barbara worked the following week, but she got the impression that Paul mostly stayed in his room during the break, reading or playing video games. To her surprise, she had to nag him into going to the New Year's Eve dance. The next day he'd seemed to be in a better mood, telling her about the girl in the ward who was interested in Chad and how he'd seen the two of them dancing. She laughed out loud when he told her the advice he'd given Janice about how to get Chad to notice her.

And then Saturday hit, and he took off again for a while. After he got back, he seemed really upset. And he didn't take the sacrament again the next day. She thought back on those statistics about depression and gay teens and wondered just how worried she ought to be.

School started on Monday. They went through the next week without Barbara getting any new ideas about what she ought to do or whether she needed to do anything. And then, on Sunday, Paul told her he'd be staying after to talk to the bishop. She couldn't help but hope it might make a difference.

Richard Mortensen had seen Paul Ficklin in a lot of different moods over the years. As the father of Paul's best friend — and, he believed, a kind of stand-in father at times — he'd seen Paul happy, silly, nervous, frightened, stubborn, angry, sad — many of the different moods common to boys as they grew up. Last July in this very office, he'd watched with concern as a scared but determined Paul had made sure his bishop knew about his feelings for other boys before accepting a calling of responsibility in his priesthood quorum. He'd seldom felt prouder of any young man than he'd felt of Paul that day.

Today, though, things weren't looking so good, judging by the expression on Paul's face. Richard had seen that particular mix of self-directed anger, embarrassment, and shame before. Not so much on Paul up to now, but on other boys he'd had in his office since becoming bishop.

Paul needed to confess something.

Sure enough, the first words out of his mouth, after Richard had closed the door and gestured him to sit, were, "I need to be released as teachers quorum president."

What do I do now? he asked within himself, as he always did. He'd learned never to proceed in situations like this without a prayer of that kind in his heart.

"Why?" he asked.

Paul dropped his eyes. "I'm not, uh, worthy anymore."

Bit by bit, the story came out. How Paul had started spending time with Jared, a junior he'd met in the gay-straight club at school, which Paul had started attending that fall. How he'd explained that he wouldn't ever be his boyfriend because he was Mormon. How Jared had seemed to accept that and was okay hanging out with Paul anyway. "He's a friend, you know? And he has this great sense of humor, and . . . well."

They'd been over at Jared's house, looking at some pictures of hot guys. "Just models, you know? Not like naked or anything." Then—

"Then he asked if I wanted to look at some porn. And I, um, said yes." And things had proceeded from there.

Richard sighed inwardly. He hated this next part, but he'd learned that he needed to get a clear idea of just how serious the problem was. The only way was by asking questions.

Had clothes come off? No.

Had hands gone underneath clothes? Um, yeah.

Had the other boy's hands touched Paul's sexual organs? Yes.

Had Paul's hands touched the other boy's sexual organs? No.

Had it happened again? Yes. A week later.

The same thing, or more? The same.

How long ago was this? A little over a week ago, the second time.

Richard remembered that the last couple of Sundays, Paul had assigned other boys to prepare the sacrament but hadn't helped himself. Now he knew why.

Had anything else happened since then, with this boy or anyone else? No.

Had he looked at pornography any other times? Once, a few days after the first time with Jared.

How did Paul feel about what had happened?

Ever since the conversation began, Paul had been looking down at his hands with a bleak expression on his face, but his voice had been steady. At this latest question, though, he closed his eyes and swallowed. Richard leaned forward.

"It was—I never felt anything like that before. Not even when I'm by myself and—anyway. And then it was all over, and I felt so awful. I, like, stood in the shower for a half-hour, just scrubbing, because I felt so dirty."

"But you did it again a week later."

"Yeah."

"Do you think it'll happen again?"

"I don't know." Paul opened his eyes and looked Richard in the eye for the first time since the questions had started. "I don't want it to happen, but I can't stop thinking about it. I've tried to pray, but I just feel so awful." He turned away again. "After the first time, I thought, I'm never gonna do that again. I was so sure. And then I went back a week later." Paul swallowed. "Yeah, I think it's gonna happen again."

Inside himself, Richard felt a great sense of frustration. Right now, he felt that if he had this—this Jared boy—in front of him, he'd be hard pressed not to physically attack him. *I wonder if this is what a father feels about the boy who knocked up his daughter?* he thought to himself. With difficulty, he kept his feelings from showing on his face. *It won't do any good if Paul thinks I'm angry at him.*

"Paul?"

"Yeah."

"Do you have faith in Jesus Christ? That he can help you?"

"I don't know," he whispered, and looked down again.

Richard contemplated the young man who sat before him. Paul's hands were shaking slightly, he realized. He hadn't noticed it before.

And suddenly in his mind's eye he saw a different scene. Paul, head still down, shaking the bishop's hand and walking out of his office. Paul going into the house where he and his mother lived. Paul opening the medicine cabinet in the bathroom, pouring pills from a bottle into his open hand, swallowing again and again—

The fleeting mental vision broke.

"Paul." He stood and held out his arms. "Come here."

Paul stood, but hesitated. Richard took a step toward him. With a gasp, Paul flung himself forward and clung to Richard as if he were a much younger boy.

"Paul," Richard said again, his arms wrapped around the boy's shoulders, which were shaking now with sobs. "Heavenly Father loves you. And so do I."

They stood there a long time, five minutes at least, while Richard's shirt grew damp with the boy's tears. Finally Paul released him and pulled away. "Thanks," he whispered.

Richard clasped an upper arm. "Hey, you. You're a good kid."

"I don't feel like it."

"That's Satan trying to get you to feel like you aren't worth anything. Like you can't change. Like you aren't worthy of God's love, or anyone else's." Richard cleared his throat. "There's a scripture I memorized back when I was about your age. 'For I am persuaded, that neither death, nor life, nor angels, nor principalities, nor powers, nor things present, nor things to come, nor height, nor depth, nor any other creature, shall be able to separate us from the love of God, which is in Christ Jesus our Lord.' That's what the missionary who interviewed me for baptism quoted when I told him I didn't think I could ever be good enough to be a member of the church."

"But you weren't gay."

Richard paused. How to handle this one? "I'm not completely sure you are, either."

"But—"

He held up his hand. "I don't doubt that you're attracted to other males. I'm not convinced, though, that it has to mean you're *gay*. I take gay to mean someone who's chosen to live a homosexual lifestyle, one that's not consistent with the gospel."

"But I—"

"You committed a sin. You made a mistake. You did something that naturally makes you feel bad, because you weren't living up to your own standards, God's standards. It made you feel rotten. Now Satan's jumped on that. He's trying to convince you that you're garbage because you made a mistake. He wants to convince you that you can't help acting that way. He wants you to think you're stuck. But you're not."

"I don't think I'm gonna stop feeling the way I do. About guys and stuff."

"I didn't say you would."

They were still standing. Richard gestured Paul to sit, then sat down himself. He no longer felt that same frightening sense that the boy might be on the edge of deciding life wasn't worth living anymore. Now all he had to do was convince Paul that being the way he was didn't mean he had to leave the church.

He began again. "Paul, God doesn't expect more from you than you're able to do. At this point, the only thing that's expected from you is the same thing that's expected of all young men in the church. Basically, that's to keep your hands and your body to yourself and do your best to train your thoughts and personal behavior not to go where they shouldn't." He softened his voice. "Do you have a testimony of the gospel?"

"I—I believe it's true." Paul looked down at his hands. "I've felt the Holy Ghost, sometimes. I think."

"Do you want to stay in the church?"

"Yes."

"Do you want to serve a mission, get married, have a family? I'm not talking about whether you think it can happen. What I'm asking is, do you *want* it?"

"Yes." The boy's voice was very quiet now.

Richard hesitated for a few seconds, then continued. "I don't know what you're going through. I've never been attracted to other men. But I do know that each of us encounters hard things in our lives. This thing you're struggling with is really tough. I don't know if you will ever be free of those feelings in this life. But I do know that being gay isn't part of your eternal character. Someday, whether in this life or the next, you can be married to a woman you love. You can have a family." He paused. "God can do this. Can you believe in him enough to give him a chance?"

Paul still looked hesitant, or maybe fearful. "I don't know if I can."

Richard thought some more. "There's another scripture I like. Let's see if I can find it . . . Here it is. Alma is talking to the Zoramites. 'But behold, if ye will awake and arouse your faculties, even to an experiment upon my words, and exercise a particle of faith, yea, even if ye can no more than desire to believe, let this desire work in you, even until ye believe in a manner that ye can give place for a portion of my words.' That's what I hear in what you're saying to me. You're not sure if you believe. You don't know if you can do it. But you *want* to believe. You *desire* to believe. My challenge to you, Paul, is to let that desire work within you, the way the scripture says. Do an experiment on the Lord's words, and on my words. Give them a try. I promise that God won't let you down. Will you do that?"

Slowly, hesitantly, Paul nodded.

"Okay." Richard took a deep breath. "So let's set some ground rules, some things you can do that will give you strength to make sure this doesn't happen again. Have you been reading your scriptures?"

"Most of the time."

"I want you to commit to reading your scriptures each day, at a regular time. Can you do that?"

"Yes."

"What about your prayers? Have you been saying them, each morning and evening?"

"Not always."

"I want you to commit to saying your prayers every day. Each morning, ask Heavenly Father specifically for his help in getting through the day. Each evening, report back to him about how things have gone. Can you do that?"

"Yes."

And now the tougher ones. "Paul, I think we need to make sure you don't ever find yourself in situations where this might happen again. How can you do that?"

"I don't know."

Richard shook his head. "I don't think it's a good idea for you to see this Jared person or keep going to this GSA group. But at the least, you definitely need to make sure you don't get into situations where you're alone with Jared or any other gay person."

Richard paused. He wanted to make sure Paul understood the reasons for these boundaries. "The impulses you've talked about—they're the product of opportunity and temptation. You may not be able to get rid of the temptation, at least not right away or all at once, but you *can* remove the opportunity. What you need to do is make sure that when those feelings come, you're not in a situation that makes it easy for you to act on them. No looking at porn, either alone or especially with someone else there. No intimate situations with other guys. No personal conversations, even, with someone you think might be same-sex attracted, unless another person is there as a chaperone. Can you do that?"

Paul swallowed. "Yes."

Richard looked at the youth sitting in front of him. Paul had made the commitments but didn't sound too happy. *He needs a lifeline,* he thought. *Something he can grab onto and hold onto when things get tough. Someone who can be there for him. He needs a dad, but I can't give him one.*

Richard guessed he would just have to do as a substitute.

"You have a cell phone, don't you?"

"Yeah."

"I want you to call me. Call me each day at"—he mentally flipped through his daily calendar—"3:30. Here's my number." He pulled out one of his business cards, circled the number, and handed it to Paul. "Call me, tell me how things are going. How your day is going. Even if it's just a minute. All right? Or I'll be calling you. Can you do that?"

"Yeah." Paul blushed and nodded, but he didn't seem angry or upset. *He really wants someone he can talk to about things,* Richard realized, *even if it's just the bishop.* Once again, as on numerous occasions over the years, Richard felt the temptation to seek out Barbara's ex-husband and smack him for leaving her to raise a boy pretty much on her own. *It's a good thing he lives in Minnesota.*

"Call me any other time as well, anytime day or night, if things start getting tough for you. If you start feeling bad about yourself, or if you feel like you might give in and make some bad choices. Or even if you just want to talk. Okay?"

"Okay."

Richard thought again for a moment. "Paul, there's one other thing I'd like to do before we leave today. Will you let me give you a blessing?"

"Yes."

Richard got out of his chair and put his hands on the boy's head. "Paul Eric Ficklin, by the authority of the holy Melchizedek priesthood which I hold, I lay my hands upon your head . . ."

As the words flowed, Richard could feel Paul relaxing under him. Somewhat to his own surprise, the main thrust of the blessing was admonishment to follow the counsel of his leaders — a reference, Richard assumed, to the things he'd just told the boy — with a promise of spiritual protection as he did so. Nothing about the larger issues of same-sex attraction or how Paul should lead his life in general. *Maybe just getting him past this is enough for right now.*

Soon the blessing was over. Paul stood, wiped tears from his face, seized Richard in a great hug, and then let him go. As the boy left the room, there was a tentative smile on his face — the first Richard had seen from him that afternoon.

It was Monday afternoon, and Chad was working on his algebra when the doorbell rang.

Paul was at the door. "Can I come in?"

"I thought you weren't talking to me right now," Chad answered, without moving from where he stood blocking the doorway. Part of him was happy to see his best friend. Another part was angry at the way Paul had lit into him that Friday before Christmas and even angrier at the way Paul had been avoiding him since then.

"Yeah, well, I'm sorry," Paul muttered, looking down. "I was wrong. And — well, I need some help with stuff."

Slowly, Chad opened the door all the way, then led the way up to his bedroom. Paul closed the bedroom door behind him and dropped onto a chair. Chad sat on the bed.

"So," Chad began. "Want to explain why you've been such a jerk the last couple of weeks?"

"Not really," Paul said, still looking away.

"Well, too bad, jerk-off."

Paul winced. "Yeah, well." He drew a deep breath. "At first, I was ticked off about all that stuff you and your friends were saying and 'cause you were pretending to be okay with me being gay when you really weren't. I still think you were being a real loser about that, by the way."

"And then?"

"I, uh, didn't want to hang out with you, because . . . I did something really stupid. And I didn't want to talk about it."

"This I gotta hear. Something stupid enough to make *you* not want to tell *me* about it?"

"I did stuff with Jared. That guy from GSA."

For a minute, Chad couldn't figure out what he meant. Then it all came clear. "Geez, Paul! What the fuh — I mean, why the hell did you do that?"

"Keep it down!" Paul yelped. Then, more quietly, he added, " 'Cause I was dumb. And horny."

Paul sat there looking at his best friend, who was staring back at him from his bed. He looked mad, which Paul had expected, but mostly he just seemed exasperated — as if Chad couldn't believe Paul had been so stupid.

Paul still couldn't believe it either.

Chad spoke. "So, you been to talk to my dad yet? Or does this favor you need have something to do with that?"

Paul stared at him. "Huh?"

"Come off it, Paul! We've been friends for seven years. Remember that time we stole those soda pops when we were nine? Fifteen minutes later, you were going all guilty on me about it. You didn't last an hour before you were telling your mom. Got me into trouble too. I was mad at you for a week.

"I figure there's no way you won't tell my dad about this sooner or later. So the question is whether you told him already or decided to talk to me first." Chad paused. "Except that doesn't make sense either. There's no reason why you'd talk to me about this unless you had to. So I'm guessing you already talked to my dad." He peered at Paul suspiciously. "What's this favor you need from me?"

"You're right. I talked with your dad yesterday."

"And?"

"And he gave me some rules."

"Yeah? Like what?"

"I have to have someone else with me if I'm gonna be alone with any gay guys."

"Well, duh."

"What do you mean?"

Chad shrugged. "I kind of wondered about that. I mean, can you imagine my dad and mom letting me spend several hours alone with a girl, with no one else in the house? But you got together with that Jared guy whenever you wanted. You were sliding by."

Paul frowned. He hadn't thought about it that way before.

Chad continued. "So how does this affect me?"

"I really need to talk with Jared."

"Uh-uh. No way. I am not gonna stick around just so you can tell your ex-boyfriend why you're breaking up with him."

"It's not like that. I mean, he's really *not* my boyfriend."

"So basically your hormones got out of control and you jumped the guy?"

Paul could feel his face reddening even more. "More like I let him jump me."

"Geez, Paul, you're a dumb shit." Chad paused. "So if he's not your boyfriend, why do you have to talk to him about it at all?"

"Look, I just do, okay?"

Chad closed his eyes. "So when're you planning to deliver this bit of news to the fair Jared?"

"After school tomorrow. Either before or after the GSA meeting."

"Oh, great. You want me to go to this GSA thing, then hang around trying not to look like a homophobe while you tell this friend all about the new rules my dad said you have to follow."

"Look, I know you're not a homophobe. I'm sorry for saying it, okay?"

"I wouldn't be too sure about that. Right at the moment, I'm feeling pretty pissed at most of the gay people I know."

"Me, you mean."

"Well, yeah, you. Not to mention that pea-brain jerk-off Jared." Chad shook his head. "You're gonna owe me so bad for this."

"I know," Paul muttered.

• • •

Jared was having a good day. He'd been in a good mood generally, ever since Christmas.

Christmas vacation had been surprisingly good for him and his family. A few days after the holiday, to his great surprise, his dad had pulled him aside and talked with him about college. He'd told him they were still planning to support him at the University of Oregon if he did his best to earn good grades. "I know we haven't talked a lot, since . . . well," his dad had said, obviously uncomfortable. "I want you to know that you're still our son, and we'll support you in all the good things you want to do with your life." He'd looked away then. "I'm sorry. I've just had a hard time getting used to this." It wasn't a declaration of gay pride or even complete acceptance, but it was a sign that things were finally starting to get better—after Jared had pretty much given up hope that it would ever happen.

And then there was the stuff with Paul.

After Paul had come out at GSA, Jared hadn't seen him again before school let out for the break. So he was surprised when Paul called him up the Saturday after Christmas and asked if they could hang out. They'd talked for a while, then started looking at some mags and online pictures. Seeing how excited Paul was getting, Jared had made a snap decision and put his hand on Paul's back.

Things had progressed from there.

At one point Jared had stuck his hands down Paul's pants. He worried for a minute that he might have gone too far, but the other boy hadn't objected.

After it was all over, Paul had taken off pretty quickly. The next Saturday, though, he'd come over again, and pretty much the same thing had happened.

Since then, Jared had found himself thinking. His original idea had been to have some fun without going too far with the other boy. He didn't want a boyfriend right now, and he knew Paul wasn't up for one.

And that was all it had been the first time. Paul was cool, he was a good guy, he was cute. And he seemed to like what they'd been doing. The way Jared saw it, it wasn't like it was real sex. Just messing around.

The second time, though . . . Jared had felt something that second time, a kind of connection that hadn't been there before. Several times since then, he'd caught himself thinking about the other boy at odd moments.

Paul was cute. He was friendly, and he had a good sense of humor, without the extra layer of sarcasm Jared had found in a lot of the gay people he knew in GSA and elsewhere. Paul was . . . *nice.* Wholesome. Good natured. It was a combination, Jared was starting to realize, that he found a lot more attractive—at least in the case of Paul—than he ever would have guessed. He couldn't really explain it.

Jared was even starting to think maybe he could live with having a boyfriend he couldn't have sex with if the boyfriend was Paul. If it came to that. *After all,* he reminded himself, *it's not like I'm having sex with anyone right now anyway.*

Paul hadn't been at the first GSA meeting after Christmas break. Jared was surprised but didn't read too much into it. After all, Jared himself didn't come to all the meetings. He also hadn't expected to see the other boy this past weekend, since school had started up again and they hadn't talked about getting together. It had been a casual, one-time thing that happened to be repeated. It was only this past weekend that he'd started to realize he might want to find out if it could turn into something more than that.

And so Jared was hoping to see Paul at GSA today and maybe get a chance to talk to him afterward and see whether they might spend some more time hanging out together. That was where things stood when Jared spotted Paul and his friend standing outside the GSA room. Paul had an uncomfortable expression on his face, and his friend didn't look terribly friendly. "We need to talk," Paul said, and that was when things started going rapidly downhill.

Talking to the bishop had been hard. Talking to Chad had been embarrassing. But talking to Jared was turning out to be a lot worse than Paul had expected.

Seeing Jared walking toward the GSA room, Paul couldn't help but notice the smile on the other boy's face as he caught sight of Paul standing in the hallway. To Paul's surprise, he could feel his own breath speed up. Jared was—Paul had to admit—pretty good looking. A mental picture flashed in Paul's mind replaying what had happened the last couple of times they got together. His body definitely remembered and was reminding him of that fact.

Paul realized that Chad being there was a good idea for its own sake, not just so he could say he was following the bishop's rules. *Stupid teenage hormones.*

"So, Paul," Jared began. "Haven't seen you for awhile. You wanna introduce me to this guy?"

"This is my best friend, Chad. I told you about him."

"I guess you two are cool again."

"Yeah." Paul sucked in his breath. "We need to talk."

Jared was quiet for a long moment. "You wanna do this after GSA, or right now? We can skip out on the meeting."

"Right now would maybe be better, if that's okay with you."

"Okay."

They walked out into the courtyard. The minute they got there, Chad started. "Look, this all has nothing to do with me, okay? So I'll just go sit over there, and you two can talk about what you need to talk about, and I'll walk home with Paul afterward. Deal?" Without waiting for an answer, he walked over to a table about twenty feet away, then pulled out a textbook and started reading it, very obviously not looking their way.

"Well. I guess that tells us, doesn't it?"

"Yeah." There was an uncomfortable silence.

Paul drew a deep breath. "Jared. About the time we spent over Christmas." He swallowed. "I, uh, I crossed a line. A line I shouldn't have crossed."

Jared didn't say anything. Paul couldn't meet his eyes.

"I was . . . I, uh, talked to you that one time about the standards I'm supposed to keep. What we did was way beyond what I should have been doing. The porn and, um, the other stuff."

There was a pause. "Yeah. So, I guess that's good to know," Jared said finally. Paul couldn't tell anything from his expression.

"There's, uh, more. I kind of, um, talked with my bishop about it. My minister, you know?"

Jared closed his eyes. "And he doesn't want you hanging out with faggots like me anymore."

Paul winced. "Not exactly. But I'm, um, not supposed to be alone with any other gay guys."

"Shit. So now we need a chaperone just to get together and talk." He jerked his thumb over toward Chad. "That's why he's here, then?"

"Yeah."

"Well, that really sucks."

"It's — don't think — " Paul's words ran out then, as he realized he wasn't really sure what he was trying to say. He started again. "I still think you're a cool dude. This doesn't change that."

"And let's still be friends, that whole crap." Jared's voice sounded sarcastic and vaguely bitter. He glared over at Chad. "What happens to you if you don't go along with this?"

"It's not like that. I mean, yeah, I made an agreement with the bishop, but it was my choice really. It's a way that I can keep the promises I've made."

"Like that really makes me feel so much better, knowing you and your church think I'm some kind of chemical contaminant you have to be protected from."

"That's not it at all." Paul was now feeling thoroughly miserable.

"Sure feels like it."

"Look, I'm sorry if it makes you feel bad. That's really not what it's about, though. It's about making it easier for *me* to be sure I'm keeping my commitments." Paul laughed nervously. "I mean, it's not like we were boyfriends or anything."

Jared stared at him for a moment, then slapped one hand against a tree trunk. "Yeah. Of course. Well, thanks for letting me know, anyway, instead of just avoiding me like you've been doing the past two weeks." He picked up his backpack and headed toward the courtyard exit.

"Hey! Aren't you going to GSA?"

Jared paused. "Somehow, I just don't feel like going to a meeting right now about how we're all supposed to be happy being gay, or straight, or Mormon-in-the-closet, or whatever." He turned back toward the doors again. "See you, man. Hopefully not too soon, though." Then he was gone.

Paul stood staring after him for a minute, stunned.

"Well, looks like that went well." It was Chad.

"Not really."

"I was being ironic. Moron."

Paul looked at his watch. "Dang. I'm late for my call with your dad." He pulled out his cell phone and started pressing buttons.

"Dammit." Jared pounded a fist against his bedroom wall. "Dammit," he repeated.

Paul had warned him. Hell, he'd warned himself. *It's not like we're boyfriends.* No duh.

For one fleeting moment, the thought crossed his mind that really, this was all pretty ordinary stuff. Teenagers found out all the time that someone they liked didn't like them back. The fact that he and Paul were both boys didn't really have anything to do with it. *Yay for equal-opportunity disappointment.* Somehow it didn't make him feel any better.

Chapter Eleven

CHAD AND PAUL TOOK THEIR TIME walking over to Chad's house, despite the gathering dark and cold of the winter afternoon. Neither of them said very much. After his conversation with Jared, Paul didn't feel like talking. Besides, now that the whole thing with Jared was over, he realized that things were still kind of awkward between him and Chad.

Paul had been surprised when Chad invited him over. When he asked if Chad's mom would be upset, Chad replied, "I'm tired of waiting for things to be okay with her. She needs to just get over it."

Once they got to Chad's house, though, it didn't seem to be an issue. On the way up to his room, they stopped in the kitchen to grab some chips and salsa and a couple of root beers. Chad's mom wasn't in the kitchen, but on the way out they passed her in the hall. She stopped and put a hand on Paul's arm.

"We haven't seen you much during the last couple of months. It's good to have Chad's partner in crime back with us again."

Paul looked at her. She was staring at him, still holding his arm. It looked like she was waiting for him to say or do something. "Thanks," he said at last.

She nodded and let go. He nodded back, but inside he was trying to keep from showing just how upset he was.

"What was that all about?" he demanded as soon as they were in Chad's room with the door closed.

"Heck if I know. I guess you don't have cooties anymore."

"First she doesn't want you to spend time with me, and then suddenly everything's all okay?"

"Hey, at least it's over now. Don't complain."

I should be happy about this, Paul thought. *I don't have to feel anymore like my best friend's mom thinks I might infect her family.* He was uncomfortably reminded of Jared's complaint earlier that afternoon that Paul's church thought he was some kind of chemical contaminant. *Chad's mom thinks that way about me. She thinks I'm the one who's dangerous.*

It wasn't a new thought. He just wished he knew why it was bothering him so much right now.

"Hey! What's up? Looks like you're a million miles away."

"Dunno. Just thinking."

"About my mom?"

"I guess."

Chad made a vague gesture. "Sometimes my mom gets upset. Then she gets over it. I sure as heck don't know why."

That was what bothered him the most, Paul realized. The unpredictability of it all. *It wasn't anything I did or said that started it, just finding out about what I am. Now apparently it's over, and I don't even know what changed so things are okay now.*

Chad's voice interrupted his thoughts. "Hey, Paul! Wanna try out *Warcraft 3* on my computer? My folks got me it for Christmas."

"I still can't believe they got you a Mac."

Chad rolled his eyes. "Safer from computer viruses, they said."

"I guess. Too bad it's missing so many good games." Paul shook his head. "The thing I don't get is why they got a Mac for you when your family already has a PC downstairs."

"The day my family makes sense is the day I'll check myself into a mental hospital." Chad double-clicked something on the computer desktop, then stood and waved Paul toward the chair. "C'mon, let's get you started. We only have about half an hour before you have to get home."

Downstairs, Sandy was in the kitchen standing in front of the sink, staring out the window but not really thinking about what she was seeing. Every now and then, sounds would erupt from the family room where Jeffrey was playing one of his endless video games: bursts of noise from the game itself, alternating with shouts from Jeffrey when his character died. But she wasn't paying attention to that, either.

That was hard, talking to Paul like that.

Sandy hated apologizing. She hated feeling like she was in the wrong, and she hated other people knowing about it. She'd gotten into a lot of trouble as a child because she simply refused to acknowledge that anything she did was ever wrong. She'd received a lot of punishments from her parents and lost several friends because of that.

It had all come to a head Sandy's junior year in high school. She'd lost her first job as a sales assistant at a toy store because she refused to smooth things over with a customer whose child was throwing a temper tantrum. "But it wasn't my fault!" she insisted to the store manager after the woman stormed out.

"Doesn't make any difference whether it was or not. There isn't any being right when the customer's unhappy." The store manager had shaken his head. "I can't afford to have you here if it means people will be looking like that when they leave." And that was that.

Afterward, Sandy had taken a grim look at herself. Over the previous year, she'd been trying to change some of the personality traits that made other people dislike her, such as her habit of making sarcastic comments. Clearly this was another area she'd have to change, especially if it was getting in the way of her keeping a job.

It had taken a lot of work. She'd been most of the way through college before she'd been able to successfully fake a gracious apology, even when she was seething inside. *And I still don't like it.*

Part of her, amused, reminded herself that technically she still hadn't apologized to Paul. *Shut up,* she told herself.

Sandy had been surprised earlier that afternoon to hear Chad talking and laughing as he came in the door. When she heard Paul answering him, she understood. *Teenage boys really are herd animals,* she'd thought. Chad was in a good mood because his best friend was here. It was as simple as that.

Then she met them in the hall. As soon as he caught sight of her, Chad's face had turned to a mask, while Paul looked wary.

I did this, she thought. *With my reaction and my attitude. And now my son won't talk to me except when he has to, and his best friend — a harmless kid I've known since he was nine years old — looks at me like he's scared of me.*

On an impulse, she grabbed Paul's arm. "We haven't seen you much during the last couple of months. It's good to have Chad's partner in crime back with us again."

Internally, she winced. *I wonder if that sounded as stupid and fake to the boys as it did to me?*

"Thanks," Paul responded after a minute. Sandy nodded, abruptly dropping Paul's arm when she noticed she was still holding onto it.

The boys clattered past her and up the stairs. A minute later, she heard the sound of Chad's door closing. To her surprise, she realized that the two of them being together in a closed room didn't bother her. *I guess I really do know that Paul isn't going to turn my son gay.*

Over the next two weeks, Paul got used to his new routine.

Most days after school, he'd go home with Chad. Usually his time to call Bishop Mortensen would come during their walk. He'd pull out his cell phone, and he and the bishop would talk for about thirty seconds. When it was raining, which it often was, he'd duck inside a convenience store and call from there.

The first day after his conversation with Jared, Paul went back to his own house the way he'd been doing pretty much all that year. He'd been home for only about fifteen minutes when he found himself staring at his computer and thinking about the kinds of pictures he'd looked at with Jared. After several minutes of mental struggle, he'd realized that if he wanted to keep his promises to the bishop, he needed to not be alone in the house. Shortly after that, he was riding his bicycle over to Chad's house.

Chad had asked him about it exactly once. "So why are you hanging out around here all the time, anyway?"

He asked, Paul thought. "So I don't spend the afternoon looking up gay porn on my computer."

Chad's eyes had widened, and he quickly looked away. *Got him that time*, thought Paul, amused. *Someday Chad's gonna have to learn not to ask questions if he doesn't want to know the answers.*

Paul didn't plan on going back to GSA. Unfortunately, that didn't turn out to be as easy as he'd expected.

"Missed you at GSA again yesterday," Sarah told him at lunch on Wednesday, about a week after his conversation with Jared. Paul noticed that she'd been careful to approach him as he was leaving the lunch table, so no one else heard her question.

"I, uh, didn't really feel like coming yesterday."

"Jared wasn't there either. Does this have anything to do with that argument you and Jared had last week?" Paul stared at her. "Ellen saw you," Sarah continued.

I guess I can't pretend it didn't happen, then. "Kind of." He paused, then continued. "Look, I don't think I'm gonna be coming out to GSA that much anymore." He winced at the accidental pun. "It's just not really my thing, I guess."

"That's stupid," Sarah replied. Paul blinked. "You loved it at GSA. I could tell." She tilted her head to one side and looked at him. "Whatever happened between you and Jared, you should both just get over it."

"Like that's the way girls act when they have an argument with someone."

"I do," Sarah responded. Paul looked at her with disbelief. "Last year I had this big blowout with Ellen, but I kept coming to GSA. Eventually we got over it." Sarah's eyes narrowed. "Unless the real reason is you've decided we really are all going to hell, and you don't want to go with us. Or maybe you're all nervous now that you're out."

"That's not it. Really."

"Whatever." She shrugged. "Well, you're the one who has to choose. Whatever your reason is for not coming to GSA, though, I think you're being stupid. GSA is all about helping you feel comfortable with who you are."

That wasn't the end of it, of course. A couple of days later, Jared caught Paul at the end of a school assembly. "Can we talk a couple minutes?"

Paul looked around. The hall was full of people, but no one was paying much attention. Chad had already taken off to his next class. "Sure, if we make it fast. I don't wanna be late for fourth period."

"Look. That stuff I said . . . I didn't mean for you to stop coming to, uh, the club, you know. It's okay." He looked away.

"Sarah talk to you too?"

"Yeah."

Paul shook his head. "Look, it's really not because of what you said." *Not completely, anyway,* he added mentally.

"See, though, that's it." Jared looked back at him. "Yeah, I was pretty ticked off about it all. Sarah's right, though." He lowered his voice. "GSA's a place everyone needs to feel like they can go. I think maybe that's especially important for you."

"What do you mean?"

"Look, you don't have any friends that're gay besides the people you know in GSA, right?"

Paul shook his head.

"So, maybe you wanna be all religious and stuff. Still — is being gay something you can talk about with your other friends? Like that Chad guy?"

"Not really."

"I know how it would be for me if I didn't have someplace where I can, I dunno, just be myself."

He's got a point, Paul admitted mentally. He didn't say anything, though.

Jared sighed. "Just come, okay? I mean, you can decide you don't wanna associate with us lowlifes later on, sometime when Sarah won't get on my case about it."

"I told you, it's not like that."

"Whatever." Jared walked away.

Chad nearly blew a gasket the next Monday when he found out Paul was thinking about going back to GSA.

"That's stupid! First you get in trouble for doing gay stuff, and then you wanna go back to this gay club where the guy hangs out and everybody else knows you're gay? It's — look, Paul, you're being an idiot. Besides, what about my dad?"

"He didn't say I couldn't go." Chad stared at him, a look of disbelief on his face. "I mean, look, it's not like I'm gonna make out with someone in the middle of the GSA meeting."

"Do some of them do that?"

"Not that I've seen." Actually, from what Paul could tell, it seemed like the straight couples were more physical with each other than the gay couples. All he'd ever seen from the gay couples was some hand-holding, plus a very occasional quick kiss.

"Still," Chad said. "I mean, what's the point?"

"Maybe because they're friends of mine?"

"With friends like that . . ."

"*I'm* like that."

Chad looked away. Exasperated, Paul hit him on the leg. "Come off it, Chad! It's not gonna go away just because you pretend it's not there! I'm gay. Got it?"

"Yeah, well, it's not like I could have missed it," he muttered. "Not the way this school year has gone."

Paul felt his eyes narrowing. "You know, I'm pretty sure the real reason you're all upset about me going to GSA is because it reminds you that I'm gay, which isn't something you like to think about."

"Not this stupid argument again!"

"Huh?"

"It's like, every time I say something you don't like, suddenly it's all about how uncomfortable *I* am with this."

"But you're *not* comfortable with me being gay."

Chad was quiet for a moment. Finally he said, "You're right. I'm not comfortable with it. But you know what? This isn't about that. It's about you doing something I think you're gonna be sorry about later on."

"They're my friends. I can't just ditch them like that."

Chad stared at him. "You know, that's the same thing I thought back in eighth grade when I was hanging out with Steve Sessions and his friends. It was a stupid reason then, and it's a stupid reason now."

"And yet you still spend time with Tyler and those guys."

"It's not the same."

"Sure it's not."

"I haven't had a make-out session with any of those guys."

Paul winced. "Yuck! I just—that's gross."

"No argument from me."

"Though come to think of it, Tyler—"

"Shut. Up."

Paul snickered. Revenge was sweet. Besides, it had let them both cool off.

"See, this is what I mean," Chad complained. "Going to GSA's turned you into a pervert."

Paul rolled his eyes. "Like you're one to talk about being a pervert. I saw the way you were looking at Christy Winters the other day."

"Well, yeah. But I'm a *straight* pervert." Chad shook his head in mock sorrow. "And you used to be such a nice little boy, too. Now you're all gay and perverted."

"Oh, please," Paul answered. Chad was snickering at him.

Then Chad turned serious. "I used to get all jealous of how you never got into trouble."

"The way I remember it, we both got into plenty of trouble."

"Well, yeah. But still, you were always the good kid."

"Yeah. Too bad I turned out to be gay."

Chad snorted. "You're still the good kid, Paul. You just do dumb things sometimes."

"Like going to GSA?"

"You got it."

Paul was silent for a moment. Why was this bothering Chad so much? Finally he said, "They're just ordinary teenagers, you know."

Chad snorted again.

Paul was starting to get irritated. Chad could really be an ass sometimes. "You know, you could come and find out for yourself."

"No way!"

Paul grinned, ignoring his own misgivings at the idea. "Sure you can. In fact, I think you really need to if you're gonna spout ignorance about GSA."

"Not happening."

"Wanna bet?"

As it turned out, Chad didn't go to the GSA meeting with Paul the next day. After Paul had calmed down, he wasn't sure whether he should be ticked off or relieved about that. Chad plus GSA wasn't necessarily a good combination.

"Hi, Paul! Good to see you back!"

It was Sarah, of course, waving and smiling from halfway across the room. Paul winced. Judging by the number of people who came up to say hi, though, he suspected that sneaking in wouldn't really have been possible even without Sarah and her loud mouth.

Jared was over where he usually sat, in a group that included Trevor, Nara, and a couple of others. Paul took a spot a few seats away. He could tell from the look on Jared's face that Jared wasn't fooled by Paul's attempt to act casual, but it wasn't really Jared he was trying to fool anyway.

"So. Took a vacation from GSA?" Trevor smirked. Of course, Trevor was almost always smirking at someone.

"Something like that," Paul agreed.

A shout came from the front of the room. "Okay, everybody. Time to shut up now . . ."

The meeting was pretty normal. There was the usual round of announcements. Then Jessica, the club president, spent a couple of minutes talking about statistics on gay teenagers, depression, and anorexia. From the glance she gave Ms. Allington before she started, Paul guessed their advisor had been the one who decided to add that to the agenda. *At least Allington's not standing up there and lecturing us about it herself. She'd be a lot more longwinded about it.*

Then came the planning part. Apparently, GSA was helping out with some things for Black History Month in February. Paul was relieved to find out that most of what they were doing didn't have a gay focus. *I've had enough of that for a while.*

Before he could say anything one way or the other, several people volunteered him to work with the poster group. "That's the thing," Trevor told him, smirking again. "Do something well, and you're stuck with it until you die. You'll be doing posters forever now."

As the groups were getting settled, Paul glanced at his watch and saw it was time for his call to the bishop. He told the others he'd be back in a couple of minutes, then stepped outside and made the call.

"Bishop."

"Paul," the bishop responded.

Just then a couple of kids passed by, talking loudly. Paul moved down the hall to where it was quieter. "Sorry about the noise. I'm still up at the school."

The bishop asked his usual question about how things were going. Then he asked what was keeping Paul at the school later than usual.

"I'm at the GSA meeting."

"That gay club thing?"

"Yeah."

There was a pause.

"Are you following the rules we talked about?"

"Yes, sir." Paul imagined Chad laughing at him for calling his dad *sir*. Somehow, though, it seemed appropriate. "No being alone with any gay guys."

"And no doing anything else that makes it harder for you to keep your commitments."

This time the pause was on Paul's end. "I really don't think this is gonna do that," he finally responded. "GSA isn't just about being gay. It's just . . . a group that's about treating people right. Like putting a stop to bullying, and not disrespecting other people just because they're different." *And I like spending time with them,* he thought but didn't say.

"Some of them thought it was pretty weird I'm a Mormon," Paul continued. "It's like they thought Mormons were all about going out and bashing gays. I hope maybe they'll see Mormons aren't that bad."

Several seconds passed before Bishop Mortensen responded. "I'm not at all convinced this is a wise idea. You need to focus on the things that will keep you spiritually strong. Stay on the Lord's side of the line."

"I'll be careful."

"Just don't do anything you'll regret."

After they wrapped it up, Paul went back to the meeting.

After GSA, Paul took off, telling the other kids he couldn't hang around. Mostly, he didn't want to wind up in a group with Jared—or break his promise to the bishop.

As soon as he got home, Paul took off his shoes and dropped his backpack on the floor, then pulled out his Book of Mormon.

Just after New Year's, Bishop Mortensen had challenged the youth to read the Book of Mormon during 2004 and gain a testimony. When someone pointed out that they were already reading the Old Testament in seminary, he'd looked embarrassed for a moment but then repeated the challenge. "Of course, I want you to stay caught up with your reading assignments," he'd said. "But if you really want to develop a testimony of the restored gospel, there's no substitute for reading the Book of Mormon."

Paul had been too worried about the whole Jared thing to think much about it at the time. Once he'd gotten that taken care of, though, he remembered the bishop's challenge and thought maybe he should give it a try.

Before his parents split up, Paul remembered they used to go to church only a few times a year. Usually it wasn't an LDS church. In fact, Paul hadn't really known that his mom was a Mormon until after the two of them moved to Oregon.

Because he'd been raised without knowing about the church, someone—Paul imagined it was their bishop at the time—had decided he should be taught the missionary discussions before he was baptized. Chad's dad sat in on the discussions. Paul guessed that in reality the lessons had been at least as much for his mom as for him.

Paul couldn't remember asking any questions or wondering if what the missionaries were telling him was really true. It was kind of like math: the teacher taught you the way things were, and you accepted it. You didn't argue whether three times four really equaled twelve—at least, not if you wanted to stay out of trouble. Listening to the missionaries when he was an eight-year-old had been like that.

Since then, he'd never really doubted the church's teachings. They were just a given, like breathing air or drinking water. He knew a lot of the other kids in the ward didn't take it as seriously as he did, but mostly he just thought they didn't care about doing the right thing. *Maybe they followed Satan in the pre-existence and snuck their way down here somehow,* he thought with a snort.

Now, though . . . Paul was starting to think that just believing because it made sense and felt right to him wasn't enough anymore. Especially with him being gay. He needed a testimony. So he decided to try out what the bishop had said.

The idea of praying to know whether the scriptures were true and whether Joseph Smith really was a prophet felt uncomfortable to Paul. Maybe it was because asking the question was like admitting that he wasn't sure what the answer might be, which wasn't the case at all. At least, Paul didn't think so.

It wasn't like Paul was going to leave the church, even if he didn't get a testimony right away. He'd probably just keep on trying, though part of him wondered if that was really honest. *If I'm going to ask if the church is true, shouldn't I be willing to accept it if the answer I get is no?*

He shook his head. He wasn't going to worry about that right now.

He opened up his Book of Mormon to where the bookmark was. *And it came to pass that I, Nephi, returned from speaking with the Lord, to the tent of my father . . .*

Chad wasn't sure whether he was more excited or terrified about taking Janice Taylor to the multi-stake Valentine's Day dance.

It wasn't like it had been his idea, of course.

Several weeks before, Janice had come up to him after Sunday school. "You haven't thought about inviting me to the Valentine dance, have you." It wasn't a question.

"Uh, no."

She rolled her eyes. "Okay. Dating 101 here. We're dating." Chad opened his mouth, but Janice just kept on talking. "Yeah, we're just dating casually, blah blah blah. But we've been on a couple of dates.

So we're dating. Now, when you're dating someone, you don't really have a choice anymore about taking the person you're dating to the Valentine's dance. Not if you still want to be dating that person afterward."

Janice speared him with a look. "So, are you taking me to the Valentine's dance?"

"Only one answer won't get me in trouble, right?" Even to himself, his voice sounded a little sullen.

"You got it."

"Sure." He sighed. "Janice, will you come to the Valentine dance with me?"

"Why, Chad. I thought you'd never ask." She batted her eyelashes at him. Despite himself, Chad laughed.

She patted him on the head. "You have potential. Somewhere out there, I hope there's a girl who's cluing in the boy I'll eventually wind up with, the same way I'm doing for you." Then she walked off to Young Women.

Chad stood there a minute, staring. *She's so scary* was his only really coherent thought.

So now it was Valentine's night, and they were at the dance, and it was all kind of . . . weird.

The whole cultural hall was decorated with paper hearts. It looked unbelievably tacky. The music was really lame as well. About halfway along each wall, there was a little table with a bowl of nasty heart-shaped candy. The same candy had been used in the decorations.

The dance was officially formal wear: Sunday clothes, including slacks, button-up shirt, and tie. Beside him, Janice looked really nice in her dress. That was one of the few pleasant things about the evening so far. *Yeah, she looks nice. But it'd be a lot more comfortable if we were watching a movie or something like that.*

Chad couldn't decide which was worse: the fast dancing, which meant hopping around like rabbits, or the slow dancing, when you put your hand on the girl's waist and she put her hand on your shoulder, and you kind of turned around in a circle while standing as far apart as you could. School dances were almost as lame as church dances, but at least you got to *feel* the girl you were dancing with.

Don't go there, his mind warned. *You may not be standing right up against Janice, but there's no guarantee she won't be able to tell if you start getting . . . excited. And then she'll look at you and maybe make a com-*

ment, and you'll die of embarrassment. And if Paul finds out about it, he'll mock you forever.

Chad and his folks had been watching a TV program once when a character said something about teenage boys thinking about sex every seventeen seconds. His mom had snorted. "That's so unrealistic. C'mon. Nobody thinks about sex that often." Chad hadn't said anything, but he exchanged glances with his dad. *She really doesn't know, does she?* Even if his mom didn't understand what boys were like, though, that didn't mean Janice was equally clueless. Unfortunately.

Think about something else, his mind advised. *Think about the decorations. Think about the paper cupids that are stuck all over that giant pink heart. Oh, yuck.*

"I think I'm going to be sick." He didn't realize he'd said it out loud until he heard the words.

"What?"

"That heart over there." He nodded toward the wall.

Janice snickered. "Pretty bad, isn't it?"

"Bad? It's awful. Craptacular, in fact."

Chad hadn't bothered to keep his voice low. Another girl dancing nearby scowled at him. "I think maybe she helped with the decorations," Janice said, laughing, as the dance ended.

"Let's go get some punch."

"Even though it's Pepto-Bismol pink?"

Chad glanced at the clear plastic cups that a few other kids were holding. Janice was right. He shuddered. "I did *not* need to think about that."

"So, should we go anyway?"

They wandered to the room where the refreshments were, then spent a while relaxing there before going back to the cultural hall.

"These cookies are really awful," Chad commented. They were heart-shaped, of course, with pink frosting. "My mom makes better cookies than this. Heck, *I* could make better cookies than this." He frowned. "At least, I think I could."

"I make cookies. Sometimes. When I'm bored out of my mind doing math." She took a bite. "You're right. Mine are better than these."

"You spend a lot of time doing math?"

She didn't say anything for a moment. Finally she spoke. "I'm in calculus. It's a lot of work."

Chad was surprised. "Calculus? But you're just a junior!"

"Yeah. All my friends think I'm an alien, but honestly, I like math."

"Proves you have a brain. More of a brain than I do, anyway."

"Whatever." She looked at him. "Just don't get all weird on me."

"Why would I do that?"

Janice gave him a measuring look. "A lot of guys don't like it if a girl is as smart as they are. Especially if it's in something like math that guys are supposed to be better at. It intimidates them." She took another bite, then dropped the rest of her cookie in the trash. "Are you going to be like that?"

Chad swallowed. "I'm, uh, fine with it." His voice didn't come out quite as confident as he wanted.

She sighed. "Right. So . . . have you recovered enough for another dance?"

As Chad let himself be dragged back to the cultural hall, he glanced again at the girl who was walking at his side. *She looks really . . . pretty, I guess,* he thought. *As well as smart and intimidating.* His body started to react again, and he quickly looked away. Then out of nowhere he thought, *I wonder if this is what it feels like for Paul when he's around a good-looking guy?* The idea seemed utterly alien to him.

Chapter Twelve

THE DAY AFTER VALENTINE'S DAY, the bishop called Paul into his office to let him know he was being released as teachers quorum president.

"Don't worry—this is an honorable release," Bishop Mortensen said. "It's not because of anything you've done wrong."

"Time to put me out to pasture?" Paul grinned at him.

"You got it."

"Great." Paul smirked. "Alan'll make a great teachers quorum president."

"I didn't say it would be Alan."

"Oh, c'mon."

The bishop cleared his throat. "Regardless, it's good to know that the new teachers quorum president will have your support, whoever it may be. Right?"

"Right," Paul agreed as he walked out of the office. *And it'll be Alan. No way it won't be.* He laughed.

Richard found himself encouraged by Paul's reaction. He'd worried that their conversation back in January and the daily check-in calls since then might have made things awkward between them. Instead, if anything Paul seemed to have become more comfortable with him than before.

Young men really do want adult guidance in their lives. Then Richard thought of some of the other teenagers in the ward, and even Chad at times. *Well, some of them want it,* he mentally corrected.

Richard had expected to release Paul right away following their conversation the month before. After thinking and praying about it, though, he just couldn't feel good about that. Instead, he'd spent a few minutes the next Saturday talking with Paul while he was over visiting Chad. He asked how Paul was doing on his commitments, and Paul told him. Then he informed the surprised boy that as long as he kept doing the things he was supposed to do, he'd stay on as teachers quorum president—"until you turn sixteen or the Lord tells me otherwise, whichever comes first. The Lord doesn't call perfect people into his service," Richard had added. "Instead, he calls imperfect people and then helps them become better."

He'd known right away that his decision was the right one, just from the expression on Paul's face. All the next day in church, each time Richard looked at Paul there was a kind of glow around him. Clearly, this evidence of the Lord's trust in Paul's determination to change—and his own trust as bishop—had made a big difference to the boy. Richard didn't agree with all the choices Paul was making—he thought the boy was fooling himself if he didn't realize that sticking around that GSA group would only cause him more grief—but overall, it seemed to him that Paul was doing better than Richard could have hoped a few scant weeks ago.

I could probably stop the daily phone calls now, Richard thought. *Paul seems to be doing okay.* Then he reconsidered. *If it's working, don't fix it.*

And now it was Alan Thompson's turn to serve as an Aaronic priesthood leader.

Sitting on the stand one week, it had occurred to Richard that Alan—who was helping out the deacons that week passing the sacrament—would make a good teachers quorum president, even though he'd just barely turned fifteen. Richard had put the idea aside as an idle thought, but it kept returning. Finally he decided that maybe God wanted Alan to start serving now instead of later. *Every now and then I get the message—after God pounds on my head long enough.*

Richard's counselors had been surprised when he suggested the call. It almost seemed as if his counselors viewed the leadership positions as a kind of rotation based on seniority in the quorum. Richard guessed that was how the boys saw it, too. It would be good for all of them to realize that it didn't necessarily happen that way. A learning opportunity for everyone.

Back in January, Richard had dedicated some time to thinking about how they'd done as a ward in 2003. Overall he'd been pleased, but there were a lot of areas where they could be doing better. He'd pushed each of the ward organizations and Melchizedek priesthood quorums to set ambitious goals for the coming year. Just last week, they'd presented their goals in ward council and agreed to support each other in achieving those goals.

We have to lengthen our stride, he thought, remembering the slogan of Spencer W. Kimball, who'd been president of the church when he was baptized. *I've been bishop for more than two years now. It's time to be doing more, working harder, performing at a higher level.*

Paul wasn't sure what he thought as he watched Alan Thompson shake hands with the bishop and their quorum advisor after he'd been set apart as the new teachers quorum president.

It wasn't like Paul was jealous of Alan. That would be stupid. After all, the quorum president didn't really do that much. Mostly, he just made the assignment for who was supposed to come early and prepare the sacrament—and then made sure to come early himself so he could fill in when the boys he'd assigned didn't show up. And the teachers quorum president got to sit at the front during opening exercises in priesthood meeting and then welcome everyone out to quorum meetings before turning the time over to the adults who ran things. And once the lesson was done, he got to call on someone to give the closing prayer.

It really wasn't that big a deal. Still, it felt strange to realize that from now on the quorum president would be Alan, not him.

"She dumped me."

It was Monday, President's Day. Chad and Paul were over at Paul's house enjoying the day off from school. Paul had just told Chad about being released as teachers quorum president.

Chad had grinned and asked whose poodle Paul had killed to get himself kicked out two months before he turned sixteen. The whole time, though, he was looking kind of half-distracted and grumpy. So Paul started teasing Chad about the dance on Saturday and asking whether he and Janice had a good time.

And that's when Chad had growled out his news.

"Huh?"

Chad gave him a sour look. "We went to the dance. It was great. She gave me a kiss on the cheek and told me it was fun but we probably shouldn't date each other anymore. Then she left."

Paul was stunned. "That sucks."

"Tell me about it."

"She say anything else?"

Chad shifted. "I guess. Yeah. She likes me, but she doesn't think we should be dating anymore. Stuff like that."

Paul shook his head. "Isn't she the one who said you guys were, like, going out together? Just a couple weeks ago?"

"Yeah." Chad took a drink of root beer. "I think maybe the problem was this other guy who asked her to dance with him. All the rest of the night, she kept looking at him. It pissed me off." He scowled. "Maybe she decided to ditch me so she can hook up with him."

"That doesn't seem like Janice."

"Yeah, well, apparently you're wrong." He finished off the root beer.

Paul decided to change the subject. "So how's the grade improvement project coming?"

Chad groaned. "You know how my dad's always all 'If you persist in what you should be doing, you'll come to like it over time'?"

"Yeah."

"Doesn't work with homework."

"Well, duh." Paul took a drink of his orange pop. "Sometimes I think your dad says things because he wants them to be true, not because they really are true."

"You're telling me."

"So how's it going?"

Chad scowled again. "Okay, I guess. Still mostly getting B's. A few A's, some C's. I don't think I'll ever get much better than that."

"Sucks."

"Yeah. It's just, I can only work on homework for two or three hours a night before my brain starts to melt." He shrugged. "If I can't get into BYU, I guess I'll go somewhere else."

Paul shook his head. "Sucks," he repeated. Another pause. "So, we gonna play some video games?"

"Sure," Chad agreed.

"Calling to order this meeting of the Arcadia Heights High School Gay-Straight Alliance, Tuesday, February 24, 2004 —"

"Ahem."

" —in the unavoidable absence of Jessica, our lovely club president—"

"Ahem!"

" — who's busy in the corner trading gossip and fashion tips — "

"Blake Travers, I am *not* gossiping — "

"Oops. Now backing away from the podium, this is Blake, your friendly and about-to-be-massacred club vice-president — "

Right about then, Blake tripped and fell over backward. Paul couldn't tell whether it was on purpose or not, but he laughed along with the rest of the club. Meanwhile, Jessica, with a glare on her face, was still advancing toward Blake. Just before she got there, he scrambled to his feet, grinning.

"Blake."

"Yes, Jessica?"

"Please at least pretend to be a senior, whatever your mental and emotional age may be."

"Whatever you say, Jessica."

"You're hopeless." She shook her head and turned to face the group. "So, yeah. Welcome out everyone. If it's your first time, please don't hold Blake's performance against us too much. He hasn't had his meds today."

"Hey!"

"I'd like to thank everyone who helped out with our activities for Black History Month. I'd like to especially thank the poster group. We got some good comments on our posters."

Several people gave Paul a smile or thumbs up. He grinned back.

"So now, let's talk about what's coming up next . . ."

The rest of the meeting was more of the same: announcements, kids talking and goofing off, and a little bit of planning in between everything else. Trevor kept several people entertained describing his run-in with a bunch of goth wannabes at the mall last Saturday. Gwenyn told about her cousin's wedding several weeks before. It was out in the woods, and there'd been drumming and belly dancing and a kind of group chant. Paul thought it sounded very strange.

They also talked some about the Day of Silence, which was coming up in April. "It's one of our biggest events," Jessica explained. "Students who participate are silent all day to protest the silencing of gays, lesbians, bisexuals, and transgendered people." Paul vaguely remembered something like that from the year before, but he hadn't known what it was all about.

Toward the end of the meeting — after all the business was done and people were pretty much just socializing—Trevor turned to him. "You haven't said much today."

He shrugged. "Not a lot to say."

"Not everyone's as big an extrovert as you are, Trevor," put in Elaine. "Maybe Paul's the strong, silent type." She batted her eyelashes at him, and everyone laughed.

And then the meeting was over.

It was drizzling and cold as Paul walked home after GSA. It wasn't really walking weather, but this was the easiest way to make sure he wasn't alone with another gay guy. He'd told several of the GSA kids who'd asked that he liked walking in the rain. They stared at him. *I wonder how many points a lie like that costs against keeping my promise to the bishop?*

About twenty minutes later, he was home. He toed off his sneakers, hung up his dripping raincoat, then made his way upstairs for his daily scripture reading.

A couple of weeks earlier, Paul had been up late working on homework. Before he went to bed, he decided to do some reading in the Book of Mormon. It was one of the places where Nephi was quoting Isaiah, and he hadn't understood it very well. For some reason he'd gotten really upset about that. He wound up imagining himself reading the Book of Mormon but never getting a testimony, and then, after graduation, leaving the church and moving away to Seattle, where he'd have to support himself working as a busboy in a local restaurant.

Since then, Paul had been more cautious about his Book of Mormon reading. He was still trying to read about a chapter each day, but he was doing his best to be patient about the whole getting-a-testimony part. He'd also decided not to stress out too much about those quotes from Isaiah.

He started reading.

And now, Jacob, I speak unto you: Thou art my first-born in the days of my tribulation in the wilderness . . .

It was all familiar stuff. Lehi's last words to Jacob. Congratulations to Jacob for following Nephi. Lehi's explanation about knowing good from evil. Some verses about why Christ's atonement was important. The opposition-in-all-things part that was always quoted in church.

And then about a page later, Paul found another verse he'd heard quoted in church a lot: *Adam fell that men might be; and men are, that they might have joy.*

Paul thought for a moment. *I wonder what it means to have joy for someone like me. Someone who's gay.*

The church tells me I can't be really happy if I do stuff with other guys. Most of the people at GSA would say I can't be happy unless I follow my feelings. That didn't leave a lot of room for compromise. *So what is it that will really make me happy?*

What Paul had told the bishop about what he'd done with Jared was true. He tried not to think about it, but that stuff had felt really, really good while it was happening. Afterward, though, he'd felt really, really guilty. Like he'd been surrounded by darkness somehow. He hadn't been able to get rid of those feelings until he finally talked to the bishop.

If the church is right, then having sex with guys, no matter how fun it might be, isn't a way that I can be permanently happy. If God's plan is all about having joy, then having sex with guys must not be something that's necessary for me to have joy. Even if it seems that way now, it can't be something I really want.

Times like now, it was easy to imagine himself staying in the church, living the commandments and never doing anything against church standards with another guy again. Just this past week when he'd been shaking hands with the bishop, he felt a kind of warmth bubbling up inside him when he realized he'd been keeping all his promises and didn't have anything to be ashamed or disappointed about that week. He imagined feeling that way all the time. It was a feeling he wanted to keep.

And then there was the whole getting-married-to-a-girl part.

He could imagine being married. He could imagine having a wife and a family. But not falling in love with a girl. A woman.

It wasn't about sex, Paul realized. He could have sex with a girl. It would be a physical release, without any real emotional connection, kind of like masturbation. But he could do it. That minute of half-response when he was hugging Sarah in the GSA meeting was enough to make him pretty sure about that.

But would I really feel happy living that way?

Deep inside himself, there was a part of Paul that really wanted to be with another guy. Not just to have sex but to feel all romantic and, well, sappy with. Someone to snuggle up next to. Someone to hug and be hugged back by. Someone to have fun with and to understand him and make him feel better when he was sad. Someone to be with him all the time and share his life with.

Paul could imagine himself falling in love with a guy really, really easily. But that wasn't what the gospel said would bring him joy.

Something's gotta change. If I can't be with another guy, then the change has to come in what I want. Somehow, sometime.

Paul could accept in his head that it might be possible, but he couldn't imagine how it could happen.

The question is, can I live the gospel and the church standards, feeling like I do now but hoping that things will be different someday? Even if someday doesn't ever come in this life? Can I be married to someone I'm not really in love with, or else never get married at all and not have anyone I can spend my life with?

Paul sat on his bed, staring at nothing.

It was raining outside, Richard saw as he looked out from the mezzanine lobby in the building where he worked. No surprise there — after all, it was February in western Oregon.

Work was going okay. About six months before, he'd been put in charge of a new group of salesmen — *and saleswomen,* he reminded himself. *Sales people. Gotta use that gender-inclusive language.*

It was fun teaching them how it was done. Of course, sometimes they got into problems they couldn't figure out how to handle. Then he'd come in and fix things — or try, anyway.

As much as possible, he ran it as a team effort with people sharing positive and negative experiences and learning from what happened to each other. He thought they were starting to catch on to the advantages of cooperating that way. That part was all good.

What wasn't so good was how much time it all was taking, especially since he kept being asked to help with sales to customers he'd worked with in the past. *Or when they need an idiot who's just too good-natured to say no,* he grumbled mentally. He was taking work home quite a bit and coming back to the office several evenings a week.

He pushed back the resentful thoughts. *I just need to learn to work a little smarter. It's not my job to worry about how hard other people are or aren't working.* His attempts to convince himself weren't completely successful.

Sandy was bored.

Part of it, she was sure, was because it was February. February in Oregon always seemed to make her stir-crazy. For one thing, there was the rain, drizzling down in a kind of endless Chinese water torture. And then there was the fact that Sandy seemed to be spending all of her time at home by herself, as usual, with Richard nowhere to be seen.

Sandy had been shocked when the stake president had called them in a little over two years ago with the news that they wanted to make Richard a bishop. In her mind, bishops were people like her father: kindly but stern, devoted, spiritual, steeped in knowledge of the gospel and experienced in how things were done in the church. Richard . . . well, he just wasn't like that, to put it charitably. Honestly, she'd known more than he did about how a ward worked.

Richard's first few months as a bishop had been a learning experience — for them and for the ward as well. During his first three weeks, he'd offended Sister Archibald, the Young Women president at that time, with a comment about the young men being his primary responsibility, without any mention of the young women. The Relief Society president had been upset when one of her counselors was called into Primary without any warning. And an innocent statement from Richard about how most teenagers didn't pay attention during Sunday school had been taken as a criticism by one of the Sunday school teachers, who had then insisted on being released. Richard had to spend forty minutes talking with Brother Jeffries before he'd agreed to stay on as a teacher.

And those were just the incidents she knew about. She was sure there'd been plenty of others as well.

Richard's first year as a bishop had been tough on all of them. Looking back on it, though, she realized it had been kind of exciting as well. He'd been learning new things, developing in ways she'd never expected to see from the half-clueless but eager convert she'd married. She'd been forced to grow as well, both in order to deal with the increased demands on their family and to live up to the kind of person she thought a bishop's wife should be.

And then the new school year had started, with Jeffrey going off to first grade and all three children in school most of the day. Sandy had taken a deep breath, congratulated herself on surviving fifteen years of motherhood, and looked forward to having more time to do the things *she* wanted to do.

Except that it hadn't turned out that way. Sure, Sandy had more time, but there wasn't an awful lot to do with it. Not that she wanted to do, anyway.

She didn't like it. This wasn't the kind of person she'd wanted to become back when she and Richard got married: tied to her home, tied to her husband, tied to her children, without anything to fill up her life when they weren't around. It was scary to think how easy it had been for her to lose the person she'd always been.

One time back when Chad was three years old, Richard had come home from work, taken a look at the messy house, and asked what Sandy had been doing all day. Sandy had snapped. For about thirty minutes, she'd yelled at Richard while he stood there looking at her with wide eyes, telling him about how hard her day had been and how much she *hadn't* gotten done that she'd planned to do and how he was the one who had things easy. Afterward, he'd quietly apologized and offered to watch Chad while she got dinner ready. They wound up eating takeout that night. He never asked that question again.

And now I'm the one trying to figure out how to keep myself busy all day.

Sandy had remodeled the kitchen—something she'd wanted to do for years. She'd also redecorated a couple of other rooms in the house, including their master bedroom. But there were only so many times you could redo a room. Besides, she liked them the way they were now and didn't want to change them again right away.

She'd tried volunteer work. Most of it was unbelievably boring, no matter how necessary or valuable it might be. She'd helped out at the elementary school Jeffrey and Emily attended, but after a while she got tired of making photocopies and laminating pictures and lesson materials. She went to a couple of PTA meetings but soon realized she didn't get along with several of the women who ran things there. She joined the candy stripers at the local hospital—*excuse me, the hospital volunteer auxiliary*—and helped out there for ten hours a week. She actually enjoyed that one and was still doing it, but aside from that she'd stopped trying to be Sandy Mortensen, Volunteer Queen.

She thought about getting a job, even though they didn't particularly need the money. She'd even gone so far as to look at the help-wanted ads a couple of times. But looking at what was available just made it clear that she didn't want to work just for the sake of having a job. Maybe it would be different if there were something available in the field she'd studied in college. Sandy suspected, though, that in order to get back into interior design in any professional way after all this time, she'd have to put a lot of effort into getting up to speed. Right now, she wasn't sure that was what she wanted.

Sandy shook her head. *What I really want isn't to have a job. It's to not be bored and to have someone — preferably Richard — around to do fun and exciting things with. And to have his help when I want it and to not feel alone and by myself and like I'm losing a popularity contest against his stupid job and his church calling.*

Well, yeah. But that's not what I get to have, is it?

Chapter Thirteen

Wednesday, March 3, 2004.

"And in local news this evening, earlier today the Multnomah County commissioners voted four to one to grant marriage licenses to same-sex couples. Although she played no official role in the decision, Portland mayor Vera Katz issued a statement praising the move and stating, 'It is now time that the barrier to the right of two consenting adults to marry comes down.' . . ."

Barbara sat listening as the newscaster went on describing the legal opinion behind the decision, opposition from one county commissioner who claimed not to have known that anything like this was even being considered, positive responses from gay groups, and negative reactions from conservative local ministers and from the Catholic Church. Then she turned off the TV and sat a few minutes, trying to figure out her reaction to the news.

Based on what the other LDS women said whenever the issue came up, Barbara supposed that as a Mormon, she ought to be horrified by the thought of two men or two women marrying. Really, though, she found it hard to work up much indignation about the issue. *Maybe that's one of the things I missed by not growing up active in the church.*

Admittedly, marriage between two men or two women seemed quite strange to her. But then, a lot of what she encountered in everyday life was strange, in her opinion. *It doesn't really seem any stranger than teenagers with eyebrow piercings and blue hair.*

Part of her was simply happy that gays would have the opportunity to be in relationships that were acknowledged by society. One of the women she knew at work was lesbian. She and her partner had been together for three years. It was nice, she supposed, that they'd be able to say they were married now, assuming they did get married. She didn't know if that was what they wanted.

And then there were all the contradictory feelings that came from thinking about the issue in connection with her own son. Speaking of which—

"Hi, Mom!" Paul bounded into the room, still drying his hair after his shower, although he'd already put on a shirt and pants. "How much time do I have before Young Men?"

"Twenty minutes before Chad picks you up." The next words popped out of her mouth without her thinking about them. "If you weren't Mormon, would you want to get married to another man?"

Paul stopped toweling his hair. "Huh?"

"I just heard on the news that up in Portland, they've started issuing marriage licenses to gays."

"Wow."

"So what do you think about it?"

Paul sat. "I, uh . . . I dunno."

"But you do want to get married someday?"

"Not to a guy!"

"Really?"

Paul's face took on a trapped expression. "Look, it's not gonna happen, okay? I told you that before."

"But is it something you would want?"

"What I want or don't want has nothing to do with it!" Paul yelled. They stood there a moment, staring at each other. Then Paul dropped his eyes. "Look, I gotta go get my stuff ready for scouts," he muttered, before running back upstairs.

Well. That was interesting.

When Richard heard about gay marriage in Portland on the way into work Thursday morning, he had to swallow some words he was supposed to have stopped using after he'd joined the church twenty-five years before.

Richard remembered four years earlier, back in 2000 when there'd been that big campaign about gay marriage in California. The church had been in the middle of that, encouraging its members to become publicly involved in defeating it. Here in Oregon, the members hadn't been directly affected, but it had been impossible to miss just how nasty things got. Now it looked like the same thing was about to happen right in their own backyard.

If Richard hadn't been a member of the church, he guessed that he wouldn't have had any problem with gay marriage. *They want to get married? Fine! Let 'em do whatever they want.* Certainly that would be an easier opinion to hold publicly, living in a place like western Oregon. But he was a member of the church—a bishop, even—and this was something the church had taken a pretty clear stand about.

Even if Richard had disagreed with the church's position, he would have felt it was his duty to support it. *They're the prophets and apostles. They have the right to receive revelation for the whole church. If I don't understand things the way they do, it means there's something I'm missing.* He honestly believed that.

Besides that, though, given the importance of marriage from a gospel perspective, he could see why the church thought it was so important to try to preserve the *idea* of marriage. *Each individual can achieve his or her true, divine potential only through marriage. Gay marriage is . . . a counterfeit. Something that will only make people miserable if they embrace it, thinking it can give them something that it really can't in the eternal scheme of things.*

Over the years, Richard had become convinced—from his observations and from hearing some gays talk about their relationships—that there was real, true love in some homosexual relationships. Maybe it wasn't the same kind of love that could exist between a man and a woman, but it was something that came close, at least in terms of what it meant to the people involved. In some ways, that only made it more tragic. How would someone feel, caring about another person but eventually coming to know that because they were both men or both women, they couldn't be together in the eternities? Gay marriage was a lie—even if it was a lie that only Mormons were really in a position to understand, because only Mormons knew that marriages were *supposed* to be eternal.

He sighed. Explaining that to non-Mormons wasn't really possible. Which meant the church's position on gay marriage wasn't something that really made sense to other people. Sure, there were plenty of non-Mormons out there who didn't approve of gay marriage, but a lot of that was for reasons Richard didn't feel terribly comfortable about. Even many members of the church, he suspected, didn't get beyond "Homosexuality is disgusting and unnatural" as their reason for thinking gay marriage was wrong. Richard probably would have thought that way himself if it hadn't been for the gays he'd known through his work.

It wasn't really true that the only thing men wanted out of a relationship was sex. Sure, there were men who were like that, though even in those cases Richard suspected sex might be a substitute for the emotional intimacy they really wanted. But most of the men he knew were looking for a real partner, someone they could share their lives with. He didn't see any reason to believe that wasn't true of gays as well. Which made it a lot harder to look them in the eye and tell them he didn't think society should recognize their relationships the same way it did his.

Chad didn't spend much time thinking about the whole gay marriage thing. He didn't *want* to think about it, to tell the truth.

And then Sunday came: the first Sunday of the month, fast and testimony meeting, when adults and kids and old people and everyone else stood up and talked about being grateful for the gospel and everything it gave to them—along with whatever else happened to come out of their mouths while they were standing there. On some Sundays, that meant Chad got to hear way more than he really wanted to know about people's latest trip to Guatemala or the state of their intestines, which was one of the reasons why sometimes he didn't listen very hard to what people said in their testimonies.

This Sunday, predictably, it included gay marriage in Portland.

"And we can truly see the signs of the times and the hold that Satan has upon the people, just like the days of Sodom and Gomorrah . . ."

Chad snuck a look over at Paul. He had an emotionless expression on his face, almost like he was wearing a mask. Chad sighed.

Gay marriage was all that anyone seemed to be talking about at the next GSA meeting, though to Paul's surprise not all the kids were enthusiastic about it.

"Why should we even care what the straights do?" argued Trevor. "I mean, yeah, they're all about marriage. Does that mean it's the best thing for gays?"

"What, are you looking to try out, like, multiple partners?" one of the other guys asked.

"Really, Trevor, you need to get at least one guy interested in you before you start fantasizing about orgies," put in Nara. "See if you can get as far as monogamy first."

"Right now, Trevor's the only one who's interested in himself that way," added Jared, grinning.

"Burn!"

"I hate you all," Trevor said in an even voice while flipping them off.

"Calm down, people." It was Ms. Allington. Paul was surprised she'd noticed, sitting over at one side of the room typing on her laptop.

"Really, though," Nara said. "Don't you want to, like, have a boyfriend and be a couple and stuff like that?"

"Sure." Trevor shrugged. "I just don't see why I need to make this big commitment to stay with another guy for the rest of our lives. I guess it makes sense when you've got kids to raise, but there's no way I'm gonna be getting my boyfriend pregnant."

"There's no way you're ever gonna *get* a boyfriend," said Sarah.

"What, is this pick-on-Trevor day?"

"Every day is pick-on-Trevor day."

"Whatever." He flipped them off again.

"So Trevor isn't going to be tying the knot with his nonexistent boyfriend anytime soon," said Jessica. "Is anyone else against gays getting to marry?"

"I'm not against the idea," Trevor insisted. "I just don't get what the attraction is. But if that floats your boat, then whatever."

"Right. It's all about having options," said one of the girls.

Paul didn't say anything. The church's position on gay marriage wasn't anything he wanted to get into at GSA.

The meeting broke up a little while after that.

Paul realized he hadn't seen Jake—the kid he'd hugged that one day in GSA—since Christmas. On his way out, he asked Sarah about it.

"You're right. I don't think I've seen him since then, either."

"You didn't track him down and tell him how he needs to keep coming to GSA?" Paul tried to make it sound like a joke.

"Look. No matter what you may think, I don't go around chasing everyone who stops coming to GSA."

"Coulda fooled me." As soon as he said it, Paul realized it was a mistake.

Sarah glared at him. "I did with you because I thought we were *friends*. Also, I felt kind of responsible, since I was the one who dragged you out to begin with. Though from the way you've been acting since then, I wonder why I bothered."

Whoa. Major-league irritation. I wonder what I did to cause it? Paul decided not to ask.

"Look," he began instead. "I'm just saying I wonder what happened to him, okay? I mean, the kid didn't look like he had a lot of friends while he was here."

She snorted. "Like you would care."

Paul stopped in the hallway. They were about thirty feet beyond the door into the GSA room. "What is with you, anyway? Why're you acting like I'm all the enemy or something?"

She glared back at him. "You know, when you started coming to GSA again, I thought things were okay. I thought you were back to accepting us as your friends."

Paul shook his head. "I seriously have no idea what you're so ticked off about."

"This sort of thing! It's like—today, when we were talking about gay marriage. You didn't say anything about it, even when Melanie asked what your opinion was."

Paul could feel himself starting to get angry. "So just 'cause I don't want to talk when people ask me a question, that means I'm like a traitor to the GSA or something? Geez, Sarah! Do I have to get your permission now just to be quiet?"

She shook her head. "That's not what I meant. It's just—it doesn't seem like you're even there sometimes. People talk, and you just kind of watch and don't say anything. And then you smile sometimes like you think you're better than the rest of us. I know it's not because you're shy, since that's not how you are at the lunch table. Or the way you used to be at GSA." Her hands twisted together, and she looked away. "It's just—I'm sorry for making a big deal about this. I'm in a crabby mood anyway, and when I saw you just sitting there today and smiling and not saying anything—" She broke off, then continued in a lower voice. "I hoped you really did feel comfortable here, since I nagged you into coming back. Like there was a place you could talk about what you're really thinking. I'm sorry," she repeated, then quickly walked off, leaving Paul gaping after her.

This is so frustrating, Paul thought once he got over the surprise. *I come back to GSA, I help out with the posters, I smile—I guess I smile—because I don't know what to say and don't want to get into an argument with anyone. And it still makes people upset.* He shook his head again before turning down the hallway to start his walk home. *It's like trying to make things better just makes them worse sometimes.*

• • •

"So Richard's back in the doghouse."

Sandy looked up at her friend, who was just sliding into her seat at the restaurant. "I hate it when you do that," Sandy said. "How can you just look at me and know what I'm planning to rant about?"

Ella answered without looking up from her menu. "Sandy, when you're ticked off, your face is a megaphone. They can tell you're mad from here up over into the state of Washington. Maybe Montana, if you're facing east. You never get that particular look on your face unless it's Richard." Ella looked up. "Chicken primavera for me today. And peach pie. I feel like living dangerously."

The waitress came and took their order.

"So what did he do this time?"

Sandy shook her head. "It's not so much what he did. It's just . . . he's never around anymore. Long hours at work. Long hours at the church. Even when he comes home, he spends long hours in his office downstairs."

"You sure he isn't having an affair?"

Sandy stared at Ella blankly. "I—you can't really be asking me that. I mean, this is Richard."

"Yeah. So what?"

Sandy shook her head again. "No. I really can't see it." Trying to match her friend's matter-of-fact tone came hard. The more she thought about Ella's suggestion, though, the harder she found it to believe. "I just—not Richard. If he ever did have an affair, he wouldn't be acting this way."

"Huh. Well, you'd know better than I would."

"Do you really think it's likely?"

"No."

The conversation wandered. Then the food came, and they both started eating, Ella taking swift, efficient bites that made the food disappear faster than Sandy thought ought to be possible without looking like a pig.

"So you don't see Richard around as much anymore," Ella continued after her food was mostly gone. "Is that really such a big deal?"

"He's not there when I need him. He's no help with the kids or household stuff. When I ask his opinion, he just waves his hand and tells me to do whatever I like."

"Sounds like a dream come true."

"It's a nightmare!" Sandy snapped. "If I wanted to be a single parent, I would have adopted!"

Ella gazed at her speculatively. "You don't like your kids very much, do you?"

Sandy made a cross-hatch with her fork in the pureed squash on her plate. "Not always," she admitted. "Sure, I love them. I try to be a good mother for them. But Richard's the one who actually likes kids." She looked up. "I've never told him that. I don't think he'd believe me."

"So basically, you got into the whole mom thing because Richard wanted kids and because that's what good Mormon girls do. And now Richard's not around to help."

Sandy grimaced. "Pretty much."

"And Richard isn't around as much for intimate moments, I'm guessing?"

Sandy blushed. "Yeah."

"So you're turning into a bitch."

"Pretty much."

Ella laughed at her. "Serves you right for getting yourself into this mess to begin with." She shook her head. "So babies and Band-Aids aren't what you really wanted to do with your life. Fine. You did it anyway. But nobody said you have to stop being yourself just because you picked up some brats along the way. Get out and live a little, girl! Unless you want to keep moping around until Richard's patience runs out and he really does have an affair, or he trades you in for a newer model."

"You think he'd do that?"

"How the hell should I know? You're the one who married him, not me. As far as I'm concerned, he's this alien that my best friend from high school hooked up with for some bizarre reason." Ella sniffed. "Never thought you'd wind up with George Mormon."

Sandy snickered. "It's not George Mormon. It's Peter Priesthood. Molly Mormon and Peter Priesthood."

"Oh. My. Gosh. You have got to be kidding."

"No."

"So when Mormon girls say that the guy they're dating is a dick—"

"Don't go there."

Ella's voice went up several notes in clear imitation of a teenage girl. "Wow! He's got such an impressive . . . priesthood."

"No. Stop." By now, Sandy was giggling helplessly.

"If you say so."

"You really are wicked, you know."

"Yeah. Makes up for you being such a saint." Ella grinned for a moment. Then she got more serious. "You know, if you really want things to be different, you have to do something. Not just moan and bitch to me about it. Find something *you* want to do. Talk to Richard. Peter. George. Whoever. Work out a way that things can change."

Sandy snorted, and Ella continued. "I know you, girl. You get too bored and frustrated, you'll sabotage your own life and make yourself and everyone around you miserable. So use your brain and figure out what *you* want to do instead."

Ella dropped a few bills on the table, then stood. "Gotta run, hon. Next time, you get to hear the saga of the handsome deadbeat three cubicles down from me. Ciao." Then she was gone.

Sandy sat there for a few minutes, slowly finishing her diet Dr. Pepper.

Figure out what I want to do. Like that's so easy.

Back when Sandy first started college, she didn't have any idea what she wanted to do with her life. About a year and a half into her bachelor's program, she'd more or less stumbled into interior design. It was a good match for her interests. She'd always cared about making her personal space look nice, and she was frustrated to no end with her mother's bland ideas about the way rooms in their house should look. Sandy shuddered, remembering the "celestial room" white-with-gold-highlights theme of their living room back in her early teens. That room had been creepy.

For a while after Sandy and Richard got married right after Sandy graduated from college, she'd worked at a local store that sold home furnishings. The theory had been that her interior-design background would let her help customers who needed ideas for how to decorate their house. Things had just been starting to pick up when dealing with morning sickness and settling into their new house had gotten in the way.

Sandy never really got back into it after that. The time just hadn't ever been right. Over the years, Richard had been pretty good about letting her experiment with the different rooms in their house, and she'd helped a few friends figure out their homes, but that was as far as it went. Sandy still subscribed to several home-design magazines, though, and enjoyed thumbing through them from time to time.

So maybe now's the right time. Go down to the local library, look at a few magazines, maybe dig out my old notes and designs from college. It's a place to start.

Chapter Fourteen

Spring break. Unfortunately for Chad, that turned out to mean babysitting his little brother and sister pretty much full time instead of hanging out and doing fun things with his friends, the way he'd been planning.

Chad had no idea what his mom was busy with all the time. Sure, there was her volunteer work at the hospital. She spent an awful lot of time, though, on the computer playing Spider Solitaire or looking things up on the Internet. She also spent a lot of time talking with friends on the phone and reading boring-looking magazines and books with pictures of bedrooms and living rooms and furniture and stuff.

He shook his head. It really wasn't fair that he was being cheated out of his vacation just because she didn't want to take care of Jeffrey and Emily. It wasn't like she had a job to keep her busy. He'd said as much on the first morning when she told him to stick around and watch the kids instead of playing soccer with his friends.

She hadn't reacted very well. "When you're the one cooking the meals and cleaning the house and doing the laundry and tucking the kids into bed every night, then maybe you'll have the right to make that kind of comment. In the meantime, consider yourself grounded for the rest of the day." As he opened his mouth to protest, she added, "Want to make it two days? Didn't think so." Then she walked off to do whatever she was doing on the computer.

Chad had kept his mouth shut since then. It was hard, especially when she said no to a couple of things he'd wanted to do, but he knew his chances of getting to do anything fun later in the week depended on it. So he managed.

She'd let him out of jail for a few things. Basketball with some friends on Tuesday. The mall for a couple of hours on Wednesday. Tony's house on Thursday to listen to music and shoot the breeze.

Paul had been with him pretty much all day Wednesday and Thursday. Chad really appreciated it, not just because it kept him from being bored out of his mind but also because Paul was generally more patient with his little brother and sister than he was. Fortunately, Chad was past the six-month point on his license, so he was able to drive Paul with him over to the mall and to Tony's. It also gave him a chance to tease Paul about still being only fifteen and not having his license yet.

And now it was Friday . . .

Wednesday night, Chad had approached his dad about spending Friday over at Paul's house. He'd been careful to mention how he'd been doing a lot of babysitting and how Paul had come over to keep him company, but they hadn't been able to spend any time at Paul's house yet this break. He didn't mention being grounded on Monday, figuring it wouldn't help his case.

Chad's dad had agreed that he could spend the day at Paul's. His mom yelled at both of them when she found out, but the decision held.

So now he was over at Paul's house, playing video games again. But at least they were different from the ones he had at his house. And he wasn't responsible for any rug rats, which was worth it all by itself. He settled in for another round of *Soulcalibur II*, the new fighting game Paul had gotten for Christmas. He was determined to enjoy at least part of his break.

Paul stood beside the pool, blinking water out of his eyes while he ignored the sting of the chlorine. *Tim's doing better now,* he thought. *Finally.*

Back in February, their ward and the two others that met in their building had all gotten together one Saturday to put on a half-day workshop for all the younger scouts who hadn't yet earned their First Aid merit badge. Paul and several other older scouts had been recruited to man the stations where different skills were taught, do demonstrations, and work one on one with the kids until they were ready to pass off something with an adult merit badge counselor. It had been kind of fun, despite all the inevitable noise and confusion.

Paul guessed he must have done a good job. That was why he was here at the high school pool on Saturday morning, spending his last day of spring break helping Tim Osterling learn how to swim.

Apparently, several younger boys weren't advancing the way they ought to because they couldn't meet the swimming requirements for the different scouting ranks. So someone had the bright idea of organizing another workshop, this one focusing on swimming skills for the eleven-year-olds and twelve-year-olds. And of course Paul had been volunteered to help.

At least Tim wasn't completely hopeless or afraid of the water, like some of the others. Most of his problem was that he got flustered, was uncoordinated, and had some bad habits he needed to get rid of. It took quite a while for Paul to get him not to turn his mouth up to the sky when he was trying to breathe, instead of just turning to the side. He ended up having Tim hold onto the edge of the pool while the boy kicked to keep his body straightened out. Then Paul made him practice turning his face to the side while Paul kept one hand on the back of Tim's head to make sure he didn't turn too far.

And it was finally starting to work. No one would call the boy a champion swimmer, but at least it wasn't painful now to watch him.

"That's good, Tim. You did great that time. Just a couple more times, and then I think we can get you signed off on this requirement."

"Great!"

He sure has a lot of energy, Paul thought. *Was I that hyper when I was twelve?* For a minute, Paul wondered just how insane he was to want to spend all next summer as a camp counselor for a bunch of kids this age.

About thirty minutes later, they got the word to wrap things up.

Paul thought it was funny how most of the younger scouts showered in their bathing suits and then went back to the locker area to change. The older scouts, of course, didn't have any problem with stripping down and showering naked. High school gym classes made you get over that type of shyness real fast.

Through long practice, Paul had learned how to navigate through gym showers and getting dressed without letting his gaze—or his mind—linger on the naked bodies around him. He didn't think of it as self-discipline but more as a kind of deliberate ignoring. It just wasn't that big an issue, if you were careful.

Not that it would have been an issue today even if he wasn't used to it. *It's easy to ignore the temptations of the flesh when you're sur-rounded by a bunch of scrawny preteens. Just not very tempting, really.*

"Hey, dickhead! Watch where you're putting that!" It was one of the older scouts, yelling at a twelve-year-old who'd just dropped his wet swimming suit on top of the older kid's socks. *Stupid place to leave them, if he didn't want them to get wet.*

"Sorry," the younger kid muttered, quickly picking up his suit. In the process, he inadvertently mooned several of the other scouts.

One of them—an older scout from another ward—laughed. "Thanks for the invitation, but sorry, I don't swing that way."

By now, the poor kid was blushing with embarrassment, though from the look on his face Paul guessed that he really didn't under-stand what the older boy was implying. Farther down the row, Paul saw Tim watching, his eyes round and his mouth a large O. *Looks like he got it.*

Paul snickered to himself. Being perpetually embarrassed about contacts with the adult world, or even the teenage world, was one of the parts he really didn't miss about being a middle schooler. *Actu-ally, I don't think I miss any of it,* he thought, looking quickly around the locker room. *Poor little idiots.*

End of March. Another day, another set of problems.

Richard stood in the mezzanine for a couple of minutes watch-ing the play of clouds and sky, then checked his watch. Time to get back to work.

Everyone in his department knew he liked to take off for a few minutes early in the afternoon. Each day that he could, he'd leave his cell phone on his desk and come to the mezzanine or stroll out-side. Sometimes he'd go to the bakery around the corner to get a doughnut. "My noncoffee break," he called it. No one seemed to mind, and he always made sure he didn't take more than fifteen minutes. *Maybe they've decided it's worth it to keep me in a good mood.*

The minute Richard got back to his office today, Bill Lister poked his head around the doorframe, a frown on his face. "Richard. I've been looking for you."

Of course, there are always a few people who seem to think you're slacking if you aren't there anytime they want to talk to you. "Yes?"

"Things are getting really tight on the Tucker presentation for tomorrow. Can you stay late tonight to give us a hand?"

Richard mentally sighed. It was Wednesday night—a joint Young Men/Young Women activity—and he'd been planning to be at the church. Still, a jam was a jam, and he always tried to say yes whenever he could. "Sure thing," he forced out.

"Great! I knew we could count on you."

Richard was even less happy later that night when one by one everyone else who was supposed to be working on the presentation took off. It was 9:30 before all the files were done and he was ready to leave. He bought a burger from Wendy's, then headed home.

Richard had called Sandy as soon as he knew he was going to be staying late. She hadn't said much at the time, but he figured she'd be upset. Sure enough, the minute he came inside, she started in on him about it. "I thought you were supposed to be out of that sales group, now that you're supervising the trainees."

"They needed some help with a presentation."

"Uh-huh."

"What was I supposed to do?"

"Maybe tell them you already had something else planned for tonight?"

"Brother Rasmussen was able to take care of things at Mutual."

"I meant, here at home."

Richard couldn't think of anything to say.

"Emily had some things she wanted to show you today from school. Jeffrey was a nightmare. I had to threaten to spank him three times. Chad I only saw three times: once on the way up the stairs after school, once when he was grabbing some food on the way out the door to Mutual, and finally after he got back from Mutual about an hour ago. Actually, I take that back. I didn't see him that time; I just heard his footsteps going up the stairs, and then the pounding of that stuff he calls music. He's been in a bad mood ever since I made him help out last week instead of just running off whenever and wherever he wanted."

Richard winced. He didn't want to get Sandy started again about him giving permission to Chad to go over to Paul's house without checking with her first. "Our parents didn't like the music we listened to either," he reminded her, attempting a grin.

"That's *not the point*. The point is that I never know when you're going to be here. I'm sick and tired of being the lone, solitary parent. Particularly when it comes to things like communicating with moody teenage boys and other aliens." Sandy was shaking, Richard realized—whether with anger or frustration he couldn't tell.

A couple of weeks ago, Sandy had stated that now the kids were all in school, she thought it might be a good time to get back into interior design. Richard had been surprised, but he'd done his best to be supportive. Anything that would keep her happy and productive, he'd thought. So far, though, it seemed like she'd been even more irritable since then.

He didn't think mentioning that would help with this particular conversation.

"Look, I'll try to spend some more time at home this weekend." As soon as Richard said it, he remembered this was the church's general conference weekend. He also had a summary report due for the V.P. of marketing that would take up pretty much all his free time that weekend. He'd been looking forward to a Sunday without extra meetings and appointments, in fact, because he would need the time for his report. He looked at Sandy helplessly. There just never seemed to be enough time for everything.

Sandy shook her head. "Something has to change," she said softly. "This just isn't working."

Richard gave a short, humorless laugh. "It's just too much. Work. The ward. My calling."

"What about your family?"

"That too." He shook his head. "I can't deal with this right now. I'm stupid tired, and you're upset. We should talk about this later."

"We never *do* talk about it later, Richard. It's always 'Let's talk about it later,' and then later never comes. You just won't deal with things you think are upsetting, or things you think I'll get upset about."

"Is that such a bad thing?"

"It means things never get solved!"

"Yelling about things doesn't solve anything either."

"Fine! I don't even know why I try sometimes." Sandy stalked back toward the kitchen.

Richard hesitated. He wanted to go after her but didn't know what he could say to make things better. Finally he sighed, took his cold burger with him, and headed into the study to get things ready for tomorrow.

"Thanks for your help on the presentation."

Richard looked up. It was Jerry Entwood, one of the junior consultants. Richard had been in meetings most of the morning, and by the time his first break came the Tucker presentation was already underway. "So how'd it go?"

"Better than I expected." Entwood paused. "Sorry I ditched out on you last night. I told Lister I could stay and help, but he said you'd be fine on your own." Richard's eyebrows climbed, but he didn't say anything. The other man, not noticing, continued. "I really don't know what they were doing, springing this on us at the last minute. I told them we'd need another couple days to get ready, but they said it would be fine. Put me off schedule for the rest of the week—next week too, probably, unless I come in over the weekend."

Hmm. So I'm not the only one they're jerking around with these schedule changes. "I suppose something came up."

"Nah." Entwood snorted. "Just shuffling things around because they didn't do a good enough job of planning, I expect."

Richard didn't say anything. At some level, he felt it was his job to support the other sales managers. On the other hand, he suspected Entwood was probably right.

"So back to the salt mines, yeah?"

"I suppose."

After Entwood left his office, Richard tried to get back to the figures he'd been working on, but his thoughts kept going back to his conversation with Entwood. After yesterday's late night, it was odd that he'd been the one to come by and tell Richard how things had gone with the Tucker presentation. And what was this about Lister telling Entwood he didn't need to stay and help?

He shook his head. *Not something I should be making myself upset over.* Still, it was hard not to get mad when he thought about his conversation with Sandy last night and how Lister apparently didn't think it was any big deal for Richard not to be able to spend time with his family.

Chapter Fifteen

Sandy pushed the books and magazines over to one side. *If I don't take a break, my brain will — what is it Chad says? Leak out my ears.*

Back in college, Sandy had hit on the strategy of making comments during class as a way to keep her mind from wandering. As a side benefit, she'd found that talking about what she was supposed to be learning helped her remember and understand it a lot better. By the time she turned twenty, she'd realized she was a social learner. She learned best by talking about things, by hearing other people's ideas and responding to them.

Which probably was one of the reasons why just reading books and magazines wasn't making her feel any more prepared to jump back into interior design. She'd tried to compensate by pretending to have conversations with the authors, mentally telling them when they were being stupid and jotting down questions and comments in the margins. But it wasn't enough.

She needed someone to talk to about this stuff. Someone to trade ideas with.

Even more than that, she needed to get off her duff and stop just thinking and reading. Interior design wasn't about knowing; it was about doing. She wasn't going to get any better until she started doing something—preferably with someone else who could help her get up to speed.

Sandy stood, walked over to the telephone table, pulled out the phone book, and started flipping through the yellow pages. As she dialed the first number under "Interior Decorators and Designers," she asked herself, *Why didn't I do this to start with?*

• • •

Richard's week had been a long and exhausting one.

Things got off to a discouraging start with the ward council meeting on Sunday. Richard had hoped to have the council members report on the goals they'd shared back in February. Instead, the whole meeting was taken up with other issues: correlating schedules, cliquishness among the young men and young women, and figuring out how to help a couple of families who'd lost their jobs and were in danger of losing their homes. The last part really should have been taken care of in welfare meeting, but the families involved hadn't said anything until their eviction was less than a week away, which didn't leave much time for doing anything about it.

The ward council also spent far too much time talking about the problem of kids making noise at the end of the three-hour meeting block, which one of the other wards had complained about. The Primary was convinced the problem was the young men, while several other people thought some of the Primary classes were being let out too early. Everyone wound up saying something about it— including the Sunday school president, who spent several minutes talking about the importance of reverence in general even though technically the problem didn't have anything to do with his area of responsibility. It was all very nice, but they didn't need a sermon. What they needed was a hall monitor.

Richard had been able to grab only a couple of minutes at the end of the meeting to talk about goals. He got the depressing impression that several of the ward council members were having a hard time even remembering what their goals had been. He'd encouraged everyone to review their goals and redouble their efforts, but he doubted anyone was really paying attention.

People take their cues on how important something is from how much time you spend talking about it. The message here is that we talk about goals just enough to claim that we have them, but not enough to change our behavior. Not a good start on Richard's great ambitions for improving the ward's performance in 2004.

Things at work hadn't been much better. Richard had been scheduled to leave on a business trip down to the company's central California office on Wednesday night. The first part of the week, people kept streaming in and out of Richard's office, trying to get a week's worth of work out of him before he left. By the end of the day on Wednesday, Richard had been more than ready to take off for Stockton.

Richard had been hoping things would get better after that, but

Thursday and Friday wound up just as busy as the first part of the week had been. Still, it was nice spending time with people in the Stockton office that he didn't see that often. And best of all was the chance to visit his in-laws, who lived nearby in Manteca.

"You're looking good," said Charles, his father-in-law, when he showed up on their doorstep Wednesday evening.

"Come in and give your favorite mother-in-law a hug," Rose chimed in with outstretched hands.

There wasn't much time to talk that evening, since Richard had to get up early for a meeting the next day. Thursday night he had a business dinner, followed by a quick shower at his in-laws' and several hours putting his notes together before he finally got to sleep. Friday night, though, he was able to relax and spend the evening just sitting and talking with Charles and Rose. He'd have to get up early the next morning to catch his flight back, but the lack of sleep was worth it for a chance to visit.

Rose dismissed herself for the night, giving Richard a hug and saying, "I'll just leave you two to talk about whatever it is men talk about till all hours of the night." Richard watched as she left the room.

"She's a wonderful woman," his father-in-law commented.

"That she is."

"A better person than I am. I tell you, Richard, the older I get the more convinced I am that if we men make it to the celestial kingdom, it'll be by hanging onto our wives' coattails."

"If they don't just flick us back where we came from," Richard responded ruefully.

Charles looked at him a moment. "We didn't talk much at Christmas. How have things been, what with work and a young family and your calling and all?"

Richard squirmed a bit mentally. Talking to his father-in-law was a bit like getting a personal priesthood interview from the stake president. A kindly, gentle personal priesthood interview, but still it always made Richard think about areas where he wasn't doing as well as he should.

"Not as well as I'd like," he admitted. "Work's been taking a lot of time recently. I'm not around as much as I'd like at home. Sandy's been holding up really well, though. She's a trouper."

"What about the ward?"

Richard sighed. "Frustrating."

The older man quirked an eyebrow at him. "Oh?"

"Home teaching isn't where it ought to be. The ward mission leader wants more ward missionaries, but he wants to do it by drafting people who already have callings in other organizations. My Young Women president can't talk to my Young Men president without yelling at him. The Primary presidency keeps experimenting with ways to split up their classes to get just the right chemistry in each class. The Relief Society president is wonderful, but I keep getting these half-hour-long calls from her with way more detail than I need about the families in our ward."

Charles chuckled. "Sounds pretty normal to me. A lot like when I was a bishop." Richard looked at him skeptically. "No, really. Except you haven't mentioned half the ward yelling at you or getting offended at something you said."

"It's not that bad."

"Maybe not for you." Charles shook his head. "Remember that I didn't have your experience managing people when I was made a bishop. I wasn't the most diplomatic person around."

"Huh." Richard had a hard time imagining his father-in-law being tactless or losing his temper, but he didn't want to argue.

Charles gave him a measuring look. "What are your core responsibilities as a bishop? The things no one else can do?"

Richard thought. "Working with the youth. The young men, especially. Deciding worthiness issues. Approving disbursements from fast offerings and the bishop's storehouse. Presiding over the ward."

"How have you been doing in those areas?"

"Not so bad," Richard answered after a moment, to his own surprise. "Though some of what I've had to deal with—" He shook his head. "I don't know. Maybe I was more sheltered than I realized during my growing up. Maybe things have just gotten that much worse since I was a teenager."

Charles raised an eyebrow, and Richard continued. "Drugs, some, though mostly I hear about that from adults with their prescription addictions. Alcohol. Vandalism. One of the girls is a chronic shoplifter. She takes things she doesn't need or even want—they're trying counseling with her, but I don't know if it'll do any good. Earlier this year they found a gambling ring at the middle school. A couple of our kids were involved. They didn't think they were doing anything wrong."

"I'm surprised you didn't mention pornography."

"Oh, yes. I don't know of any of my older teenage boys who

haven't had a problem with that. They're all good kids—" Richard frowned. "Well, a lot of them are good kids. They want to do the right thing. They just have problems. Challenges." He paused. "I suppose all teenagers do. Goodness knows I did. But the problems seem worse than when I was their age. Or different, at least." Richard shook his head. "You could have knocked me over with a feather when a kid who I was calling as teachers quorum president told me he was gay."

Charles looked surprised. "You're right. That's not something I ever had to deal with as a bishop. How'd you handle it?"

Richard shrugged. "Asked him the standard questions. It turned out he was worthy, so I went ahead and extended the call."

"How has he been doing?"

Richard hesitated. "There've been some challenges. I've worked with him. We set some boundaries, and I believe he's keeping to them. He's going out to this gay-straight tolerance club in school. That has me a little worried. So far, though, it doesn't seem to be a problem. I'm just concerned that it'll end badly—that he'll wind up feeling pulled in two directions. Even if he chooses to stay true to himself and the gospel, it seems very likely that he'll end up hurt somehow."

"I suppose this is Chad's friend that Sandra was so unhappy about a few months ago?"

"She told you about that?"

"She talked to Rose, and Rose told me."

Richard hesitated. "I really don't feel like I ought to say," he answered finally.

Charles held up one hand. "Believe me, I don't want to know any more about the situation than I do already. Still, I can't help but wonder if your sympathy for the young man has made you lose sight of some of the bare truths involved. That's especially likely since you already know and like him.

"It's one thing to accept and be sympathetic about the boy's efforts to live a gospel life," Charles continued. "It's another thing to accept homosexuality itself." He shook his head. "Homosexuality is a perversion. The more space and sympathy we give it, the more we treat it like a normal part of everyday life, something you can talk about openly in a club at high school no less, the more ground we yield up to Satan. You don't do any good to your young man if you water down the message of the Lord and his prophets and the scriptures on the subject."

Richard sat there a moment. A lot of what his father-in-law was saying was true, but— "I really don't think that's what I've been doing," he replied softly. "Maybe I'll bear some blame if I haven't been as clear with Paul as I should have been." Oops—he'd mentioned the name. Oh, well. It hardly seemed like it made a difference at this point. "But you weren't there, looking into his eyes as he struggled to believe in the atonement's power for him." Richard felt his throat tightening. "This was a young man who didn't need to hear that he was evil or wrong or perverted. He already thought that. What he needed was to know that God loved him, that I loved him. He needed to know that he wasn't beyond the boundaries of God's love and acceptance as long as he kept trying to do the right thing."

"So you let him go somewhere where they teach him it's okay to be that way?"

It was a strange thing. Though the tone of the conversation was thoughtful, this was probably the closest Richard had ever come to having a real argument with his father-in-law about a gospel topic. Yet even though he respected the older man's insights and acknowledged his far superior experience in the church, Richard realized that he didn't doubt or regret how he'd handled things with Paul. Certainly he'd made some mistakes—he even knew what some of them were—but he'd done his best to follow the Spirit, and he couldn't find it in himself to doubt the guidance he'd felt.

"Paul has some choices to make," Richard said at last. "I'm not so worried about what'll happen this year or next year. What I'm more worried about is where he'll be in two years, three years, ten years—whether he'll choose to do the right thing when it's time to go to school and go on a mission and everything after that. Will he take the risk of getting married? How will he find the strength to stay in the church if it means being single the rest of his life?" Richard shook his head. "I don't want to be the one who gives him a deadline, who tells him, 'You have to figure all this out right now,' with only the spiritual strength and wisdom he's accumulated in less than sixteen years of life."

There was a long pause before Charles responded. "Well, I'm not the boy's bishop," he said at last. "And I guess it's a good thing too, if things really are the way you've said. I can't imagine myself reacting the way you did."

"Believe me, I never would have thought I'd react that way either. Not until it happened, and I started doing and saying things that were a complete surprise to me."

"That can be a sign of inspiration, too."

The older man fell silent. Richard thought for a moment, then decided to ask a question he'd wondered about since becoming bishop. "Back when I was first dating Sandy, why didn't you and Rose ever encourage me to serve a mission?"

Charles looked startled by the change of topic. "That was . . . what, spring of 1986?"

"Fall of 1985, I think."

"That's right. You met in that Institute class, didn't you? Back when you were both attending Oregon State."

"Yes, that's right." Richard nodded, remembering. "I was so nervous meeting Sandy's family for the first time."

The older man chuckled. "We could tell."

"Sadist."

"No, just protective father. You'll see what that's all about with Emily one of these days."

Richard grimaced. He suspected there was more than a little truth in his father-in-law's prediction.

"Ricky, as I recall, was a complete brat. And then when I spilled the punch all over the couch . . ." Richard shook his head. "I wanted to make a good impression so badly."

"You did. Mostly, anyway."

"I sure couldn't tell it at the time. That was one of the most awkward evenings I've ever spent."

Charles shrugged. "We hadn't even known she was dating someone until the day before, when she told us you'd be coming over on Christmas Eve. All we knew was your first name, the fact that you didn't have any family in the area, and that the two of you met in an Institute class. From that, we assumed you were a member of the church." He chuckled again. "We also had orders from Sandy not to 'screw things up,' as she put it. Believe me, Ricky paid later for the way he acted. And Sandy cross-examined her mother afterward about whether she'd somehow engineered that accident with the punch. She was pretty offensive about it, in fact."

There was an uncomfortable pause. "What you have to understand," Charles said slowly, "was that things weren't terribly good between Sandy and the rest of the family right then. Did you know we offered to let her stay at home without paying any rent while she was attending college?" Richard shook his head. "She wouldn't have any of it. Wanted to be independent. We hardly even saw her after she started college, except when she came home to do her laundry.

"Sandy wasn't too happy with the church growing up. She had a testimony, I think, but a lot of times it only seemed to make her angry. She resented the church, she resented the rules, she resented the time the church took away from us as a family . . ." Charles frowned. "When Sandy was seventeen and just starting her senior year, she informed us that she was going to have a career and not marry anyone until she was in her thirties at least. We didn't take it completely seriously. She was always making dramatic pronouncements she didn't necessarily mean. But still . . . At one point, she actually said she'd rather die than live the kind of empty, wasted life her mother had led. When she left home, I admit I wasn't entirely sorry to see her go.

"By the time you showed up, she'd mellowed a lot. Still, we more than halfway expected she'd wind up marrying a non-Mormon, go inactive, and move somewhere far away where we'd see her maybe once a year, if we were lucky. We were surprised — but very, very pleased — that she ended up with you instead."

Richard didn't know how to react. On the one hand, he couldn't help but feel somewhat defensive about the way his father-in-law was talking about his wife. On the other hand, it honestly sounded like Sandy had been something of a brat before he knew her. And he had to admit that what he was hearing explained a lot that had never really been clear to him before about the way Sandy got along with her family. It also shed some light on a few character traits that Sandy and Chad shared and why they didn't get along much of the time.

Charles continued, "I suspect the fact that you were a convert and didn't act just like all the Mormon boys she'd grown up with was a point in your favor. And I also guess that in the end, she couldn't just ignore what she knew about the church being true. I'm just glad she found someone she could stand to stay in the church with."

"So me being a returned missionary wouldn't necessarily have been a good thing from Sandy's point of view," Richard guessed.

"I don't know. But if you'd gone off and served a mission, I doubt she would have been waiting for you when you got back. Besides that, you have to remember what you were like back then. You'd just finished college. You had a job, a plan, and a direction you were going in your life. You'd been baptized a few years before, but you really didn't know that much about the gospel. That Institute class was a sign you wanted to learn more, but really it was just a first step.

"When it came down to it, I just didn't feel good about trying to push you to go on a mission when I wasn't sure it was the right choice for you. Especially not when I thought it might cost us the best chance for our daughter to lead a happy, active life in the church." Charles spread his hands. "Maybe I did wrong. I know some other young men in similar circumstances delay marriage and careers to serve a mission. But each case is different. I can't find it in myself to regret the choice that felt right at the time."

Richard nodded. "Like me with Paul."

Charles gave him a sharp look. "I also considered that I wasn't your bishop. It wasn't my job to figure out whether you ought to delay your plans in order to go on a mission."

"I would have paid more attention if it came from you than from my bishop at the time."

"Did he ever say anything?"

"Not really. At least, nothing I ever noticed as such."

"There you have it, then. Maybe he felt the same way."

"Perhaps," Richard agreed.

They were both quiet for a moment. Richard wondered what Charles was thinking. At last he said, "Richard, the thing you have to remember as a bishop—the thing I didn't remember nearly often enough—is to focus on the big issues, the things that only you as a bishop can do. The things that make a real difference in the lives of your ward members. Let the details take care of themselves."

The older man stood and stretched. "Time for me to pack these old bones into my bed. It was good talking with you, son."

As Richard returned his father-in-law's firm embrace, he thought what a blessing it was that he had someone like this in his life, someone who—unlike his own father—could be an example of the kind of man Richard wanted to be. Honestly, if he and Sandy ever divorced, Richard thought he'd miss his relationship with Charles almost as much as he'd miss her.

Paul felt like he was floating on air the whole day he turned sixteen and was made a priest.

That morning, he got up extra early to make sure he was at church on time. His mom gave him a big smile as he came down to breakfast after his shower. "French toast for the birthday boy," she said, pointing to the tall stack. He smiled back and ate several platefuls, then drove them slowly and carefully to church in the drizzling rain, arriving a few minutes before sacrament meeting.

Paul had been assigned to help prepare the sacrament that morning. "We have to get some work out of you while we still can," Alan had said with a grin. First, Paul filled the tray insert with plastic cups, using quick, experienced motions. He turned on the water to a slow trickle and moved the tray insert from side to side underneath, then tilted it to drain off the extra water from between the cups. Watching the water falling made him think of the rain outside, of water spraying their breakfast plates clean in the dishwasher, of water from the showerhead streaming over his body that morning, washing off soap and sweat and dirt. His chest and shoulders tingled under his white shirt.

Brother Rasmussen was conducting the meeting that day. After a few announcements and callings, he said, "The bishop has a matter of business." He sat down, and Bishop Mortensen took his place at the podium.

"Brother Ficklin, please stand up." Paul stood.

"Today is Paul's sixteenth birthday. I've interviewed him and found him worthy to be ordained a priest in the Aaronic priesthood."

Bishop Mortensen was looking straight at Paul, a slight smile on his face. Paul smiled back. He'd had his interview with the bishop on Wednesday night. It had felt really, really good to be able to answer each of the questions the way he was supposed to.

"All those who can support this ordination, please show by raising your right hand." Paul's hand rose with the rest. The bishop raised his hand as well. "Any opposed, by the same sign." No hands came up. "We'll take care of the ordination after the meetings."

Paul sat. Beside him, his mother gave him another big smile as she squeezed his arm. From behind the sacrament table, Chad smirked at him. Paul smirked back.

The meetings progressed. Between sacrament meeting and Sunday school, several of the older members of the ward came up to Paul and shook his hand, congratulating him. His friend Janice smiled and gave him a thumbs up.

After priesthood opening exercises, Paul followed Chad to the bishop's office, where the priests quorum met. Troy Simpson, the quorum's first assistant, welcomed Paul to the quorum. Then they had a lesson on the duties of a priest—"Good information for Paul, but all of you can use the review," the quorum advisor said.

After church, Paul and his mom and Chad and Bishop Mortensen and Brother Sanders, the Young Men president, all filed back into the bishop's office. Paul sat in a chair while Chad, Brother Sanders, and the bishop all stood in a circle around him and put their hands on his head. Paul closed his eyes, and Bishop Mortensen began to speak.

"Paul Eric Ficklin. In the name of Jesus Christ and by the authority of the Aaronic and Melchizedek priesthoods that we hold, we lay our hands on your head and ordain you to the office of priest in the Aaronic priesthood, together with all the rights and privileges involved in this office of the priesthood . . ."

Paul tried to concentrate on the words, but despite his best efforts his mind started to wander. Bits and pieces caught his attention, though.

"The experiences of your life have been a trial of your faithfulness. But the Lord is pleased with you and encourages you to press forward in his path. The priesthood will be a blessing to you as you learn how to be the kind of man God wants you to be . . .

"As a priest, you have a responsibility to prepare for a mission and become the kind of man who can serve our Lord faithfully . . .

"It will be your job to sit at the front of the congregation and kneel before God and offer up the ordinance that signifies we are striving to be the people of God. As such, you must live a life that is pure and clean and right before Him, so you can perform the ordinances of the priesthood in righteousness . . .

"The Aaronic priesthood holds the keys of the gospel of repentance. At this time in your life, repentance is an important part of what you need to learn. This includes the process of recognizing where you fall short of our Heavenly Father's expectations and then learning how you can improve and become a better person. This is a process that will continue throughout your life . . ."

And then it was over. Paul shook Brother Sanders's hand, then stretched his hand toward the bishop. Bishop Mortensen ignored it, instead pulling him into a tight hug that Paul returned. He and Chad shook hands, both trying to control their snickers. Then his mom gave him a hug, and they all walked out except the bishop, who had another appointment waiting for him.

The rest of the day was good. Paul spent most of the afternoon downloading favorite songs from his CDs onto his new iPod, via the computer. Dinner was roast chicken with potato wedges and Paul's favorite kiwi-and-mango salad, followed by a yellow cake with chocolate frosting. Even after a full dinner, Paul ate about half of the cake, grinning at his mom's pretended disgust over teenage male appetites. Then Paul read the Calvin and Hobbes book that Chad had given him. There was also a telephone call from his dad in Minnesota, during which Paul made sure to say how much he liked the iPod, and he had short but enjoyable thirty-second conversations with his little brother and sister.

It was all very nice. Somehow, though, the part of the day that lingered most in his memory was the press of three pairs of hands on his head and the warmth that flooded through him afterward while he was being hugged by Chad's dad—the man who had reached out to him in love and acceptance just a few months earlier, at what had been the lowest time of his life so far.

Chapter Sixteen

PAUL THOUGHT FOR A LONG TIME before he finally decided what to do for the Day of Silence.

There had been a lot of discussion in the GSA about whether they should all wear a Day of Silence shirt, or a scarf, or a hat, or wear tape across their mouths. Each idea someone came up with was shouted down by the other GSA members, usually because they hated the way it would make them look. *It's really unbelievable just how much teenagers care about their clothes and appearance,* thought Paul, conveniently ignoring his own almost-violent reaction to some of the T-shirt designs that had been passed around.

Finally Jessica simply decided that since they couldn't agree on something to do as a club, everyone could come up with his or her own thing to do. Surprisingly, this solution seemed to make everyone happy. It soon turned into a contest to see who could come up with the cleverest or most unusual way of communicating the idea of silence, homophobia, or intolerance in general.

On Tuesday, the day before the Day of Silence, one of the girls brought a little clamp-type device to GSA for making buttons. All you had to do was supply a paper circle with the design you wanted. For his pin, Paul carefully lettered the words *In Silent Support* on a piece of paper. Then, after getting home, he dug through his shirt drawer until he found an old T-shirt he'd gotten at school for Earth Day several years ago. On the front it had a cartoon-type drawing of the world, with paper-doll-cutout kids holding hands all around the outside. In the middle were the words *Love the World*.

Paul snickered. Back in sixth grade, he'd thought the shirt was very cool. Chad had too — until some of the older kids made fun of it. The next day Chad had thrown his shirt out. Paul kept his, though.

He tried it on. Tight but still wearable, with no really embarrassing holes. *This must have been, like, fourteen sizes too big for me back then.*

Chad was already in the seminary room when Paul got there. The minute Chad saw him, he groaned. "Oh, no. Not the hippie shirt."

Paul smirked. Then he pointed to the button he was wearing.

"In silent support? What the heck?" Then Paul pointed at his own closed mouth. "Oh. Right. That Day of Silence thing." Chad shook his head. "I can't believe you wore that shirt, though."

Having Chad know about the Day of Silence came in handy later, when the seminary teacher called on Paul to answer a question. He shook his head and pointed at his button.

Beside him, Chad sighed. "It's this thing he's doing for school. He has to go all day without saying anything."

Several other members of the class looked puzzled. Paul knew there'd been enough talk about the Day of Silence at school that some of them probably knew what it was about, but if so, they weren't saying anything. Paul was glad. He was sure he'd get comments over the course of the day, but he'd just as soon the whole GSA thing not come up during seminary.

As they were leaving the church, Janice came up and pointed at Paul's button. "Ha! I was wondering if you'd do anything for that."

Paul shrugged and spread his hands. Inside, he was laughing. *The great thing about hand gestures is they can mean so many different things.*

Much to Paul's surprise, when he got to school he saw kids wearing black armbands with the words *Stop the Intolerance.* Then in the school entryway, he saw a table where several students — not GSA members — were passing out the armbands, though it quickly became apparent that many of the people wearing them didn't get the part about being silent.

The mystery of the armbands was revealed at a school assembly later that morning. Ms. Wilson, one of the assistant principals, spoke first. She droned on for about fifteen minutes about tolerance and understanding and how the school had a zero-tolerance policy for bullying and harassment.

Finally she was done. Mr. Whittaker, the principal, started clapping. Taking the hint, everyone else started clapping too. Paul joined in as well, though he felt somewhat irritated when he realized she hadn't said anything about gays except for when she listed sexual orientation as one of the things that you couldn't discriminate or harass other people about.

Then it was the senior class president's turn. She explained how their class had chosen the theme of "Tolerance for All" and how the class council had decided to pay for the armbands to show their solidarity with oppressed peoples. Paul rolled his eyes. *Oh, please.* More polite applause.

Finally, Jessica stood at the podium. Instead of saying anything, she handed a set of papers to Ms. Allington, who had stood up to join Jessica. Then Ms. Allington spoke.

"Hello. I'm Donna Allington, one of the school counselors and advisor to our school's gay-straight alliance. What I have here are a few words from Jessica, the GSA president, which she's asked me to present for her today." She looked down at the papers and started reading.

It was a good talk, Paul thought. Ms. Allington—or rather, Jessica—talked about how silence was part of an environment of fear and how, if people were afraid of expressing who they were, it meant that bigotry and intolerance had won. She mentioned gays as an example of things society could pretend weren't there because people were silent about them. She finished by saying, "The truth is, you don't know who might be gay: your friend, your neighbor, the boy or girl who sits next to you in class, the person sitting next to you in this assembly. As students, it is our choice this day to be silent, so we can all try to remember to speak more carefully, more supportively, more respectfully in the future, so that our speaking may make our world and Arcadia Heights High School a better place to be, not just for gays but for all of us as well."

As soon as Ms. Allington stopped reading, Jessica stepped back up to the podium. She pointed to her shirt, which read *Speaking Out to End Injustice, Day of Silence 2004*, then she raised a fist and grinned.

Paul attracted several stares with his enthusiastic clapping. He didn't care. He felt as if Jessica had somehow managed to put into words what he felt about today, why he felt like the Day of Silence was worth supporting even if he disagreed with a lot of what the other kids in GSA believed. *It really is all about tolerance and acceptance. Speaking out so other people don't have to suffer in silence.*

Mr. Whittaker stood and thanked everyone who had taken part in the assembly. He announced that there would no penalties in the day's classes for anyone who chose to be silent, but everyone would be expected to complete all other class assignments and participate in other ways as directed by their teachers. Then he dismissed the students. *That's pretty smart,* Paul realized as he walked to his second-period class. *He lets other people be windbags so he can be the one who tells us we can leave.*

Paul was amazed just how easy it was to get used to not talking. When people said things to him, he'd smile and point to his button. If they asked a question, he'd try to answer without words. If it was too complicated, he'd shrug or spread his hands the way he'd done with Janice. He had the idea that not speaking was supposed to make him feel all angsty and marginalized, but really it was more like a game. He guessed it would be different if being silent hadn't been his own choice.

There wasn't anything in math, science, or P.E. that had to do specifically with the Day of Silence. In social studies, though, the day's theme seemed to be persecuted minorities. Come to think of it, they'd been focusing on ethnic groups, religious minorities, and even the treatment of women quite a bit all year, though Paul supposed that women didn't qualify as a minority in the strict mathematical sense. At the end of the class period, the teacher, a white-haired lady named Mrs. Stimpson, made the point explicitly:

"It's a basic part of human nature that we define ourselves by splitting people into groups, *us* versus *them*: people who are like ourselves versus those who are different in some way. Early religions, as best we can tell, were generally tribal religions, worshiping gods who were the patrons of particular tribes and groups. If you look back at the origins of our legal traditions, they go back to codes that were for settling differences within the group, not outside of it.

"Possibly the greatest social challenge humans have faced during our recorded history has been the struggle to get past this kind of tribal thinking. Efforts to create governmental systems that are based on the rule of law are part of this. In a similar way, many of the world's great religions have attempted to persuade people to broaden their definition of *us* and to train people to think about good and bad in terms of abstract standards of behavior that apply equally to everyone.

"This is why communication is so important, as well as learning about foreign cultures and the experiences of people living in different lands and circumstances. The hope is that by learning all these things, we'll come to feel a greater sense of kinship with others. The world can't afford tribal thinking."

Walking to English class, Paul couldn't stop thinking about what Mrs. Stimpson had said. *That's one difference with not talking. You can't really socialize with other people, so instead you think about things.* It was kind of nice as a change.

Back in Paul's freshman year, they'd studied church history in seminary. Paul had been shocked when he found out about the laws that Congress had passed back in the late 1800s dissolving the LDS Church and seizing church property. He'd wondered if the government had ever done something like that with other religious groups. He even asked about it in his U.S. government class, but the teacher had denied that such a thing had ever happened to Mormons or anyone else. His teacher hadn't wanted to talk about the Extermination Order in Missouri either, when the Missouri governor said that Mormons had to be either driven from the state or killed.

Everyone thinks about the times their own group was persecuted. No one likes to admit that persecution happens to other groups as well. At least, not to groups they don't like.

Paul walked into English class a few seconds before the bell rang. As he stepped in the door, Ms. Steinbraun grabbed him, put a finger to his lips, and pointed him toward one of the desks. He took his seat, a little confused, and watched while she did the same thing to the other students who were still coming into the classroom. Every now and then she'd put her finger to her lips again as a reminder to the students who were already sitting. Once, when one of the boys at the back of the room started talking, she rapped her knuckles against the whiteboard, then pointed to where she'd written *Talking* = *Detention* in big red letters. The boy stopped talking.

Finally everyone was seated. She closed the door, then stood staring at them from the front of the room. One minute. Two minutes. Then she spoke.

"How many of you are participating in the Day of Silence?" To Paul's surprise, almost a third of the class raised their hands.

"Good. I commend those of you who are doing this. Everyone else will be expected to participate in the class discussion. Those of you who are silent will be expected to listen attentively and take part in a writing assignment later in the class period. If you're being silent but you want to make a comment, raise your hand and I'll call on you. You can come up to the board and write it." She smirked. "Anyone who claims to be participating in the Day of Silence will receive a zero for class participation today if I see you talking here or anywhere else in school.

"So let's think about silence for a minute. What does being silent represent when we're talking about communication?"

One of the things Paul liked about Ms. Steinbraun was the way she could tease comments out of the class without making people feel stupid. By the time the discussion was over, they'd talked about silence as an absence of communication, silence as a product of fear, silence as a replacement for communication, silence as agreement, silence as disagreement, and silence as a way of hiding what people really thought.

Partway through, one of the other boys in the class — Evan, who was rumored to be gay but who Paul had never seen at GSA — raised his hand, then came up to the board and wrote the word *frame*.

Ms. Steinbraun tilted her head to one side. "Can you elaborate on that a little more?"

Evan stood there for a moment looking frustrated. Then he started writing again. Half a minute later, he turned around and pointed at what he'd written: *Speech is surrounded by silence.*

"Very good," Ms. Steinbraun commented in a thoughtful voice. "Yes, it's certainly true that silence can be a frame for spoken words. I see what you're getting at now." She paused. "Okay, people. I think we've brainstormed enough ideas that you should be ready to put something down in writing."

About half the class groaned. Sometimes when a discussion was going really well, they could get her to forget when she had a writing assignment planned. Not today, though.

"I'd like each of you to start writing something about silence and language. You can take one of the ideas we've been discussing here or another idea of your own. Develop it into two to three pages, using your own insights and experiences. Since we have only twenty minutes left today, I'll expect you to turn in the completed essays tomorrow at the beginning of class." Another pause. "Hop to it, people! Or I'll be taking off class participation points."

Paul started writing. Partway through class, he'd realized what he wanted to write about. *Silence can be used as a part of communication. Hand gestures. Things like that. After all, who says language has to be spoken? What about those chimpanzees who learn sign language? Silence isn't the same thing as not communicating. There are lots of ways to communicate without saying anything out loud.*

It was a clever idea, and Paul knew it would get him a good

grade. His mind kept drifting off, though, to other thoughts about the Day of Silence, including what silence meant to him and all the different places and situations where he felt like he couldn't say what he was really thinking.

Paul couldn't tell the people at church he was gay. They'd freak out, just like Chad's mom had done. Chad knew, but Paul couldn't really talk to him about the way it felt to be gay either.

On the other hand, there was an awful lot Paul felt like he couldn't say at GSA about being Mormon and following Mormon standards. Paul's mind drifted back to the meeting a few weeks ago when he hadn't felt comfortable talking about the church's position on gay marriage. *They know I'm Mormon, but they don't really know what that means. I don't feel like I can share it with them. That's a kind of silence too.*

The bell rang. Paul put away his writing stuff and took off for his next class.

By the time school was over, Chad was sick and tired of the whole Day of Silence crap.

First it was Paul that morning, with that stupid shirt and button and the weird hyper grin on his face. Chad did his best to make it sound like a routine school thing when he explained Paul's silence to the seminary teacher, but that was blown as soon as everybody got to school and saw the seniors passing out those stupid armbands. *So now all the kids in our seminary class know why Paul was being quiet today. Great.*

Sometimes Chad wondered just how badly Paul wanted to keep people from knowing he was gay. Paul *said* he didn't want anyone to find out, but then he did stuff like this that was guaranteed to make people wonder.

Not to mention coming out to the whole freakin' GSA. *Smart move there, bonehead.* Sometimes it seemed like Paul believed that church and GSA and school and scouts were all these separate bubbles, and what happened in one bubble couldn't spill over into the other bubbles. Chad was afraid of how things might turn out if the truth leaked out — and not just for Paul. Things could get really bad for him too, as Paul's best friend.

The day hadn't gotten any better after that. There'd been that stupid assembly with all the boring talks, including that nutcase from GSA who had their advisor read her talk. How lame was that, anyway?

Actually, the speech had been kind of hard to hear because the guys he'd been sitting with kept snorting and making comments about fags getting what they deserved. Chad knew it was mostly hot air, but the whole thing reminded him of that time before Christmas when Paul got all upset about the comments he and the other guys from the soccer team had been making.

It was true that what Chad said hadn't been that bad compared to a lot of stuff guys said to each other all the time. But it was also true that Chad had been a jerk and trashed his best friend, even if he didn't know Paul was listening at the time.

Chad hated feeling that Paul's getting into trouble with Jared might have been partly Chad's fault, just because he hadn't been a good friend. It was a feeling he never wanted to have again. So Chad hadn't joined in with the comments the other guys were making, even though the assembly really was very lame and he was sure Paul wasn't sitting anywhere near them. He hadn't cracked any jokes of his own, and he'd done his best not to laugh at theirs.

The other guys had noticed.

At one point, Blake Castle made a rude comment about the GSA president's looks. Then he glanced at Chad as if he was expecting him to agree. When Chad didn't say anything, one of the other guys poked him.

"Whaddaya think, Mortensen? She goes for other girls because she's too ugly to get a boyfriend?"

Chad hesitated a second. "I think she looks pretty good." Actually he didn't have much of an opinion one way or the other, but he figured it was the safest way to sidestep the issue.

"I guess. If you get all excited about girls getting it on with each other."

"Just shut it," Chad said. A couple of the other boys snickered.

As soon as the assembly was over and the other guys had left, a girl who'd been sitting right in front of Chad started tearing into him for how disrespectful and rude he and his friends had been. Chad tried to defend himself without actually saying, "Look, chick, my best friend is gay," but she wasn't having any of it. Afterward he wondered if the reason she'd approached him instead of the other guys was because he was less intimidating. *Great. I try to be more tolerant, and all it gets me is that now people think I'm the one it's safe to get mad at.*

Most of Chad's classes didn't end up doing anything special for the Day of Silence. Unfortunately, one of the exceptions was his

English class, where Mrs. Alder seemed offended that most of them weren't observing the Day of Silence. She spent the whole time talking about persecution and intolerance and AIDS and how homosexuals had been an oppressed minority in Western civilization. Chad wasn't impressed. He was sure she wasn't gay. Besides, he knew what kind of car she drove. Nobody was oppressing *her*. She just got off on talking about how other people were oppressed and showing off how liberal she was, and then she came down like a ton of bricks on anyone who disagreed with her.

Mrs. Alder wasn't Chad's favorite teacher. By the time class was over, he was desperately wishing *she'd* decided to be silent that day.

Day of Silence. What a pain.

Another week.

Paul's Tuesday hadn't been going terribly well. First, he overslept and had to rush through breakfast and getting dressed for school. He'd missed some questions on his Spanish quiz, and he hadn't been really happy with how his social studies assignment turned out either. He was looking forward to going home after GSA and curling up with the next book in Orson Scott Card's Ender series — he'd loved *Ender's Game* back when he was in sixth grade but had only recently started reading Card's follow-up books.

So he was surprised and a little annoyed when Jessica asked him to hang around and talk with her after the meeting. *What's wrong now? Have I been too quiet? Not quiet enough? Wore the wrong kind of underwear for the Day of Silence?*

He wasn't expecting to be asked if he wanted to be next year's GSA vice-president.

"The club constitution says we have to hold elections in the spring so we can hit the ground running in the fall. Penny's going to be the president, but we need a vice-president as well."

"You want *me* to be the vice-president?" Paul knew better than to ask why they weren't just waiting to see who got elected at the club meeting. No telling who they'd wind up with if they did that.

"We've been talking — Penny and me and a couple other juniors and seniors. Jared thought you'd do a good job."

Paul controlled his wince. Things were still awkward between him and Jared. The other boy was friendly enough when they interacted in groups, but both of them carefully avoided saying much to each other directly.

"Why doesn't Jared do it?"

"He refused." She shrugged. "Besides, it's not a good idea for the president and vice-president both to be seniors. Or both guys or girls, or both straight or not. Things work better if there's a kind of balance. You'd be a good balance for Penny. You're a guy, you'll be a junior next year, you're . . . well, kind of out, even if you're not really. Out inside of GSA, anyway. You're good at organizing people. And you're not as loud and bossy as Penny and don't get on people's nerves as much."

"Hey!" It was Penny, who'd come up and joined the conversation while Jessica was talking.

The other girl grinned at her. "If the shoe fits, let it pinch."

"So why am I taking this job again?" Penny grumbled.

"Because you want to? Because I asked?" Jessica shrugged again. "You'll do a good job. Loud and bossy isn't always a bad thing in a club president, you know."

"As you often demonstrate."

"Besides, if we can get Paul here to be your partner, he can be the nice cop who gets people to calm down after you've been yelling at them." She looked at Paul again. "So, what do you say?"

"Uh . . ." Paul hesitated. "I'm, uh, not really sure. Can I get back to you later?"

"Sure. The elections aren't until June first."

"Okay."

Walking home, Paul thought about the irony of it. *Sarah bawls me out for not talking enough. Then Jessica says I'll make a good vice-president because I don't talk too much.*

Thinking about Sarah made Paul grimace. If they wanted someone who was less intense than Penny, he could see why they didn't ask Sarah. She was pretty good at bossing people around but not at getting them to cooperate with each other. And she didn't listen very well to what people were saying. He shook his head, remembering that Sarah had said something similar about Penny after his first time at GSA.

Thinking about Sarah reminded him of the real problem with agreeing to be V.P. *Just how well do I really fit in at GSA, anyway?*

Paul remembered his thoughts from the Day of Silence—how he'd felt like he had to be silent about being Mormon at GSA, just like he had to be silent about being gay everywhere else. He wasn't sure how well he'd do at being vice-president of a club where he felt like a big part of himself wouldn't be accepted.

So why not do an experiment? See if GSA can handle me being Mormon before I decide whether or not to be vice-president. Heck, once they know more about me being Mormon, they may not even want to have me in the club anymore.

Part of himself thought this was one of the stupidest ideas he'd ever had. *I hate conflict. And now I'm planning to deliberately do something I know people won't like, just to see how much they hate it?*

No risk, no benefit, he thought, remembering a saying of Chad's dad. *If I don't do it, I'll just be waiting for things to go bad some other time. Sarah's always saying GSA's a place where we can be accepted for who we are. I guess I'll find out if that's really true.*

Chapter Seventeen

ON THE NEXT SATURDAY MORNING, Paul woke up with a headache. That was pretty normal for fasting. He hoped it didn't get so bad that he had to take an Excedrin before he got his patriarchal blessing.

A few weeks ago, during his interview to be made a priest, the bishop had asked Paul if he'd thought about getting his patriarchal blessing. Paul said he would think about it. The more Paul thought, the better he liked the idea. So he got his recommend and called the patriarch from another nearby stake to make an appointment, since their stake didn't have a patriarch right now.

A patriarchal blessing was supposed to give direction for a person's life. Paul thought he could use that right now, especially with all his confusion about GSA and being gay and everything.

Still lying in bed, Paul picked up his Book of Mormon. He'd managed to make his way through 2 Nephi despite all the Isaiah chapters, though sometimes his brain felt scrambled after just a few verses. He'd read through Jacob and his lecture to the Nephite men about chastity, which reminded him uncomfortably of all those general conference talks about pornography. Then there was a lengthy and almost incomprehensible chapter about olive trees and the House of Israel. *Maybe I'd understand it better if I had more experience with gardening.*

And then there was the book of Enos, which he'd read just a couple of days ago. It made him feel like a slacker.

Enos prayed all day and all night to get a testimony. I haven't done anything dramatic like that. He just hoped that what he had been doing—saying his prayers and reading the Book of Mormon—would be enough.

• • •

Barbara had been pleased when Paul asked her to go with him to get his patriarchal blessing. It was such a personal thing. She wouldn't have blamed him if he hadn't wanted anyone else there at all.

Barbara couldn't remember much about when she got her patriarchal blessing. She'd been fourteen at the time, and her family was mostly inactive by then. Maybe the other girls her age had been getting theirs and her mother thought it was time for Barbara as well.

It wasn't until shortly after Paul was born that Barbara had come across the folded sheet of paper in a box of personal things, reread it, and realized for the first time just how insightful her blessing had been about the challenges and experiences she'd faced so far in her life. Later on, when things started to go sour with Frank, she'd reread it from time to time. Even though she hadn't done anything back then about returning to activity in the church, the blessing had given her hope that someday things could get better, with its promises about enduring trials and then receiving joy and happiness and its assurance that God would always be there for her whenever she was ready to reach out to him.

Even now, Barbara would reread her patriarchal blessing whenever she felt like she needed to recapture her sense of balance. Over the past year, she'd read it several times since Paul's . . . unexpected announcement. Each time, she'd felt a sense of reassurance, both about Paul's future and about her own ability to deal with the challenges of being his mother. She hoped Paul's patriarchal blessing would do as much for him as hers had for her.

The patriarch wasn't as old as Paul expected. He looked like he might be retired, but he wasn't all bent and white-haired like Brother Jespers, who'd been their stake patriarch until he died a couple of years earlier.

Brother Hoskisson greeted Paul and his mother with a firm handshake, then led them into his study. He talked to Paul for a few minutes, mostly going over what a patriarchal blessing was and asking if Paul had any questions. Then he switched on a tape recorder, put his hands on Paul's head, and began speaking.

"Our Father which art in heaven, by the authority of the holy priesthood, I lay my hands upon the head of thy son, Paul Eric Ficklin, to give unto him a patriarchal blessing . . ."

As the words washed over Paul, along with the weight of the

patriarch's hands he started to feel something else, a kind of cool tingling that flowed over his skin. At the same time, there was a tight, focused feeling inside him, a feeling that grew as he did his best to listen to what the patriarch was saying.

"As you allow yourself to be made an instrument in the Lord's hands, your weaknesses will be turned into strengths and you will have the opportunity to share your experiences and insights and the wisdom you have gained, at the proper times that you are prompted to do so by the Spirit of the Lord and under the direction of your leaders in the priesthood. And this will be a great blessing unto you and a means by which you can be of service to your brothers and sisters while you are here on this earth, in helping them to see the tender mercies and the salvation of the Lord which he has wrought for all his children . . ."

The blessing continued. After a while, Paul realized that his headache was starting to come back and he was having trouble focusing on the words.

"Listen to the voice of the Lord, the words of His holy prophets, and the direction of your priesthood leaders, together with the whisperings of the Spirit, and you will know and understand the paths that you should take, despite all the confusing and erroneous philosophies of men and the lies of the Adversary. Always be loyal to the cause of truth, to God and the church and to the priesthood you bear . . ."

There was more of that type of thing, all about church callings and things Paul was supposed to do in his life. A lot of it sounded kind of vague. Maybe it would make more sense once he was able to read the words on a printed page.

After what seemed like about fifteen minutes, Brother Hoskisson finished. "Now I seal these blessings upon you on condition of your faithfulness, advising you to always remember that God is your eternal Father and that as his son you have the potential to become like him if you will but live faithfully. In the name of Jesus Christ, amen."

Paul blinked and stretched his neck. And then unexpectedly, as he was standing and shaking the patriarch's hand, Paul felt a sudden blaze of fierce joy leap inside him, as if the world and everything in it was momentarily filled with molten gold that only he had eyes to see.

Wow.

• • •

As things turned out, Paul had a chance to try out his tolerance-for-Mormons experiment at GSA sooner than he'd expected.

It started, not surprisingly, with posters. Partway through the next week's GSA meeting, someone suggested they should make posters about gay marriage, particularly since some groups were trying to get an initiative on the November ballot that would make gay marriage illegal in Oregon. Paul tried to argue that they should wait to find out if it was going to be on the ballot first, but he was overruled.

"They'll get it on the ballot," Ellen argued. "This way, though, we can talk about the issue itself, not the ballot measure. We're not just responding. Instead, we're talking about a general principle, which is: Why can't two women or two men get married, if a man and a woman can get married?"

"Won't there be problems if we take sides on a political issue?" asked Paul a little desperately.

"I don't see why there should be," Ms. Allington broke in. "Especially since it's simply a matter of making people aware about the issues."

Paul wondered what the difference was between taking sides and making people aware about the issues. *Probably whether Ms. Allington thinks you're on the right side or the wrong side.*

Ellen looked at him. "So why does the idea of making posters about gay marriage bother you so much?"

He hesitated. "Look. My church doesn't accept gay marriage, okay? I really can't work on this kind of a poster."

"No one has to know that you worked on it," Ellen said.

"Besides, you need to do what you think is right, not what your church says," argued Sarah, who had joined the discussion by then. Several other people nodded.

"You can't let the church your parents go to define who you're gonna be," put in Trevor.

Paul felt like he was being backed into a corner. "But what if I don't think gay marriage is right either?" he finally asked.

The room grew quiet.

"You're a gay guy. And you don't think gays should be allowed to get married?" Trevor shook his head. "You know, I think that may just be the most messed-up thing I've ever heard."

"You really don't support gay marriage? Just because your church tells you not to?" Ellen demanded.

"Basically, yeah."

"That's bullshit."

Paul looked around. Everyone was staring at him.

"I mean, that's the type of attitude that's led to gays being repressed all these years," Ellen said. "Being denied equal rights with straights, just because some religion says so. That's the sort of thing GSA was created to fight against."

"So you're saying I can't be a member of GSA and be against gay marriage?"

It looked like Ellen wanted to say something, but Nara responded first. "You can have whatever opinion you want."

"Yeah," said Trevor. "It's just a stupid one."

"It's a f—"

"Language," interrupted Ms. Allington.

"—crock of shit!" yelled Jose, his face twisted with anger. He was a freshman who'd showed up at GSA a couple of months before. He claimed not to be gay, though apparently something had happened that made his parents think he was. Whatever it was had left him really mad both at his parents and at churches in general.

Paul was starting to get upset. "And that's such a *tolerant* point of view."

"Look, Paul," put in Jared. He'd been listening but hadn't said anything up to now. "You have your reasons for believing what you do. But we don't share those reasons. We're not Mormons. You can't really expect us to be happy about what you're saying, that gays can't have the same rights everybody else wants to have, just because your religion thinks being gay is wrong. And it sounds really hypocritical to say that at a GSA meeting when we know you're gay too."

Ouch.

Paul tried to respond. "Look! It's not—it doesn't—I didn't choose to be gay. I'm not gonna change my ideas about right and wrong just because of who I'm attracted to!"

"Pretty piss-poor religion if it teaches you you're a bad person just because of something you can't control," Ellen said.

Paul thought about trying to explain that being attracted to other guys didn't make you a bad person unless you acted on it, but he decided it wouldn't really help matters any. *They wouldn't get it. Even if they did, it wouldn't make them any happier about it.*

"I think we've managed to get pretty far afield from the official focus of this meeting," Jessica announced. "So Paul doesn't want to work on a gay marriage poster. Fine. Who's willing to head up the poster group for this?" And with that, the meeting continued, much to Paul's relief.

Paul was silent for the rest of the meeting, his hands shaking less as time went by. Afterward, he went up to Jessica, who was talking to Penny and Sarah and a couple of others.

"I'm guessing you don't want me for V.P. next year," he started bluntly.

Jessica got an embarrassed look on her face. "No."

"That's what I figured. Well, better now than after I was elected." He turned to walk away.

"Wait!" Sarah hurried after him. "They were talking to you about being the vice-president of GSA next year?"

"Yeah. Not anymore, obviously."

"Well, no. Not if you're against gay marriage."

"Like I say, it was worth finding out beforehand."

"So that was on purpose, bringing up that stuff today?"

"Kind of. I also wanted to find out for my own sake, you know? Find out just how much I *really* am accepted at GSA. Turns out, not much."

"That is so not fair!"

He shrugged. "I thought it was fair." Paul thought he sounded pretty calm, like the whole thing was mostly a polite difference in opinion. Inside, though, he realized he was still pretty upset. In fact—

"Hey, Sarah!" a girl called from down the hall. "What's going on?"

Saved by one of Sarah's random friends.

"Oh, hi, Francine. Um, Paul—"

"Time for me to get home anyway. See you later." With that, Paul took off toward his house.

"So what did you expect? A round of applause?"

It was later that evening. Paul had just finished telling Chad about the GSA meeting. Chad, to Paul's irritation, was less than sympathetic.

"I mean, it's not like you didn't know what side of things they're on," Chad continued. "The chances were, like, a zillion to one they were just going to say, 'Omigosh, you're right! How could I ever have been in favor of gay marriage?' "

"Look," Paul growled, "I wasn't expecting them to agree with the church's stand on gay marriage. I just—I guess I was hoping they'd be a little more open-minded about it."

"Dude, I'm telling you. Open-mindedness about other people isn't really what the GSA is about. What they're looking for is open-mindedness about themselves." He shook his head. "You just—you've been living in a dream world, man."

"What do you mean?"

Chad looked at him for a moment. Paul felt a tightening in his gut. It was the kind of look that told him Chad was about to say something he didn't think Paul wanted to hear but that Chad thought he needed to hear anyway.

When Chad finally spoke, his voice was gentler than Paul had expected. "You're straddling the line, man. I think you have this kind of fantasy that you can be gay with your gay friends, but not really, and then be Mormon the rest of the time." He shook his head again. "That's not the way things work. Being a Mormon, man—if you don't want to go against what the church says, you'll never be accepted completely. Even just trying, it'll rip you apart if you let it." Chad snorted. "I can't believe I'm the one saying this stuff. I mean, I'm the one who usually tries to fit in with the other guys, you know? But you gotta make a choice."

Chad fell silent and looked away. Paul thought about what he'd said. *Is that really what I've been doing? Straddling the line? Trying to be two different people? Well, yeah. I mean, pretty clearly. The thing is, it really is true. There really are two different parts of me. At least two.*

I'm Mormon. I don't want to stop being that. I don't think I need to stop being that. And I'm attracted to other guys. That's not something people in the church will understand.

I thought the kids at GSA could help me with that part, even if they don't understand about the church part. But being attracted to other guys doesn't mean the same thing to me that it does to them, since I don't plan to do anything about it.

They're right. By their standards, I really am pretty weird. A hypocrite, even, since I'm not willing to accept the gay part of myself the way they think I need to. But that's because I know something else about myself that they don't know. At least, if I accept that the gospel is true.

Paul's feelings during his patriarchal blessing, his feelings when he'd been ordained a priest, were a lot like what people said the Holy Ghost felt like. It wasn't the kind of full-blown testimony that he wanted to have someday, but it was close to that. He couldn't turn away from those feelings.

At the same time, he really didn't want to lose the sense of friendship and acceptance he'd felt at GSA. It made him feel more . . . normal. Like it really was okay for him to be the way he was and feel the way he did.

Except now they think I'm weird because of my religion.

"Paul! You okay?"

"Yeah. I guess. Yeah." To his frustration, Paul's voice wavered. *I sound like I'm going to cry.*

"Oh, crap! Damn it, Paul, you can't—I mean, you know it's not—"

"It's okay." Stupid, stupid voice, cracking like that. "I mean—I—" And then the ultimate embarrassment, as tears spilled out of his eyes and onto his cheeks.

Out of the corner of his eye, Paul saw Chad looking as horrified as Paul felt. Quickly Paul closed his eyes and put his head in his hands, but the tears kept trickling through his fingers. A minute later, he felt his friend's arm resting awkwardly on his back, which only made him feel worse.

It was several minutes before he was able to say anything. "I don't know why I'm all upset about this."

Silence.

"I mean, you're right about the whole GSA and Mormon thing. It's just, I, I—" He took a deep breath, his face still hidden behind his hands. "I just want to be accepted, you know?" he mumbled. "For who I am. It's like, going to GSA, it made me feel like I wasn't a freak." Paul's voice shook on the last word. For a moment, he felt Chad's arm pressing harder on his back.

"It's not—I'm not trying to dodge around church standards, you know? Not since that stuff with Jared and my promises to your dad. I guess I was just hoping . . . I don't know, maybe I could find some kind of balance. Some way I could stay in the church and do what I'm supposed to do, but still spend time with people who understand what it feels like to be gay, who won't get all freaked out about me liking guys. Someplace I wouldn't have to pretend." Paul lifted his head and looked at Chad, barely noticing as the other boy withdrew his arm. "I'm really sick of pretending, you know?"

Chad nodded. After a minute, he spoke. "I guess I can see that. Doesn't look like it's working out that way, though."

"No."

• • •

By the time next Tuesday came around, Paul still hadn't decided whether he was going to keep going to GSA. On the one hand, part of him wanted to see just how bad things were and whether he'd still feel any of the sense of belonging he'd felt over the last year. On the other hand, the thought of walking through the door made him feel like he wanted to throw up. *I'll skip it this week and figure out my decision later,* he finally decided.

The next day, Paul saw Sarah give him a speculative look at the lunchroom table. "Don't even say anything about it," he told her.

Her eyes widened. "Fine," she snapped, and turned to talk to someone else.

I didn't need to be that obnoxious about it. But I'm not in a mood to be nagged about this right now.

The next week, Paul skipped GSA again.

If I keep this up, there won't be any decision to make, he thought as he pushed his way out the school doors instead of staying for the GSA meeting. Oddly enough, the thought didn't make him any happier.

At the lunch table the next day, Sarah glared at him but didn't say anything. She didn't have to. Paul already had a pretty good idea of what she would say. He just wasn't sure that GSA was worth it anymore—not if it was going to be like the last time he went. He still didn't think being in GSA had to conflict with church standards, but his little experiment had certainly proved that people there weren't terribly open to the church's ways of understanding homosexuality and marriage. *If I have to spend all my time defending the church's position, then GSA won't be the kind of place I want it to be for me. And if I have to keep quiet about things like that in order for me to be comfortable at GSA — and for other people to be comfortable with me being there — that's not good either.*

Conflicting loyalties. That was what this was about, really. A lot of the people in GSA wouldn't see why a religion might deserve Paul's loyalty—especially one they didn't think allowed them equal rights. But he wanted to be loyal to the church, like his patriarchal blessing said.

Every group demands that we make choices. Heck, the soccer team was worse than GSA in a lot of ways, with all the cussing and bullying and stupid practical jokes that everyone else on the team was expected to keep quiet about.

Eventually, Paul decided he really needed to go to the next GSA meeting, which was the next-to-last meeting for the school year. Go one more time and see how things went before deciding for good. *I owe them that much at least. And I guess I owe it to myself as well.*

The phone call from a sister in another ward — someone Sandy had served with in the stake Young Women organization a few years back — arrived just as she was coming in the door from another design consultation.

Calling random interior designers out of the phone book and telling them, "Hi, I'd like to be your assistant" probably hadn't been the smartest way to go about things. She'd been more than halfway down the list before she found someone who was even willing to hear her out. But it had worked in the end. Sandy had already learned a lot from Margaret Pericelli in the few weeks since she'd started working with her.

"Hi, Sister Hart. What can I do for you?"

"Sandy! It's so good to talk to you!"

The tone of the woman's voice — and the fact that she hadn't said what she wanted yet — instantly made Sandy cautious.

"So how can I help you?"

"First, I should make it clear that this isn't something that's coming from the church."

"Okay." Sandy tried to make her voice as noncommittal as possible.

"You know this gay-marriage thing they've got going on in Portland . . ."

And suddenly it clicked. Sandy wasn't surprised at all by the woman's next words.

"There's a group that's putting together a ballot initiative to reverse that and clarify the law so no one else can just decide gay marriages ought to be legal in Oregon. Right now, they're still working on getting the ballot language approved. Once that happens, there won't be much time to collect all the signatures that'll be needed to get the measure on the ballot in November."

"So how can I help?" Now that she knew what this was about, Sandy was willing to sound a little more positive.

"We figure we'll need a lot of people to collect signatures."

"Door to door?"

"Probably, but also just talking to people we know are likely to sign. You know, like church members."

Inevitably, Sandy's thoughts went to Paul and his mother. She wondered what they thought about all this. Then she shook her head. Being sympathetic to gay people was one thing. Changing the whole definition of marriage was something else entirely.

She gave a cautious thought to her schedule for the next several weeks. "I could help with that."

"That's what I was hoping. I've talked with Sister Randolph from the third ward, and I've got some possibilities lined up for other wards. Do you have any suggestions for the Spanish ward?"

"Sister Menendez, maybe."

"Who's she?"

"Relief Society president, I think."

"She might do."

"So when will things be getting started?"

"Well, first we have to find out about getting the ballot language approved. That should happen in the next few days. Then we'll have to get petitions distributed. The whole thing basically has to be done by the end of June."

"That should work for me. I can't put in a lot of time, but I should be able to collect signatures from some people in our ward."

"That's all I was really hoping for. Thanks."

"No problem. It's something that needs to be done. Sometimes it's just important to take a stand."

"Exactly."

Chapter Eighteen

Paul couldn't help but feel nervous as the May twenty-fifth GSA meeting got closer.

The meeting started out well. Trevor was telling stories again. Everyone seemed to be in a good mood. Paul got cautious looks from time to time, but no one was hassling him about the whole poster thing or what he'd said at the last meeting. At least, not at first.

Then the discussion switched to the ballot initiative prohibiting gay marriage and how the group sponsoring the initiative was now collecting signatures. The question was whether they'd be able to collect enough signatures to get it on the ballot in time.

"They won't have any problem with that," Ellen predicted. Paul remembered that she'd been pretty positive on that point at the earlier meeting, too.

Steve snorted. "Plenty of bigots around. Homophobes, religious wackos . . ."

"Mormons," sneered Jose. Several people glared at him. "Oh, c'mon, you're all thinking it," he added.

"Just why do Mormons have such a problem with gays anyway?" asked Nara. She seemed sincere.

Paul thought a moment. He'd imagined often enough what he might say if he ever had a conversation like this. *If I really want to try and bridge both groups, I need to explain as well as I can. One time, at least.*

"It's like this," he started. "We believe that God is married—"

"What a bunch of shit!"

"Shut up, Jose!" Nara snarled. "I want to find out what Paul's church believes, not what you think about it."

"I kind of like the idea of God being married," murmured Gwenyn. "Mr. and Mrs. God."

Paul did his best to ignore Jose. Instead, he focused on the part of the room where Nara and Gwenyn were sitting. "We also believe that humans are children of God. If we make the right choices, we can become like him. That includes being married eternally."

"I heard that Mormons believe they'll be gods someday," put in Sarah.

Paul grinned to hide his nervousness. "Yeah. It's kind of a trip."

"That really doesn't sound like what most churches believe," Trevor observed.

So Paul described Joseph Smith and how Mormons believed that a lot of stuff had been revealed to him that the rest of the Christian world didn't believe—stuff Christ originally taught that had been lost over the centuries. He was sure no one agreed with what he was saying, but at least they were polite enough to hear him out.

"So what does all this have to do with gays?" someone asked.

Paul could feel his nervousness returning. "That's the thing. It only, uh, counts if it's a man married to a woman."

A girl whose name Paul didn't know gave him an angry look. "So if you're lesbian or gay, you're just out of luck, right?"

"I—" Paul hesitated. "I think the idea is that no one is really gay, deep down. I mean, yeah, some people are gay in this life, but no one is really gay forever."

Several people were staring at him. "Sorry, but that makes absolutely no sense," put in Penny.

Paul tried again. "Even if people are gay in this life, we don't believe they have to be gay in the next life."

"You mean, like, reincarnation?"

"No. I mean that the person we really are, the person I am at the most basic level, isn't really gay at all, no matter what it might seem like in this life. After we're dead and then resurrected, even if we've been gay in this life, we'll have the opportunity to be normal and straight later on."

To Paul's surprise, Ms. Allington spoke. "That sounds unhealthy, denying your feelings that way."

Paul bristled. *What the heck is she doing butting into this conversation?* "It's not a matter of denying my feelings," he responded sharply. "It's a matter of believing that there's more to who I am than whether I'm attracted to guys right now."

Several people responded at once.

"Bullshit!"

"That's putting gays right back where—"

"Great! Homosexuality isn't real, so we can just ignore—"

"You can't really believe that stuff—"

"Just because your church says—"

"You're, you can't just—"

Jessica's voice rose above the others. "Look, Paul. You can't just pretend to be a certain way, just because that's the person your church wants you to be. You have to be true to yourself!"

Finally Paul had had enough. "Will you all just *shut up* a minute!"

They were quiet.

Paul shook his head in frustration. "You all just don't get it!"

"What don't we get?"

"Look! It's not just because my church says it, all right?"

"But—"

"See, this is the thing. I don't think any of you really believes me when I say I'm a Mormon, just as much as I'm gay."

That quieted them down again. "What do you mean?" asked Nara.

"I mean—I *believe* it, you know."

As Paul spoke, to his surprise he felt something warm begin to burn through his body, starting in his chest and spreading outward through his arms and legs. It was like the peaceful feelings he'd had when he was being ordained a priest and receiving his patriarchal blessing, except stronger.

"See, I believe all that stuff about Joseph Smith and the Book of Mormon, about God speaking to people and my church being led by a prophet. Because of that, there's a lot of other stuff I just can't accept, like it being okay to be gay and how you have to accept that part of yourself. I *don't* accept it. I know that's the way I am, and I know it's probably not going to change in this life. But I don't believe it's who I really am. Being gay—being attracted to other guys—yeah, that's part of who I am *now*. But being Mormon, that's who I am forever."

As Paul stood there at that moment, there was no room for doubt in any part of him. He knew. He simply knew.

And then he looked around and saw the impatience and lack of comprehension on everyone's faces. *They just don't understand.*

"You know what? This really isn't working." He picked up his backpack. "I thought maybe if I explained where I was coming from, that would help. Instead—" He shook his head. "It's pretty clear there's just too big a difference between what I think and what you all believe. And I don't feel like the person I really am is welcome here. So—"

Several of the girls spoke at once.

"You can't leave!"

"It's not—"

"We don't—"

Paul was more interested to notice the people who weren't saying anything, including Jared, Trevor, and Penny. To Paul's surprise, Jose's face was twisted with something he could only call hatred. *What on earth did I do to him?*

And then Ms. Allington spoke. "Paul. Have you really considered this thoroughly? I can't help but think you're making a mistake here."

Paul stared at her, shocked. *Where does she get off having an opinion on whether I stay in GSA or not?*

"You can't let your parents' religious expectations get in the way of—"

"I already said, that's not why I'm quitting GSA!" He took a deep breath. "Anyway, it's my choice, right? That's what GSA's all about, right?"

Before Ms. Allington could respond, Penny started in. "It's about not having to hide who you are! Not going back into the closet and hiding things!"

"So I guess you're all in favor of personal choice, until someone makes a choice you disagree with. Is that it?" Despite the way Paul's words sounded, he realized he wasn't that upset. The calm sense of certainty he'd felt earlier was still with him, at least a little.

Ms. Allington's lips thinned. "I think we're all just concerned about *this* choice you're making, to please your family and your church by trying to change who you are."

Paul shook his head again. "You're just not listening to anything I say, are you?" He picked up his backpack again. "Bye, everyone. It was nice being here when I thought this club was really about accepting other people." Then he left, ignoring the half-dozen or so shouted objections behind him.

Paul had expected to feel some regret after the adrenalin of the confrontation ran out. To his surprise, after he got over the annoyance and anger of having everyone jump on him all at once, what he felt was something more like . . . relaxed. Like he'd had a weight taken off him. That, more than anything, convinced him that he'd made the right decision after all.

They're not bad people, he reminded himself. *I mean, yeah, Jose seems like a nutcase. Most of the rest of them, though, they're just ordinary kids.*

But their beliefs are different from mine. They really can't see where I'm coming from. There's half of me they don't understand and can't understand. Not understanding that part means they don't really understand the rest of me either.

Paul's calm mood lasted until Sunday. When he saw various members of the GSA, mostly they avoided saying anything to each other. Sarah had started sitting at different lunch tables on different days, so it wasn't all that unusual that she didn't show up at Paul's table for the rest of the week.

Then Sunday came, and Paul's peaceful feelings evaporated.

It started when Paul's Sunday school teacher went off on a long rant about homosexuality and the evils of the last days. Then a class member started talking about the Day of Silence at school and how there was a club for gays at the school.

"Paul! Weren't you part of that? The whole Day of Silence thing?" It was Agatha Timms.

"Yeah."

"Does that mean you're gay?" someone else asked.

"It's not about being gay!" he answered sharply. "It's about tolerance and not hating people."

No one answered him, and the discussion went on from there, though several class members looked at him a little strangely. By the end of the class period, the whole thing seemed to have been forgotten—except by Paul.

He was still in a bad mood the next day when Chad came over to hang out. Since it was Memorial Day, there wasn't any school.

"Why are you so surprised?" Chad responded after Paul told him about the GSA meeting and the Sunday school class. "People are jerks. So what? It's pretty much true anywhere you go."

"You should know. Jerk."

Chad grinned and punched him on the arm.

The next week was more of the same. Each time Paul saw one of the kids from GSA, he felt frustrated and angry. He never really doubted that he'd made the right choice in quitting GSA, but part of him felt like it wouldn't have had to be that way if only the other GSA kids had been a little more open-minded and Ms. Allington had kept her nose out of it.

At the same time, Paul's reactions were almost as negative whenever he caught sight of the other LDS kids, especially the ones from his Sunday school class. *Do they think I'm gay? Or am I just being paranoid?* Either way, he was glad seminary was over for the year so he didn't have to see them each morning. *I'm really ready for this school year to be over.*

Paul woke up the next Sunday vaguely sick to his stomach and with the beginnings of a fast Sunday headache. He wished he could stay home from church, but he realized that was mostly just because he didn't want to hear what the other kids might say. So he gritted his teeth and made himself go anyway. The only negative thing that happened was that Karl Olsen called him a fag lover, but that was pretty normal for Karl, who didn't need any excuse to act like a jerk.

And then Monday morning came and everything fell apart, just three days before school let out for the summer.

Paul had taken the bus that morning, grumbling to himself the whole time. *I've got a license. Chad's got a license. Why am I stuck in this yellow tin can?* Paul knew, though, that there was basically no chance Chad's parents or his mom would give up use of a family car during the school day just to let them drive themselves to school. And as for either of them getting their own car—

Paul was walking through the school courtyard about fifteen minutes before first period when he saw a large group of students standing over by one wall. It was the GSA kids putting up a banner that read *Support Family Values: Marriage Is for Everyone.*

And then from the direction of the GSA kids, he heard Melinda Larson from his ward loudly exclaim, "But marriage is supposed to be between a man and a woman! Not between two men or two women!"

Paul's immediate impulse was to keep walking. He really didn't want to see what was going to happen. Inexplicably, though, he found himself drifting closer. *Kind of like how cars slow down when they're passing an accident. I just hope I don't get hit by any flying pieces when this explodes.*

Paul didn't catch the response to Melinda's statement, but he couldn't miss what she said in reply. "Yes, so I've got religious reasons for what I believe. But that doesn't mean those reasons are wrong!"

Paul sighed. Melinda undoubtedly had the courage of her convictions. And the diplomacy of a large, stubborn boulder.

"Look. You can believe what you want. But why should other people have to be limited by the kind of marriage you think is right?" It was Ellen from GSA, sounding more patient than Paul would have expected.

"You're a Mormon, right?" Sarah put in. "Didn't you guys used to believe in polygamy? So how can you criticize other people for having marriages that aren't traditional?"

"It's not the same!" Melinda insisted. It looked like she was biting her lip. She looked around, obviously trying to figure out what to say next, and she caught sight of him. "Paul! You know what I mean, right? You explain it!"

Paul immediately started feeling sick to his stomach. "This really isn't a conversation I want to get dragged into," he forced out.

She stood there looking at him, her mouth open.

Jose laughed, a sharp, sneering laugh. "Yeah! Paul's such a perfect Mormon, he doesn't want to get involved. Doesn't want everyone to know that he's a faggot too, just like he was telling us at GSA two weeks ago."

Jose's voice was very loud. It cut through all the sounds in the courtyard. Paul, panicked, looked around quickly. There were at least a dozen people watching from other parts of the quad. Several were people he knew. And Melinda . . . she was still staring at him, but now she had a horrified look on her face.

Oh, crap.

Paul stood there a moment with no idea what to do. Then suddenly he felt his stomach lurching, and he was running in the direction of the nearest bathroom.

Oh, crap.

When Chad had first come into the courtyard, he noticed a group of kids over to one side putting up a banner. It sounded like some kind of argument was going on. He didn't pay much attention until he realized that one of the people arguing was Paul. That was just before some Hispanic kid shouted out Paul's name and said something about him being gay.

Chad froze, watching his friend. For a moment, Paul just stood there with a look on his face like someone had chopped him with an axe. Then he took off running. Chad hesitated only a second before running after him.

Paul was leaning over a toilet. He hadn't thrown up yet, though he felt like it might happen any moment. In his rush, he hadn't even bothered to close the stall door behind him.

The restroom door opened. There were some footsteps. Then he heard Chad's voice right behind him. "How you doing?"

Paul didn't bother turning around. "You saw?"

"Yeah. I got there about the time everything went to hell."

Paul chuckled weakly. "That's one way to put it."

There was a pause. "Paul, do you need me to—I dunno. Go talk to someone at the office, see if you can go home the rest of the day?"

Before Paul had decided one way or the other, he heard the restroom door open again. More footsteps, then someone sneering, "Hey! Two guys in the same stall! What, you both fags?"

"He's my friend, and he's sick," Chad yelled back.

"Let's get out of here," Paul muttered.

Chad backed out of the stall, holding Paul's backpack in one hand. Paul stood and followed him.

Chad sighed. *Well, it's finally happened. Now the whole school knows Paul's gay.*

It hadn't been very hard to get the nurse to agree to let Paul go home for the day. Apparently, there was some kind of twenty-four-hour flu going around. Nobody wanted to keep people around who might throw up at any moment. The only problem had been figuring out how to get him home. Eventually, they'd called Chad's mom. She agreed to pick him up, and Chad had gone off to class with a note excusing him for being late.

The news about Paul spread quickly. A couple of people tried to ask Chad about it. "Get lost!" he snarled. They all backed off.

Chad wasn't in any mood for comments from the other soccer players he usually ate lunch with, so he spent lunch period wandering around outside and thinking.

"Hey, Mortensen." It was Rich Grober, one of the guys he and Paul had their traditional end-of-school sleepover with.

"Yeah?"

"You coming to the party this year?"

Chad stared at him. "Is Paul invited?"

"That faggot!"

I guess they heard already.

"If he's not coming, I'm not coming." Chad heaved his backpack onto his shoulders and started walking again.

"You a faggot too?"

Chad hesitated. He thought about telling Rich to eff off, but his sense of self-control got the better of him — something he'd noticed was happening more often these days — and he pushed on without saying anything.

I should be more upset about this, he thought as he walked. *It's, like, social suicide. At least with the guys I hang out with, the ones on the soccer team and people like that.* He knew for sure that if the school had found out Paul was gay back in eighth grade, Chad would have ditched him so fast people could have seen the skid marks. *Heck, if I'd known he was gay back in eighth grade, I probably would have ditched him even if other people didn't know.* But things were different now.

A lot of it, Chad was sure, was just because he was older now. He'd made choices that had turned him into a different person. Part of it, though, was simply because Paul had been such a great friend to Chad.

Friendship's worth more than popularity. More than having an easy time of it with the other kids. Sometime during the last few months, in the middle of all the drama with Paul, that had become really clear to him.

Chad had never thought much about friendship and what it meant. He still didn't feel really comfortable thinking about it. Friends were just . . . people you did things with and liked to spend time with. People you could make dumb jokes with. You could punch them and they'd punch you back, and somehow it wouldn't really matter. Friends weren't something you thought about; friends were part of the way you lived.

So what does being Paul's friend do for me? Paul listens. He calms me down. Helps me get past things when I feel so frustrated I could yell and scream and punch walls. Instead, he says something stupid that makes me laugh.

Paul was pretty much always there for him.

And then last year, he'd told Chad he was gay.

Chad remembered the panicked look on Paul's face when they'd talked. He hadn't recognized it at the time, but thinking about it now, it was clear that Paul had been wondering if Chad would still be his friend after finding out that he was gay. But he'd told him anyway. It took a lot of guts to do that.

He trusted me. Before he trusted anyone else in the world. After something like that — after everything we've been through this last year — I don't think I could ever choose not to be his friend.

Barbara was surprised to see Paul home already when she got off work at 3:00.

"So what happened?" she asked.

Paul grunted. "Sick."

"Really sick, or nervous-stomach sick?"

He gave her a . . . subdued look, she guessed she'd call it. "Nervous stomach, I suppose." There was a pause. "I'm out at school now," he mumbled.

"You're what?"

"I'm out at school now," he repeated, a little more loudly. "They know I'm gay."

"How? Who?"

Paul told her all about it. The tension in GSA since he started going back. The big argument about gay marriage. The scene with the banner that morning, with the other boy shouting that Paul was gay in front of the whole school. How Chad found him in the restroom and helped him to the nurse's office, then called Sandy to bring him home.

Partway through, Barbara put her arm around Paul. He scooted up next to her on the couch. Slowly she stroked his hair as he explained.

Finally he finished.

Barbara waited a moment to try to figure out what to say. "So just how bad is this?"

Paul took a deep breath. "Maybe not that bad. I mean, this is a pretty liberal town. Several GSA kids are out at school. I haven't heard about much bashing at school. Gay-bashing, I mean. Yeah, they get rude comments from some people, but that's pretty much as far as it goes, I think."

"That's good, I suppose."

Paul was staring off into the distance, like he hadn't really heard what she said. "It's just—I didn't want it to happen this way, you know? I wanted people to know only if I told them, if I felt like I could trust them."

"You thought you could trust the other kids in GSA."

"Yeah. And then—" He looked at her. "I don't think I've ever had someone be mad at me just because I'm a Mormon."

"But now someone has been."

Paul nodded.

"And now everyone knows you're gay."

"Yeah."

"Are you okay going back to school tomorrow?"

"Yeah. I think so." He couldn't completely hide the look of dread on his face.

"Paul."

"Yeah?"

"We'll get through this, all right? You let me know if this—all this stuff starts getting too hard, all right? I've seen those statistics about gay teens and depression. Promise me you'll talk to me if things start getting worse."

"Okay."

"Do you promise?"

"Yeah. I promise."

"All right then." Barbara pulled him closer to her. He leaned in and put his head on her shoulder. She was reminded that he was taller now than she was.

She spoke softly into his hair. "You know how the gospel tells us that families can be together forever?"

"Yeah." His voice was equally soft.

"I don't know exactly what that means. Children grow up, after all, and stop living with their parents. Maybe it means that you and—that your house will be in the same subdivision as mine in the celestial kingdom." Her voice turned momentarily sour. "I surely am not interested in being married to your father eternally, so if you're holding out for that, better think again. Eleven years with him was long enough."

Paul gave a shaky laugh. "I kind of figured that, Mom."

"Anyway, my point is that whatever it means to be together with your family eternally, the thing that makes me happiest in this life is the thought that, somehow or other, you'll stay connected to me after this life." She shook her head. "Maybe sometime, somewhere, I'll find someone else to marry, someone to share my life with. Even if I don't, though, just being together in a family with you would be reason enough to feel like it was all worth it. That was true when you were a child, and it's become even truer as you've become a young man. Your being attracted to boys hasn't changed that at all."

Barbara could feel Paul shaking as she talked. *Crying into my shoulder.* It had been years since he'd done that. Finally, he pulled away from her, wiped his eyes, and smiled at her a little blearily.

"Thanks," he said. "I needed that." Then Paul went upstairs to do—something, maybe blow his nose—and Barbara got up to work on her errands of the day.

I thought that all went without saying, Barbara reflected as she was putting together her shopping list. *I was sure he knew without me telling him. I'm glad I decided to say it anyway.*

The next day wasn't quite as bad as Paul had expected.

"Always knew you were a fag" was probably the most puzzling comment he got. He heard it twice: once from someone he'd known on the soccer team, and once from a girl in his Spanish class. He couldn't think of any time either of them would have had a reason to speculate about his sexuality. As far as he could remember, neither of them had said anything about him being gay before.

And then there was his conversation after school with Janice, walking home by way of a park that was nowhere near the direction of his house. *Why is it that when I walk with girls, I wind up going the way they want to go, instead of the way I want to go?* Paul guessed it was one of those male-female mysteries he'd never figure out.

"Look," Janice said. "If you want me to, I can pretend we've been dating. I can even make the girls think I've had to, um, discourage you from going too far."

Paul hesitated, looking for a diplomatic way to turn her down. "I doubt it would help that much. Anyway, I'd just as soon not lie to people. I'd have to keep on lying for the next two years until I graduate. I'm not that good of an actor."

"I'm just saying. If you want to give it a try."

"No, thanks."

She nodded, as if his response was what she'd been expecting.

They'd almost reached the edge of the park. Instead of continuing on toward her house, though, Janice turned onto a path that looped off toward the left. Apparently she didn't think the conversation was over yet.

"Look," Paul blurted. He figured this might be his only chance to ask without Chad being around. "There's something I've been wondering . . ."

"What?"

"Why'd you ditch Chad after the Valentine's dance?"

Janice didn't say anything at first. "I like Chad," she finally started, a little hesitantly. "He's a good guy. I thought it would be fun to date him for a bit. Good experience for me, good for him. Nothing too serious. And I was pretty sure he wouldn't turn into an octopus on me. You know. Wandering hands and everything."

Paul nodded, though internally he wasn't so sure. He guessed that Chad would be pretty grabby if he thought he could get away with it. But then, Janice had Chad pretty intimidated. If he ever did get out of line, Paul was sure she'd be able to handle it without any problem.

"It was kind of like play-acting," she continued. "Not really real. Just practice. That's how it was supposed to be, anyway."

He looked at her. "That's pretty cheap, isn't it? Dating a guy when it doesn't mean anything to you?"

She shook her head. "Look, this is one of those places where I think the church standards make sense. Kids our age aren't supposed to be in real relationships. We're trying things out. Not sex," she continued as Paul opened his mouth to make a smart comment. "But dating. Guys talking to girls. Girls getting used to spending time with Neanderthals—I mean, guys."

Janice paused. "You know how church leaders are always telling us we're supposed to date a lot of different people?"

Paul nodded.

"I don't know how it is in other places or for you guys, but for girls in our school, that's social suicide. You date a lot of different guys, you'll get labeled as a slut. Hanging out's fine, but once you start dating it's all about monogamy and faithfulness. You date someone twice and then date someone else, you're cheating on him."

"So why'd you dump Chad, then?"

Her smile faded. "It seemed to me . . . I thought he was starting to get attached. Taking it seriously, you know? That wasn't something I thought would happen."

"And you were interested in pursuing other options," Paul guessed, remembering Chad's unhappy speculations about the other guy at the Valentine's dance.

Now it was Janice's turn to blush. "Yeah. Guess you know about that."

"*Chad* knew about that. You must have been pretty obvious."

"Hey! I've got hormones too, you know. I notice good-looking guys."

Paul shook his head. "I can't believe I'm talking to a girl about her hormones."

"You're not. You're talking to Janice. A person, not a girl." Her tone was a little sharp.

"You know, that's still a pretty crappy way to treat someone. Pushing a guy away because he's starting to like you more."

"Better to get it over and done with, I thought."

"Maybe." He looked at her skeptically. "And of course you were thinking about Mister Distracting from the dance."

She rolled her eyes. "Tony Culvert, from the third ward. I danced with him a couple times at the next stake dance. He didn't take his eyes off my chest the entire time."

Paul grinned. "Too much information."

"It was pretty creepy, believe me. I felt like I was just a pair of boobs attached to, well, nothing he was really interested in." She shook her head. "I would have done better to stick with Chad."

"You know, I'm pretty sure Chad likes boobs too. In fact, as his best friend I can definitely state that Chad notices boobs on girls."

"Yeah, but at least he made an effort not to talk *to* my boobs."

Paul shook his head. "So Chad has some manners. Who would have thought?" They grinned at each other.

Out of the corner of his eye, Paul noticed several guys approaching from another direction—including Randy from the soccer team, one of the guys from the poster incident back in December. *Time to get out of here.* "Anyway, thanks for the offer. About pretending to be my girlfriend, I mean. I wish that was something I could do for real." Then he quickly walked off in the direction of his house.

Janice watched Paul go. His sudden departure surprised her, until she noticed the other guys approaching. She guessed he wanted to leave before they noticed him and started hassling him.

Janice clenched her fists. *It's always the nice ones who seem to get it the worst.* Fortunately, it seemed the three boys hadn't seen Paul, since they passed without making any comment.

She was glad, mostly. *I don't have to find out if I'm mad enough to punch someone if I hear a fag comment. No matter how satisfying it might be.* Shaking her head, Janice took off for home.

Wednesday morning, June ninth. Telephone call from Sister Hart.

"Sandy?"

"Yes?"

"We have the petitions. Can you come around and pick them up?"

"Sure."

"Great! Then you can just let me know when you've had a chance to collect signatures from your ward."

"Will do. Thanks for thinking of me."

One more thing to juggle, thought Sandy. *But it's for a good cause. And it'll make a nice break from interior design and taking care of kids. A refreshing change from trying to tell people tactfully that their design ideas are garbage and getting into power struggles over chores and schedules.*

Chapter Nineteen

THE DAY AFTER SCHOOL LET OUT, four days before Paul was scheduled to go work as a counselor at Beaver Lodge Scout Camp, he tripped going down the front steps of his house.

"No doubt about it," said the doctor after examining his foot and taking an x-ray for good measure. "You'll be in a cast for a good six weeks." And that was the end of Paul's plans to be a camp counselor that summer.

His response was a massive teenage sulk.

His mom made a vain attempt to cheer him up, but he wouldn't have any of it. Finally she snapped. "You know what? You're right. Every single bit of your summer is going to be completely miserable, so there's really no point in me doing anything to make it any better." Then she stalked out of the room, leaving Paul with the uncomfortable feeling that although he might have succeeded in his short-term goal of showing just how unhappy he was, he'd made a rather bad strategic blunder in terms of his own long-term interests. Fortunately, after they'd spent a few hours apart, several apologies seemed to bring him out of the danger zone.

Chad told him he didn't know a good thing when he had it. "I mean, look. No lawn mowing. No job. No putting up with twelve-year-old brats. No summer chores to speak of. Just as much time as you want sitting around playing video games."

Chad was starting a job with the grounds crew that took care of the city parks. They'd liked the work he did for his Eagle project the previous summer. "Mom and Dad got into a big argument about it," Chad said. "Mom wanted me around so I could help with the kids while she's doing her interior design stuff. Dad said it was more important for me to get a job and learn responsibility."

"Huh."

"At least I'll get paid for it. I figure it's gotta be better than watching Jeffrey and Emily."

Paul didn't really agree, but he could see how it might be that way for Chad.

What it all added up to, though, was that there wasn't a lot Paul could look forward to doing over the next month and a half. Most of the time, Chad wouldn't be around because of his job. And after the whole blowup at school, Paul didn't feel like calling around to find out just how wrecked his social life was.

He certainly didn't feel like contacting any kids from GSA. When Jessica and Penny had talked to him just before school let out, he'd done his best not to show just how upset he was. Things hadn't gone as well, however, when Sarah tried to apologize.

"Paul! You have to know I'm really, really sorry about what Jose did—"

"Whatever," Paul had interrupted. "So GSA is this place where you can be safe, huh? Where everyone's so tolerant and respectful. Tell me that one again!"

"Like I said, I'm sorry!"

"Yeah, well, sorry doesn't exactly fix anything, does it."

Sarah hadn't made any answer to that, and Paul hadn't been in a mood to talk about it any longer.

Sitting with his cast stretched out on the coffee table in front of him, Paul shook his head. *It's not like I want to hang out with them anyway. After everything that's happened, I'd be just as happy if I could get through high school without seeing any of them ever again.*

Sandy had hoped things would get less hectic after school let out for the summer and Chad was more available to help out. Instead, her schedule was starting to look more impossible than ever.

Margaret had been pleased with how the first few consultations went, so now she'd started sending Sandy off on her own more often. The older woman would do an initial survey, jot down some notes, and then dispatch Sandy to work with the client more in depth. It was the sort of thing Sandy had hoped would happen, but the timing could have been a lot better—especially considering Chad and his summer job.

The very thought made her want to grind her teeth. Apparently, Richard thought it was more important for her teenage son to have a pointless, dead-end summer job, even if it ruined her chance to do something with her interior designing. She really should have known better than to believe he'd support her decision to get out and get a job of her own.

Sure, it's fine just as long as it doesn't get in the way of me being a perfect housewife, mother, maid, tutor, chauffeur —

Sandy rubbed her forehead. She was getting a headache.

Several more consultations today. And then —

She glanced at the calendar. *I really need to collect some more ballot petition signatures next week. I'll have to fit that in somehow.*

Richard looked out over the ward.

Second Sunday in June already, he thought. School had let out earlier that week, and several families were already gone on summer vacation.

The prelude music ended. As Richard's first counselor stood to start the meeting, he saw Sister Ficklin enter the chapel, followed by Paul on crutches. *I wonder what the story is behind that?*

As the two of them made their way toward their normal place near the front of the chapel, Richard noticed a sudden buzz of whispering and staring from the youth of the ward. He glanced over at Chad at the sacrament table. From his son's tight jaw and clenched fists, it looked like Chad had noticed — and like he was angry about it.

This doesn't look good.

Richard didn't find out what it was all about until priesthood meeting.

During opening exercises, Richard noticed Paul and Chad sitting together off to one side, pretty far away from any other young men. *Whatever's wrong, I guess it isn't a problem between the two of them.*

Then the priests filed into the bishop's office for their quorum meeting. Once again, Richard noticed that Paul was sitting on one end with Chad between him and the other boys.

The Young Men president asked what had happened to Paul's foot. He blushed as he told them about tripping on his front steps. The boys snickered. One made a comment Richard didn't catch, but it made Paul and Chad both turn red — Paul with what looked like embarrassment, and Chad with anger.

The lesson that day was on practical preparation for a mission.

Partway through, one of the boys raised his hand. Smirking at Paul, he asked, "So what about fags? Gays, I mean? Are they allowed to serve missions?"

I guess Paul's secret came out.

The shuttered look on Paul's face tightened, while Chad glared at the speaker. If it hadn't been for the two adults in the room, Richard was sure that words—and probably fists—would have started flying.

Richard spoke briskly. "Whether someone is attracted to other males or to females is irrelevant, if they're worthy to go on a mission. That's an issue that should be discussed between the bishop and the young man involved." He continued without a break. "So, can anyone suggest other ways to prepare in the area of household skills?"

And that was it until the end of the meeting, when a couple of boys knocked against Paul on the way out the door as he was getting onto his crutches. The second time, Chad kicked the boy on the back of his calf.

"Ow! Jerk!"

"Oops. Sorry." Chad's voice was full of insincerity as he repeated what the other boy had just spoken as he knocked into Paul's crutch.

Later that evening, Richard got the complete story from Chad. He winced when he heard about the scene in the school courtyard.

"So just how hard is this going to be for him, do you think?"

Chad shook his head. "I dunno. All I can say is, it's a good thing he's not playing soccer anymore."

"The team's pretty worked up about it?"

"You know it."

"Will it be okay for you, being his friend?"

Chad looked him in the eyes. "If it isn't, I'll deal with that."

Richard nodded. "Good."

Boring and uncomfortable. That pretty much summed up Paul's first full week of summer vacation.

He tried reading, but somehow now that he had plenty of time to read, he couldn't seem to get into anything. *I guess I'm not really a genuine bookworm after all. Just a geek who happens to like books.*

He tried poking around in his video games. A couple of summers back, he'd spent a lot of time playing RPGs—role-playing games. His dad had given him some more RPGs that next Christmas, so there were still a couple he'd never played. He flipped a coin between the two games in the Final Fantasy Chronicles set and started playing one of them.

Six hours later, when Chad walked in, he was still playing.

"What you playing?"

"*Chrono Trigger.*"

"What's it about?"

"It's this fantasy/science fiction thing. I'm in the past rescuing Queen Leene so I can get Marle back. Just shut up and watch."

So Chad did, for about ten minutes. Then he started whining about how boring it was sitting there watching someone else play a video game and how it was Paul's fault for not being a better friend and keeping him entertained.

"Fine. Just let me make it to a save zone. Then we can get out *Soulcalibur II.*"

"Ha! Prepare to get your ass whupped."

They played for a couple of hours, until Chad had to go home.

Paul was playing *Chrono Trigger* again the next day when Chad stopped by.

"So where are you now?" Chad asked.

"Back in the year six hundred. Rescuing Queen Leene again"

"I thought that's what you were doing yesterday."

"Yeah, well, when I got back to the present, I got arrested and sentenced to death for kidnapping the princess. So I found an FAQ online. It said that if I do some things different at the beginning of the game, the jury'll find me innocent instead of guilty."

"That's lame. You mean you had to restart the whole game?"

"I didn't *have* to. No matter what I do, I'll still get thrown in prison and have to escape, even if the jury decides I'm innocent. But it's cooler if I'm innocent. Besides, I got the doll of me first this time, so I can get rescued after I get killed later in the game."

"The doll of you?" Chad shook his head. "Whatever." He paused. "So what're you going to do with your summer besides play the perfect *Chrono Trigger* game?"

"I dunno. Wait for my foot to heal, I guess."

"That's lame."

"Yeah, literally."

Paul reached a stopping place and saved the game. Chad spoke again. "How's your Eagle coming along?"

Paul hesitated while popping in the *Soulcalibur II* disk. "I've still got a couple merit badges to finish up. That and my project. Didn't think I'd have time for it this summer."

"You've got plenty of time now."

"Yeah. And a big fat cast." Paul's original plan had been to do something like what Chad had done last summer with clearing the brush in one of the parks. But there was no way he wanted to try something like that while his foot was broken.

"There's gotta be something you can do, even with a cast."

Paul snorted. "Yeah. Sure."

"Really. Think about it, okay?"

"Mom?"

"Yes, Chad."

"You do a lot of volunteer stuff, right?"

"Yes." She sounded . . . wary, Chad decided. As if she was waiting to find out if he was trying to trick her into something. *Not this time.*

"I was just wondering if you had any ideas for something Paul could do for his Eagle project with his broken foot."

His mom's eyes narrowed. Not the look that meant she was mad, but one that meant she was thinking.

"He's in a cast, right?"

"Yeah."

"On crutches."

"Yeah."

"Hmm."

Chad waited a few seconds. "Mom?"

She blinked. "Oh. Yes. I'll, um, think about it, okay? Let you know what I come up with."

"Great!"

Chad smirked to himself. *No way does Paul get to sit around the house playing video games while I'm working. Besides, it'll be good for him to do something constructive with his time. Really, he should thank me for being such a good friend.*

Now that was a good meeting, Richard thought. *It's really inspiring the way the church is using new technologies like that.*

It was Saturday morning. Richard had just spent a couple of hours up at the church watching a training broadcast from Salt Lake

City about bishops and the Aaronic priesthood. President Hinckley's talk had been especially inspiring, but really the whole meeting had been very good. Richard had taken a good six or seven pages of notes, and he was looking forward to reading the transcript when it came out.

He pulled into the driveway, parked the car, then went into the kitchen to make himself a sandwich. On his way in, he saw Sandy sitting on the couch in the living room. He poured a glass of milk and put his sandwich on a plate, then went in to sit with her while he had a quick lunch.

"Where's everyone?"

"Out." Sandy sounded distracted, like she was thinking about something else. "Jeffrey and Emily are out with friends, Chad's over at Paul's house." She paused, then looked at him more directly. "Did you know some of the ward members think Chad is Paul's boyfriend?"

Richard almost choked on a mouthful of milk. "What?"

"It's true. I was calling around, asking people if they wanted to sign that petition for the anti-gay-marriage ballot initiative. Sister Cutler said she was surprised, since our son is gay."

"You know that's not true, don't you?"

She shook her head irritably. "It's obvious Chad's not gay."

You didn't seem so confident about it last year, Richard remembered, but he didn't say anything. Instead he asked, "So what did you do?"

"I told her Chad wasn't gay and left it at that. Later on, though, Janet Moseley told me the rumor is that Paul and Chad were both outed at school and are boyfriends. She said she didn't believe it but thought I ought to know." She looked at him again. "Did you know that's what people are saying?"

"No one mentioned it to me. I did know that Paul was outed at school, just before school got out."

"And now it's spilled over onto Chad."

He gave her a sharp look. "I would think you'd be happy that our son is loyal to his best friend, despite social rumors."

She snorted. "I'm not happy with anything about this whole situation." Richard was going to respond, but she continued. "I'm not saying this is Paul's fault, though getting outed at school is just plain idiotic. I also know it wouldn't make the slightest bit of difference if I told Chad to stay away from Paul. He made that abundantly clear last fall."

"He's a lot like you. Once he decides something, no one really stands much chance of changing his mind."

She gave a short, humorless laugh. "Oh, fine. So you're saying our oldest son has inherited a trait that's gotten me into trouble pretty much all my life."

"It's not a completely bad thing, either in him or in you." Richard paused. "So how many signatures did you get?"

"Some. I'm going to try for more tomorrow. I've got a couple of consultations today, plus some errands. Emily needs new clothes, and I need to go online and get the automatic payment straightened out on the electric bill."

"Tomorrow'll be another long day at the church, I'm afraid. I'll be home long enough for dinner and family home evening, but then there's a fireside I need to go back for."

And just like that, what had been a pleasant and relaxed conversation went up in flames.

"Well. Nice of you to stop by. Let me know the next time your busy schedule lets you drop in for a short visit."

"It's not—"

"Not what?"

"Look, you know our family is my highest priority—"

As it turned out, that was possibly the worst thing he could have said.

"You're right, I do! That's why you spend all your evenings at home with your family. That's why you come home after church on Sundays. That's why you spend Saturdays playing with your kids and helping out your wife around the house. Except, wait—you don't do any of those things after all, do you?"

Sandy's glare could have cut through metal. "A couple months ago," she continued, "Ella asked if I thought you were having an affair. I laughed it off, because I knew—I absolutely *knew*—there was no way you were having an affair with anyone. But—"

"Sandy, I swear—"

"I *know* you're not having an affair!" It was almost a scream. "I *know* the reason you aren't home has nothing to do with wanting to spend time with someone else!" Her eyes flashed. "I almost wish you *were* having an affair! At least that way I'd have something to point to, something to look at and say, there, that's why he isn't home!"

They stood there for a moment, staring at each other. Richard had no memory of when they'd moved from sitting to standing.

"Why didn't you tell me, if you need more help at home?"

Another mistake. "I've been telling you that for the past year!" she shouted. "But you never listen! Just last week I was saying how much I need Chad to stay home and take care of the kids while I'm consulting, but oh, no, Chad had to have his summer job. You didn't even talk to me about it—you just announced that was the way it was going to be!" She took a deep breath. "Richard, it's really not about me needing more help. It's about you not being here when I need you to be here, when the kids need you to be here!"

"I'm doing what I can!" Dimly, Richard realized that he was shouting back. "I do what I have to do at work. I've got things I have to do as bishop—I just spent two hours hearing about all the things I need to be doing as a bishop. The very *last* thing I need is for my wife to tell me oh, so sorry, I'm starting my *career* now, so hey, you need to put your responsibilities on hold, put our children's lives on hold, just so I can—"

And then, horribly, they discovered they weren't alone in the house after all, as Chad stormed in from the TV room.

"Shut up! Just shut up, both of you!" Chad's face was dark red. "You're both— You—" He closed his eyes and swallowed.

"I thought you were over at Paul's house." The minute Richard said it, he realized how stupidly unimportant it was.

"Paul's mom brought us back."

The sick feeling in Richard's stomach grew. *We really blew it this time.* "Paul's in the TV room?"

"Yeah." Chad glared at them both. "We could hear you shouting." He swallowed again. "Just—try not to be so loud. Work it out, okay?" Then he turned and stomped off. A few seconds later, the door to the TV room slammed shut.

Richard turned to look at Sandy. Her face was cold and blank. In the early days of their marriage, he'd thought that look meant she didn't care about things. Finally, he'd realized it was a mask she put on when she was upset and didn't want to seem vulnerable.

Richard knew he had a choice. If he just walked away from this argument the way he wanted to—just went off by himself so he didn't have to be in the middle of this, somewhere he could just not think about all the nasty things he and Sandy were saying to each other until the adrenalin had time to pass—

That might help him feel better right now. But what kind of marriage would he have tomorrow, next week, next year—whenever Sandy finally got tired of waiting for him to talk?

Sometimes a man had to put his hand into the fire.

"Can we go upstairs, Sandy?"

Sandy stared at Richard.

She had a choice. She could hold onto her anger and watch things sink a little bit more. Or she could—well. She couldn't just pretend this was okay, the way Richard always wanted to.

I'll let him talk. But if he tries to avoid the issue or make it all my fault—

Chad threw himself onto the couch next to Paul and scowled.

"I can't believe it. They get after me for being all immature and not controlling my temper—"

He noticed that Paul wasn't looking at him. Instead, he was staring at the floor. Looking at Paul more carefully, Chad could see that he was shaking slightly.

The door opened. His dad poked in his head. "Your mother and I are going upstairs now." His voice was quieter than usual. "You can come out and get snacks from the kitchen, if you want." Then he closed the door again.

"This really sucks," Chad said. Paul didn't say anything.

Richard looked at Sandy carefully. They were up in their bedroom. He was sitting on the bed, and she was sitting on the chair near the side table.

He had to get this right. But he had no idea what to say.

Asking a woman to tell you more about what she's feeling is never a mistake.

"What's the worst problem—the thing that's bothering you the most right now?"

Sandy examined Richard through narrowed eyes. *Well, at least he had the brains to ask me a question and not just charge in like he already knows everything. I guess I should give him a useful answer.*

She waited a good half-minute, to give what she was saying more emphasis. "The biggest problem," she started finally in a clipped tone, "is simply that you're *not home* enough. I'm tired of it. The kids are tired of it." She could see his mouth tightening, no doubt biting back whatever comment was in his mind. "You're just plain *not here*."

Richard swallowed. Opened his mouth and closed it again. Licked his lips. "I—" He swallowed again. Sandy watched, fascinated. *I wonder what's going through his head?* "So . . . what, exactly, is the problem with me not being at home?"

Sandy stared at him. Before she could say just how stupid Richard's question was, he continued. "I'm not denying there's a problem. I'm just trying to understand exactly what the problem *is*."

Sandy stared at him some more. "This family doesn't work as well when you're not here. *I* don't work as well when you're not here. I'm not as good as a mom. I'm not as patient. I get snappy with the kids. I get snappy with *you*. I feel like I'm on my own." She drew a deep breath, struggling to steady her voice. "I don't know what you want. I don't know what *we* want. There's no sense of *us*. I feel like I'm flying blind." She managed to laugh. "We both make stupider decisions when we don't talk to each other. And I *miss* you." She could feel her mouth tightening. "Me doing my thing and you doing your thing wasn't our bargain back when we got married. We were supposed to be partners." She was appalled to hear her voice waver on the last few words.

"You're doing great as a mother."

Sandy's temper flared. "When I tell you I'm *not* doing well as a mother, I expect you to respect my judgment instead of just dismissing what I say!"

Richard looked like he'd been slapped. *Good. Shake him out of his optimistic little fantasy world.*

"But every time we talk about the kids, we wind up arguing."

"Well, that's a pretty good clue that we need to talk some more, isn't it?"

"You sure don't act like you want to hear about it when I disagree with you."

Sandy closed her eyes and took a deep breath. "*Of course* I don't like it. I especially don't like it when you just make decisions without *talking to me* about them, which is something you've been doing way too much lately." She snorted. "You talk a good game about unrighteous dominion and not ordering people around, but when it comes right down to it, things end up going your way whenever we disagree."

Richard's nostrils flared. *Good. He's taking this seriously.* "Oh, that is *so* not fair," he said. "Mostly when we disagree, I end up just letting you do things your way. And there's *lots* of things you decide without ever talking to me about them, like that whole 'Chad has to stop seeing his best friend' thing back last fall."

"I admit I lost my temper over that." Sandy grimaced. "It didn't help that Chad was in brat mode at the time. But at least I was talking to you about it. I was telling you the way that I thought things *should* be. And they didn't wind up going that way, did they?"

Her voice was rising. She tried to calm herself before continuing.

"The worst thing isn't the times you make decisions on your own. It's actually a lot harder when you're not around to help with decisions at all. And the very worst part is when you *are* there, but instead of actually giving an opinion you just say, 'Yes, dear,' or 'Whatever you decide is fine with me.' "

"Don't you want me to support your decisions?" Richard asked.

"It's not called *supporting* me when you just sit back and force me to decide everything by myself! That's more like—I don't know. Abandonment. Acting like you don't care at all. Making it my fault if something goes wrong. It's like—*every time* we disagree about something, you just back off and become even less involved. Leave me to do it all on my own!"

"I thought that was what you wanted. Just to be left alone so you could do things the way you wanted."

Sandy closed her eyes in frustration. "Did you ever *ask* if that was what I wanted?"

There was a long silence. Sandy opened her eyes. Richard's face looked—frozen, though whether in anger or shock or frustration Sandy couldn't tell. She was reminded again just how much Richard hated conflict and how badly he'd reacted whenever they'd gotten into shouting matches early in their marriage.

Well, too bad. Conflict exists, and he just needs to deal with it. Not for the first time, she wondered how he ever handled managing people at work. *Except I know how he does it. He gives everyone whatever they ask for, even if it's unreasonable. Whatever the customer wants, that his motto. Whether it's ward members or coworkers or—whatever. Richard simply cannot say no.*

"No," he said at last. "No, I never did ask. I guess I just—assumed," he murmured. There was a kind of bitter, twisted smile on his face that she wasn't sure she'd ever seen before.

Then his expression changed to an earnest, sincere look that she imagined he used in talking to dissatisfied clients. "What can I do to make it better?"

She would never have imagined that such apparently reasonable words could make her quite so angry.

The question hung in the air between them. Then Sandy exploded.

"You—I—" Her eyes narrowed. "This is *not* something you can just make better! I'm not some upset eight-year-old you can distract by getting her an ice cream cone!"

She looked completely furious. Richard had no idea why. "Why are you getting mad at me for trying to fix things?"

"Richard, it is *not your job* to just fix things! It's our job to *work together* on problems like this."

"That's what I thought I was doing!"

"No. You said, 'What can *I* do to make it better?' *I*, not *we*. That's not a solution, it's the same damn problem all over again."

Oh.

"You have a nasty habit of trying to take care of things by doing more yourself, even when you're already doing more than you can handle! It's the same thing that happens whenever you try to make up for someone else's bad planning by paying for a ward event yourself or staying late to help out with a report that it's someone else's job to write. You've got an obsession with solving things. Anytime someone asks you to fix a problem, you try to fix it—*whether or not* it's your job. As a result, you can't be relied on for things that really are your responsibility."

Sandy's comment hit him like a punch to the gut. It was true. And he'd never thought of it as a problem before.

Wait a minute. There's something here that's not making sense. "Look. If you're so overwhelmed by things, then why on earth did you decide to start with this whole interior-decorating thing?"

"Because I was so damn *tired* of it all! Because I was sick of just staying at home and feeling left behind with the kids while you live your life! Because I want to fill up my time with something worthwhile instead of just sitting and *waiting at home* when you aren't here!" She drew a deep breath, then slowly let it out. More quietly, she continued, "And because I like it. I figure it's time I get to do some things that I like, for once."

That's really not fair, Richard thought. *You do a lot of things you want to do. Like redoing the kitchen with the money I earn.* Of course, he didn't say what he was thinking.

And then Richard realized there was something important in what Sandy had just said that he hadn't processed yet.

Sandy's not this perfect, flawless stereotype of the perfect Mormon wife and mother. She puts on a good mask. But she's faking it.

"Richard? What are you thinking?"

"Am I really the person you wanted to marry back when we were twenty-two?"

She stiffened. "What do you mean?"

Richard tried to explain. "It's just—I don't know. I can't really tell if I'm the person you want to be married to right now. And so I was wondering if I ever was that person, or if I've changed, or if you've changed."

Sandy shook her head. "You're making no sense at all."

"Is this really the life you wanted when we first got married?"

She stared at him. "Why would you think it wasn't?"

"Us arguing like this. You wanting to go out and get a job. Resenting the time I put in as bishop." Sandy's face gave a definite twitch when Richard mentioned that one. *First Chad, then Sandy. How did I miss that my family isn't happy with my calling?* "How can that be good?"

Sandy paused before answering. "I don't think arguments are the worst thing that can happen in a marriage," she said at last. "The worst thing is when two people *stop talking* to each other." Her voice lowered. "You asked me if I wanted to be married to you. Is this your way of telling me I'm not the person *you* want to be married to?"

"*No!* That's not what I'm trying to say at all." Richard ran his hand through his hair. "Somehow we just seem to keep talking past each other."

"It's a simple enough concept. *I need you at home more!*"

And then it all started clicking in Richard's mind. What his father-in-law had said several months ago, what Sandy had been saying. It had been right in front of him all this time, he realized, but he'd never really understood what he was seeing.

Being in the church, being married with kids — this is all hard for Sandy. That's the thing she's faking. She tries to pretend it all comes naturally when really it doesn't.

She stayed at home for seventeen years when it wasn't really what she wanted to do. She did it, though, because I thought it was right. Because the church said it was right. Because she believed it was right. And she's been a good mom. Well, mostly. With my help. Her helping me, and me helping her.

She did it because —

Richard remembered Charles telling him about Sandy resenting the church and its expectations when she was growing up. Even though she had a testimony, she hadn't been happy about it.

I had this idea in my head that she was the one who was strong in the gospel. Just because she was raised in the church, just because she knew a lot more than I did about so many things. Just because so many people in the church say that women are more naturally spiritual than men. That had always made Sandy mad whenever someone said it, and Richard never could figure out why.

Maybe she felt like she had to be a perfect Mormon wife and mother because she thought that's what I expected her to be. Looking at Sandy now, he knew that it was true. He could see the fear lurking just underneath Sandy's anger.

Richard had never really thought about what being married to him did for Sandy. Sure, they had fun together, though he felt guilty when he realized just how little time they'd spent doing things together since he was made bishop. *I know what she does for me. I know she makes me try harder to be better. For me, she symbolizes all the things I want to be, all the things I feel like I can become with her help and couldn't be otherwise.*

But what he did for her . . .

He couldn't really put it into words. He just knew somehow he was *important* to Sandy — not just as her husband, but as part of what made it possible for her to be the person *she* wanted to be. He was a necessary part of Sandy's balance.

And then when I was made bishop . . .

She'd said it. *This wasn't our bargain back when we were married. We were supposed to be partners.*

And he'd thought things were fine, thought she'd actually do better if he let her take care of house and family and all that stuff on her own while he was off doing bishop-type things.

He'd been utterly clueless. And then the final piece clicked into place. *Yeah, she likes interior design. It's probably even a good idea now that the kids are in school a lot of the day. But part of why she's so desperate is so she can have something else to do with other people, other grownups. Because I'm not around.*

• • •

Like most women she knew, Sandy liked to talk about just how dense her husband was, especially about communication and relationships. Despite that, she knew that in reality Richard was a bright man. In fact, he was very good at figuring people out, when he took the time to do it. Watching the distracted look on Richard's face reminded her of that fact again.

I wonder what he's thinking.

And then his eyes focused, and he was looking at her.

"I think I get it now," he said in a quiet voice. "I am so very sorry." He held out his arms, and then the two of them were embracing each other, his hands stroking her back.

"We can work it out," he whispered into her hair. Feeling his tears splash on her neck and shoulder—and her own tears run down her cheeks—Sandy began to hope. *Something has changed,* she thought. *I think he really has figured out what I was trying to say. Maybe we actually can work things out.*

Chapter Twenty

Wow. I had no idea Chad's folks ever argued like that.

Paul was having a hard time understanding why Chad wasn't more upset, until his friend explained.

"They used to get into shouting matches like that all the time back when I was, I dunno, seven or eight. It's calmed down a lot since then." He shrugged. "Sure, I don't like it when they yell at each other. But maybe this way they'll figure something out, you know? I mean, it wasn't really working with them not talking about things and my mom just getting mad all the time. Maybe this'll be better."

It didn't make any sense to Paul. The only memories he had of his mom and dad arguing were from the year or two before their divorce. But apparently it worked for Chad's parents.

The day after the argument, Chad told Paul about some of the changes his parents said they'd be making. Chad's mom was still going to do interior design, but only some days of the week. Chad would help with babysitting, but he'd also have time to hang out with friends when he wasn't working.

Chad's dad, meanwhile, was going to spend more time at home and less time at work and up at the church. Chad was skeptical about that, saying he'd believe it when he saw it. But at least they seemed to be trying.

Is that what marriage is all about? Yelling and getting mad, and then making up again? I thought that if people really loved each other, they wouldn't have arguments like that to begin with. Paul hated conflict. The thought that it might be something couples couldn't avoid in a marriage made him wonder if he even wanted to be married at all.

Not that I'm certain I'll be able to get married anyway. What with being gay and all.

A few weeks ago, Paul had been looking over his patriarchal blessing when he started to wonder whether it said anything about getting married and having kids. During one of their priesthood lessons, Brother Williams had said that your future family was usually mentioned in a patriarchal blessing.

So he'd looked and found . . . nothing. Stuff about sharing the gospel and serving in the church and developing his talents, about priesthood callings and blessing the lives of others, but no mention of kids or being married.

I don't know what that means, he'd told himself. *It doesn't necessarily mean anything.* But it made him nervous.

Wednesday night. Activity night for the youth. Three weeks since Paul had come crashing out of the closet like a stack of heavy Christmas boxes, complete with the tinkle of broken ornaments and people yelling at each other to be more careful.

By the end of the evening, Chad felt like yelling at someone. Or killing someone, maybe.

It had all started the minute he and Paul came in the foyer. About half a dozen kids were milling around, waiting for the meetings to start. One of them—Elaine Simpson, a sophomore—sneered, "It's the fag couple, I see."

"Chad's not the fag," Paul said, tightlipped, as he maneuvered his crutches. "That would be me."

She shrugged. "Friend of a fag, same thing."

"Don't let him get too close to you!" This was one of the other priests.

"Don't bend over or he'll—"

"That's quite enough!" interrupted Brother Williams, first counselor in the Young Men presidency. He'd popped up, unnoticed, at the back of the group. "Isn't it time for opening exercises?"

The rest of the evening had been more of the same.

It was a combined activity, which meant in this case that all the teenagers were together in one group doing glow-in-the-dark indoor Siamese-twin soccer. Paul and Chad wound up being tied together as one pair, which Chad admitted to himself was probably for the best, the way things were going. After the lights were turned off, the only way to see where people were—or where the ball and goalposts were, for that matter—was by the glow bracelets that had been tied around everyone and everything. Despite that, a lot of people were evidently able to tell who was who, based on the number of shoves and under-the-breath fag comments they got.

"I'm outta here," Chad muttered as soon as the lights went back on. He didn't even bother to wait for the closing prayer and blessing on the refreshments. Pushing his way out of the cultural hall and into the parking lot, he had to keep reminding himself not to move too fast for Paul's crutches.

"Sorry that had to happen," Paul said on the way home, looking out the passenger window.

"Nothing you should be sorry about. Except that they're a bunch of assholes."

"Yeah. Well, I'm sorry they wound up being assholes in your general direction."

Chad took a deep breath. *My dad's going to hate this, but —* "So whaddaya say we find something else to do on Wednesday nights from now on?"

Paul looked surprised, but grateful. "Sounds like a plan to me."

There were pluses and minuses to having July fourth fall on a Sunday.

Firmly in the plus category, in Richard's opinion, was the excuse it gave to cancel the extra leadership meetings before church. And there seemed to be an extra fervor in the ward's singing of patriotic hymns.

On the minus side was that several ward members apparently felt that July fourth gave them permission to include veiled political endorsements as part of their testimonies.

While Richard had no intention of voting for John Kerry in the fall, he knew there were some good members in the ward who were also Democrats — such as Brother Flanders, who taught at the local university. Richard had seen him spout church history for a full twenty minutes with examples of how church leaders had taken different sides in national debates. He was always insisting that everyone should know you could be a good Mormon and not agree with the Republican party line on everything. *And he's right,* Richard acknowledged. *I just wish he'd find a way to say it without provoking Brother Richie and Sister Rasmussen into returning fire.* They'd lost whole Gospel Doctrine class periods to that in the past.

For the closing hymn, everyone stood to sing "The Star-Spangled

Banner." Then, before everyone could escape to their different Sunday school classes, Richard sent the deacon who'd been assigned to pass messages for the bishopric that day to round up the scoutmaster, the Young Men president, the elders quorum president, and the high priests group leader and ask them to meet briefly in his office.

The men arrived. He greeted them, brought them into the office, and closed the door. They all sat.

"Brethren."

"Bishop."

"I won't keep you very long. I just have a challenge that I need to share with you. One I'm sure the priesthood in this ward are up to accomplishing."

"Just ask, and we'll do it," said the elders quorum president. The others nodded.

"Good," said Richard, smiling. "I'm glad you said that. You know that Paul Ficklin's been working on his Eagle project, cleaning and repairing the children's books at the library." He'd been particularly proud of Sandy for suggesting that idea, which hadn't been done in their area before, as far as he could tell—and which was something Paul could handle with his broken foot.

"I was disappointed to hear that for the group cleanup session this last Friday, the only two people who showed up were Paul himself and my son Chad."

Richard noticed the looks that were exchanged between the scoutmaster and the Young Men president. He continued, "I've told Paul that perhaps the problem was having the cleanup session on a Friday, when people were working. I've suggested that he should ask for volunteers for several afternoons and evenings this coming week and all day Saturday and set up a schedule for people to help out whenever is convenient for them.

"I remember last summer just how pleased I was at the level of support for my son Chad's Eagle project and just how pleased I've been with the level of support for other young men's Eagle projects in the past. All fine young men, just like Brother Ficklin."

Richard leaned forward. "This is a kind of service project that young men can help with, but also older priesthood brethren, sisters, and even children. Anyone older than about eight or so. It's a fine project, a service to the community. It's a good thing for our ward, a good way to be involved and heighten positive recognition for the church. And it's a chance to support one of our fine young men in his worthwhile goals.

"I've asked you here to make sure we continue with this good record of supporting our young scouts. In particular, I'd like each of you to accept an assignment to make sure there'll be people from your groups ready to volunteer when Paul asks for help in priesthood meeting in" — he glanced at his watch — "a little more than an hour from now. Can I count on your support with this?"

They all agreed. *Not that I gave them much choice in the matter.*

That's fine. If I have to remind the priesthood holders about their duty to support one another, then that's something I'm prepared to do.

"Thanks for your help with everything."

Sandy waved a hand dismissively. "It was nothing. Really."

"No. I'm serious." Barbara Ficklin sat down carefully next to Sandy on the bench outside the library. "I know how busy you are these days. I really appreciate the time you've put into it, and I know Paul does too."

Sandy grimaced. She still felt more than a touch of guilt about how she'd first reacted to the news that Paul was same-sex attracted. It was worse now that she knew what it was like to have someone say something like that about her own son, even though it wasn't true.

Back when she first heard one of the ward members calling Chad gay, her initial reaction had been fury. *But he's not gay!* She'd started feeling angry at Paul again for getting Chad into this whole mess. Then she'd seen something that changed her mind.

It had been later the same afternoon when she and Richard had their knock-down-drag-out argument. Chad was holding the car door open for Paul so he could get out more easily with his crutches. They were talking to each other, both of them laughing about something — Sandy couldn't hear through the living-room window. Both of them seemed completely comfortable with each other, just like the friends they'd been for years.

Watching them interact that way, suddenly it didn't make any sense to think of one of them as hers and one of them as someone else's. Instead, the two of them seemed like some kind of collective *they*: two boys helping each other out in the tough business of becoming adults.

Thinking about it from that perspective, Sandy had realized that standing by your friend when the chips were down was simply one of those things boys had to learn in order to become decent men.

She'd been ashamed, then, of her earlier feelings and reactions. When the chance came up for her to help with Paul's Eagle project, she'd seized the opportunity.

"How do you deal with it?" she asked Barbara suddenly. "Not just Paul being . . . whatever. But the attitudes of the ward members. Of people you know." *Of people like I was,* Sandy thought but didn't say.

Barbara gave her a measuring look. "When it comes down to it, it's not really that hard to choose between your child and the rest of the world," she said at last. "You do what you have to do. *Whatever* you have to do."

Sandy couldn't think of anything to say.

"So how are things for you these days?" Barbara asked.

Sandy considered. She wasn't really close to this woman. On the other hand, this was a chance to make things better between them. The two women had never talked about what had happened when Sandy found out about Paul, but there'd been a distinct chill.

"I've been doing interior design consulting with another woman here in Arcadia Heights. We've managed to split it up so I do some work on evenings and weekends, but not all the time."

"That must be challenging. Balancing all those schedules like that."

"Richard's been helping."

It was true. After they'd calmed down from the initial blowup, the two of them had talked for quite a while about how to manage their family's schedule more successfully. It hadn't solved all their problems, but since then, Richard had clearly been trying to be more available for her and the kids. Most important, he'd started *talking* to her, asking questions and listening and actually saying what he thought, though sometimes she still had to push him a bit. And she'd been trying to be more patient and less demanding as well.

Each marriage has to be constantly reinvented, she reminded herself. *What works today won't be the same thing that works tomorrow. I think maybe that was part of the problem all along. We weren't thinking or talking about the way things had to change, but instead we just hoped or assumed things would go on the way they were.*

"That's good," replied Barbara. Sandy had been so involved in her own thoughts that it took her a moment to remember what they'd been talking about. When she did remember, she nodded. *Yes, it's good. Things are good.*

• • •

Bill Lister poked his head into Richard's office. "Richard. I need your help this weekend to shepherd that account through."

Richard groaned internally. On Saturday he was supposed to watch the kids so Sandy could meet several of her clients for some consultations. Saturday evening, they were planning to do something together as a family. And Sunday was . . . Sunday.

Then he said what he knew he had to say. "Sorry. I won't be available."

"Excuse me?"

"You heard what I said. I've got other commitments for this weekend, and I'll be keeping them."

There was a short silence. "You've got prior commitments here."

"No, actually, I don't. The way I see it, I have a commitment to do a job to the best of my ability during my regular work time. That doesn't mean handing over my weekends or my life."

Lister didn't say anything. Richard didn't know if he was just too surprised, or angry, or if he was trying to figure out what to say next.

What the heck, Richard thought. *I might as well get it out in the open.* "The way I figure it, Bill, the company hasn't been keeping its commitments to *me.* I told you when I hired on: no Sundays. You said that was fine. Richardson said it was fine. Then about a year in, you asked if I could help over the weekend with that Elliott account, since things had gone sour at the last minute. I thought, sure, I can give up one Sunday to help us get out of a bind. A one-time thing, you called it. Soon, I was coming in one weekend a month.

"Then this new job in my church came up. I told you the weekends would have to stop. You said sure, fine. And they did stop, for about six months. Then there was the Hoover account. After that, it seemed like you and Richardson figured it was okay to count on me whenever that little extra push was needed.

"I admit, it's largely my fault. Clearly I was too accommodating. I shouldn't have let it go this far. But now I've seen that the more I say yes, the more you assume you can get from me. So now, I'm saying no."

Lister's mouth hung open. More than once, he'd complimented Richard on his straight-talk manner, the way he could switch from being Mister Agreeable and simply lay it out for a customer whose expectations became too unreasonable or with an employee who had screwed things up. Apparently it had never occurred to him that he might be on the receiving end someday.

"Another thing. I know there've been sales bonuses going to some people for accounts I've worked on, bonuses that I haven't received. You can't have it both ways, Bill. If you want me to do the work of a sales rep on top of my regular job, I get a sales rep's pay."

Richard shook his head. "The company's been saving a bundle by having me do half the work of a sales rep on top of my full-time job as a supervisor. I'm okay with that. I think it's good to keep my hand in with sales. Helps me stay current as a supervisor. But you've been treating me like I'm too stupid to notice it. That's not smart. And I haven't been smart to let it go on as long as I have.

"I'm a salesman, Bill. I know my value to this company. I'm no longer sure you do. So run the numbers. If you think you can get better value by hiring someone else to fill my spot, then you do that. Let me know if I've still got a job when you're done."

When Richard left the office, Lister was still standing there looking like someone had knocked him on the head with a two-by-four.

August fifth through seventh. Campout near Topaz Lake for the older boys in Paul's ward. Mostly fun, especially now that Paul's cast was off, except for —

"Fag."

Paul sighed. *This is getting really old.* He turned from where he'd been standing, looking out over the lake.

Two of the other boys were standing about a dozen feet away. The one who'd spoken was Steven Call, one of the older priests who'd been quite vocal about not wanting to be around "queer-o Paul." Beside him was Alan Thompson, the boy who'd replaced Paul as teachers quorum president.

"Hey, fag. I'm talking to you."

Paul rolled his eyes. "And yet you haven't said anything worth listening to."

"Don't know how you got Mortensen fooled, a fag like you."

"Maybe you should ask me," came Chad's voice. Paul couldn't deny the relief he felt as he saw his friend stepping out of the woods. "Not that I'd expect a sausage head like you to actually understand anything I might say." Chad jerked a thumb toward Alan. "Thompson. What're you doing hanging out with a lowlife like Call?"

Steven's fists clenched. "Look, Mortensen. I don't get it. He's the fag, not you. Why're you still sticking up for him?"

"You know, Call, I don't really want to know about your girl-friends and your sex life, which I'm guessing is mostly with your right hand anyway."

Paul couldn't help but snicker at Chad's words. It looked like Alan was trying to hold back a laugh as well.

"I think it's weird that you seem to care so much about another guy's sex life," Chad continued. "Looks pretty gay to me."

Steven's face was bright red. "Shithead," he hissed. Then he turned and stomped off. Alan shot Paul and Chad what looked like an apologetic look, then followed.

"Well, that was really sucky," Paul said as they began walking along the lakeshore.

Chad gave him a disgusted look. "I can't believe you used the word *sucky* in a sentence."

"Well excuse me, Mister Correct Grammar."

"It just sounds so, uh —"

"Gay?"

"You said it, not me."

"Sorry you have to put up with all those dickheads." Paul hesi-tated. "Sure you still want to share a tent with me?"

Chad grabbed Paul's arm and turned him so they were facing each other. He looked almost angry. "Look. We've been over this. Over and over again. I went through that whole 'Can you be best friends with a gay guy?' thing last year. I made my choice."

Paul couldn't think of anything to say. After a few moments, Chad turned away, and they started walking again. Finally Paul responded, "Still, it sucks that *you* have to take all this crap just be-cause *I'm* gay."

"Well, yeah, sure it sucks. Sucks even more for you. Not much of anything we can do about that."

"You could stop hanging out with me."

"And once again I'm telling you that isn't gonna happen."

Another silence. "Thanks," Paul said at last. They finished their walk in silence.

It was Friday night, time for the bishop's campfire devotional.

The idea for the two-and-a-half-day mini-campout with the old-er boys had come from Brother Sanders. "The boys who care about scouting are already making good enough progress," he'd argued. "They've got the high-adventure stuff. Let's just have a campout where the boys can relax and have fun." With difficulty, Richard had persuaded himself to let Brother Sanders make the decision. *Remember what Charles said. Don't try to do his job for him. He's the Young Men president.*

Since they'd hiked in Thursday afternoon, the boys—and their leaders—had swum, hiked, and canoed. There'd been a bit of work done on merit badge requirements too, but it hadn't been the main focus. Judging from the grins and the relaxed attitudes of most of the boys, it seemed to have worked out pretty well, though Richard had noticed that Paul and Chad were keeping their distance from some of the others. Still, at least they were here. It had taken a major sales job to get the two of them to come at all. Richard was pretty sure he wouldn't have succeeded if it hadn't been for Paul's eagerness to do something outdoors now that he finally had his cast off.

"It's been a good day today," Richard said to the assembled group. There were seven young men—three teachers and four priests, counting Chad and Paul. Brother Sanders was there as well, together with his first counselor. "I know it's been a lot of fun for me."

Richard paused, and his voice grew softer. "So let's talk about standards tonight. And guilt, and forgiveness, and being good to other people and to ourselves."

He looked around the campfire. "Who here is perfect?" He waited a second. "No one raising your hands? Surely we've got at least one or two perfect people here."

"You aren't raising *your* hand," Alan Thompson pointed out.

"That's exactly right. And there's a good reason for that. I'm not perfect, no more than anyone else here is. I know all about not being perfect. I didn't grow up in the church, but even without knowing the church standards, it still seemed like I spent a lot of time during my teenage years feeling guilty about the kind of person I was, compared to the kind of person I thought I ought to be."

Richard paused again for emphasis. "Every one of us falls short of where we know we ought to be. I do. You do. Your parents do. The prophet does. I'm sure President Hinckley comes a lot closer than most of us, but I'm also sure there are times when he's disappointed with himself. And I'm sure that back when he was a teenager, he messed up sometimes, just like I messed up when I was a teenager, just like you all mess up sometimes, just like every teenager who ever lived on the face of the planet has messed up—except Jesus, I guess. Joseph Smith messed up too when he was a teenager."

Richard pulled out a folded-up photocopy. "A few years after I joined the church, before I married Sandy, I took an institute class about church history. One of the things I found out was that the First Vision account in the Pearl of Great Price wasn't the only version Joseph wrote. Back in 1832 — six years before the version that's in the Pearl of Great Price — Joseph Smith dictated another account, which is the earliest one we have.

"What's interesting to me is the way the 1832 account focuses on different things from what we usually think about in connection with the First Vision." Richard started reading. " 'I felt to mourn for my own sins and for the sins of the world . . . therefore I cried unto the Lord for mercy . . . and the Lord heard my cry in the wilderness and while in the attitude of calling upon the Lord . . . a pillar of light above the brightness of the sun at noon day came down from above and rested upon me and I was filled with the Spirit of God . . . and I saw the Lord, and he spake unto me, saying, Joseph, my son, thy sins are forgiven thee, go thy way, walk in my statutes and keep my commandments.' "

Richard folded the paper back up again. "It doesn't bother me that the two accounts are different. Whenever any of us talks about something that's happened to us, we tell it a little bit differently from one time to the next, depending on who we're talking to and what we're focused on at the time. That means we can learn different things, sometimes, by looking at different accounts of the same events. That's one reason why we have four different versions of the life of Jesus in the New Testament.

"Anyway, back to Joseph Smith's story. The thing that impresses me about his 1832 account is that the way he tells it here, Joseph's original purpose in going before God had a lot to do with his concern about the welfare of his own soul. He was worried that he wasn't right before God. And the first part of God's message that Joseph tells us about in 1832 is how the Lord reassured him that his sins were forgiven and told him to go his way and keep the Lord's commandments.

"Every one of us labors under a burden of sin and unworthiness. Each of us is guilty before God. We all feel it. In our heart of hearts, a lot of the time we don't really believe that we *can* be worthy."

He paused. The only sound was the crackling of the campfire.

"That's why the atonement is such a miracle. It cleans us. It makes us into better people, people who *want* to do right, who want to be better than we are. And it makes us capable of *becoming* those better people.

"The change doesn't happen all at once. It strengthens every time we pray in sincerity, each time we do something good for other people or make a right choice. The process continues throughout our lives. The miracle is that it *can* happen, that God will reach out to us and bring us along if we will just work with him, despite all our failings and mistakes and weaknesses.

"Each of you has weaknesses. I have my own weaknesses. Some of you have had occasion to talk to me about some of the specific weaknesses you struggle with." Past the glare of the fire, Richard saw small winces from several of the boys, including a couple where he wasn't expecting it. He made a mental note to try to talk to those particular boys sometime in the next few weeks.

"What I'm here to tell you tonight is that all that doesn't matter as long as you keep working with God to get past those weaknesses. The Lord told Moroni, 'I give unto men weaknesses so that they may be humble.' He wants us to come unto him. He wants us to see the path. He wants us to walk the path with him. The pits and snares and potholes we have to get past aren't the important part."

Richard waited to make sure the point had sunk in, then continued. "The other thing is that knowing we're all sinners, knowing we're all guilty and none of us is perfect, means that none of us gets to judge anyone else either."

Richard looked around the fire again. Paul was looking at him, as were Alan and Brother Williams. The others were staring at their feet or at the fire.

"Some of you know about the challenges that some of the rest of you face. Some of those challenges are things that maybe you think are strange or that maybe make you feel uncomfortable. The point is that we don't get to judge other people's weaknesses. God judges you. You don't get to judge anybody else. When it comes to other people's sins and other people's guilt, you have only one responsibility. Can anyone tell me what that is?"

Richard looked around the campfire. To his surprise, Alan raised his hand. Richard was impressed. *A kid who actually volunteers an answer in a heavy-duty discussion.*

He nodded in the boy's direction.

"To, uh, help the person, I guess."

Richard nodded again. "That's right. You help the person in whatever way you can, and you make sure you're not standing in the way of that person repenting and improving. That means you don't make fun of someone because of the challenge that person faces. You don't avoid the person, and you try to be a good friend and not make things harder for that person in any way. Especially, as priesthood holders you have a responsibility to help your fellow quorum members when they're facing challenges. I hope you all will do that."

No one was looking at him. Richard sighed. *I wonder if I succeeded in doing anything except embarrass Paul again in front of the other boys. But I had to try.*

"In the name of Jesus Christ, amen."

Chapter Twenty-One

Even before Paul began cleaning books at the library, he'd finished all his remaining merit badges and started collecting the paperwork he needed to become an Eagle Scout.

For his project, he used the official project workbook to record his plans and the hours everyone put in, with a special emphasis on how he'd called up people and coordinated them to come at different times and bring the various supplies that would be needed, since one of the purposes of the project was to show his leadership skills. Then after that was done, he'd spent quite a few hours writing his statement of ambitions and life purpose and filling out the application form. His goal was to get it done in time so he could have his board of review before taking off to his dad's house the last couple weeks of summer break.

And it had worked. Everyone had cooperated with getting the forms reviewed at the ward level. The people he'd asked to be his references had all agreed. And now it was late Wednesday afternoon, and he and Brother Ellis, his current scoutmaster, were meeting with the board of review up at the stake center.

The first part seemed to go pretty well. There were three men on the board of review, including two who introduced themselves as Brother James and Brother Caldwell and a third who introduced himself as Jim Weaver. They asked about his experiences at different scout camps, earning merit badges and serving as a patrol leader, and about his work as a counselor-in-training the previous summer. Then they spent at least fifteen minutes just asking him about his Eagle project: how he'd gotten the idea, his initial contacts with the library, how he'd recruited people and organized them to help out. He figured they were mostly trying to make sure he'd really done the work, but he didn't mind talking about it. It was kind of fun actually, especially when he got to talk about how tough it had been getting around on crutches and how he'd dealt with that. Several times he noticed them nodding approvingly at something he'd said.

Then Brother James leaned forward and asked, "So what's this we hear about you being a homosexual?"

Paul could feel his stomach clenching. "What do you mean, sir?"

"He means, is it true?" Mister Weaver growled.

Hesitantly, Paul admitted that he was attracted to guys. "But I'm committed to following my church's teachings. That means not living a homosexual lifestyle."

"But you're part of that gay-straight club at school," put in Brother James again. "That Day of Silence thing."

How did he know about that? For that matter, how did they know about me being gay in the first place? I can't believe the bishop would— He swallowed. It probably *was* the bishop. He might not even have seen anything wrong with it. After all, it was an example of Paul's involvement in the community, wasn't it? Or he supposed it might have been his English teacher, who he'd listed as his educational reference. She'd been really pleased with the essay he wrote for the Day of Silence.

Which left the question of how to answer their question.

"That isn't about being homosexual. It's about being tolerant. At least, that's the way I see it." The fact that the GSA group had turned out not to be as tolerant of Paul's Mormonism as he'd hoped was something he didn't want to get into.

"I see." They asked him a couple of other questions about his time in scouting, then asked him and Brother Ellis to leave the room.

About twenty minutes later, they were called back in.

"You've done very impressive work as a Life Scout," Brother Caldwell began quietly. "Your service project meets the standards, and you've filled all the formal requirements to become an Eagle Scout. However, we're concerned about whether you can really be the kind of positive example of scouting and its standards that an Eagle Scout should be, with the kind of involvement you've had in the gay community in your school. And with being known to be homosexual."

"GSA isn't just the gay community!" Paul blurted out. "There's lots of straight kids in it too!"

"Be that as it may, on considering all these factors, we don't feel that we can in good conscience approve you to be advanced to the highest rank in the Boy Scouts." He paused. "I'm sorry."

And that was that.

Paul didn't remember much about the drive home. At first, he felt kind of numb. By the time he got home, though, he was starting to get angry. Going inside the house, he felt grateful that his mom was working late that evening. He really didn't want to see anyone right now.

I did everything I was supposed to do. I earned the stupid merit badges. I did the service project. I put in the hours. I helped with the younger scouts. But they're worried about making me an Eagle Scout because I'm attracted to other guys. He snorted, thinking about some of the other boys he'd spent campouts with. *If they're that worried about scouts being a good example, they really shouldn't have given Zach Peterson an Eagle.*

Thinking about it that way helped him calm down a little. *It's just scouting,* he thought. *Nothing big. Nothing really important in my life.* His thoughts backfired, though, when he started thinking about all the time and effort he'd put into scouting, ever since he was twelve years old and he and Chad had decided they'd make Eagle together. He felt his chest growing tight.

Stupid scouting. Stupid board of review. Paul's mind flashed back over the campouts he'd been on, the overnighters, the day hikes back when he'd been eleven and twelve, including the time he and Chad had been talking so much they didn't catch Brother Timms's instructions and wound up getting separated from everyone else. By the time they got back to the camp, they were an hour late and the others had split up into teams and started looking for them. They were both grounded for a week after that, and Brother Timms wouldn't let them partner up or even sit next to each other for half a year.

And then there was that horrible campout when he was thirteen and had gotten diarrhea. He'd run out of underpants and Chad had loaned him an extra pair. Later, he'd found out that Chad wasn't wearing any himself. When Paul called him a pervert, he shrugged. "I kind of like it," he'd said. "Maybe I'll go like this from now on."

"Yeah, right. Like your mom'll go for that."

"She won't care if she doesn't know." Chad's voice became more enthusiastic. "I could change in the bathroom at school before first period, then change back before we catch the bus or first thing after I get home. She'll never find out."

"You don't think people'll think it's weird for a seventh grader to be stripping in the bathroom? People can see under the stalls, you know. And what if someone sees you carrying your underpants around in your backpack?"

"You worry too much." By which Paul understood that Chad couldn't think of any answers but also didn't care.

Paul suspected Chad had actually gone commando a few times. He shook his head. Chad could be a wild man sometimes.

Thinking about the good times got him feeling better again. He smiled.

The good feeling lasted until the phone rang. He picked it up and heard Chad's voice asking, "So how'd it go?"

Paul froze.

"Dude," Chad laughed. "All I'm hearing is heavy breathing. So tell me about it."

More silence.

"Paul, this zombie-imitation stuff is getting a bit old. Just tell me how it went."

"They didn't pass me."

"What?"

"They didn't pass me."

"Why not?"

" 'Cause I'm known to be a homosexual. That makes me a bad example of Boy Scout values."

"You're shi—you're kidding me."

"That would be a no."

"I can't believe—how did they know about that?"

Paul shrugged. "I dunno. I figure one of my references mentioned something, maybe. Or maybe they heard the rumors on their own."

"That really sucks."

"Tell me about it." And then Paul could feel his throat tightening up, which he absolutely did not want to have happen while he was talking to Chad. "Talk to you later," he choked out, and he hung up. Then he went back to lying on his bed, wishing that his closed eyelids could somehow block both the stream of memories and the tears that were sliding down his cheeks.

When Paul pulled into the clinic parking lot to pick up Barbara, all it took was one look at his subdued expression to tell her something was wrong.

"What happened?" she asked.

For about a minute, Paul didn't say anything. Then he answered, "I'm not a good example of the Boy Scouts. Because people know I'm gay and because I was involved with the GSA."

"What does that mean?"

"I can't be an Eagle Scout."

Barbara took in his quiet voice and the sunken look on his face. *This isn't good. This isn't good at all.*

But the day's problems weren't over yet.

As they were eating a late dinner—Chinese takeout they'd picked up on the way home—the telephone rang. Barbara picked it up.

It was Frank, her ex-husband. "Just calling to congratulate the new Eagle Scout!"

Great. Just what we need.

"Frank," she began carefully. Across the room, she heard Paul draw in his breath. "It's not—things didn't work out so well with the whole Eagle Scout thing."

"What do you mean?"

"The board of review didn't approve his rank advancement." She'd learned the terminology over the years.

There was a pause. "Put Paul on the phone."

Silently, she held out the phone. Paul looked at it like it was a snake that was about to bite him, but he took it anyway.

Barbara tried to stay calm as she listened to Paul's side of the conversation.

"Dad?"

"Yeah, I know."

"I know, Dad."

"Well, it wasn't—"

"It wasn't anything about the Eagle project."

Paul swallowed and looked at his mom. "It's because I'm gay."

"Yeah. That's what I said."

"It got out at school just before summer break."

"No, Dad."

"*No,* Dad."

"Dad, I wouldn't *ever*—"

"Just listen to me, Dad!"

He stood there silent for several more seconds.

"Here." Paul handed the phone back toward her, tears starting down his face.

She took it. "Frank?"

"Barbara." It was Frank's flat, businesslike voice—the same voice he'd used when he told her he'd be staying in Denver from now on. And oh, by the way, the lease was about to lapse on their apartment, and she and Paul would need to find somewhere else to live.

"In light of what Paul just told me, I don't really think he should come out to Minnesota next week."

"What? But his plans—"

"I think it's unwise for someone like him to be around Mikey and Susan."

It was several seconds before Barbara could find her voice. "You think he would do anything—*anything*—to hurt his little brother and sister?"

"That's not something I choose to risk."

Barbara lost the battle to keep her composure. "You—complete—*bastard*," she hissed. "Just because you—"

There was a click, followed by a dial tone.

I could murder the man. I could slice him up into little pieces with a pair of sewing scissors and smash all the pieces in a hydraulic press. But Paul needed her right now.

God tells us to forgive. I'll forgive when my son isn't weeping in my arms because he's just had half his family ripped away from him.

"Bishop, I'd like to get a blessing."

It was Sunday after church. Sister Ficklin had asked if Richard could squeeze in a few minutes to meet with her, and he'd agreed.

"What are your reasons?"

So Richard got to hear all about Barbara Ficklin's current life, from her stresses at work—which she didn't feel she could tell Paul about, since she thought he was dealing with enough already—to the whole nightmare with Paul's board of review, which Chad had already told Richard about, and then the whole appalling thing with Paul's father, which Richard *hadn't* heard about.

Richard had a hard time believing in evil as the result of deliberate malice. Evil as the result of stupidity and pride, on the other hand . . . *Poor kid. Each time things look like they're getting better for him, something like this happens.*

"So. If you could choose what kind of blessing Heavenly Father would give you, what would it include?"

Barbara's eyes closed, as if she was thinking. "A blessing of wisdom, to know how to be a good mother to my son. A blessing of strength, so that I can do and be who he needs me to be. A blessing of charity . . ." Her voice faded.

He waited for a few seconds. When she didn't say anything, he prompted, "Charity?"

Her eyes opened. "Charity. To forgive those who would do such a thing to my child. Especially the man who should have acted as his father and the ward members who should be supporting him, not making his road harder."

"Those are certainly worthy desires." Richard hesitated. "I apologize if there's anything I've done or not done that's made things more difficult for the two of you."

"You don't have anything to apologize for. Unless you're the idiot who told the board of review about Paul's orientation and his involvement in the GSA."

"The subject never came up."

"You—your help, your understanding and acceptance—they've made such a big difference to Paul. Just letting Chad be his friend . . ."

"I doubt I could have done anything to prevent that. Chad hangs on tight."

"He's turning into a fine young man. Like his father."

There wasn't anything really to say to that, so Richard just nodded. Then he asked, "So, are you ready to receive this blessing?"

"Yes."

"What's your middle name again?"

"Elaine."

"Sister Barbara Elaine Ficklin. By the authority of the holy Melchizedek priesthood which I hold . . ."

After Barbara left, Richard sat back in his chair and closed his eyes.

The whole thing about Paul's board of review was immensely frustrating. Richard remembered the look on Paul's face when, as a younger scout, he'd earned his earlier ranks. His enthusiasm. His dependability. The way that he always wore his scout uniform to meetings, something no one else except the leaders could always be counted on to do. His help with the younger boys. How he and Chad had joked about which of them would finish his Eagle first, and how Paul had almost put in more hours on Chad's Eagle project than Chad himself had.

Scouting was a good program. Richard was convinced of that. It could help boys in so many ways. *But how am I supposed to feel good about trusting my boys to scouting when something like this happens?* The more he thought about it, the angrier he got.

I may not be able to do anything about Paul's dad being an S.O.B. But we'll see if I can't do something about Paul's Eagle.

Next morning during Richard's work break, he called up the Boy Scout district commissioner.

"Rex Knight here. Lower Willamette district, Boy Scouts of America. How can I help you?"

"Hi. I'm Richard Mortensen. I'm the bishop of the Arcadia Heights First Ward in the LDS Church. One of my scouts was up before an Eagle board of review last Saturday. Paul Ficklin is his name." Richard did his best to sound crisp and businesslike. *I can always rip his head off later if he gives me any grief.*

"Yes?"

"His rank advancement was refused on grounds that had nothing to do with his qualifications or fitness as a scout. I'm wondering what can be done to correct this clearly mistaken and damaging decision."

Richard heard Knight muttering, "That's right. Weaver talked to me about this." Before Richard could respond, the other man continued in a louder tone, "The boy is gay, right?"

"I don't see what that has to do with his Eagle qualifications."

"Look." The commissioner's voice took on a harder edge. "The scout oath says that boys have a duty to be physically strong, mentally awake, and morally straight. Boy Scouts of America takes the position that being morally straight means not homosexual. That's a position the Mormon church has always supported. Seems pretty odd for a Mormon to be asking for an exception to that rule."

"What rule is that, exactly?"

"Boy Scouts is on record as saying that avowed homosexuals aren't appropriate role models for the values in the scout oath and the scout law. Even went to the U.S. Supreme Court. Part of an Eagle Scout's job is to be a good role model for younger scouts."

"As the boy's pastor, I can tell you in no uncertain terms that Paul is *not* an avowed homosexual."

"He was part of that organization up at the high school, wasn't he? One of his own references mentioned it in the letter! The board even asked him, and he confirmed it!"

"He said he was gay. He never said he'd chosen to live a homosexual lifestyle." Richard shook his head, frustrated. Clearly this wasn't getting anywhere. "Look. Do you ever see a woman and think she's good looking?"

"Every guy has thoughts. Every normal guy, anyway."

"You aren't married to her. Do your thoughts make you unfit to be a scouting leader?"

"Not unless I act on them. But see, this isn't about your boy's actions. They never even asked him about those. It's about what kind of an example he is, what values he's associated with in the community."

"I see. Scouting cares more about a boy's reputation than it does about the person he actually is."

There was dead silence on the other end of the phone.

"Look," the other man said at last. "Ficklin can always file an appeal at the council level. I'm not saying they won't overturn the board of review's decision. That's where he'd have to go to get the decision changed. I couldn't do anything even if I wanted to."

"What are the procedures for that?"

"There's a publication, the *Advancement Committee Policies and Procedures*. Your scoutmaster should have a copy." Richard could hear the other man's sigh. "Look. I sympathize with you and the kid both. It sounds like he's a great kid. But why the hell did he have to be stupid enough to get himself outed at school in the middle of a big political campaign about gay marriage, just before he went up for his Eagle?"

"If you know that much about it, you should know it really wasn't his choice."

"Be that as it may." The commissioner sighed again. "Go ahead, do whatever you want. Who knows what the council will decide."

"Thanks for your help." Richard forced his tone to be civil.

"I don't want to appeal."

Richard looked at Paul, astonished. He'd swung by after work, happy to deliver some good news. "Why not?"

"It's just . . ." Richard waited, noticing the dark shadows under Paul's eyes. "I really wanted it, you know? To be an Eagle Scout. But now —" He swallowed. "They didn't want me. Just because I'm attracted to guys."

Then Richard understood. It wasn't about the award. It was about being rejected for something Paul couldn't control.

"I mean, thanks for calling the district guy and everything. But right now I just—" Paul didn't finish.

Maybe if Paul's dad hadn't hit him with the whole not-coming-to-Minnesota thing right after the board of review, he'd be up to this, Richard thought. But given the boy's current frame of mind, Paul's reaction didn't really surprise him, now that he thought about it. The idea of talking to people Paul didn't even know about whether or not he was homosexual couldn't be very attractive.

I tried. This is one of those times, though, when I can't just wave a magic wand and make it better.

Barbara was surprised to find Paul sleeping when she got back from work. *It's only 8:00. How can a sixteen-year-old be sleeping at 8:00 in the evening during the summer?*

"So how'd your day go?" she asked, as she started putting together a late dinner for them.

"Meh."

"Meaning?"

"Okay."

"You do anything with Chad?"

"Nah."

"So what did you do today?"

"Played some video games."

She waited for the details that usually followed. Nothing. "Is everything okay?" she asked.

At first, there was no answer. "No," Paul finally said in a tight voice.

Then she remembered. Today was the day Paul was supposed to be flying to Minnesota.

Barbara sat on the couch beside him. To her surprise, he put his head in her lap. She stroked his hair while tears slowly leaked from his closed eyes. Eventually, they stopped.

The telephone rang. Reluctantly, Barbara slid off the couch, leaving Paul sleeping.

It was Chad. Barbara walked to the couch, shook Paul awake, then handed him the phone.

The conversation was a short one, as teenage phone calls went. Barbara was shocked to hear Paul tell Chad not to come over the next day.

Come to think of it, she didn't think Chad had been over at all since Paul's board of review. That was really odd.

Barbara felt suddenly uneasy as she remembered all those symptoms of teenage depression. Changes in behavior, low energy, sleeping more than usual, withdrawing from people . . . Paul was displaying pretty much the classic checklist.

It wasn't like Paul didn't have plenty of reasons to be depressed. Being outed. Not getting his Eagle. His dad rejecting him. Being cut off from his little brother and sister. He got to see them only a few weeks each year, but Barbara knew they were important to him.

So he's depressed. What am I going to do about it?

Barbara couldn't change all the things that were going wrong in Paul's life. But that didn't mean she was completely helpless.

"I thought I said not to come over." Paul sounded like a grouchy eight-year-old who hadn't gotten enough sleep.

Chad wasn't impressed. "Dude, my best friend starts acting like an alien, you gotta be sure I'm gonna check it out." *You look like a zombie*, he thought but didn't say.

Paul didn't reply. Chad continued. "So how are things going?"

"Why don't you just go away?"

"Whoa! Mister Bad Attitude here." Chad paused. "You wanna play some video games?"

Paul ignored him. Instead, he was fiddling with something. It looked like a pill bottle.

A spike of fear went through Chad. "What's that?" he demanded.

"Nothing." Paul shoved it into his pocket.

"Dude, I'm telling you. That had *so* better not be your mom's sleeping pills."

"Just shut up!"

"Dude." Chad pulled out his cell phone. His hand was shaking. "I am like ten seconds from calling the paramedics if you don't hand over that fuh—that damn pill bottle."

"It's nothing like that!"

"One."

"I swear, Chad, you—"

"Two."

"Fine!" Paul jammed his hand into his pocket, pulled out the bottle, and threw it hard at Chad's head.

"Sh—ow!" Chad exclaimed. "What the hell—I mean, what the heck did you do that for?"

Paul, glaring at him, didn't answer.

Chad picked up the bottle. "Citalopram? What's that?" Then he saw something else. "Dude. This is for *you*?"

"They're my new meds, jerk. Happy now?"

"I don't get it."

Paul glared at him. "Antidepressants. Mom got tired of me sleeping all day long and not talking to anyone, so she dragged me off to the doctor this morning. He gave me these. Got it?" Paul grabbed back the bottle and shoved it into his pocket.

"Oh." Without really thinking about it, Chad rubbed the spot where the pill bottle had hit his forehead. "That's good, I guess."

Paul rolled his eyes at him. "Jerk," he repeated.

Even with Paul looking like he wanted to punch him, Chad still couldn't be sorry he'd reacted the way he had. What if Paul really *had* been thinking about offing himself? He was just glad he'd been wrong.

Richard tried to be conscientious about his yearly interviews with the youth. At the same time, he knew that sometimes real problems couldn't wait for the annual interviews. If one of the youth needed to talk to him, he didn't want to make it any harder by forcing them to schedule an interview with the executive secretary. So each Wednesday night whenever he was there during Mutual, he tried to make it clear that if any of the youth wanted to talk to him, they were welcome to grab him in the hall or poke their head into his office. It didn't happen very often, but occasionally someone would show up.

Still, it was a surprise when Tim Osterling, the twelve-year-old son of his second counselor, hesitantly turned up at his office door a few minutes after opening exercises and asked if they could talk. Richard closed the door and had the boy sit, then he sat down on another chair just a couple of feet away—he hated having a desk separate him from someone when he was trying to have a personal conversation.

"So, Tim. What can I do for you today?"

The boy looked down and scuffed his shoe against the rug. It could have been a Norman Rockwell painting about a kid fessing up to sending a baseball through a window. Richard bit his lip to keep from grinning. He felt his hopes rise that this might be something small and easily handled, at least compared to the other things he'd been worrying about that week.

Then the boy spoke, and Richard didn't feel like smiling anymore. "I'm gay," he said, looking up. "Like Paul."

Oh, well. It was a nice fantasy while it lasted. Richard pushed the thought to the back of his head as Tim explained.

A few weeks before, Richard had challenged the young men to reread *For the Strength of Youth*, or read it for the first time if they hadn't read it before. Apparently that's what Tim had done. This time, when he got to the part about same-gender attraction, the boy had a better idea what it was talking about. "So I talked to my folks. And I'm supposed to talk to my bishop, I guess. So here I am."

"Do they know you're meeting with me now?"

He shrugged. "Nah. We talked about maybe me coming to talk with you sometime. But tonight, I dunno." He scratched his head. "I saw your door open, and I felt like maybe I should just get it over with."

Sounds about as close to a spiritual prompting as you're likely to get from a twelve-year-old, Richard thought to himself.

"What makes you think you might be same-gender attracted?"

Tim blushed, a bright, fiery red. "I — um, I get all horny when I see boys who aren't wearing shirts and stuff, like when we play shirts and skins with capture the flag. Or when I go swimming. And I think about boys when I, uh —"

"Masturbate?" Richard prompted.

Tim struggled to maintain eye contact. "Yeah."

I always tell the boys I want them to be honest with me. I guess I shouldn't complain about getting what I ask for. "Do you look at pornography?"

"Nah."

"Have you ever done anything sexually with another man or boy?"

"No!"

"You know that's not allowed, right?"

"Yeah."

"Glad to hear it." Richard paused. "I'm going to tell you the same thing I tell other boys who are struggling with masturbation.

The church teaches that this is something you shouldn't do. You need to develop self-discipline. I don't want you to get all down on yourself about this, but you need to do your best to avoid temptations." He paused. "Are there any particular times when it happens?"

Tim hesitated. "After school when I'm taking a shower. At night when I'm going to sleep."

Richard thought a minute. "See if you can come up with some ways to reduce the temptations at those times. Maybe at night, for example, you could leave your bedroom door open when you're falling asleep. Talk to your dad about this and see if he has any suggestions."

"Do I have to talk to him? It's, well, embarrassing."

"I think he'll be more understanding than you think."

Tim looked doubtful.

"Try not to obsess about masturbation, either. Sometimes worrying about it too much can just make you think about it more." Richard knew all about that from when he was a teenager. "Instead, do your best to think about positive things, like sports or things you like to do. Video games, maybe."

"Sure."

Tim, he saw, was starting to tune him out. *Twelve-year-olds and their attention spans.*

"I'll expect a report on how you're doing at our interview when you turn thirteen. That's, what, November, right?"

"Yeah. November thirteenth."

"Do you mind if I talk about this with your parents? Not any details, just in general about being attracted to boys," he hurried on, seeing the worried look on Tim's face. "Maybe we can all talk together about it."

"I guess." Not really an enthusiastic response, but Richard supposed it would have to do.

After Tim left the office, Richard sat a minute, rubbing one hand over his face. *First Paul, now Tim,* he thought. *I wonder how many more conversations like this I'm going to have before I'm released as bishop?*

Chapter Twenty-Two

THIS TIME PAUL WENT BY HIMSELF to see the patriarch.

He'd been thinking again about families and his chances of ever having one, especially after—

He swallowed. He'd told himself that he wasn't going to think about his little brother and sister and the fact that he wasn't being allowed to see them this summer. Or maybe not ever again, if his dad didn't change his mind.

But that wasn't what he was here about this afternoon.

Paul had read over his blessing again, trying to figure out if maybe he'd missed something before. Nothing. Finally he'd decided to talk to the patriarch. So he called Brother Hoskisson and asked if he could come over and ask him a question about his blessing. The man had seemed reluctant but finally agreed.

Paul knocked on the door. Brother Hoskisson opened the door and let him in. They sat down in the study where Paul had received his blessing.

Before Paul could ask his question, the patriarch spoke. "I should start by telling you that it's very unlikely I'll be able to answer your question, whatever it is. It's my privilege to speak the words. But pretty much everything I know is what's in the blessing itself. You're the one who has the right to pray and receive inspiration about what the blessing actually means—not me."

Paul nodded. Brother Hoskisson had said something like that when they were talking on the phone. "I was just wondering . . ." His voice trailed off.

"Yes?"

"About having a family. Getting married. Whether or not I'll have kids someday. I thought maybe my patriarchal blessing would say something about that. But I couldn't see anything about it any-where." He looked down at the envelope that held the printed copy of his blessing.

The patriarch held out a hand. Paul handed him the envelope. Brother Hoskisson opened it, unfolded the paper, and started read-ing. A couple of minutes later, he looked up again at Paul.

"You're right. I don't see anything here that talks directly about being married or raising a family." He handed it back.

Paul tried to hide his disappointment. "What does that mean?"

The patriarch spread his hands. "I don't know."

"Does it mean I *won't* have a family?"

"I doubt that. But as I said, I really don't know." He paused. "Is there a reason you're particularly worried about whether or not you'll be able to have a family?"

Paul hesitated for a few seconds. "Yes."

It looked like the patriarch was thinking. Finally, he spoke. "We don't really know why some things are mentioned in a patriarchal blessing and some things aren't. It's my belief that Heavenly Father includes the things that will be especially helpful for us to know in our lives. Other things he may leave out because he wants us to discover them on our own or go to him at some point in the future for answers. Or sometimes because the answer he might give isn't one that we'd understand correctly, even if he told it to us."

I think "You'll get married and have some kids" would be pretty easy to understand, Paul thought. He swallowed.

"One thing we do know from the scriptures is that the way of exaltation is open unto all. If you live the way you should, if you live a life of righteousness and service to the Lord, there's absolutely no reason why you won't be able to be married and have a family in the eternities, whether or not you have the opportunity to have one in this life."

The patriarch shifted in his seat and refocused his gaze on Paul. "My best counsel to you is that you study your blessing, pay atten-tion to the things that you *are* told, and do your best to live the kind of life Heavenly Father wants. If you do, then just like all the rest of Heavenly Father's children you have his promise that in the eterni-ties, all the righteous desires of your heart will be fulfilled, whatever challenges you may struggle with in this life."

Paul couldn't be sure, but something about the patriarch's last words gave him the feeling that maybe Brother Hoskisson knew or had figured out just what Paul's problem was.

And then Brother Hoskisson led him out again. All together, he'd been there only about ten minutes.

I don't really know anything now that I didn't know before, Paul realized on his way home. *I guess I'll just have to wait and see.* For some reason, though, he felt comforted.

"Thanks for coming to meet with me." Richard closed the door, and the Osterlings sat, Tim and both of his parents.

"Tim says he told you what we talked about a week ago Wednesday," he said, nodding at the boy.

"Yes. We were . . . surprised that he'd gone ahead and met with you without even letting us know. But then, he's always doing things that surprise us." As she spoke, Sister Osterling looked at Tim, a rueful expression on her face. He squirmed in his chair.

"I imagine this whole same-gender thing was a surprise," Richard said.

"Not so much. Not for me, anyway." She looked at her husband. "Ever since that day in second grade when he came home talking about how cute one of the other boys was, and then we got a note from the teacher asking us to explain to him that most boys don't like to be kissed by other boys."

"Mom!" Tim's face was crimson.

"It was a surprise to me," muttered Brother Osterling.

"You're not always the most observant person, dear, when it comes to things outside your own experience."

Richard cleared his throat. "You all need to understand that simply feeling *attracted* to other boys isn't a sin." He continued carefully, "The sin comes if you choose to act on those feelings. And they might still go away or change to liking girls as Tim gets older."

"But they might not," put in Sister Osterling.

"Yes." Richard continued. "Ultimately, Tim, the goal is for you to reach a point where those feelings aren't an active part of your life anymore. Until then, though, you need to exercise self-control." They were all nodding.

"Tim and I have talked about what kind of behavior is and isn't allowed, according to church standards. I wanted to meet with all of you to answer any questions you might have, if I can, and to let you know I'm here to support your family as you deal with this particular challenge."

The parents looked at each other. "Is there . . . any kind of treatment the church offers, to help people deal with same-gender attraction?" Sister Osterling asked.

Richard noticed her use of *same-gender attraction*, which was the church's latest preferred term. They'd been doing some research, he realized.

"Not really, no," Richard replied. "LDS Family Services sometimes offers counseling for people dealing with same-sex attraction, but there's no specific program endorsed by the church. I can hook you up with them if you'd like."

"It still seems early to be talking about that kind of thing," Brother Osterling put in. "I'd hardly even started thinking about girls when I was twelve. Let's wait a couple of years and see about it then." Sister Osterling nodded, though from her pursed lips it didn't look like she fully agreed.

"Tim, what do you think?" Richard asked.

He shrugged. "Whatever." From Tim's body language, Richard was pretty sure the boy would rather not even be in the same room with the three of them, let alone talk to another adult about the topic. Clearly, though, he didn't feel like he could say so — particularly with his parents right there.

Richard made a sudden decision. "Tim, I'd like to talk with your folks a bit. Will you wait outside?" Tim nodded and quickly got up. On his way out the door, Richard saw him pull a Game Boy out of his pocket.

"What did you want to talk to us about, Bishop?" Brother Osterling asked.

"First, are there any questions or concerns you have that you didn't want to raise while Tim was here?"

They looked at each other — they did that a lot, Richard had noticed — then shook their heads.

"Tim seems like a fine young man. In my view, it's a very positive sign that he came to talk to you about this. And I'm glad you seem to be handling this so calmly and supportively." He paused. "Have you thought about what kinds of rules you might want to put in place?"

"What do you mean?"

"Monitoring Tim's computer use. Deciding whether he should be at a friend's house if there aren't any adults there. Leaving the door open when he's playing with other boys. That sort of thing." Richard hesitated. "I'm not saying you need to get paranoid about this. But boys do sometimes experiment with each other sexually at this age. I can't help but think that could make it harder for Tim to deal with this particular challenge." *I only wish I'd thought about that when I first talked with Paul.* "It's your decision, whatever you think will work best. But I think you should consider it."

"We'll keep that in mind," Brother Osterling responded. He seemed a little paler than when he came in, Richard thought. He guessed the whole thing had just gotten a little more real to him.

"So how are you both holding up with this?"

Brother Osterling shrugged. "Okay, I guess. I think I'm still trying to wrap my mind around it, you know?"

"It gives me more appreciation for what Barbara Ficklin must be going through," his wife added.

Brother Osterling's eyes met Richard's. An item of concern at their last bishopric meeting had been the gossip about Paul and his mother that had been spreading through the ward.

"Tim was really upset when people first started saying Paul was gay," Sister Osterling continued. "At first we thought it was because Paul had helped with his swimming earlier this year. I asked if Paul had ever done anything Tim was uncomfortable with. He was quite indignant that I would even ask. Then I told him just because people were saying Paul was gay, it didn't necessarily mean it was true, and that even if Paul was attracted to other boys, it didn't make him a bad person."

"It really made a big impression on Tim when Paul spent all that time with him," Brother Osterling added softly. "Most older boys aren't that patient with the young ones."

"There was definitely some hero worship going on," his wife agreed. "And then people started saying all those things. I think Tim felt like they were attacking him as well as Paul. He thought that if they knew how he felt about boys, they'd say the same things about him."

"Actually, that reminds me of one thing we'd like your opinion about," Brother Osterling said. "When we were talking to Tim, he said he wished he could talk to Paul about all this. I guess he asked Chad if it was true that Paul was gay."

Richard winced. He could imagine what had happened, given how protective Chad had become.

"The way Tim tells it, Chad threatened to punch his lights out if he said anything to Paul, so he hasn't. But I think it could make a real difference, being able to talk to someone he admires who's facing this same challenge—if you think it would be a good idea."

Richard considered for a moment. "I'll think about it and maybe talk to Paul, and then get back to you," he said. He felt a little bad when he realized he was more or less confirming that Paul was same-sex attracted. But that cat was clearly out of the bag, down the street, and halfway to the river by now.

"We appreciate it," Sister Osterling said. "Thanks for talking with us."

And when I had said this, the Lord spake unto me, saying: Fools mock, but they shall mourn; and my grace is sufficient for the meek, that they shall take no advantage of your weakness. . . .

I give unto men weakness that they may be humble; and my grace is sufficient for all men that humble themselves before me . . .

Paul had continued with his Book of Mormon reading over the summer. Since so many of his other plans had fallen through, he'd had a lot of time for it. He was almost done with Ether. And after that came Moroni, and then he'd be finished.

Reading the book of Ether had been like watching a ship full of people on a high-speed collision course with disaster. Like the *Titanic*. It was the whole Book of Mormon pride-and-destruction cycle on steroids.

Then Paul had gotten to where Moroni was being insecure about whether the Gentiles would ignore the Book of Mormon just because the Nephites weren't good at writing, or something like that. And that was when Jesus said that stuff to Moroni about weaknesses.

Paul had heard the scripture before, like on the campout where the bishop had quoted it. Reading it now, though, it struck him in a very personal way.

Being attracted to other guys is a weakness to me. A weakness God has allowed me to have, for some reason.

He wanted to believe the scripture about weakness sometimes being a good thing, but it was hard for him to imagine any good purpose that might be served by his having gay feelings.

And then he got to the scripture about the Gentiles developing charity. *If they have not charity it mattereth not unto thee, thou hast been faithful; wherefore, thy garments shall be made clean. And because thou hast seen thy weakness thou shalt be made strong, even unto the sitting down in the place which I have prepared in the mansions of my Father.*

Paul thought a moment.

I don't know what all of that means. Part of it, though, is that even if other people don't understand — ward members, other kids at school, the GSA kids, Boy Scouts, even my dad — that won't make a difference to God. I have a promise from God. It doesn't depend on them.

It's not my job to help other people develop charity toward me. My job is to have charity toward them. That's enough.

The doorbell rang downstairs. A moment later his mom called out to him. "Paul! The bishop's here!"

"Just a minute!" He pulled on a better T-shirt and ran down-stairs. "Hi, Bishop!"

"Paul."

He was still dressed in his Sunday suit, Paul noticed. *Hasn't he gone home yet? It's 5:00 in the afternoon! I sure don't ever want to be a bishop.*

Paul followed the bishop into the family room, away from the kitchen where his mom was cooking. "I've been speaking to another young man in our ward who's facing a challenge similar to yours."

It took a moment for Paul to figure out what he was saying. Then — *I'm not the only gay kid in the ward?*

"He's several years younger than you are. He and his parents thought it might be good if you could talk to him, tell him a little bit about how you've managed to meet that challenge."

"Who is it?"

"Tim Osterling."

A memory flashed before Paul's eyes. It was the kid he'd taught how to swim. "Sure. If you think it's a good idea."

"I think it could be. Tim's the one who wanted it."

"He's a cool kid."

"Just make arrangements for a time you want to go over."

Paul thought a minute. "Bishop, could you come with me when I go over?"

"Why?"

"I'd . . ." He hesitated. "You said I should have someone else with me if I—"

"Got it."

"I mean, I suppose his folks'll be there and everything, but—"

"All right." The bishop pulled out his cell phone. "Maybe we can just go over now."

"I guess the two of you have things to talk about," Tim's mom said. "You want to go upstairs and talk in Tim's room?"

Paul noticed the sliding glass door leading onto a deck, with steps leading down to the backyard. He glanced at Tim. "You wanna go outside?"

"Sure."

They walked out onto the deck and then down onto the lawn, while the bishop stayed behind with Tim's folks. Paul was careful to make sure they didn't go past the area that could be seen from the house. He waited for Tim to say something, but the other boy was silent.

I guess it's up to me to start things off. I wonder what I'm supposed to say?

"So, I guess you like guys," Paul began. Mentally, he cringed. *Wow. That's so lame.*

"Yeah."

"You're pretty sure you're gay?"

"Yeah."

"You think that might ever change?"

The younger boy shrugged. "Dunno." Then he looked at Paul. "You think it'll ever change for you?"

"I don't know either."

There was a pause.

"So what's it like? Being out and everything?"

"Pretty crummy." Paul took a deep breath. "For a while, I was going to the GSA club—that's, uh, this club in high school where it's supposed to be okay whether you're gay or straight or bi or whatever." From the look on Tim's face, this was going right past him. "Anyway, they were some of the first people I told that I was gay. But that didn't, uh, work out very well for me. A lot of them got mad at me for being a Mormon. One of them was the guy who outed me to the whole school."

"Was that 'cause you wouldn't be his boyfriend or something?"

Paul's eyes narrowed. "No."

"Do you have a boyfriend?"

This is really embarrassing. "I did, kind of. For a while. But then I realized I couldn't be a good member of the church and have a boyfriend, so I stopped."

"Was it Chad?"

Paul almost choked. "No. He's just a really good friend." He paused. "Not to mention that he's not even gay."

"I didn't think so," Tim said.

"You know you're not allowed to have a boyfriend or do anything gay with anybody if you're a church member, right?"

"Yeah," the younger boy muttered. "It would've been cool, though, if you had one."

Paul didn't know how to respond to that, so he decided to ignore it. *I see interesting times ahead for Tim's parents. And for the bishop.*

"So, Tim. How are you handling it? The whole thing with liking other guys?"

Tim looked away again. "It's . . . kinda scary actually," he admitted.

"Yeah. I know what you mean. Being different."

The conversation stalled again. Paul decided just to ask straight out. "So why did you want me to come over and talk?"

"I dunno." The other boy kicked at the ground. "It's just— I mean, you're this really cool guy, y'know? And, like when you helped me out with my swimming . . . I mean, here I already kinda had a crush on you and everything." Tim turned bright red, but kept on talking. "And then I found out you were gay like me and, like, wow. I mean, it's not like I'm thinking we should be boyfriends or anything. It's just—"

"It's nice to have someone else who understands," Paul finished, when it looked like Tim was just digging himself in deeper. He did his best to ignore the part about Tim having a crush on him. *The poor kid's embarrassed enough already.*

"Yeah! 'Cause sometimes it's like you see this really hot guy, or you have this crush on your friend and you wanna tell someone really bad, but it's like you know if you did no one else would understand and your friends might hate you or beat you up or something." Tim paused, then continued in a quieter voice. "And liking other guys that way really *is* weird, I guess, and g-gross." He choked on the word. "And I really don't want my friends to hate me or to get beat up and killed like that guy in Wyoming or Texas or wherever it was . . ." His voice trailed off.

In the space of about thirty seconds, he'd gone from hyper to seriously upset. *Wow. And Chad talks about my mood swings.*

"Tim."

"Huh?"

Paul considered all the things he'd like to say—about being careful and getting a testimony and finding out who his real friends were and discovering that you really couldn't be both Mormon and gay, at least not in any way that would be accepted by people on both sides. Looking into the younger boy's face, though, he knew Tim wouldn't understand. He was just too young. Paul himself wouldn't have understood a lot of it before his experiences of the last year.

What did Tim really need? *What did I need back in middle school when I'd just figured out that I liked guys?*

"Tim," Paul repeated. He put one hand on the other boy's shoulder and shook it gently. "Don't worry too much about it, okay? I mean, yeah, you need to be careful about telling people and probably not tell even your best friends until you're older and you have a better idea if they'll freak out on you. But the main point is that you don't need to feel bad about yourself or scared, as long as you're careful. There are good people out there who'll accept you the way you are, even with the way you feel about guys. It looks like your parents are okay about this, yeah?"

"Y-yeah."

"And the bishop's pretty cool too."

"He says I shouldn't be gay. That I need to not think about guys or doing stuff with guys."

"Well, yeah. That's pretty much what the church says, though it's up to you whether you decide to live it or not." Paul thought a moment. "Look. All of us have to make choices. No one can make the choice for you about whether the church is more important than being gay. I've decided the church is more important to me, but you need to make that choice for yourself."

"I don't wanna go without sex my whole life!"

There's not really any filter between his mouth and his brain, is there. Then Paul thought, *What brain? He's twelve.*

"You know, there's more important things in life than sex."

"How would you know? You haven't ever had any."

Paul bit his lip. Tim definitely did *not* need to know about his experiences with Jared.

"I'm just saying. Think about the choices you want to make. Listen to your parents and the bishop. Don't be in too big a rush to decide—well, *anything* really." It felt very weird to Paul, trying to be Mister Good Role Model and say all the approved things. Chad'd be laughing his head off.

Well, maybe he wouldn't. After all, he was the one who was always telling Paul just how much of a straight arrow he was. *Even though I'm not really straight at all.*

"Just—don't be dumb. Okay? I mean, you're only twelve, so I know you can't help being dumb most of the time—"

"Bite me!"

" —but just try not to do dumb things. I don't want to hear about you getting beat up at school or running away from home or anything stupid like that."

"You mean like getting outed at school?"

"Watch it, kid!" Paul took a playful swipe at him. Tim laughed.

"Really, though. Just be careful, okay?"

"Don't worry. I'm not stupid!"

Why don't I find that completely reassuring?

Paul waited a moment, but Tim didn't say anything else. Finally Paul asked, "Was there anything else you wanted to talk about?"

"Not really." Tim looked down at his shoes. "Thanks for talking to me."

"We can talk again sometime." Paul saw the glum look on the younger boy's face. "Come here." He grabbed Tim and pulled him into a hug.

"This is embarrassing," Tim mumbled after a moment.

"Hey! Hugs are good. Don't ever be embarrassed to accept a hug."

"Whatever. Can you let go now?"

"Your parents are watching. The bishop too."

Tim groaned. "I hate you." Despite his earlier words, he was the one still holding on.

"Sure." Paul let go, tousled the younger boy's hair, then dodged his fist. "Let's go back up to the house now, okay?"

"Okay."

Chapter Twenty-Three

IT HAD BEEN ONLY A COUPLE OF WEEKS since Paul started taking his meds, but to Chad it seemed like he was doing a lot better. And then came the first day of school.

When Chad arrived at seminary that first day, Paul was already there. Chad sat next to him. As the room filled up, no one took any of the seats next to theirs. At one point a girl from another ward started to walk in their direction, but her friend frowned and tugged her over to another spot. Chad heard the other girl start, "Didn't you hear? He's—" Then her voice dropped.

Beside him, Paul clenched his jaw. Chad had to fight the urge to say something that would probably get him kicked out of seminary for the year.

To Chad's relief, the lesson was normal, with Sister Olsen calling on Paul to answer questions just like everyone else. Then at the end of class while everyone was gathering their stuff together, Tony Westergren—a basketball freak from one of the other wards—came over and chatted with them.

"Hey. How you guys doing?"

"Pretty good," Chad answered.

"Chad, you on the soccer team again?"

"Yeah."

"How about you, Paul? Anything special going on?"

"Things are cool."

"Great. See you around." With that, Tony clapped one hand on Paul's shoulder for a second, then let go. He sketched a quick wave at Chad and went over to pick up his backpack. Then he was out the door.

"What was that all about?" asked Paul.

"Dunno." But Chad was pretty sure he did know. Clearly, Tony was making a statement. About tolerance, or something.

It made Chad angry. *Calm down,* he told himself. *Tony's just trying to be a good guy. He's not the one you should be mad at.* It didn't help.

This is gonna be another long year.

Being back in school was different than Paul had expected. Stressful, yeah, but mostly just . . . isolated.

Back during the summer, there'd been a week when Paul stayed home sick from church. Chad told him later that the priests quorum advisor had ripped them all a new one for the way they'd been treating Paul. After that, the comments and shoving had pretty much stopped, at least when adults were around. Aside from Janice and a few of her friends, though—and Chad, of course—none of the other teenagers in the ward would get into any kind of real conversation with him. Some would nod and say hi, but they wouldn't stick around to talk. *It's like they think I'm contagious or something.*

Seminary was turning out to be the same way. There weren't that many kids who were being nasty. Most of them just left him alone. He was sure part of it was that everyone was still half-asleep at that hour of the morning, but he couldn't help feeling a little bitter about the way people kept their distance, like he was surrounded by some kind of glass ball.

And then there was school.

Not very many people harassed him for being gay, though he got sneering looks from some soccer players and from some of his and Chad's other ex-friends. But Paul didn't really have anyone to hang out with, either.

At lunch the second day, Paul sat at a table next to Bryan Walters, a kid they'd called Apple Boy the year before because he made a big production out of eating apples for lunch each day. He'd bite off the bumps on the bottom, then peel off long strips of skin with his teeth before eating the rest of it. He was a year younger than Paul and seemed to be pretty much a loner.

"So how are things going?" Bryan was sitting by himself that day, and Paul thought he might as well be friendly.

"Fine."

"Classes okay?"

"Look." The other boy seemed nervous. "I'm not gay. I don't have anything against gays. But I'm, uh, having enough problems without everyone thinking I'm gay on top of it. So I'd really appreciate it if you, like, wouldn't sit by me, okay?" He picked up his lunch and moved to another table, while Paul stared after him in shock.

After that, Paul more or less kept to himself.

Chad was doing soccer again this year, so Paul was on his own after school, which sucked. Classes were harder than they'd been the year before—at least, he seemed to have more trouble getting the work done. He also seemed to need more sleep than he remembered from the year before.

A little more than a week after school started, Jared came up to him after lunch. He asked how Paul was doing, then told Paul he'd wound up as the GSA vice-president. Paul congratulated him and asked how things were going in the club.

"Okay. Lots of stuff right now on Measure 36, of course." That was the ballot measure about gay marriage.

There was an awkward pause.

"Listen. I, um, heard about the whole Boy Scout thing. About you not getting to be an Eagle Scout."

How did he hear about that?

"I just wanted to say I'm sorry."

"Why? It's not your fault."

"Well, but if it hadn't been for that lowlife Jose—"

"Yeah. Fine. Gotcha." Paul didn't want to think about it any more than he had to.

"Speaking of Jose, did you hear what happened to him?"

"No, what?"

"I guess he went to some kind of religious camp over the summer. First week back, he shows up at GSA and says that all us fags are going to hell."

Paul shook his head. "That kid has serious problems."

"Tell me about it. Finally Allington told him he couldn't come out to any more meetings unless he promised he wouldn't be verbally abusive. He started swearing at her. Wound up with a three-day suspension."

"Couldn't have happened to a nicer guy."

"So, you think you might ever come back to GSA?"

Paul stared at him. "You're kidding, right? I'm a Mormon, in case you forgot. Who was publicly outed by someone in the GSA."

"Like I said, he's not there anymore."

"But I'm still Mormon. You know, one of those people who's going to vote for Measure 36."

"You're too young to vote."

"Bite me." Paul gave him a sarcastic smile. "Anyway, I already got a taste of just how open-minded GSA is when it comes to opinions different from theirs."

Jared looked at him a moment. Finally he said, "The whole GSA thing really didn't work out so well for you, did it."

"No. It really didn't."

"Bitter about it?"

"I'm not bitter," Paul replied. Jared just stared at him. "Okay, maybe I am a little bitter. Mostly, though, it's just because I thought I'd found a place where people would accept me for who I am." Paul tried to keep his throat from tightening. "And then it turned out it wasn't true. It's kind of hard to get past that."

After a moment, Jared hesitantly put a hand on Paul's shoulder and squeezed it. "Like I said, I'm sorry," he said quietly. Then he turned and walked off.

Over time, things got a little better. A couple more kids from church started talking to him. One day at school, Alan Thompson—the kid who'd replaced him as teachers quorum president—came up and asked how things were going. Paul felt like he should have been happier about it, but he just couldn't seem to care anymore.

Paul Ficklin was one of the nicest guys Janice knew. Certainly the nicest guy in her ward. And so of course he was gay. *I wonder if that's some kind of natural law, that all the nice boys are the ones there's no point in dating?*

Or maybe it was another kind of cause and effect, and the fact that he was safe was part of what made her see him as nice. Janice grimaced. Sometimes it was inconvenient having the kind of mind that insisted on searching for alternative explanations for everything. Especially when those explanations suggested uncomfortable possibilities about herself.

All of which didn't give her any ideas about how to help him.

Every group had its idiots, and the youth in their ward included more than its fair share. Still, it was really only a few kids who were actively harassing Paul. Most of the others just didn't know what to say, or were uncomfortable around him, or didn't want to be made fun of themselves. So they left him alone.

The way Paul was reacting didn't help matters. Janice was alarmed when she noticed how he'd started actively avoiding any interaction with the other teenagers in the ward, sitting by himself and staring off in other directions whenever anyone got near. She couldn't really blame him, but she also didn't think many other kids were likely to try being friendly as long as Paul kept sending out such strong stay-away-from-me vibes. She doubted it would do any good for her to talk to him about it, though.

And then she heard about Paul and his mom moving, and she thought maybe she *should* have tried to do something about it after all.

Barbara had expected that the start of school would be hard for Paul, with the entire school knowing he was gay. She was dismayed, though, to see how quickly things went downhill. Already after only two weeks, Paul was having trouble staying caught up with his homework. That had never been a problem before. And he just seemed generally . . . listless. Subdued. Almost like he'd been before starting the antidepressants.

Part of it was that Paul seemed to lack any kind of social life. He still spent time with Chad, but Chad was in soccer, and both of them had heavy class loads. As far as she could tell, Paul didn't have any other friends.

Several times, Barbara thought about telling Paul that he needed to go out and make some new friends. Explore new interests. Each time, though, she remembered what happened last year with GSA. Paul had found new friends, and it didn't turn out very well.

Today, she'd come home to find Paul just sitting on the living-room couch. His schoolbooks were beside him, but it didn't look like he was studying.

"How are things going?"

"Kinda hard to concentrate," Paul mumbled.

"Why?"

"School sucks."

Barbara raised an eyebrow. "Aside from the inappropriate way you expressed it, what's that supposed to mean?"

Paul didn't say anything for several moments. Finally, when Barbara had started to think he wasn't going to answer her, he spoke. "I don't get why it has to be so hard, you know?"

"Classes?"

"Not just classes. The rest of it, too. I mean—" Paul seemed to hesitate. "I made my choice. I did the right thing and stood up for the church. But it's just so hard. Being around people. People not liking me. People pretending I'm not even there."

"At school, you mean?"

"Not just school. Church, too." He paused. "I still wanna go on a mission and everything, but sometimes I really wonder why." He gathered his books and trudged upstairs, leaving Barbara to think over what she'd just heard.

Part of it was probably still the depression. Maybe the dosage needed adjusting again, now that Paul had started school. But it seemed like more than that.

As for the notion of Paul making new friends . . . thinking about it now, she decided the idea was remarkably naive. Maybe it would have been possible if he hadn't been through everything the last few months had thrown at him. Or if his social situation hadn't been the source of the problem. Or if they weren't in the middle of a nasty political controversy over gay marriage, with everything becoming polarized, *us* versus *them*, whether *us* meant the gays or church members.

If Paul was still in the GSA, they could be a support system for him. But he's not.

It was ironic. He'd quit GSA because of his commitment as a member of the church. But now apparently he wasn't welcome among the other kids his age at church either.

Only six weeks and the election would be over. Except that it *wouldn't* be over. Regardless of the results, people on both sides would be bitter for months and years to come.

There's not much Paul can do to make this better, she realized. *He could be the best-adjusted kid in the world, and still most of this would be completely beyond his control.* Changing his meds might mask the symptoms, but it wouldn't change the underlying problems.

Enough. Just—enough. Sometimes you just have to walk away from a toxic situation.

She picked up the phone and dialed. One ring. Two rings.

"Hi! Aunt Muriel? This is Barbara. Say, are they still looking for physical therapists at that hospital near you?"

"So you're leaving. Just like that." Chad could hear the flatness in his own voice. It sounded like anger. It *was* anger. Here he'd been doing his best to stick things out despite all the stupid comments on the soccer team, which Paul wasn't even on, and —

Sure, Chad. Tell yourself how much worse it is for you than it is for Paul. He swallowed.

"Yeah." Paul shrugged. "Gonna stay with my Great-Aunt Muriel in Utah until my mom finds an apartment for us." He gave a weak smile. "You should be happy. No more fag boy to drag you dow —"

Chad punched him in the arm. Hard. "Don't *ever* say anything like that again!"

Paul stared at him, an astonished look on his face. Chad waited for Paul to hit him back. Instead, after a few seconds his eyes dropped. "I guess I deserved that."

"Yeah, I guess you did. Bonehead."

They both stood silent for a few seconds.

"So why do you have to leave now, anyway?"

Paul was quiet for a moment. Then he shrugged again. "My mom thinks stuff is getting to me again."

Chad looked at him. "Has it really been that bad?"

"Dunno." Paul wouldn't look back.

"Dang it, Paul, why didn't you say something —"

"It's just a lot of stuff, okay! Classes and seminary and the way everybody keeps staring at me at church. Not to mention all the ads about Measure 36 and everyone arguing about gay marriage all the time."

"I thought the meds were supposed to help with you being all stressed."

"I guess. The doctor and my mom, they're saying maybe I need a higher dose. But a lot of this stuff isn't gonna change, no matter how many happy drugs I take. It was actually a relief when my mom started making noises about leaving." Paul shrugged. "Besides, she says she's having problems at work. Dunno if it's true. Maybe she just made it up so I wouldn't feel bad about us moving."

"I didn't think you'd just give up," Chad blurted out before he could censor himself.

And then Paul exploded. "Give up?" he shouted. "You think that's what I'm doing? You've got a lot of balls saying something like that to me."

Chad noticed Paul's fists clenching as he continued. "I *didn't* give up. I'm *not* giving up. What I'm doing is moving someplace where my whole life doesn't revolve around being gay and everyone else knowing about it. You know what? Being here in Arcadia Heights, I feel like an ant with a pin stuck through me onto some kind of stupid bulletin board in a science classroom. I'm just out there for everybody to look at, you know? I mean, yeah, I can wiggle my arms and legs as much as I want, but I can't *get* anywhere. I want to get off the freaking pin!"

There was a long pause. Finally Chad spoke. "So when are you leaving?"

"Saturday, October second."

"Two weeks from yesterday."

"Yeah."

"That sucks."

"Yeah."

"I hear that you and Paul are leaving us."

A brief, fierce look crossed Barbara's face. Richard was reminded of the young mother who'd moved to Arcadia Heights almost ten years before, still in the middle of an ugly divorce. "It seems like the best thing to do."

"I'm sorry." He paused. "Can I talk with Paul for a few minutes?"

Soon, Richard and Paul were sitting alone in the Ficklins' living room.

Paul looked exhausted. He'd smiled when he came in and shook hands, but the smile hadn't reached his eyes. More than ever, Richard felt certain he'd been prompted to see Paul before they left.

Now if he could only figure out what to say.

"I was looking forward to sending in your mission papers."

Paul's eyes widened. Richard himself was more than a little surprised at the words coming from his mouth. "I would have told the missionary committee that you've overcome great challenges to be able to serve a mission. I would have said you were one of the most spiritually aware young men I've had the privilege to know. I would have mentioned your sense of humor and the way you have of making other people feel at ease." He hesitated. "I would have said that I'd be proud to consider you my son."

Paul swallowed and looked away.

Richard continued. "Back in January, we talked about what you want out of life. Before you take off for Utah, I'd like you to give me a quick rundown of what your goals are at this point, what you want your life to be like moving forward."

There was a pause. "I dunno," Paul finally said. "I mean, right now, mostly I just want to get through the next couple of years. Survive high school, you know?" The boy drew a deep breath. "I want to do what's right. Be a good person. Be happy. Not be alone." The last few words were so quiet Richard could barely hear them.

Richard thought a moment. "I can't guarantee all of that. But—" He stopped himself. "I believe—I think—" He shook his head in frustration. This wasn't working right.

"Do you mind if I give you a blessing?" he asked at last.

"That's fine," Paul replied softly.

Richard stood and moved behind Paul's chair. "Your middle name's Eric, right?"

"Yeah."

Richard drew a deep breath. "Paul Eric Ficklin. By the authority of the holy Melchizedek Priesthood, I lay my hands on your head to give you a blessing of—to say the things I think Heavenly Father wants me to say.

"The first thing I have to say to you is that you're a good person. You're a child of God. You—" Richard choked, swallowed, then tried again. "He loves you. Your mother loves you. Your friends love you. I love you."

It was hard. Richard wanted so badly to be able to say something that would help. He just didn't know what.

Let it go. Let the words come. Don't try to wrestle it into the shape YOU want. Just open your mouth and speak.

"Heavenly Father has things for you to do in this life. He has blessings and tasks for you. He will comfort you and be beside you, and you will never be alone.

"Though opposition and trials may rage, he will be with you. And you will find friends who know who you are and will help you to live his teachings. Some of them will understand and be able to help you deal with this great burden you've been given to bear in this earth life, this—these feelings, this attraction to other men.

"As you do the things God wants you to do, you'll find that your capacities will expand. You'll be able to do more than you believed you could. And you will experience great joy in this life, and in the eternities all your righteous desires will be fulfilled.

"Take courage and faint not, but be believing.

"In the name of Jesus Christ, amen."

Neither of them hesitated as they moved into a hug. They stood there a long moment before separating.

"Thanks." Paul was crying, but there was a smile on his face.

Richard hesitated, then made a decision. "You have my cell number. I won't be your bishop anymore, but—well, call me if you need to talk to someone."

"Yeah. I will."

They left the room, Richard's arm draped over Paul's shoulders.

It was the last Sunday in September. Because next Sunday was general conference, it was also fast and testimony meeting. And with only one month to go, it seemed like almost everyone was talking about the election.

Lots of them were going on about corruption in the last days and the sins of homosexuality and gay marriage. Each time they did, Chad noticed glances in Paul's direction from all over the chapel. *I guess I can see why Paul and his mom wouldn't want to stay here right now.*

Not everyone was ragging on gays. Brother Flanders had gone on for several minutes about tolerance and people making up their own minds. It seemed like a pretty safe bet that Brother Flanders would be voting against Measure 36. At one point, he'd glanced in Paul's direction while he was saying something about understanding people who were different. Paul had gotten a look on his face like a trapped cat. Chad would have snickered, except that mostly he wanted to smack Brother Flanders for being stupid.

It was getting close to the end of the meeting. Brother Rasmussen looked like he was about to get up and announce the closing hymn, when old Brother Schmidt stood and slowly made his way up to the podium from the second pew on the right, where he always sat.

"My brudders and sisters," he began. "It is fifteen years now dat my beluffed Margarete is taken from me. Later dat year, I listen to de missionaries of de Church of Cheesus Christ of Latter-day Saints. Den de Berlin Vall comes down and I come to de United States, vere my daughter and her husband are.

"Now I tink to say someting about de homos dat I hear on de news vant to get married."

Chad cringed. He couldn't stop himself from looking over at

Paul, but he couldn't tell anything about how Paul felt from the look on his face.

"I am seffenty-seffen years old. Back ven I vas a boy, de Nazis vere ruling over Germany. Dey tell us dat de Chews and de Communists betray our country, so dat ve lose de var. And ve beleef dem. And so de vorld knows dat millions of Chews die in de concentration camps because uff de lies uff de Nazis.

"My mutter had a brudder who vas younger dan she. My uncle Otto. She luffed him." Tears were starting to run down the old man's face. "I luff him. I do not know dat he is a homo. But de Nazis, dey come and dey take de homos to de *Konzentrationslager*, de concentration camps. And dey take my uncle Otto. And he dies in de camps."

Toward the back, a toddler was loudly complaining about something. Aside from that, the chapel was silent.

"And now I hear de people on de news talk about de homos. And I hear de hate in de voices, and I tink about my uncle Otto. And den I remember de message dat de missionaries bring to me, uff Christ and his atonement, and how I can be vit my Margarete again, and my mutter and fater. And I hope dat my uncle Otto is dere too.

"I do not say dat de homos should be marry. But I say dat ve must luff dem, because dey are Gott's children chust like ve are.

"In de name uff Jesus Christ, amen."

The *amen* that echoed from the congregation was quieter than usual. The silence continued while Brother Schmidt made his way back to his seat.

"Look. I'm just not up to talking about it now, okay? I mean, I really don't want to talk about it."

"But—"

"Look, are you gonna help me with these boxes or not?"

Chad was exasperated. "Geez, am I supposed to just pretend I'm not gonna miss my best friend?"

The two of them stood staring at each other over the pile of boxes in Paul's room. Chad snorted. "This is stupid."

"Yeah."

"Should we go out in the yard and have a fistfight? Prove we're just as mature now as back when we were nine?"

"Eight."

"That's right. It was eight for you. You're the *little* kid."

"Watch it!" They were both grinning now, but Paul's smile didn't look terribly convincing. Chad was sure his wasn't any better.

"It's gonna be weird not having you around," Chad said at last into the silence.

Paul shrugged. "Yeah, well."

"How am I gonna get by without my best friend?"

"You jerk." Paul's face was turned away, and Chad guessed that he was close to crying. Chad felt that way himself. "I'm the gay guy, y'know," Paul continued. "I'm the one who's supposed to be all mushy. Not you."

"Right," Chad said. Paul still wasn't looking at him. "Oh, c'mere, you bozo." Chad grabbed him by one arm and pulled him into an awkward hug.

How does my dad make hugging another guy look so natural? This is, like, the weirdest thing I think I've ever done.

The hug lasted only a few seconds before they both let go.

"So is this the part where we call each other fags, like in *Bill and Ted's Excellent Adventure?*"

"You know, Paul, I wonder about you sometimes."

"Yeah, well, it's mutual."

Getting a hug from Chad felt unbelievably awkward. *That's probably because it's never happened before,* thought Paul. *I wonder if Tim felt this awkward when I hugged him?* But the younger boy had hung on anyway, the same way Paul felt like holding on now.

Paul hated a lot of things about this situation: hated the reasons he was leaving, hated the awkwardness between him and Chad, hated the fact that part of that awkwardness had to do with Paul being attracted to guys and Chad knowing about it. But he wouldn't have traded Chad's hug for pretty much anything.

And then Paul was gone.

It was the second Sunday in October, a couple of minutes before sacrament meeting was supposed to start. Chad was sitting behind the sacrament table, watching the teachers as they rushed around getting the water trays filled. One of them tripped and almost spilled before catching himself and setting the tray down on the sacrament cloth.

Chad snickered. Paul had done that once. Actually, what Paul had done was a lot worse. One time when he was still a deacon, he'd been assigned to pass the sacrament to the bishop and everyone on the stand. On the way down the steps, he'd tripped and sent the bread flying onto the floor. Bright red, he'd knelt on the carpet to pick it up. The second counselor had come down off the stand and told him to leave it there to be cleaned up later. Paul had been so embarrassed that he refused to pass on the stand for months after that.

Paul should be sitting next to me right now, poking his elbow to get me to be reverent before the meeting starts. But he's not. He's in Utah.

His dad stood. "Brothers and sisters. We are met in the name of the Lord Jesus Christ . . . ."

As his dad continued with the announcements, Chad's eyes wandered. Seeing the faces in the congregation, he couldn't help but remember all the teenagers who had made Paul's life so miserable. The adults who kept going on about how evil homosexuals were. Everyone at church and school who spread gossip about him and Paul. Whoever it was that told Paul's board of review about him being gay.

The opening song began: "The Day Dawn Is Breaking." Chad choked on the words.

I hate them. I hate what they did. I hate them for making it so Paul couldn't stand to live here anymore.

All through the callings and releases, Chad sat on the bench, shaking with anger. When the sacrament song began he stood, hands automatically breaking the bread while his mind kept displaying pictures of everyone he was mad at. Members of the ward. Paul's former GSA friends. The guys in school and seminary who'd made fun of him. All the people who were making such a fuss about Measure 36. Paul's own father. Chad's hands ripped the bread into smaller and smaller pieces until he made himself stop.

The sacrament hymn ended. Chad stood as the other priest knelt and said the prayer on the bread. Then they both sat. Shortly afterward, Chad took a piece of bread from the tray the deacon held in front of him. It was dry and dusty in his mouth.

And then it was his turn to kneel and bless the water.

He tried to say the words, but his throat was too tense with all the emotions he was feeling. He opened his mouth, then closed it again. Seconds passed. In desperation, he lifted his eyes from the printed card, up and over to the side pews, where he saw —

Brother Schmidt, head bowed, callused old hands folded. Praying. Listening. Waiting.

Chad swallowed. Finally, he felt the tightness in his throat start to relax.

The church includes other people too. Good people like Brother Schmidt and Janice and Paul and even my dad. I need to remember that.

Chad opened his mouth again. This time the words flowed. "O God, the Eternal Father . . ."

Paul's great-aunt's ward was very different from any other ward he'd ever seen.

There were almost no youth in the ward. Looking out over the chapel from behind the sacrament table, he saw a few families with small children. Most of them, though, were at least as old as his great-aunt. Lots of gray heads. Lots of single sisters. It looked like this ward must have as many widows as President Monson's ward that he was always talking about, back when he'd been a bishop.

Certainly the bishop in this ward had been quick to draft Paul into helping with the sacrament. Talking to him, Paul had seen a gleam in his eye. *I bet he wants me for a calling in the priests quorum. I guess I'd better tell him we're moving as soon as Mom finds us a place of our own.*

The prelude music stopped, and someone—one of the counselors in the bishopric—stood at the podium.

"Welcome, brothers and sisters. It's good to be with you this fine Sabbath morning . . ."

Paul let his mind drift. The sight of his mom sitting beside Great-Aunt Muriel a few rows back in the center section reminded him of their conversation on the long drive out to Utah.

"So how do you feel about this move, really?" she'd started. "I know you said you were okay with it, but . . ."

"Too late now if I'm not okay with it," he'd replied.

"Still."

Paul had hesitated. "At first, I was pretty much numb about the whole thing. You know? Now, though, I guess I'm just relieved."

"Relieved?"

"That I don't have to keep on trying to make things work back in Arcadia Heights. That I'm going somewhere no one knows I'm gay."

She hadn't said anything for several minutes. They'd been driving through the Blue Mountains between Pendleton and La Grande, and parts of the road were tricky for a U-Haul.

"How do you want things to be different?" she asked finally. "Now that we won't be in Arcadia Heights anymore?"

It was a good question.

"For one thing, I don't plan on getting myself outed at school. Aside from that . . . I don't really know."

"Do you want to get back involved with Boy Scouts?"

"I don't ever want to have anything to do with scouting again."

"Why not?" she'd asked.

Because I don't wanna get stomped on again. He didn't want to say that, though. "Things can't be the same as before," he'd said at last.

From the quick glance his mom had given him, that wasn't an answer she'd been expecting. "What do you mean?"

"It's just—things are different now, you know? I can't just go back to the way things were."

It was true. He wasn't the same person anymore, after everything that had happened in the last year and a half. Being back in the closet wouldn't change that.

Paul's attention was brought back to the present as the opening hymn finished. The opening prayer was said by a man with a round face who sounded a bit like a five-year-old. *Down syndrome,* Paul realized.

His attention drifted during the callings and releases. He and his mom stood and were welcomed into the ward. Then it was time for the sacrament hymn.

Paul stood, along with the older man beside him. Together they pulled back the cloth and started breaking the bread as the music flowed around them. It was the same routine he'd done a dozen times or more back in his old ward. Chad had been the one who showed him what to do his first time, just a few months ago.

Paul blinked. He missed Chad. He shook his head, trying to get rid of the sudden tightness in his throat.

And then suddenly a feeling of peace swept through him, together with a small but definite rush of warmth. It felt like the time Paul had borne his testimony at the GSA meeting—and how he'd felt when Chad's dad was giving him that blessing before they left, when he said he'd be proud to call Paul his son.

The feeling lingered as Paul stood while the older man said the prayer on the bread.

Things *wouldn't* be the same here, he realized as he sat there watching the "deacons" — about half of them grown men — pass the trays to the ward members. What happened back in Oregon had left Paul less optimistic about being accepted for who he was. Even before he told Chad he was gay, he'd known it wouldn't be easy to be gay and Mormon. The last year and a half had given him a lot clearer idea of just how hard it might be.

But there'd been good things too. Chad. The bishop. His mom. Tim, even. Getting a testimony. He couldn't turn his back on the spiritual experiences he'd had and his hopes for the future — whether those hopes were fulfilled during this life or afterward. The whole GSA mess had helped him realize he couldn't just walk away from the church, even if that might make his life easier in a lot of ways.

And he didn't want to give up the warmth and comfort and familiarity he was feeling right now, looking out over his new ward. Watching as each of them took a small piece of bread and ate it as a symbol of a promise that bound them together with each other and with God.

He knew some of them would shun him if they knew how he felt about other boys. He knew that hearing people talk with hate about homos would be hard for him — even if they didn't know he was one of the people they were talking about. When that happened, he hoped he'd be able to remember the warm feeling he was experiencing right now. He hoped he'd be able to remember that he was loved and accepted by God and by the people who were most important to him.

When it was time for Paul to kneel and bless the water, he could hardly see the words on the printed card because his eyes were too blurry.

He drew a deep breath. "O God, the Eternal Father . . ."

Epilogue

Chadster: hey
Hyperboy: hey
Chadster: howz it going?
Hyperboy: good, u?
Chadster: yeah
Hyperboy: still stuffed from t-day?
Chadster: ??
Hyperboy: turkey day
Chadster: ??
Hyperboy: thanksgiving
Chadster: ??
Hyperboy: yr a doofus
Chadster: u still living at yr gr8 ants house?
Hyperboy: yeah
Hyperboy: mom says shes 2 buzy 2 look 4 sumthing else
Chadster: oh plz
Chadster: just stop it already with the random numberz
Hyperboy: ha ha
Hyperboy: i rule
Chadster: whatever
Chadster: so u ok with staying at yr ants?
Hyperboy: yeah
Hyperboy: shes cool
Chadster: so y r we typing on computers
Chadster: instead of talking on the phone?
Hyperboy: bcuz we r so kewl
Hyperboy: lol
Chadster: i have 2 kill u now

Chadster: just for spelling kewl that way
Chadster: hey u still there?
Hyperboy: sorry
Hyperboy: wuz laffing 2 hard 2 type
Chadster: yr such a geek

Chadster: so how r things going?
Hyperboy: pretty good ac2ly
Hyperboy: better than b4 i moved
Hyperboy: there talking about taking me off the meds
Chadster: good news
Hyperboy: so what about u?
Hyperboy: school going ok?
Chadster: grades pretty good actually
Hyperboy: u mean ac2ly?
Chadster: whatever
Hyperboy: lol
Chadster: i got mostly a's
Hyperboy: !! yr kidding
Chadster: no
Chadster: u moved away
Chadster: my iq shot up
Hyperboy: hardee har har
Hyperboy: thats gr8
Chadster: yeah
Chadster: u look up yr skools gsa yet?
Hyperboy: yr joking, rite?
Hyperboy: this is utah
Hyperboy: im so in the closet
Hyperboy: nobodys even seen the key
Chadster: lol
Hyperboy: hey
Hyperboy: im in the anime club
Chadster: ??
Hyperboy: u no, japanese animation
Hyperboy: we get together, watch anime
Chadster: sounds pretty boring
Hyperboy: i like it
Chadster: yr such a weirdo
Hyperboy: takes 1 2 no 1
Chadster: so get this

Chadster: janice wants 2 date again
Hyperboy: no way!!!
Chadster: yeah
Chadster: i said no
Hyperboy: y??
Chadster: shes nice but
Chadster: dont need the drama
Hyperboy: i got that

Chadster: guess what?
Hyperboy: what?
Chadster: got yelled at by a gay kid last week
Chadster: kid w cloak
Hyperboy: trevor???
Chadster: he wuz going off on homophobes who passed measure 36
Chadster: i called him a str8ophobe
Chadster: he got mad
Chadster: cussed at me
Chadster: he got detention
Hyperboy: lol
Hyperboy: hes a hothead
Chadster: what a bunch of losers
Chadster: paul?
Chadster: u there?
Hyperboy: yeah
Hyperboy: sorry
Hyperboy: its still kind of hard, u no?
Chadster: ??
Hyperboy: u, bish, my mom
Hyperboy: u 3 were the best
Hyperboy: but i still kind of miss it
Chadster: what?
Hyperboy: feeling like i fit sumwhere
Chadster: hey man
Chadster: yr not alone
Hyperboy: thanx
Chadster: so u still coming back to visit at christmas?
Hyperboy: thats the plan
Hyperboy: dec 27
Chadster: good
Chadster: c u then

About the Author

Jonathan Langford is a freelance writer who grew up in western Oregon during the 1960s and 1970s and now lives in western Wisconsin, where he is married with three children. He served a mission to Italy for the LDS Church, has a B.A. and M.A. in English from Brigham Young University, and serves as a membership clerk in his LDS ward. For several years, he served as moderator of AML-List, the e-mail discussion list of the Association for Mormon Letters.

Join the Conversation

Thoughts? Reactions? Questions? We'd love to hear from you! To share what you thought about *No Going Back*—and for more information about the book itself, including other readers' comments—go to Jonathan Langford's website at www.langfordwriter.com.

Author's Acknowledgments

While composing *No Going Back*, I was fortunate to receive help from many sources. In particular, I'd like to thank the following:

The many people who read and made comments on part or all of this book during the writing process, including Linda Hunter Adams, Gwenyn Anderson, Gerald Argetsinger, Evan A. Ballard, Connie Bankston, Beth Bentley, Jennifer Vaughn Breinholt, Brian Burns, David Clarke, Laura Craner, Clark Draney, Rex Goode, David H., Kristine Haglund, Matthew Hamby, C. L. Hanson, Marianne Hales Harding, Larry Jackson, Eric W Jepson, Laurel Langford, C. M., Ty Mansfield, Rob McNelly, William Morris, Dai Newman, Laura F. Nielsen, Carl Olsen, Scott Parkin, Dallas Robbins, Thomas F. Rogers, Heidi Tighe, Steven C. Walker, Lotte Willian, and Brett Wilcox. This book would not be as good without their comments. Any remaining faults and errors, of course, are entirely my own. Please note that listing someone here constitutes my acknowledgement of their help and *not* necessarily an endorsement of the book on their part.

Various people who served as information sources and cultural informants, from the teenagers in my ward who helped with modern music references to the high school advisor who described activities in a local GSA club.

My family, for much patience.

Chris Bigelow of Zarahemla Books, both for his encouragement and for creating a place where a book like this could be published.

Rex Goode and the others on AML-List, the e-mail discussion list of the Association for Mormon Letters, where the conversations took place that ultimately led to this book.

"Jonathan Langford's *No Going Back* is a heartfelt, heart-breaking, and ultimately enriching tale of what it means to be a fifteen-year-old Mormon boy who truly wants only to do what is right but is faced with the terrifying fact that he is gay. The main character's troubling journey is honest and sheds light on one of the most difficult dilemmas facing hundreds, if not thousands, of young Mormons who just want it to go away. Langford writes honestly without becoming bogged down in the politics surrounding this issue."
—Gerald Argetsinger, associate professor of performing arts, Rochester Institute of Technology; former artistic director of the LDS Church's *Hill Cumorah Pageant*

"I love the way this novel brings to life through narrative what I imagine will be the struggle of many youth growing up in today's evolving culture around gay issues. Parents, friends, priesthood leaders, and peers are all a critical part of how we negotiate our sense of self-identity and life choices, and this story is masterful in how it brings to life all the tensions associated with that process. A couple of times, I even found myself forgetting this was fiction and wanting to get in contact with the main character to assure him he's not alone. Each of the characters, with their different personalities and roles in the narrative—Barbara, Sandy, Richard, Chad, Paul, the kids at church and the kids at school—offers something quite meaningful to the story."
—Ty Mansfield, coauthor of *In Quiet Desperation: Understanding the Challenge of Same-Gender Attraction* (Deseret Book, 2004)

"By telling the story simply, tying it to a particular time and place, and focusing on the teenage protagonists, Langford is able to confine the discussion of this issue to a manageable narrative—and a compelling one. The approach Langford takes is genius. I love the way he threads the middle of American Mormon mores, doctrine, and practice in a way that is in some senses mundane—this is basically a domestic drama—but also incredibly radical.

"These teenagers act like teenagers, even though they are basically good kids. Any discussion of same-sex attraction makes a lot of Mormons uncomfortable. But the novel is thoroughly orthodox. Its characters are orthodox Mormons. Its tensions and ultimate solutions and resolutions are firmly rooted in active LDS life—prayer, scripture study, repentance, the priesthood, love, charity, hope, the family."
—William Morris, founder of the Mormon arts and culture blog *A Motley Vision*

"*No Going Back* is not just for anyone with same-sex attraction. It is a must for leaders who work with those struggling with these choices, as well as for family and friends as they love, reject, support, or fail to understand what such a struggle costs."
—Linda Hunter Adams, former director of the BYU Humanities Publications Center, past president of the Association for Mormon Letters

"For perhaps seventy-two hours after reading *No Going Back*, it was almost the only thing I thought about. Langford has touched very sensitively, compassionately, and thoughtfully on a very important topic about which Mormons are almost completely silent. I see this book as an essential step in opening a viable dialogue about a struggle that is very real for many members of the church. In truth, I believe this book will save someone's life."
—Clark Draney, associate professor of English, College of Southern Idaho